Daughters of India

By Jill McGivering

Daughters of India

Daughters of India

JILL MCGIVERING

Allison & Busby Limited
12 Fitzroy Mews
London W1T 6DW
allisonandbusby.com

First published in Great Britain by Allison & Busby in 2017.

All rights ... ed,
stored ...
any mea ... er,
nor b ...
other ... .
c ...

A ...

First Edition

ISBN 978-0-7490-2182-5

Typeset in 11/16 pt Sabon by
Allison & Busby Ltd.

The paper used for this Allison & Busby publication
has been produced from trees that have been legally sourced
from well-managed and credibly certified forests.

Printed and bound by
CPI Group (UK) Ltd, Croydon, CR0 4YY

For Alice and Emily

Prologue

'You are a good girl, Asha, and a brave one.' His voice fell to a whisper. 'You have your part to play. An important part. I know you will make your baba proud. And make me proud also.'

She couldn't speak. She wanted to blurt out: already I have betrayed you and my baba both; I am serving that man, who condemned him to death. She stood, silent and ashamed.

He nodded as if he understood everything, as if he saw not just through the thick door but right into her soul. Her body ached from straining to reach to the peephole. It was hot and airless in the corridor. There was so much she needed to say, to confess to him, but she couldn't find the words.

He said then: 'Your madam. You are knowing who she is?'

She blinked. 'Isabel Madam. Her husband sentenced my . . .' Her voice faltered.

'Her husband made your baba a martyr. That is true. But she herself, you know her?'

He lifted his hand. She couldn't see but it seemed to her that he placed it flat against the wood of the door between them. She lifted her own and placed it too, flat against the worn wood on her own side, imagining that they could touch.

He began to whisper to her.

'Do you remember that day, long ago, when you were a little girl only and your baba brought you to my uncle's house? Rahul was there, my good friend, and he told you about the Britishers' house with the mango and jamun trees where you and he were children? They cast out your baba and sent him to the slum, accused him falsely of being a thief.'

Of course she remembered. Her poor baba bore it all and never spoke of it.

'That was your madam's house. It was her people who destroyed your baba's reputation. They set him on the long path that led him to a cell here and to death.'

Her hand shook on the wood. 'Her people?'

He nodded. His eyes fixed on the peephole as if he could see her.

'They are snakes, these people. Full of kind words but also of poison.'

The wood swam. She felt a sudden wave of sickness and leant her cheek against it.

He said: 'Harden your heart against her.'

She took a deep breath. 'I will leave her. Amit-ji will protect me. I'll clean pans and cook for him.'

On the other side of the door, he let out a low sigh. 'No, little sister. They are snakes but we are tigers. Be strong. Be fierce. And have faith. The day of the tiger is almost come.'

Part One

Chapter One

Delhi, 1919

The magnolia tree was too high. Its branches thinned and weakened and, now Isabel was near the top, they bowed where she placed a foot. She tilted her head and looked down through the falling shiver of leaves to the ground. The earth rose rushing towards her. Her stomach tightened and breath stuck in her throat.

'Here.' Rahul twisted back to her, stretched down a warm, safe hand.

She couldn't move. Her knuckles whitened as she grasped the trunk.

'Look up only.' Rahul climbed down to her, a shield against the dropping empty air.

She gathered a bunch of thin branches in her hands like reins, steadied her breath and pulled herself higher.

They emerged, at the top, into another world and sat, pressed together, breathing hard, trembling. Leaves stirred all around. Far below, the ground swam. The compound lay mapped out, the buildings shrivelled and unfamiliar. Fear and glory knotted into one as she lifted her eyes and looked out across India, across the world.

Rahul pointed behind them, over the angled roof of the bungalow and far beyond.

'That's backwards.' His voice was solemn. 'Into the past.'

When she screwed her eyes and stared, she saw past generations, the darkness of the ancients.

He pointed forward then, over the garden's boundary walls, out across the brown mud and lush vegetation of unclaimed land, of the jungle.

'That's forwards,' he said. 'Into the future.'

That evening, the light in the servants' shack was dim, pooled round the lamp, which was too weak to reach the corners. She kept close to Rahul as he sat, cross-legged, among his brothers and sisters on the dirt floor. Dark heads hunched forward over food. Daal, rice and subzi sat on leaves on the ground. They balled it deftly to eat and she felt her own clumsiness as daal ran down her wrist and onto her knees.

The women whispered. The sweeper-wallah was in trouble. He was a shy man with a sad face. Isabel hardly knew him.

'Where will he go?' Mrs Chaudhary said. 'His daughter's just a baby.'

Isabel looked round. There was chilli in the subzi and her lips smarted.

The wooden door creaked open. The new houseboy, Abdul, wide-eyed.

'Memsahib, at the door, calling Missy Isabel.'

She held herself so still that her body shook. She wouldn't go.

'Miss Isabel.' Mrs Chaudhary spoke to her in English now. The boys lifted their heads. 'Please be going.'

Isabel hesitated.

Rahul said: 'But her food, Mama.'

Mrs Chaudhary shook her head, repeated. 'Please, Miss Isabel. Please.'

*   *   *

12

Isabel was summoned the following day.

'Where were you?'

Her mother sat at her desk in the sitting room, one long-fingered hand stretched across an open writing case and the other clasping the gold chain around her neck, gathering it into folds and kneading it. The mid-morning sun was already strong. It reached through the French windows and made the moving necklace sparkle.

'Ayah says you ate with the servants. Is that true?'

Isabel's round-toed sandals cut red half-moons in the wooden floor. She stood two, maybe three, steps from the fringe of the rug. She could jump it in one bound if she had a run-up.

'Well?'

She shrugged. 'I was hungry.'

Her mother sighed. 'It won't do, you know.' The gold links of the chain scraped together as she bunched, then rolled them between her fingers. 'Your father and I have decided it's time for you to go Home. There's a small school that's supposed to be awfully good, just like a family, really.'

Outside, Cook Chaudhary hollered from the side of the house. Angry. The houseboy was for it.

'Are you even listening?'

She forced her eyes to meet her mother's and nodded. A bicycle bell rang down by the gate and someone whistled. It wasn't Rahul, she knew his whistle anywhere. A delivery boy, perhaps. From town. Her toes clenched in her sandals, bursting to run outside to see.

'If it hadn't been for the war, you should have gone long ago. It's a big change but you'll soon settle.'

A thought struck her. The whispers last night. 'Is the sweeper-wallah leaving?'

Her mother looked surprised, then frowned. 'Where did you hear that?'

It was true, then. 'Where will he go?'

'I really don't think—' Her mother let her necklace fall. It bounced against her blouse, then swayed and settled. 'He let us down very badly. That's all.' She turned back to her desk. 'Your father's quite right, Isabel. It's time you went Home.'

Chapter Two

'She's a plain girl.'

Isabel lay stock-still and listened. The Misses Ellison stood in the shadows, just beyond the door. That was the voice of the elder Miss Ellison, a thin woman with a sharp nose. She wore black boots and a sweeping, high-necked dress, pinned with a polished black brooch. When they met an hour earlier, Isabel saw herself reflected in it, small, pale and wide-eyed.

'She'll get by.' Her sister. A softer voice. The younger Miss Ellison had a fat bosom and powdered cheeks, doughy as buns. 'They're not without means, the Winthorpes.'

A sniff. 'The wife's the one with money. One of the Hancock girls.'

'The cloth people?'

The door closed. Footsteps and fading voices across the landing. She stretched out her feet, wiggled her toes. The sheet was cold and damp. Miss Ellison had given her a glass of milk in the kitchen, then made her take off her travelling clothes, wash her face in a basin and put on her nightdress by the fire. The milk made a stone in her stomach. She shivered, wrapped her arms round her body and curled into a ball.

'Are you plain?' A girl's voice, close by.

She turned towards the sound, strained to see. Another bed. Rustling as someone sat up. She blinked, clearing spangles of light from her eyes, peering. 'Probably.'

The sitting shape of the girl emerged from the blackness. She had an abundance of fair hair. It fell in loose waves, making a cloud round her neck and shoulders. 'I'm pretty,' the girl said. 'Everyone says so.'

A pause as Isabel considered this. 'That's lucky.'

'I expect it is.' She rose and feet slapped across the wooden floor. 'Well, shove up, can't you?'

The girl lifted back the corner of the blanket and sheet and climbed in beside her. She wrapped her arms round Isabel's ribs, her compact body hard and warm. She smelt of camphor.

'What cloth people?'

Isabel shrugged. 'My mother's people, I suppose.'

'Did you really come from India? Isn't it awfully far?'

She thought back to the sweltering train journey from Delhi to Bombay, the dull weeks on board ship, each a little cooler than the last, walking in endless procession round the worn planks of the deck with a party of other English girls, chaperoned by a hearty games mistress. When they disembarked at Southampton, the sky was dour with drizzle. Someone put a lid on the world, shut out the light, the sun, the air.

'I shan't stay long. I'm going back.'

'I thought that too, at first. Ninety-three days till Christmas, did you count?'

'Are your people in India too?'

'Kettlewell. It's in Yorkshire. We've got a farm and a beck runs right along the bottom of the garden. We had a governess but then my brother went off to school and I came here. I'm Gwendolyn but you can call me Gwen if you like.' Her breath made a hot patch between Isabel's shoulder blades. She put icy feet against the backs of Isabel's ankles where they slowly thawed. 'What's India like?'

When Isabel closed her eyes, the blackness swayed, rocked by the lingering motion of the ship. As it settled, pictures appeared.

'Hot. The lawn goes white in the sun,' she said. 'Ayah looks after me, mostly. And Cook Chaudhary. He makes me mango pudding.'

'What's mango pudding?'

'Don't you know?' She turned her mind back to India. 'My best friend's called Rahul. And I've got a pony. Starlight. I go in for the children's gymkhana. We got fifth last year.'

'You can't now though, can you?'

'And there are monkeys. The babies hang upside down, clinging to their mother's bellies. Their faces look wrinkled, like old men and—'

'Fibber.' The arms disentangled themselves and Gwen pulled away, slapped back to her own bed. The darkness settled into place between them. After a while, Gwen said: 'We have cows, by the way. And sheep.'

Isabel lay very still, feeling the chill creep back along her spine. Gwen breathed lightly, not yet asleep.

'Is it always cold here?'

'Cold?' A snigger. 'This isn't cold. Wait till winter.'

The Misses Ellison's house stood on the edge of the moor and as the weather soured, the wind rampaged across the open expanse.

In those first weeks of autumn, the heather splashed purple across the moorland and the stretches of bracken

17

faded from green to brown. In the mornings, the younger Miss Ellison walked Isabel and Gwen across the moor to the village to do her daily shop. Isabel's ears buzzed with cold.

Miss Ellison walked briskly along the mud paths. Her laced boots made light prints in the mud. Isabel and Gwen, trailing behind, made a game of stretching their strides to match hers. The wind filled with drizzle and fired it into Isabel's face. Her cheeks and fingers went numb and her nose ran, mingling with the rain.

In the village, the girls waited at the back of one shop after another while Miss Ellison made purchases. The shop assistants wore white aprons and straw boaters and slapped pats of butter with wooden paddles and shovelled sugar and flour out of lidded bins into shining brass scales. When Miss Ellison paid, the money and bill shot upstairs inside a tube to a ringing bell, only to zoom down again a few minutes later, rattling with change.

In the afternoons, they sat in the back room of the house with two stout girls with plaits, the daughters of the local doctor. The elder Miss Ellison taught reading, writing and sums. She slapped at their knuckles with a wooden ruler when she was displeased.

The younger Miss Ellison had a globe and taught them about the Empire which stretched round the girth of the world like a red corset.

'Now, girls, where is Africa?' She turned the world and made them point.

Isabel's only interest was in India. She was proud of its size, a sprawling elephant of a country, very far from the tiny smudge of England.

* * *

A letter came from her father on thin, crinkly paper. It smelt of sun and spice. He drew a funny-faced tiger with thick whiskers, dressed in britches and a self-portrait, a man sporting a topee, snoozing in a chair on the lawn. His tone was jolly. He told a story about Cook mistaking salt for sugar and how horrid the cake tasted.

Isabel kept the letter under her mattress. At night, when Gwen slept, she hung out of bed, lifted the lip of the mattress and sniffed it until it lost the scent of India.

Gwen said Isabel must be sent home to India in July, for the long summer holidays. They calculated the days and began to count them off.

Then a letter came from Isabel's mother.

Miss Ellison informs me that you and Gwen have become great friends, her mother wrote. *We thought it would be great fun for you to stay with her family for the summer. I am sorry, darling, that I can't be there myself but please be a good, polite girl and make me proud of you.*

That night, Gwen slapped across the bedroom floor and wrapped her thin arms around Isabel.

'It's too bad,' she said. 'Really.'

The view from the window seat commanded the back of the house. Gwen was on the swing. Her ankles were crossed and her loose hair flew as she cut an arc through the air, time after time, in a steady rhythm.

Isabel shifted her weight and stretched out her legs. She

pulled the cushion from its place in the small of her back and sat on it, easing off her buttocks.

At the end of the garden, beyond the dip that concealed the beck, lay a gently rising patchwork of fields. They were studded with cows and sheep and bounded by stubby lines of drystone wall, as if an artist had drawn the landscape in thick grey pencil before colouring it in.

A thin draught pressed in from the edge of the window. She pulled her cardigan closer round her chest and turned the page of the volume spread open across her knees. She knew the next picture well. The majestic elephant with flapping ears. A curtained howdah, decorated with gold and silver, crashed through the jungle on its back. A mahout, barefoot and brown-skinned, rode on its head, legs tucked behind the vast spread ears.

'Put that book down. It's not yours.'

She lifted her head. A staring boy in the doorway. He wore a blue short-sleeved shirt, serge shorts and sandals. His pale face was convulsed in a frown.

'It's not yours either. It's Mr Whyte's. Anyway, I asked him.'

'It is mine. Practically. I'm his son and heir.'

Jonathan, then. Home from boarding school. She turned her eyes back to the picture and felt him hesitate. He took a few steps further into the room and looked round.

'Where's Gwen?'

She shrugged. 'Playing out.'

'You're Isabel, aren't you? You're not as pretty as my sister.'

She raised her eyes and looked at him with cool confidence. 'I'm an Indian princess.'

'Liar.' He sounded unsure. He turned on his heel and left.

She turned her attention back to the book. The next page

showed a tea plantation. Indian ladies with silver studs in their noses and brightly coloured saris, indigo and sunshine yellow, plucked leaves and threw them into the wicker baskets slung on their backs like babies. She traced the outline with her forefinger, imagining the textures, the close, fetid smell of the tea, the warmth.

'You better put that down. I'll tell.' He was back.

'Tell all you like. I don't care.'

He came closer and peered over her shoulder. He smelt of damp earth and sweat. When he reached out a hand to the book, his fingers were stained blue with ink. He turned a few pages and pointed to an illustration. It was a set of drawings of Indian snakes, ranged in size from small grass snakes to giant pythons.

He pointed to one of the largest. 'Bet you've never seen a snake like that.'

'My mother killed one. In the bedroom. Beat it to death with her hairbrush.'

His eyes widened. 'Don't believe you.'

She shrugged, turned back to the book. 'Suit yourself, Know-It-All.'

'Know-It-All yourself.'

She held the book away from him until he pulled a face and ran out of the room.

At five o'clock, the three of them sat together round the tea table. Jonathan's eyes ranged over Isabel, looking to find fault.

The maid brought in a plate of thickly sliced buttered bread and a dish of blackcurrant jam and placed them on the cloth.

'I'll say grace.' Jonathan watched while Gwen put her

21

hands together and bowed her head. Isabel hesitated, then did the same. 'For what we are about to receive, may the Lord make us truly thankful. Amen.' He turned to Isabel. 'You didn't say Amen.'

'Did.'

Gwen looked from one to the other.

Jonathan helped himself to bread and took control of the jam dish.

'You can have some.' He spooned a dollop of jam onto his own plate, then another onto his sister's. 'Don't let her.'

'Why not?'

'She shouldn't be here.'

Gwen blinked. 'She's my friend.'

Jonathan glared. 'I'm your brother.'

'Keep your stupid jam.' Isabel took a piece of bread and bit into it. 'I don't want it anyway.'

The maid walked back into the room with a jug of water and they fell silent. Afterwards, when the maid brought slices of fruit cake, Jonathan switched round the plates so Isabel had the smallest piece.

When they were finishing, Jonathan tapped a spoon on the edge of the glass to demand attention.

'Notice is hereby given that Miss Isabel Winthorpe is sent to Coventry.'

Isabel didn't know where Coventry was. She licked her finger and gathered up cake crumbs.

Jonathan looked at Gwen. 'Cards, after?'

'If you like.'

'If it's fine tomorrow, we could take a picnic up the fell. I'll ask Cook to cut sandwiches.'

Gwen considered Isabel. 'So she can't come?'

Isabel felt herself flush. 'I wouldn't want to.'

Jonathan made a pantomime of looking round. 'Who can't come? Who do you mean?'

Gwen looked sideways at Isabel, giggled.

'Is there someone else here? I can't see anyone.'

'Neither can I.'

'You're blind, then.' Isabel hunched her shoulders. 'Blind and stupid.' Tears pricked hot. The bread in her hand blurred and swam.

When the others finished eating and scraped back their chairs, Isabel stayed alone at the table. The door banged shut behind them. A moment later, their muffled voices drifted through the wall from the sitting room. A shriek of laughter from Gwen. The thud of a chair.

Isabel counted to twenty, then followed. The others sat opposite each other at the felt-topped card table. Jonathan, his back to the door, slapped out two piles of cards. Their shoulders stiffened as she crept in but neither lifted their eyes to acknowledge her. She plucked the India book from its place in the bookcase, then retreated with it to the window seat, curled against the cold glass in the narrow hiding place behind the drawn curtain and touched the pages, one after another, in the semi-darkness.

The days settled into a pattern. Jonathan and Gwen disappeared outside together for hours at a time and came back muddy, ruddy-faced and triumphant. Isabel trailed around the silent house. Sometimes she splashed in the beck at the bottom of the garden, piling stones to make a dam, or sat alone on the swing, watching her feet rise up against the dappled green and black of the fell and slowly fall again.

In the house, she sought out new hiding places that allowed her to disappear. She lay in the thin gap between the back of Mr Whyte's desk and the lip of the window sill or sat cross-legged under the writing bureau, concealed by its chair.

With four days to go before Jonathan's return to school and six before their departure for the Misses Ellison, Mrs Whyte took Jonathan and Gwen into Skipton to visit the outfitters there. The weather turned and soured.

Long after they'd left, Isabel stood at the window and gazed out at the altered landscape. The fields smoked with low mist. The fell and the peaks above the valley disappeared in cloud. The cows shifted their feet and stamped and puffed steam.

Finally, when she sensed that they might soon return, she took her book and crawled between the legs of the writing bureau. She drew the spindly chair into place behind her and pulled down its cushion to form a screen between her hiding place and the rest of the room. It was draughty against the skirting board. Balls of dust clung to her socks like burrs. She drew her knees up, rested the book on her tilted thighs and began to read.

Doors slammed. Voices in the hall, first Gwen and her mother, then Jonathan chipping in with a short remark, a shuffling of coats and shoes. She looked at her watch. Another hour to lunch. They'd taken an early bus. The page in front of her showed the Indian jungle. It became fraught as she clenched the book, hunched her back more tightly against the wall and waited to be discovered.

The door opened. The sound of footsteps shifted from

wood to rug and back to wood as someone crossed the room. She strained low against the floor and looked through the fencing of wooden chair and table legs. Jonathan's polished, laced shoes. He stood at the window, looking out towards the hidden fell as she had done. She closed her eyes. He would sense her here, she was sure. He would know. Her breath and heartbeat boomed in the room.

A low scrape. He lifted the window by a few inches. Cold pressed in at once and the mild patter of drizzle. She strained to look. The feet turned and crept towards her. She was found then. She shrank against the wall and floor, bracing herself. The shoes stopped right in front of the bureau. She held her breath and closed her eyes. The shudder of a drawer opening, a rummage of papers, a vexed tut. The drawer closed and a second opened, then a third as he searched. He smelt of sweat and the woolly dampness of outdoors. His movements were stealthy. Whatever he wanted, it was a secret.

A sigh. He closed the final drawer and returned to the window. She pressed forward to peer round the edge of the desk to watch. He had a cigarette in his hand, one of his mother's, stolen from her case. A match scraped, bloomed into flame, and the cigarette swam with smoke. He bent over, one hand just above his knee as if he were playing leapfrog, the other holding the cigarette, and smoked in sharp puffs, blowing balls of smoke out through the raised window to disperse in the mist.

As he smoked, his body softened. Its tension seemed to gather into wisps and float out of the house in the used smoke. She wondered what it felt like to smoke, how it tasted. It was oddly intimate to observe him, unseen. Her own body relaxed with his.

It happened in a second. Quick footsteps in the hall. The door flung open.

'Jonathan!' His mother. 'What are you doing?'

The window shut with a bang. Jonathan coughed, spluttered into his hand. Finally he said: 'Just letting a fly out.'

On her knee, the book tipped and slid. She grabbed to stop it falling to the floor.

His mother crossed to the table, turning her back on him. 'I shan't join you for lunch. Cook's sending a tray up. I'm going to rest in my room this afternoon. I know the weather's a bore. You'll just have to amuse yourselves indoors.'

'Of course.' All the time she spoke, Jonathan waved a discreet arm, dispersing the smoke.

Mrs Whyte picked up her spectacles and book and turned back to him. 'Another fly?'

He nodded.

'Well, leave it, darling. Live and let live. Look after the girls, would you?'

She left the room. Once the door closed, Jonathan exhaled a stream of smoky breath, ran a hand over his hair. A moment later, he too rushed out and Isabel found herself alone once again. She stretched out her legs and bounced them on the floor. Her numb buttocks slowly prickled back to life as she rubbed them. She turned the page on the jungle. An ancient Indian fort with red clay walls appeared and she dipped her head to read the text beneath. Cigarette smoke lingered in the room.

A crack. A creaking floorboard, she thought. A wicker chair. The fort dated back to the seventeenth century. The Mughal era. She traced the word in her mind. A bubble drawing at the side of the page showed a grand Indian man in a red headdress. It was so neatly flush against his skull that it looked painted on. He was portrayed in profile with a pearl in his ear.

A pop and roar. Burning. She stretched forward to look. The waste-paper basket by the window jumped yellow and orange with flame. She shoved the cushion and chair out of the way and scrambled out on hands and knees, abandoning the Mughals. The stray balls of paper in the metal basket were alight. The rising heat caught her full in the face, pressed her back. She looked wildly round the room for water. Nothing. The flame, jumping, reached for the hem of the curtain.

'Fire!' The hall was empty. She ran down the backstairs to the kitchen. Cook would know what to do. 'Fire!'

Jonathan stood beside Cook at the kitchen table. He picked at leftovers as Cook prepared lunch. 'Don't tell fibs.' He scowled at her, went back to chewing a stray piece of ham.

'In the sitting room.' She turned to Cook. 'The waste-paper basket.'

Jonathan dropped the ham. For a moment, he looked stricken. He grabbed a basin from the shelf beside the stove and filled it with water. 'Take this.' He pushed it into her hands. She stood, dazed, then turned and rushed back upstairs. Her dress grew a dark, cold patch at her waist where the water slopped.

The sitting room was transformed. The air swam with smoke. The waste-paper basket, now a red-hot cylinder, brimmed with fire. Above it, the curtain flapped. The material was singed and dotted with rising sparks. She threw the water at the fire, soaking her feet. A shot of sooty steam caught her in the face and blinded her. She twisted backwards.

'Out of the way.' Jonathan, shouldering her to one side. He hurled a bucket of water at the sodden remains. A splash, then a final exhausted pall of smoke. They stood back. A black mess of fire-chewed pulp and a charred waste-paper basket. The soft tissue at the back of her throat pulsated.

Cook rushed in, carrying a tin tray of water. She hesitated on the rug, stared at the debris. Mrs Whyte pushed in from behind her.

'What on earth . . . ? In heaven's name!'

Jonathan drew himself up. 'It's all right, Mother.'

His mother stood between them now, staring down in horror at the singed floor, the quietly smoking heap of water and ash. 'What happened?'

Jonathan rounded on Isabel. 'Ask her.' His eyes were cold. 'I was in the kitchen. Isn't that right, Cook?'

Isabel stared. He knew, surely. He'd been the one smoking.

Mrs Whyte raised her arm and pointed to the door. Her lips pressed into a tight line. 'Go to your room, Isabel.'

Isabel opened her mouth to speak.

'At once.'

As she left the room, the atmosphere in the room punctured and sank in her wake.

'Dreadful girl.' Mrs Whyte's voice was a breathy whisper. 'Never again.'

Chapter Three

Delhi, 1933

Isabel didn't want to attend the party. The cold season was well underway and the gossip, the jokes, the faces were already stale. Isabel had been out riding much of the day. Now she wanted to bathe in a hot tub, curl up with a supper tray in her room and finish her book.

Her mother appeared in the sitting room late in the afternoon to find Isabel curled in a chair, reading, and plucked the book from her hands.

'What's this?' The corners of her mother's mouth turned down in distaste. 'Politics?'

Isabel took back her book.

'It won't give you any advantage in conversation. This isn't London.'

It wasn't. She had finally been allowed to join her parents in Delhi after endless years of exile in England. Most recently, she stayed with her aunt in London where she was paraded at dinners and parties in the search for a husband. There were few eligible young men available. The Great War had depleted the stock.

Her mother settled into her chair, picked up a magazine and rang for tea. Isabel turned her eyes back to her book.

'What are you wearing this evening?' Her mother leafed

through the magazine. 'What about the blue with the sequins?' She lifted her eyes. 'Please, Isabel. The Cawthornes matter.'

Isabel closed the book.

'You need to make more of yourself, darling.' Her mother leant forward. Her eyes, as she looked Isabel over, were anxious. 'Daphne says there may be good prospects. Bertie's bringing two unmarried lieutenants.'

'Poor things.' Isabel smiled. 'I bet the Broadside girls go. The lieutenants won't stand a chance.'

'The Broadside girls are very pretty.' Her mother hesitated, choosing her words with care. 'But you have lovely qualities, Isabel.' She paused. 'And a perfectly nice figure.'

Isabel said quietly: 'I'd much rather you went along without me.'

'Oh, Isabel.' Her mother frowned, turned her eyes for a moment to her magazine. She turned a page, then looked up again. 'And this time, please don't give away your age.'

'Is it so dreadful to be twenty-two?'

'It would be dreadful to turn twenty-three without an engagement.'

Abdul brought in the tea tray. Her mother surveyed the sandwiches and scones and took control of the teapot. Yes, said Isabel, she would wear the blue.

The Cawthornes lived in a grand bungalow on the outskirts of New Delhi. The driver, his turban scraping the roof of the car, turned in through grand gates. As they curved round to the left, the approach came into view, lit by two lines of candles, which flickered in low terracotta pots. The front door stood open, throwing a stream of light across the steps and onto the gravel beyond.

They stepped out of the car. Isabel stood for a moment, breathing in the heavy fragrance of rotting vegetation, overripe flowers and recently watered grass. The strains of stringed instruments drifted through from the back of the house. On the far side, the jungle reached towards them with its thickly clotted darkness.

The houseboy took their wraps and ushered them through the entrance hall and central passageway towards the back of the house where French windows opened first onto the verandah, then gave way to lawns and flower beds below.

The main lawn was peppered with guests, standing in clusters, drinks in hand. The vivid colours of the ladies' dresses and flashing jewels on milk-white throats shone against the sombre black and white of the gentlemen's evening dress. Here and there, military uniforms flashed polished buttons. Flaming torches stood tall in the flower beds. Servants crept silently amongst the guests, carrying trays of drinks in white-gloved hands.

A marquee on the far side of the lower lawn hinted at dinner. Across from it, a trio of Anglo-Indians sat together in front of the rhododendrons and tickled the night air with music. Isabel found herself smiling. She had no doubt that some of the conversation, some of the people, would bore her. But this, with all its cloying scents and old-fashioned conventions, was the India she loved and she was grateful to be home.

'You're here! How marvellous! Now the party can really begin!'

It was Mrs Cawthorne's standard greeting to everyone. She stepped forward to embrace Isabel's mother. She was a plump woman, the daughter of an army major and wife of a colonel. Her own sons, both recently married, had secured commissions in Indian regiments. Isabel's mother, who had seemed subdued in the car, now ignited and the two women fired off sparks of compliments and questions with easy graciousness.

Isabel hung back, watching and listening. Most of her parents' friends, who'd once seemed such a dynamic force in India, struck her now as old-fashioned. All their stories were of past exploits. All their talk was news of those who had retired to England. Their only response to India's current politics was a sad shaking of heads and frowns of confused disappointment.

She looked sideways at her father who stood patiently waiting as Mrs Cawthorne and his wife talked on. His eyes moved from one powdered face to the other but his thoughts strayed elsewhere, she could tell. His hair was thinning and his newly exposed forehead shone with sweat.

A servant paused to offer round a tray of drinks and she took a gin tonic.

She headed off alone towards the groups of younger people gathered on the far side of the lawn. Bertie and his army friends were horsing about, voices loud, faces ruddy. The Broadside girls, all attention, giggled at their sides.

Isabel joined a group nearer her own age, made up of two young married couples, including one of her oldest friends, Sarah, and her new husband, Tom Winton, and Frank, an IAS officer whose wedding date was fixed for the end of his current tour. Sarah was grilling him for details about his plans, which he clearly struggled to supply.

'Tell Amelia to come out. I had our derzi stitch all the suits and dresses for our wedding. And the linen. Saved a fortune.'

Her husband, Tom, murmured something inaudible.

'Besides,' Sarah continued, 'what's the point of her being in London when she could be here, with you?'

Frank looked over her shoulder into middle distance. 'Her parents are a bit jumpy, actually. Worried about these protests. They've been all over the papers.'

Sarah shrugged. 'It'll blow over. Just a few hotheads. Isn't that right, darling?'

Tom nodded. 'Lot of nonsense, if you ask me.'

'One of our servants actually apologised to me the other day, after that train was attacked,' Sarah went on. 'Not real Indians, that's what he said. He was dying of embarrassment.'

Tom said: 'If you gave them independence, they wouldn't know what to do with it.'

'Chaos. That's what would happen. Absolute chaos.'

'She'll be living here anyway, once we're married. They're being awfully silly.' Frank sighed. 'But they won't listen.'

The conversation turned to events in Europe and the men fell to debating the new German Chancellor, Mr Hitler, whose party had done so well earlier in the year. Isabel let her eyes drift across the party, idly reading the gestures and expressions. The pungent smell of frying onions and spices wafted across the lawn from the marquee. Servants bustled in and out with laden trays of food.

Sarah leant in to whisper. 'Who's that?' She gestured over Isabel's shoulder.

A dark-haired man of perhaps thirty looked hastily away as she turned. He shifted his gaze to the man beside him with unnaturally fixed attention. He was tall and rather thin, in need perhaps of a good feed.

'One of Bertie's crowd?'

'Not military, not the type.' Sarah seemed amused. 'Well, he seems to know you. He's been staring at you for the last ten minutes.'

'I very much doubt that.'

Isabel didn't look again until Frank announced that they should all head to the marquee for supper. As they moved off, she glanced back. He was indeed watching her. His eyes slid at once to his feet. An attractive face and rather intense brown eyes. She padded across the lawn with Frank at her side. He was probably married anyway, with several children. Whoever he was, his shyness was a welcome change from the usual boisterous crowd.

The chit arrived at the bungalow the following day as Isabel and her mother sat together in the sitting room.

'Miss Isabel Winthorpe.' Her mother twisted to look across the room. 'It's from someone at The Grand.'

'Really?' Isabel frowned and rose to take it. The envelope was luxuriously thick with The Grand Hotel's crest embossed on the fold. She examined the handwriting. Small, cramped letters.

'Well, open it, Isabel. Don't tease.'

She turned away from her mother, pulled open the flap and slid out the paper. It had the same velvety texture and The Grand's address. The letter was a single paragraph.

Dear Miss Winthorpe,
I can only apologise for writing to you in so impertinent a manner. It was such a surprise, albeit a most pleasant one, to see you again last night that I took the liberty of asking Colonel Cawthorne

for your family's address. I fear you may think me
awfully presumptuous but I wondered if you might
do me the great honour of lunching with me, here at
The Grand, on Thursday at noon? I leave Delhi next
week and would dearly value the chance to see you
before then, if only as a small token of apology for
my regrettable behaviour in the past.

    Yours in hope,
    Jonathan Whyte

'What is it, darling?' Her mother, all attention, rose from her chair. 'You're pale as a ghost.'

She lifted the letter from Isabel's hand before she could resist.

'How nice! He sounds delightful. A little unorthodox, perhaps, but well-mannered. And The Grand offers such tasty luncheons. I do recommend the fish.' She softened her tone, trying to gauge the mood. 'Isabel? Who is he, exactly?'

'Gwen's brother.' She saw it now. She simply hadn't recognised him at the party, but those brown eyes, the even features . . . She shook her head. 'I shan't go. He was horrid.'

'When did you last see him?'

'That first summer with the Misses Ellison when you packed me off to stay with Gwen's family. They're up in the Dales, miles from anywhere, remember? I never went again.' She paused, remembering. 'He must have been about ten.'

Her mother looked relieved. 'All boys are terrors at that age. And he sounds so contrite, Isabel. He's clearly embarrassed. You must accept.'

Isabel hesitated. He was about to leave Delhi, so if the

luncheon was a disaster she never need see him again. She was curious to know why he was in India and, besides, dining at The Grand was always a treat.

All the way to The Grand, past the crowded broken pavements, the street stalls and roadside hawkers, the beggars, all set against southern Delhi's ornate Victorian buildings, she thought how absurd it was to feel nervous. The lobby was hushed. Her heels clicked across the marble floor to the main restaurant and her hat bounced in and out of the gilded mirrors along the wall.

The restaurant was quiet, even for a Thursday. She stood for a moment, steadying her breathing, as the maître d' greeted her. In the centre, an Anglo-Indian in evening dress sat at a baby grand piano and tinkled old-fashioned melodies. In the corner by the door, a mother and daughter sat together, parcels of shopping heaped beside their chairs. Three young women of about her own age chatted in low voices at another table. A group of middle-aged men impinged on the quiet by breaking into sudden laughter.

Her eye was taken by a movement in the far corner near the French windows, which led out to the verandah and the gardens beyond. A chair scraped and a man rose. She recognised him at once from the party. He lifted his hand to wave to her, then hesitated in mid motion, put his palm to his mouth and coughed. The maître d' led her through the restaurant to join him, seated her on the opposite side of the table and unfolded a starched linen napkin across her lap.

Jonathan leant forward. 'I didn't think you'd come.'

She turned to the nearby waiter, expecting him to hand her a menu.

'I took the liberty of ordering for you.' Jonathan spoke in a low voice. His eyes were intense. 'The roast lamb with mashed potato.'

She raised an eyebrow. 'Roast lamb?'

'Of course, if you'd prefer something else . . .'

She shook her head. 'First you seek out my address, now you know my favourite dish. What next?'

'Let's see.' He nodded to the waiter. 'Fetch a gin tonic for the lady, would you? No lime, no lemon, no ice.'

'You have done your homework.' She drew off her gloves, finger by finger, and draped them over her bag on the chair beside her.

'And when it comes to dessert, a large slice of The Grand's signature chocolate cake but without cream.'

'Very impressive. Is there anything you don't know about me?'

He drew a cigarette case from his pocket and offered her one, then leant forward to light it for her. The waiter brought their drinks and they sat for a while, sipping gin tonics and smoking. Isabel withdrew the pin from her hat and set it on top of the gloves. She ran her fingers through her hair to loosen it.

'So tell me, what happened to Gwen? Did she take over the farm? She always said she would.'

He smiled. 'She married a schoolteacher in Ripon. Did you hear? They've got a little girl. Eva.' His features softened. 'She always loved the Dales more than I did. My father was awfully disappointed when I set my sights on the IAS.'

The wine waiter presented him with a bottle of wine for approval.

'You'll have a glass of claret?'

The crystal glasses flushed red. She drew on her cigarette, felt her shoulders slacken.

'It's all your fault, you know.'

She looked up quickly. 'What is?'

'That I'm here.' He drew on his cigarette, tipped back his head and blew a stream of smoke into the air above him. 'Remember that book, the one you studied when you stayed with us? I took it back to school with me after the hols and read it myself. Wanted to work out what had fascinated you, I suppose. Anyway, I was hooked.'

She wasn't sure how to respond. She drank the last of her gin tonic. 'You don't regret it, I hope?'

'Quite the contrary. I love India. Everything about it. The vibrancy, the craziness, the people. Even the heat.' A hint of awkwardness. 'I see now why you missed it so.'

The waiter arrived, set up his tray table with a flourish and began to serve their lunch. Jonathan sat back and watched. He seemed unable to meet her eye.

When the waiter left, Jonathan lifted his wine glass. 'I should explain why I wanted to invite you to luncheon. To give heartfelt apologies for being such an idiotic schoolboy all those years ago. And to say thank you. For opening my eyes to the Empire's greatest treasure.'

She lifted her own glass to touch his. Those weeks in the Dales seemed so long ago, from another life. They picked up their cutlery and began to eat.

'So you're based in Calcutta?'

'Port Blair.' He ate politely, taking small bites. 'The Andamans.'

'Isn't that terribly remote?'

'It's halfway to Siam. Absolute paradise. White-sand

beaches, clear blue waters, splendid fishing. But untamed. The jungle's full of savages, some of them completely uncivilised. And lots of convicts, of course. You know we have a fortified prison there? My bearer and cook are both murderers.'

'The cook's not a poisoner, I hope?'

He laughed. 'Certainly not. Strangled his wife. Hard to imagine. He's a pussycat.'

She took another mouthful of lamb. It was rich and succulent and the gin, chased down by the claret, added to a sudden wave of well-being.

'Tell me about your life there. I'd love to know.'

He lifted his eyes from his plate. His expression was one of cautious excitement. 'Are you sure? I don't want to bore you.'

'You won't.'

She settled into her meal and he took control of the conversation. He spoke with increasing confidence and speed as he warmed to his subject, describing in some detail his work as an assistant commissioner and his ambition to clear further sections of jungle and extend agriculture on the island.

Isabel prodded him with questions but mostly she took the opportunity to study him. He had an intelligent face. His eyes shone as he talked. Most young men she knew seemed to think it fashionable to adopt a rather languid, cynical attitude towards India. Jonathan sounded passionate. He was still talking when the waiter discreetly removed their plates and offered dessert menus.

'I've gone on and on, haven't I?' Jonathan looked suddenly embarrassed. 'I'm so sorry.'

She shook her head, smiled and offered him a cigarette. They sat back in their chairs and started to smoke, sipping the last of the claret. The dining room was almost deserted. Only the businessmen still lingered at their table, chairs pushed back, blurred by a haze of cigar smoke.

'I love long luncheons. I don't have them very often.'

'You will indulge me, won't you, and let me order you some chocolate cake?'

'Well, if you insist.'

The blinds on the French windows were lowered to shoulder height, the pink fabric of the top half glowing warmly with low winter sun, which protruded beneath to spread patches of light across the wooden flooring.

'But only if you tell me how you know my favourite foods?'

'Actually it was your friend, Mrs Winton.' He blushed. 'You don't mind, do you?'

'Sarah?'

'I wanted to say hello at the party but I bottled out. I wasn't sure how you'd react. Besides, that young man glued to your side seemed rather possessive.'

'Frank?' She laughed. 'Heavens, no. Anyway, he's engaged.'

'So I discovered. After you left, I finally went over to speak to your friend, Mrs Winton. She was very friendly.' He paused, leaning forward and watching her closely. 'You don't mind, do you?'

She shrugged. 'Why should I?'

It was almost three o'clock by the time they finished coffee. She reached for her hat and gloves and the waiter rushed forward to ease back her chair. Jonathan once again became agitated as they walked, side by side, towards the door and into the echoing lobby. When he spoke, his words tumbled out in a rush, as if rehearsed.

'Would you do something for me? Unless you think it's a terrible cheek. I don't know Delhi, you see. I wonder if you'd do me a colossal favour and come out and about with me this afternoon.' He hesitated, embarrassed. 'But you're busy, of course. I'm awfully sorry. It was—'

She tugged on her gloves, finger by finger. 'Why not? That sounds fun.'

He smiled, a long, lovely smile that made his eyes shine.

She led him down the hotel's broad drive to the gate and hailed a tonga there, directing it north towards the old city. As they clopped along, swaying lightly in their seats with the motion of the bony horse, the streets became narrow and dirty. The tonga vied for space alongside legions of overladen carts, stacked high with cauliflowers and bhindi and green pickles. They banged so close that she could smell the sweaty, steamy hides of the donkeys and bullocks that drew them. Thin men, all muscle, cycled through the shifting spaces, some with children or wives perched behind on the metal frame.

At a junction, she tapped the tonga-wallah on the shoulder and directed him in Hindustani. He swung the horse left into a stream of traffic and edged them across the chaos towards the mouth of a lane.

'You speak better than I do,' Jonathan said. 'And I came third in the Urdu examinations.'

She shrugged. 'It's mostly street slang.'

'Who taught you?'

'I used to play with one of the servants' boys. It wasn't

41

allowed, of course.' She peered out as the tonga squeezed into the neck of the lane and drew to a halt. A mangy dog barked round the horse's legs. 'Anyway, brace yourself.'

The mud underfoot was sticky with animal dung and discarded vegetable scraps. The stink was undercut by an intense sweetness, a cloying smell of burnt sugar.

Isabel strode ahead. Boys on bicycles wobbled through the tide of pedestrians, ringing shrill bells. A ragged toddler, naked from the waist down, took a few unsteady steps before losing his balance and crashing to the ground. An older child, her face smeared with mud, rushed to push her hands under his arms and haul him up.

The shop was little more than a stall. A long wooden counter faced the street, covered with dishes of sweetmeats in bright colours. They were piled in elaborate pyramids and a young boy sat on a stool behind the counter, wielding a long switch, which he used to knock flies off the produce even as they settled.

Isabel greeted him with a namaste. The boy slipped from his stool and ran out towards the back, bare feet slapping on the wooden planks. Minutes later, the scrap of sacking across the doorway was swept aside and a man strode out, wiping his hands on a piece of rag. He put his hands together in namaste and bowed to Isabel.

'Rahul, this is my friend, Mr Whyte.'

He glanced at Jonathan. 'Namaste, ji.'

'Hello.'

He was a young man but the belly pushing out the folds of his kurta was already rounded and his hands looked calloused by manual work.

Isabel turned from one man to the other as she spoke.

'How is Sangeeta-ji? They married – is it three years now, Rahul? I was in London, you see. By the time I heard, I'd missed the wedding. They've got a son now. Abhishek.'

'Very fine, thank you, Isabel Madam. And Mutter-ji also.'

'His baba, Chaudhary, was our cook. Rahul and I played together all the time, didn't we?' She beamed. 'A long time ago now.'

'So many years, madam.' Rahul gestured to them to go inside. 'You are drinking chai?'

Isabel followed him through into a small, rough courtyard, Jonathan trailing behind. Sangeeta, Rahul's young wife, stopped her sweeping and bowed her head with respect. A slight girl of perhaps fourteen crouched in the far corner. She held a short stick and was drawing shapes in the dirt to amuse Rahul's baby boy. Her eyes, when they met Isabel's, were piercing and hostile. She raised her dupatta to shield her face and withdrew into the building beyond.

Sangeeta set down her broom, crossed to add wood to the fire and blew the embers into life. The sickly smell of boiling sugar spilt out from a covered doorway in the far wall. In a thin line of shade, Chaudhary Madam, Rahul's elderly mother, lay on a battered charpoy. She looked little more than cloth-covered bones. White hair straggled from her long plait.

Isabel picked up a stool and sat by the charpoy. She lifted the crude bamboo fan there and began to stir the air around the old lady's face.

'Rahul's mother was so kind to me.' She spoke over her shoulder to Jonathan. 'Sometimes I trooped back with Rahul for dinner. She always welcomed me, gave me food.' The old woman stirred and Isabel bent to touch her cheek. 'It was a lark for me, being part of an Indian family. It was only later that I thought how little they had to eat. She probably went hungry because of me and I was too stupid to realise.'

Rahul brought a stool for Jonathan and placed it beside Isabel's. Sangeeta stirred chai in a blackened pot on the fire and, having served them, picked up her son and swayed him on her hip as the two guests and her husband drank their sweet milky tea from clay cups and picked at a saucer of sweetmeats.

'We ate a massive luncheon, Rahul. But I can't resist.' Isabel bit into one of the silver-topped sweets. 'Jonathan, do try one of these. Kaju barfi. Delicious. It's made with nuts, cashew nut. Now Rahul, tell me, how's business?'

He pulled a face. 'Like this, like that, madam.'

'Not good?' She nibbled at the sweets.

He glanced at Jonathan before he answered. 'These protests. So many hartals, also. No sugar, no ghee, no customers. Everything becomes closed.'

Jonathan said: 'If you really want to stay open, ask for police protection. The strikes would soon stop.'

Rahul shook his head. 'It's not so easy.'

Isabel said: 'I don't know why they have them. They seem to hurt the poor most of all.'

Rahul looked down into his chai. Isabel reached to take the baby from Sangeeta and set him on her lap. He reached for her hair.

'He's grown so much, Rahul.'

Sangeeta scolded the boy and tried to prise his fingers from Isabel's fringe as Rahul muttered: 'I'm sorry, madam.'

'You should be proud. Look at that grip.'

Isabel tickled him and he squealed. She looked over,

laughing. Jonathan stared at the ground, one hand holding a cup of untouched chai while the other pulled in a vague way at his earlobe. He looked large and clumsy and out of place.

By the time she and Jonathan left, the afternoon light was yellowing, made hazy by the smoke from cooking fires. The tonga nosed its way through a surge of traffic. Ahead, shopkeepers rushed to erect wooden shutters over their stalls. Mothers, heads and faces covered, rounded up children from the street and herded them home.

'Is there a protest?'

'Looks like it.' Jonathan sat with his shoulder turned to her.

She reached over to him. 'Look, I just thought you'd enjoy meeting them, that's all.'

He shrugged, didn't look round.

She added: 'They're lovely people.'

Bicycles and carts hurried past. She tapped the tonga-wallah on the shoulder and told him to hurry.

Jonathan said in a tight voice: 'I must say, I'm surprised. It's not safe.'

She didn't reply. The tonga-wallah slapped his switch across the haunches of the bony horse and goaded it into a half-hearted trot.

'That baby wasn't clean,' he said. 'You don't know what you might catch.'

The roadside began to look deserted. In place of the usual bustle, only a stray child in the gutter, a dog nosing through rubbish, then trotting on, a hawker pushing his barrow back home, head bowed under the weight. The quietness struck her as unnatural. Then, in the silence, something stirred. The echo of a distant noise. She strained to listen. A pulse of male voices, ghostly at first, then steadily growing. Chanting.

She faced him and raised her hand. 'Listen.'

The voices grew louder.

'It's coming from the bustee.'

Jonathan looked anxious. 'Tell the driver to get a move on, would you?'

Isabel focused on the chanting. The words weren't distinct – the noise seemed to bounce off the clouds – but the tone was clear. It had the vehemence of a battle cry and it was moving rapidly towards them. She tried to think. They could turn off the main thoroughfare and enter the labyrinth of back lanes in the hope of avoiding the protest but it would be slow going. Or they could press on and try to get out of the area before the marchers appeared.

They emerged into a broad crossroads and the swelling sound burst suddenly all around them. The intersection, normally a clutter of vehicles and pedestrians, was deserted.

'Look!' Isabel pointed down the street that ran perpendicular to their own. A dark swarm of men flowed towards them, fists striking the air, voices strident.

Jonathan leant forward and struck the tonga-wallah on the shoulder. 'Don't just sit there! Go!'

The tonga-wallah brought his switch down on the horse's back but even as the carriage lurched forward, figures detached themselves from the crowd of marchers and came running at full tilt down the street towards them, shouting and waving their arms. The horse, startled by the sting of the whip and the shouting, tossed its head and screamed. The first men were almost upon them. They were young, faces red and moist with sweaty excitement, waving staves and metal knives, which flashed in the fading sunlight.

Isabel jumped down from the carriage and ran to grab hold of the horse's bridle. Its eyes rolled white in its large head, its mouth flecked with foam and spittle where it gnawed at the bit.

'Hush, boy. Quiet now.' She hung onto the bridle as the head shook, almost lifting her off the ground. The eyes fixed on her, then veered away in terror. The switch struck its flank and the horse shot forward a few paces, dragging Isabel with it. Hooves stamped and crashed as the horse danced at her feet. She clung on and reached an arm round its neck, trying to soothe it. 'Hush, beauty. It's alright.'

Jonathan jumped out of the carriage and ran to join her. He pulled at her hands, trying to prise them off the bridle.

'Get back in the carriage.'

Isabel shook her head. 'Leave me. I know horses.'

The horse was pawing and stamping but showing signs of quietening. She hugged its neck, patted it, whispered repeatedly in its turning ear: 'Quiet now, boy. Hush now.'

Jonathan tensed at her side. The first men reached them, hot-blooded youngsters. A rank smell hung around them of toddy and ghee. Isabel turned and spoke politely in Hindustani.

'We're having trouble with the horse. Don't frighten him.'

One of the young men jeered. The shouting crowd advanced behind them. Their words grew clearer: *Jai Hindustan Ki! Inquilab Zindabad!* Beside her, Jonathan squared up.

'You've no quarrel with the horse, I hope.' She made herself laugh. 'He's a very Indian horse.'

One of the men shouted: 'Yes, under the yoke. Like all of us.'

More men were upon them now, flowing round the carriage to form a ragged, fast-growing crowd. The men waved their staves, inching closer.

Isabel kept close to the horse's head, one arm round its neck, the other on the bridle, touching its face.

'We'll get out of your way.'

She eased the horse forward, step by step, dragging the tonga behind. The tonga-wallah sat terrified on his seat.

The horse cried and reared. Isabel found herself jerked upwards, then dumped on the ground with a thud beside the pounding hooves. She scrambled to her feet.

'Who threw that?' Jonathan confronted the crowd, his face drained of colour.

Isabel hadn't seen the stone but she understood.

'How dare you?' Jonathan was shaking. 'You bloody idiots.'

A stout man, wearing only a lunghi, his bare torso showing the muscular chest and arms of a day labourer, pressed forward from the crowd and, in a sudden flash of fist, punched Jonathan in the face. The man's teeth, stained red with betel juice, grinned. Jonathan fell backwards with a bang onto his back and sprawled, winded, on the ground. He lay for a moment, too dazed to move. Isabel stood over him, trying to shield him from the advancing men to one side and the flailing hooves on the other.

'Leave him alone.' Her voice sounded shrill. 'Stop it!'

From somewhere in the crowd, a male voice rang out.

'*Esse mat karo!* Don't!'

Heads swivelled. A tall, broad-shouldered man stepped forward. His clothes were clean and neatly pressed and his face was clean-shaven. He had an air of command and addressed Isabel in English. 'Take him. Go.'

She put her hands under Jonathan's arms and helped him to his feet. Blood oozed from his nose.

He struggled to stand and glared at his assailant. 'Don't think you'll get away with this.'

Isabel tried to turn him, to push him ahead of her up into the carriage. The tonga-wallah shouted at his horse and fell again to whipping its flanks. Finally it stirred and moved.

Jonathan twisted round from the seat. 'You won't win, you know that. You think you can run this country? I'd like to see you try.'

The carriage gathered speed and drew them at last away from the crossroads and out into the deserted street. The horse, pouring its fear into its legs, reached for a gallop and the carriage swayed and creaked behind it.

Isabel looked back at the assembled men, staring after them with menace, and, in the centre, the silent figure of their leader who had intervened to save them.

Chapter Four

'Darling, what on earth were you thinking?'

Isabel's mother dipped a cotton flannel into a basin of water, squeezed it out and handed it across to Isabel. Jonathan sat on the settee. His nose was swollen and cut across the bridge.

'But why were you down there? I thought you were lunching at The Grand.'

'We did.' Isabel held the flannel against the cut. 'Does that hurt?'

'Your father sent a chit. They may have to call out the army. There's hundreds of them. On the rampage.' Her mother poured iodine onto a cotton swab and dabbed at the scrapes on Jonathan's hands.

Isabel said: 'It was all my fault. I sent the poor tonga-wallah in quite the wrong direction.'

'I thought you knew this city by now, darling. Honestly. You were lucky to escape with your lives. You must stay for dinner, Mr Whyte. Don't protest. My husband can lend you a dinner jacket.' She put the stopper back in the iodine bottle and set it on the tray. 'I do wonder what's happening to this country.'

Isabel gave Jonathan an uncertain glance. 'Mr Whyte may have other plans, Mother.'

'Of course he doesn't. Anyway, they're sure to impose a curfew. We'll send word to The Grand and say you're staying here tonight. Much more sensible.'

'Well, you were a big hit with my mother.'

'She's a charming lady. Now I know where you get it from.'

'Rot.' Isabel tutted. 'We couldn't be less alike.'

They sat side by side on wicker loungers on the verandah and smoked. The night air was cool and thick with the scent of flowers. The light from the chowkidar's hut flickered through the bushes at the far end of the drive. The grass sang with the screech of cicadas and low croaks of bullfrogs.

A rustle of paper as her mother, sitting behind them in the drawing room in a dim circle of light, turned a page of her magazine. Isabel was alert in the darkness to the low purr of her father's approaching car but it had already turned ten o'clock and there was still no sign of him.

'He's at the office all night sometimes,' she said. 'My mother tries to hide it but she does worry.'

'Goes with the territory, I suppose.'

'I wonder what's happening. The protest, I mean.'

Jonathan shrugged. 'I'm sure your father can look after himself.'

Isabel stubbed out the end of her cigarette in the ashtray and reached for her sandals. 'I should go inside and keep her company.'

'Do you have to?' Jonathan paused. She sensed that he was steadying his nerve. 'One more smoke?'

He took two more cigarettes from his case, snapped it shut, lit them both from the remnants of his ebbing stub and handed one to her.

She drew on it, tilted her head back and blew the smoke upwards into the cloud of small flies hanging around their heads. They scattered, then slowly re-formed. She sensed the turn of his head as he watched her.

'You're extraordinary. You do realise that?'

'Odd, more like.'

His teeth gleamed in the darkness as he smiled. 'You're amusing too. I like that. And courageous. I keep thinking of the way you leapt down from the carriage and handled that horse. You could've been killed.'

She smiled back. 'I doubt it. It was rather a pathetic old horse really, wasn't it?'

They fell silent for a moment. She stretched out her legs and sighed. When she drew the smoke into her lungs, it cleaned out the day's tension.

'Do you really want to stay out here?'

'In India?' She considered. 'Of course. Not sure how I can manage it, though.'

He sat very still beside her, looking straight ahead into the darkness. 'You could marry someone posted here.'

She blinked, suddenly tense.

'If you don't mind my asking, well, is there someone?'

'No. Not, you know, so far . . .'

He exhaled heavily. She glanced sideways. It was too dark to read his expression.

Behind them, floorboards creaked as her mother moved about the room. A high-pitched clink as she poured herself a glass of iced tea from the jug.

Isabel put her hand squarely on the wicker arm of the chair and made to get up. 'I really should go in. Do you mind?'

He jumped to his feet. 'Of course. How thoughtless of me.'

'It's been quite a day.'

'Hasn't it?' He hovered awkwardly. She felt him reaching for something unsaid and found herself waiting for him to find the words. Finally he said: 'I haven't offended you, have I? It's been delightful. When I suggested luncheon, I never dreamt . . .'

She laughed. 'It would go on all day? Neither did I. But I'm glad.' She extinguished her cigarette.

As she lifted her hand from the ashtray, he reached forward in a swift single movement and took her fingers, lifted them to his mouth. His lips were warm against her skin. The sudden intrusion of a noise made her jump. It was the whine of the gates being scraped open. She pulled away her hand, embarrassed, and moved forward to stand against the verandah rail and peer into the night. The thin light of a bicycle lamp wavered past the chowkidar's hut and turned down the drive towards the house, flashing snapshots of posts and bushes as it progressed.

'Mother!'

Her mother joined them on the verandah and the three of them strained to make out the dark figure cycling with a crunch over the gravel. He wobbled as he lifted a hand to greet them.

'Gerard?' Her mother disappeared inside. 'Finally!'

Her father drew to a halt in front of the verandah, dismounted from the bicycle and climbed over to join them.

He shook hands with Jonathan. 'Gerard Winthorpe. Sorry to miss dinner.' His hair was slick with sweat and his cheeks shone ruddy in the low light. 'Roadblocks. Borrowed Singh's cycle.'

'Jonathan Whyte. A difficult evening, sir?'

'I'm afraid so.' Her father looked past them to the empty sitting room.

Isabel said: 'She's gone to rouse Cook. Are you hungry?'

Her father said to Jonathan: 'How about a Scotch?'

They followed him inside and stood, watching, as her father poured drinks.

'Cigar?'

Isabel tutted as he opened the box, picked out two cigars and gave one to Jonathan. 'She'll be annoyed if you don't eat.'

'Always in trouble. Been married thirty-three years. You'll see.'

Jonathan already seemed accepted by her parents, even though they knew him even less than she did.

'What's the news, sir?'

Her father shook his head, handed Jonathan a Scotch and took a sip from his own. 'The army's out. The police did their best but it all turned rather nasty. Very unfortunate.'

Jonathan said: 'Casualties?'

'Three fatalities. There may be more. Dozens injured.' He drank again. 'Whatever game they think they're playing, these people, they certainly know how to spread mayhem.'

Mrs Winthorpe bustled in. She looked at the unlit cigar in one of her husband's hands and the drink in the other. 'Darling, you must eat. Cook's rustling something up. Don't give me that look.'

Her father turned to Jonathan. 'Come through and keep me company, at least. In the interests of marital harmony.'

The two men headed off to the dining room with their drinks. Beside Jonathan, her father looked suddenly old, his shoulders stooped.

Isabel's mother put out a hand to hold her back. Once the men were out of earshot, she whispered: 'Your father likes him.'

'They've hardly exchanged two words.'

'That's not the point. Go to bed, Isabel. Leave them to talk.'

Isabel lay awake in bed for some time, listening to the murmur of male voices from the drawing room and, beyond her window, the languid movement of the trees in the night air. Something had changed and she wasn't sure what to make of it. He had stirred something in her, a vague longing that she found hard to identify. She just sensed that when he left Delhi in a matter of days and sailed back to his life of adventure in the Andamans, she would feel herself more alone here. Her parents' bungalow seemed suddenly old-fashioned and their social world narrow and confined.

Chapter Five

Asha

The far reaches of the room stayed black with shadow. Arrows of sunshine fell along one edge, pressing in between the mud patties that held the wall together. The shafts danced with dust and swirls of smoke. The room smelt of sour breath and spices and bodies. When hands pulled back the sacking across the doorway, as people came and went, the heat swam in and drowned them.

At night, she and Baba slept huddled together in a corner, hemmed in by uncles, aunties and cousins. If she fidgeted and grew restless, Baba grumbled, 'Aram, Asha. Go to sleep.' His arm across her was dead and still as he slept. Baba's cousin, whom she called uncle, snored and sometimes an auntie also and Asha pressed her head in her baba's side to shut out the noise.

Outside the bustee was hectic with tumbledown shacks. Makeshift houses filled every space. Greasy water ran in an open channel down the middle of the street and children did their business there, for anyone to see, and played there too and it stank so badly in the heat that her stomach turned. Rats swam in it, their black eyes and whiskered noses breaking the surface. They bit, if you bothered them. And dogs, foolish with big eyes, trotted and sniffed and some let you pet them but others snapped.

She didn't have a brother or a sister or a mama even. But she had her baba and they were lucky to have a roof over their heads; her baba told her to thank the gods for it, others were worse off. Her uncle's roof was already overstretched with his wife and the other uncle and auntie and eight children between them.

The men set out early to stand for work. Even as she slept, her baba shifted and crept away, leaving empty space beside her. Then the aunties stirred and spoke in low voices, one to another, as they crouched outside and blew on the fire to boil up chai and cook rotis. Some days, all the men were chosen, even her baba. They came home late in the night, lunghis white with dust. Her uncle's face shone red with country-made toddy and the children knew to hide.

'So much work is there, nah?' Uncle boasted, hollered at his wife to stir herself and cook food. 'So many big buildings the Britishers are making, offices and whatnot. So much of money.' He clapped Baba on the shoulder. 'Come, bhai, eat. We need strength to work.'

She sat beside her baba, his thigh warm against her side, and he fed her titbits before they slept.

Other days, only the uncles worked and Baba sat the whole day long at the crossroads in the heat. On these days, he crept back to the room, ashamed, and lay alone in their corner and refused to eat even one roti.

Once Uncle hit Baba with his fists and cursed him. 'You lazy idler, when are you going to make money and pay me rent? I don't sweat in the dirt all day to keep you. Do I look a rich man?'

In the morning, the men made rough peace again. They set

out together, side by side, pale-faced and subdued, nothing but chai in their stomachs, to wait in the sun in the hope of another day's work.

'Tell about naming me Asha.'

Baba sighed. She knew already, of course. It was their secret story. The uncles were out and Baba sat alone in the dirt by the entrance to the shack, smoking a bidi and watching the street. Nearby the women crouched by a stick fire, shaped patties of roti dough and slapped them into rounds between their palms.

Asha lifted Baba's hand and measured it against her own. His skin was hard and lined. The fingernails had shredded and split with building work.

'Please, Baba.'

He lifted his hand and put it round her shoulders, drawing her to him. His breath smelt of the cigarette. 'Well, Asha, it was like this. Your mother and I were longing for a child. So many years we were married and all our cousins and neighbours in the village had three, four, five children and still we had none. The women looked sideways at your mother when she walked through the streets. Like this.' He pulled his face into a haughty expression to make her laugh. 'And the men in the chai stall gave all manner of stupid advice. Send her home and take another wife, they said. Beat her more. Make her eat coal.'

'So what did you do?'

He shook his head. 'What could we do? We lived. I hoed and planted and weeded. Your mama cooked and cleaned and drew water from the well and you know what else we did? We did puja every night, praying to Goddess

Lakshmi and Lord Hanuman for the blessing of a child.'

A fly landed on his arm and she leant forward, blew it off. 'And then what happened?'

'What do you think?'

She tugged at him to carry on.

'One day the gods were blessing us and sent you to join us. And you were so beautiful, such a tiny, perfect baby, nah? So we named you Asha. Hope.'

His voice was sad and when she tried to cuddle against him, he didn't respond. He seemed to forget that she was even there.

Baba came back to the bustee early one day. He strode out to the waste ground behind the shacks where Asha played with her cousins, took her by the arm and half-guided, half-dragged her back to the room.

'Wash your face.' He watched while she poured water into a basin and wiped at her cheeks. 'Harder.' He took a cloth and held her fast, then scrubbed at her cheeks, her chin, rubbed over her eyes.

Next he hunted through the pile of odds and ends on the room's one shelf and found a piece of broken comb. He spat on the few remaining teeth, then used it to tug at her hair.

She squirmed and kicked as it bit into the tangles. Finally he let her go, stood back to look at her. 'Is that your best dress?'

It was her only dress, a cotton kameez, handed down from an older cousin. The material showed red along the seam but faded to a grubby off-white in the centre where it was much scrubbed. She smoothed it with the palm of her hand.

He took her by the arm and led her along the narrow, twisting street. His steps were quick. She had to trot to keep up. Faces blurred as they rushed past. Women crouched over fires. Old men smoking, spitting, hugging shafts of shade. Toddlers, half-naked and grimy, raking through the filth. A dog appeared from the mouth of an alley between houses, stared, then turned and picked its way past them along the edge of the open drain.

Baba's breath was short and hard and she too began to pant. Her hair pricked with sweat. His hand, where he grasped her, was hot and slippery on her skin. Finally he pulled her up a steep bank, strewn with sodden scraps of paper and torn sacking and they emerged onto a ridge. She looked back over her shoulder as he tugged her along. The bustee lay beneath them, a patchwork of wood and tin that flashed in the sunlight, punctuated by slowly rising smoke. It looked peculiar to her. The noises were softened by distance and the squalor veiled by the lazy peacefulness of late afternoon.

'Come, Asha. Quickly.' Her baba pulled and she turned to face forward. They crossed the road and entered a neighbourhood of individual houses set in gardens and circled by high walls. After some time, Baba stopped at a tall gate and rapped on it with his knuckles. His forehead grew lines as he waited. The gate creaked open a fraction. A young man in a dark uniform peered out at them, then jutted his chin, widened the gap and let them slip inside.

The house had its back to them. Its windows were shuttered and dark. Two young men in lunghis lounged on the lawn. One, languid and propped up on his elbow, barely raised his eyes to acknowledge her. He tore up strands of grass and dropped them through his fingers.

The other, sitting with straight back and crossed legs, twisted round. His features were even, a strong nose offset by a wide mouth and creamy brown cheeks. He looked her right in the face and his gaze was frank and alert. She stared back. He smiled and she felt herself dissolve into a flush and drew her eyes at once down to the grass.

Her baba led her round the flower beds, past the bright splash of flowers, towards a narrow doorway disguised by sacking. He rapped on the door frame. An unseen hand lifted back the sacking curtain and Baba pushed her inside, his hands on her shoulders, guiding her down a short corridor and into a dimly lit room beyond.

It smelt of men, boiled chai and cigarettes. She blinked, looked round. At first, there were only shadows. Slowly they began to part and to fill. A man, older than Baba, sat cross-legged on a charpoy in the centre of the room. He smoked and the end of the cigarette winked red as he drew on it and the rising smoke softened his features and blurred them. Other men stood to the side but she daren't turn her head to look.

The man on the charpoy raised his hand and beckoned at Baba and Asha found herself pushed forwards towards him. He had sharp eyes and he stared right into her face and said nothing for some time. She wondered if Baba had scrubbed her well enough. Baba's breath sounded behind her, still heavy from the rushing.

'How old is she?' The man's voice was calm and clear.

Baba shrugged. Who knew?

'We'll say seven years old, nah? Maybe she's older, maybe not.'

He held out a hand. She looked at it but didn't know what to do.

'Come closer, girl.' He had gentleness in his voice. 'Do you know what country you belong to?'

She twisted round to look at her baba. He looked tired and shrunken beside this grander man. His face didn't give her any answer.

'This one, ji.'

'But what is its name?'

She faltered, looked at her feet.

'You live in a great country. Hindustan. Remember that. Be proud.' He tutted, shook his head. 'Do you do puja? Has your baba taught you well?'

She nodded.

'Tell me which gods are there when you go for puja.'

She thought of the temple and the statues with their snaking arms and plaster headdresses and painted faces where she and Baba prayed on holy days.

'Goddess Lakshmi and Lord Hanuman and Lord Ram.'

'Good. Never forget them. Whatever else they teach you. Do you see? You are Hindu-wallee. From birth until death. *Ye sach hai?* Is it truth?'

She nodded.

'Now go and play. Your baba and I will talk awhile.'

She didn't want to go outside on her own. She hung around her baba's side but he frowned and sent her out. The young men still lounged there and she took herself as far from them as she could. She found a piece of broken stone in the shade and crouched and watched a trail of ants run back and forth across the ground, falling and struggling and rising to run again even as she shifted the dirt into mountain ranges with her finger.

'You don't know me, do you?'

The languid youth called to her. She kept her head low.

'Your name's Asha. See? I remember.'

The young men said something to each other in low voices, then got to their feet. Her body tensed as they came over.

'My baba was cook at the Britishers' house.' He laughed. 'I gave you cocoa once on a wooden spoon and you were sick.'

The ants ran back and forth but she barely saw them now. If the boys pestered her, she would run back inside, whatever her baba said.

'It's true, little sister.' The second voice, softer than the first. The youth who had smiled. The boys settled on a low stone wall beside her, their feet big in dusty chappals. 'Your baba worked there too when you were a baby.'

She shook her head. The bustee was all she knew.

'He was the sweeper-wallah. Don't you remember anything?' the first boy said. 'The big trees with mango and jamun? My mama minded you sometimes. You called her Didi. Didi and Baba. The only words you knew.'

She raised her eyes, unsure. 'Who are you, anyway?'

The gentle boy said: 'He's Rahul. I'm Sanjay. This is my uncle's house. Maybe it will be yours too. My uncle heard what happened to your baba. He's going to give him work.'

She stared. 'Heard what?'

The boys exchanged glances.

Rahul said: 'Don't you know?' He looked across at the house to make sure no one was near. 'The Britishers disgraced him. Said he'd stolen money.'

'My baba never—'

He lifted his hand to quieten her. 'I know. They found it. Every rupee. Weeks later, when you and your baba had gone already.'

Asha frowned. 'So why didn't he get his job back?'

Rahul shrugged. 'No one knew where you'd gone. Back to the village, my baba said. You were a baby only.'

Sanjay said: 'They're like that, the Britishers. My uncle hears all manner of stories.'

Asha shook her head. Her baba never told how they came from the village to the bustee. She thought it was when her mama died.

Rahul pushed off the wall, slapped down in his chappals and pulled at Sanjay's arm. 'Come on.'

Sanjay carried on speaking over his shoulder as they moved off.

'Your baba's not built for labouring. My uncle's a good man. You'll see.'

That night, back in the bustee, everyone argued and it was all about the visit to Sanjay's uncle. She lay quiet in the corner and listened.

'Why you, anyway?' That was Uncle. 'And why now? After many years, nah?'

Her baba, hesitant. 'He heard about me, that I was here in the bustee. Some gossip.'

'Why didn't he hear before?'

'Bhai, how can I be knowing? But it's good work. Sweeper-wallah, like before. Fetching and carrying. And a place to sleep also.'

'What about us?' Auntie. 'Isn't there another job?'

'And what's all this about the girl?'

Shuffling as Baba shifted his weight. He spoke in a voice too low for her to hear.

Another auntie said: 'What's the use of learning for a girl like her?'

'She should be working.' Uncle. 'There's a man who takes girls for sewing. Maybe it's time.'

'She's just getting useful. All these years eating, eating, and finally she might be of use.'

Uncle again. 'She could weave carpet or maybe silk with those little fingers. I've got it in mind for my girls. Why not her?'

'She should marry.'

'At her age?' Baba spoke softly.

'Someone might take her.'

Baba tutted. 'She's too young.'

'Don't give the girl ideas, bhai.' Uncle again. 'What good will it do?'

Baba muttered under his breath.

'What will it cost at this school?' Auntie's low voice.

'Mind your business.' Uncle. 'Who asked you?'

'It's free. He says he knows someone there and he'll speak for her.' Baba sounded pleading. 'They get free meals, every day. Hot meals.'

'They'll make her Christian. That's their price. Is that what you want?'

'Afterwards, when she's ripe for marriage, will any decent Hindu family take her?'

Baba sighed. 'If she could learn to read, though. And to write. And to speak English also. If she has brains and works hard, all that is possible, he says. He's an educated man himself and a Brahmin. What a blessing.'

'Blessing or curse?'

'What about our daughters, Husband?' Auntie, timid. 'Maybe they too could—'

'You stupid woman. And who's going to help you to cook and clean?' Uncle turned his attention back to Baba. 'And you, if you can afford to send your daughter to school, you can afford to pay the rent you owe me, isn't it? How many years have you been here, soaking up food like a sponge?'

Baba, very quiet. 'May the gods bless you, bhai. I'll send whatsoever I can. I won't forget.'

Asha lay very still. The adults got up, shuffled to their mats to sleep. Her baba lay solidly against her, wrapped his arm round her shoulder. She tried to twist round, to see his face.

He murmured: 'Go to sleep, Asha. It's late.'

As they settled, Uncle's voice crossed the room: 'You know who he is, bhai? That man? You know what trouble he makes?'

Baba's arm around her stiffened but he didn't answer and soon the darkness became thick with snoring. Only Asha lay awake, listening to her baba's steady breathing against her neck. She thought of those people who had branded him a thief, her own baba, who never hurt anyone in his life. She curled her fists into balls with the wickedness of it. They had ruined his good name and cast them out from a world of mango trees to this stinking, overcrowded place and he had never told her, never complained. She reached her arm behind her and patted his broad side, softly so as not to wake him, comforting him as if, for a moment, he were the child and she the parent.

Chapter Six

Asha and her baba went to live in a shack at the back of Sanjay's uncle's house. When she woke, birds cawed and screeched in the trees along the back of the lawn and the mali's hose hissed water across the flower beds. The earth smelt moist and rich.

She started school, trailing each day to a brick building at the back of a church. Crows taught her, women in black robes, which covered their heads and fastened with pins at their temples. Their eyes were sharp and solemn. Asha sat on the floor with the other children and learnt letters and numbers and stories from the Bible. In the mornings, before the lessons began, they put the flats of their hands together and closed their eyes. A waxy image of Jesus hung at the front of the classroom. His head fell forwards as if he slept but his hands and feet flamed red with blood.

Sometimes, if she made mistakes, the Crows beat her across the backs of her legs with a cane. First the skin stung, then it tore and bled, then it went numb. At lunchtime, she lined up to take a flat leaf on her palm and a woman ladled first hot daal, then mixed subzi onto its surface. She took two pale rotis from the pile, tore them into strips and pinched up the food.

Each evening, Baba rolled out their mat on the mud floor

of the shack at the back of Sahib's house and she curled against him, her face pressed into the sour sweetness of his chest, his arm tucked over her shoulders.

'Tell me, Asha, what did you learn today?'

She saved up titbits of her day to feed to him: the story of a new English word she had learnt or a sum or a spelling. After too short a time, his breathing deepened and the weight of his arm became heavier as he left her for sleep. She guarded him for as long as she could. Male voices murmured low from the house. Footsteps grated the gravel paths at all hours of darkness. The stealthy footsteps of men who didn't want their coming to be known. Distantly, the wail of a wildcat and the twang of a country-made instrument playing half-remembered music.

Three years passed.

Then a day came that started as normal but went on to change everything.

Asha and her classmates sat cross-legged on the classroom floor, chalking sums, when a Crow rushed through the door and took their teacher to one side. They bent themselves together against the front wall and whispered. Finally the teacher turned to the class and clapped her hands. Her mouth showed fake jollity.

'*Jaldee*, children. School is closed for holiday.' She shooed them, flapping her broad hands. 'Go home.'

Asha stumbled to her feet. They hadn't yet had lunch. She was hungry.

The teacher held open the door. Her eyes were anxious. 'Run home. Don't dawdle.'

Asha started for home. It was too quiet. Thresholds which

usually gave into shaded rooms were stopped up with wooden doors. Shopkeepers had climbed down from their stools and hurriedly packed goods into crates, latching shutters over front-window counters. A woman hurried past her, keeping to the edge of the path. Her dupatta was pulled low over her head, her eyes downcast. The boulders by the well, usually peppered with gossiping women, were deserted. Asha broke into a run.

Several dozen men hung about the back of the house. The air was heavy with agitation. The men scuffed at the ground with their chappals, pushed at each other's shoulders in mock-fighting and smoked bidis, inhaling with nervous pecks. Sanjay was there, the young man with even features who was Sahib's nephew.

'Asha! Why aren't you in school?'

Her baba, coming out of the house, caught sight of her.

'It closed, Baba.'

'Closed?'

'They fear riots afterwards.' A thin-faced man with a prominent nose nodded at Baba. 'The bustee's always first to burn.'

'Go inside.' Baba pointed her to the shack. 'Stay there.'

As he finished speaking, those near the door shifted and made room and Sahib himself appeared. He hesitated on the threshold, looked round, as the men fell silent and turned to him.

'Well, brothers.' He smiled and it seemed a blessing on them all. Asha watched, entranced. In the bright sunlight, his skin looked wrinkled and rather sallow and she imagined saying: I will take care of you, sahib, you should eat better and come more often into the garden.

As she gazed, his eyes fell on her. 'Ah, a sister too. You are coming, nah?'

69

'Oh no, sahib.' Baba spoke up at once. 'So young, still.'

'Nay, why not?' Sahib clapped his hands. 'You want to see your Hindustani brothers, Asha? See them fight for freedom?'

'*Han-ji*, sahib. Very much.' He knew her name. She would go anywhere with him, do anything.

Baba put his hands together, pleading. 'She doesn't realise, ji. She—'

'Let her come.' Sahib turned and began to stride towards the gate. Men threw their half-smoked bidis onto the gravel, crushed them and hurried to keep pace with him. She and her baba followed them out into the street.

The men walked with proud confidence. Sahib, at the front, set the pace. He strode with even steps and his head bobbed rhythmically, rising and falling amongst the youths jostling at his side. Asha, keeping by her baba towards the rear, swelled with pride.

Along the street, heads turned to look. An old man clapped his hands. Two young men on bicycles shouted greetings. Some men rose from chai stalls and the mouths of alleys to join them. Slowly the numbers grew. Only women, watching from half-shuttered windows or from rooftops where washing hung, looked subdued and drew back from the jauntily striding men.

'Where are we going, Baba?'

His mouth was resolute. 'To the Assembly. Where they make laws.'

She considered. A new Assembly building recently opened. The Crows showed a drawing in class. It looked as round as a bird's nest. Indians, too, would meet there, the Crows explained, to help Britain to govern the country.

'Why?'

'Never mind.' He still seemed stung by his exchange with Sahib. 'Keep close to me.'

The buildings around them became more grand and the roads widened. Lawns stretched on both sides. The triumphal arch of India Gate rose ahead, then fell behind as they walked on. More and more people poured out now from all directions, crossing the expanses of grass, crowding the paths, filling the pavements. Sahib's bobbing head became more difficult to see in the growing crowd. Young men skipped in and out of the road, dodging official cars, donkey carts and legions of bicycles. Asha wanted to run, to jump in the air. Only Baba looked grim-faced.

They reached a roundabout with a central mound of grass and an imposing stone fountain. The crowd ahead flowed round it as water finds a path round a boulder. Several young men scrambled and pulled themselves onto the monument. Men in the crowd cheered and shouted. Asha laughed. The young men splashed round the fountain basin, kicked up arcs of spray, then bent and threw showers of water with scooped hands over the passing crowd. Asha wanted to stop, to watch the fun, but Baba pulled her on.

The Assembly building was ringed with policemen. The wall they formed dammed up the approaching crowd and created a lake of protesters. The police-wallahs watched with grave faces. Their lathis twitched in their hands. Sahib moved round the curve of the building, drawing his own people with him. The crowd surged and in the sudden movement, she ducked past the men at her side and followed, her eyes searching always for Sahib.

'Asha!' Baba's voice. She turned. The crowd sucked him

back but he reappeared and fought through the bodies, the arms, to reach her until she could grab hold of the cotton folds of his kurta. His body was slick with sweat.

Sahib entered a metal gate and Asha and her baba stumbled after him, squeezing through the crush and bursting out down a narrow, fenced path around the perimeter of the building to a side door. A dull passageway. Echoes in her ears as chappals and shoes slapped on stone. The sudden shift from dazzling sunlight to the dim interior shot her vision with comets and threads of bright light and she faltered. At her side, her baba was pushed on by the force of the crowd and the folds of his kurta slipped from her fingers.

'Baba!'

His face looked back, stricken, seeking hers. The gap between them widened.

She shouted again: 'Baba!'

'Come with me.' Male hands on her shoulders.

She twisted to look. Sanjay. His nose and cheeks shone with sweat. She tried to wriggle free of his hands.

'It's alright, little sister. Keep moving.'

She had no choice. The surge of bodies in the confined space was too powerful to resist.

Sanjay kept his hands on her shoulders, steadying her and keeping her upright in front of him as they moved. She glowed with shame but he held her fast. Her feet stumbled up a flight of stone steps, then along a corridor, then more steps. They turned and burst at last through a final doorway into the open shell of the building.

The sight snatched away her breath. It was cavernous. Down below, wooden benches made circles round an open kernel of space. Here, sloping tiers of benches, filling rapidly all around them, created a broad viewers' balcony.

Sanjay pushed her forward through shoving, clambering men to an empty place on a bench at one side and pushed her to sit. He sat at once beside her, shielding her with his body and claiming the space for them both even as others tried to force themselves into it. They sat in silence, panting, as the chaos around them settled.

'Good view, nah?' He smiled down at her, making her dizzy. 'Remember me?'

She nodded, too shy to say his name aloud. 'Sahib's nephew.'

'Sanjay Krishna. You've grown, Asha. And you're a great student. Smart and hard-working, that's what they say.'

She blinked. 'Who does?'

He tapped the bridge of his nose with a finger. 'Ah, little Asha. I am all-knowing.'

She drew her dupatta forward to hide her face and laced her fingers in her lap. His body was warm along her side and she shifted herself an inch away from him to avoid it. Sanjay Krishna. Of course she remembered.

He rose in his seat, pointed. 'Your baba is there, see. Not so far.'

He was right. Baba sat ahead, a few rows from the front, jammed in amongst Sahib's men. He turned and scanned the faces, looking for her. Beside her, Sanjay raised his hand and waved. Baba looked at the hand, at Sanjay, at his daughter beside him and gave a slow nod of the head. He looked relieved. Asha felt her shoulders relax.

Sanjay started to point out this and that to her. 'Here, where we are sitting, this is the public gallery, nah? Where common man can come to watch. There, that's the floor of the Assembly. That's what they call it. The politicians debate and vote down there but only the Britishers have the right to approve the laws. In our land. How is that right, Asha, when they are so few and we, we Indians, are so many? Tell me.'

She shook her head. He confused her. He was so much older than her, already sixteen or perhaps seventeen, and had the same commanding presence as Sahib. They were packed tightly on the bench and his thigh was close to hers and it was embarrassing but also exciting and that made her feel ashamed.

'Some day all this will change. You'll see.' He lowered his voice to a whisper. His breath blew warmth on her cheek as he bent towards her. 'Britishers will be packing their bags in a hurry to leave and Indians will be ruling their own affairs and Hindustan will be great again.'

She turned to look at him. He looked solemn, perfectly serious. He seemed to know so much. She twisted the hem of her dupatta in her lap and opened her mouth, then closed it again.

'Hush. It's starting.' He pointed. Men were filling the official benches below. They were Indians drawn from all corners of the country, all types and all looks, from the broad-faced of the East to the dark-skinned of the south. Sanjay dug her in the ribs. 'Listen and learn.' He sat forward, his chin resting in his hands.

The first man rose to his feet and began to speak. The Crows taught in English and she understood it well now but this man's speech was dull and his words difficult. He droned like a priest, on and on, shuffling a sheaf of paper in his hands. His subject was civil rights and a new law that threatened to curb them but he wandered around his argument like an old man lost in a forest.

She looked over the faces around her. Several men sat with

their heads tilted forward on their chests, sleeping. She tried to count the number in the pit below. Even if half of them spoke, they would still be here until sunset. She shifted her weight. She started to feel thirsty and imagined drinking cold, fresh water. She tipped her head a fraction to her left. Sanjay was rigid, paying attention. He was clever, she could tell, and kind. He had been respectful. Little sister. She must seem a child to him.

A colossal bang. Her heart stopped. Head jerked forward, straining to see. Sanjay suddenly on his feet beside her. Men in front of them jumped up too and craned into the pit. Bitterness in the air. Acrid smoke clogged her nose. Bang. Again. A second explosion. Her mouth opened to scream but no sound came. Raucous shouts rising from below. Smoke, soft for a moment, suspended like time itself, suddenly billowing in clouds, expanding upwards, outwards in a second.

In the public gallery, cries, deafening male shouts. *Inquilab Zindabad!* Long live the Revolution! *Hindustan Zindabad!* Shapes swam in and out of the fog of smoke. Sahib, tall and composed, stood in the centre of it all. His arm held high. His men around him thrust their fists into the air, screaming slogans. Some faces convulsed with anger. Some were ruddy with exhilaration.

Whistles, police whistles. Heavy feet. Men packed in tightly around them now turned, shoved, climbed past them, wrestled to get out.

A hand fastened on her arm and pulled her to her feet. Sanjay, already turning to make his way to the left, to a side exit, dragged her with him.

'Baba?'

'*Jaldee!* Quickly.'

She twisted back to look for him as Sanjay tugged her

along. Disembodied hands and heads swam into view where the smoke thinned only to be swallowed again.

'Baba!' Her voice fell into the noise and dissolved.

Sanjay swept her on. The slogans and the smoke faded as they forced their way along the bench, out of the side door and down a narrow stairway. All around fleeing men swore and shouted as they fought to escape. Behind them and ahead, police whistles screamed.

They reached the ground floor and flowed into the bright sunshine with the crowd. Men surged there, shouting. To one side, a khaki wall of uniforms curled round the edge of the crowd, penning in the crowd. Their lathis rose ready in their hands.

Sanjay pulled her to the far side, out of the path of the advancing police-wallahs. She scrambled after him. A shout went up. Deafening, drowning them. *Inquilab Zindabad!* The same cry as before but raucous now and catching fire through the crowd. Commotion. Men around them jostled and strained to see. She twisted.

Police-wallahs appeared at the exit. Prisoners marched between them, their heads pressed down to their chests by heavy hands, their arms pinned tightly behind them. Trails of blood showed at temples, foreheads. Her breath caught in her chest. Sahib was there, dignified despite the rough handling. She recognised his men around him. And there, in the midst of them, the slight figure of Baba, her own dear Baba, his head lowered, one eye puffed and swollen.

'Baba!' The sound stuck in her throat. 'Baba!'

She struggled to get free of Sanjay's grip, to run to Baba, but she was held fast. Sanjay bent and brought his face close to hers. His eyes were sharp.

'Quiet. If you want to help him, keep quiet.'

Beyond him, the police-wallahs dragged the men round the curve of the building towards their vehicles. Her baba tripped and the men at his side dug their lathis into his back, forcing him to arch in pain.

Sanjay's hot hands pinned her in position. She started to sob.

'What's wrong?' An old man beside them turned to look. 'Is she hurt?'

Sanjay answered. 'She's feverish.' He forced a laugh. 'You know how girls are. I should never have brought her.'

He marched her away. The passing bodies blurred as she cried. Slowly the press of men eased and they emerged at last into the cool of open space. Her breath juddered in her throat as she tried to stop crying. Behind them, the shouts grew wilder. The shrill notes of police whistles rose from a bed of chaos and a terrible splintering of wood on flesh, on bone.

Sanjay bundled her across the grassy lawns and, even as they rushed, the humid air made a cushion behind them and softened the sounds. They didn't stop until they reached Sahib's house. Once they were inside the gate, Sanjay turned to her, put his hands squarely on her shoulders.

'Tell no one you were there. Understand? You went to school, then you played at home only. You know nothing about Sahib. Nothing. Promise me.'

She nodded. The lawn was silent and desolate beside them. Wherever she looked, the face of her own Baba hung there, bloodied, battered and bruised.

That night, she was woken by the pounding of fists on the gate. Loud voices, shouting; 'Police! Open!' Footsteps, running. Beams of light swinging round the garden, crashing into the shack through cracks and gaps.

She sat against the wall with her knees drawn up and shivered. They hurt her baba. Now they would hurt her.

The door was wrenched open and light streamed in. A young police-wallah, holding a lantern. She blinked, twisted her face away, reached for her dupatta to shield her eyes.

'Come out!'

She tried to shrink into the wall.

He twisted and spoke to someone unseen behind him. 'A girl only.'

A deeper voice. 'Bring her out.'

The young man reached in and pulled her to her feet. She stumbled out, straining against him. The garden was unnaturally bright with lanterns. Police-wallahs swarmed across the lawn. Inside the house, lights bloomed and faded in one window after another as they searched the rooms.

Cook stood in his nightshirt by the back door. He was bleary-eyed and unshaven. His feet were bare. A police-wallah at his side held him fast at the elbow.

Another police-wallah, stout and sporting a flamboyant moustache, looked her up and down. 'Who are you?'

She shook her head, playing dumb, and braced herself for a blow.

'Where's your mama?'

'Dead.' That much was true. 'My baba also.'

The police-wallah looked at the shack. 'You live here?'

She shrugged. Behind them, there was a scuffle at the gate and a white police-wallah strode in through the gate, a Britisher.

'Who's she?' He spoke Hindustani with a heavy accent.

'A servant only. Shall we bring her?'

The Britisher looked round. He said in English: 'Bring him.' He pointed to Cook. 'Leave the girl. She looks a halfwit.'

Asha opened her mouth to shout back in English, to show what brains she had. Then she thought of Sanjay, pressing his face in hers and telling her to say nothing and she closed it again. The police-wallah dropped her arm and gave her a shove backwards. They turned and moved rapidly away across the lawn, sending pools of light swinging over the darkened grass.

She crept back inside the shack and crouched there, wrapping her arms round her body and hugging her ribs as she watched them through the half-open door. In a matter of minutes, the men and the light had gone, taking with them the old chowkidar on the gate and Cook. The house fell silent.

She sat up for the rest of the night, wrapped round in a blanket. The sky slowly lightened to grey. The shadows in the shack softened. The only evidence of her baba was the cotton bag hanging limply from a nail, bulging with the shapes of his block soap and razor and the cotton folds of his spare lunghi, soft and faded with overwashing.

When it was time, she went into the deserted kitchen, boiled up a pan of chai and ate a piece of stale roti. She opened the cupboards and checked over the food. A pail of rice. Spices. Sugar. Flour. In the cool larder, a round slab of butter.

Afterwards she washed her face, smoothed down her clothes and went to school. She never saw Cook or the chowkidar again.

Chapter Seven

After some weeks living alone, she came home from school to find the gate locked. She put her eye to the narrow gap and tried to make out the shapes of the garden, the house. A movement inside. She twisted her body to get a better angle and watched. A man, there, on the ground floor.

The figure moved here and there through the house, sometimes disappearing from view, then reappearing. She couldn't make out his features. The sun fell hard on her head and made her dizzy.

Finally the back door opened and Sanjay Krishna emerged, cigarette in hand. He stood and smoked, looking out over the garden.

She banged on the gate and called: 'Over here! Let me in!' She was afraid to use his name.

He started, dropped his cigarette and ground it into sparks with the toe of his chappal. Then he crossed the lawn and opened the gate a fraction.

'Are you alone?'

She nodded.

He led her across the garden to the house and then down the corridor to Sahib's room at the front. It was shuttered and dim. Dust hung thick in falling arrows of light. He made his way round the room, touching small objects on the table and mantelpiece as he passed. A heavy glass ashtray, which Sahib liked to use. A leather-bound book. A pencil.

He turned and looked her over. 'You still live here?'

She didn't answer. He must have seen that food was missing, that the pans in the kitchen were used.

'You are going to school? Every day?'

She nodded. It was comforting to be at school, and besides, she needed the meals.

'You can sleep inside if you like. There's no one here.'

Her shoulders relaxed a little. He wasn't angry, then.

'I'd rather sleep outside.' When her baba came home, that's where he'd look for her.

'As you like.' He pulled out a chair and sat down, swinging himself round to face her. 'You know what's happened?'

He sighed. He pulled out a cigarette case and lit another cigarette. He looked older than ever, smoking in Sahib's room.

'Sahib is fighting against the Britishers. Did you know that?'

She shook her head. She was glad. The Britishers disgraced her baba, that's what Rahul said.

'He is fighting for the freedom of our people. To drive the Britishers away and let us take control of our own land again. That's why he threw that bomb. That's why he and his men stayed to face the police-wallahs when they came. Do you see? They could have run away but they chose to stay. To fight them in their own courts.'

She considered. 'Where's my baba?'

He blew out a trail of smoke. 'In prison. Your baba and many of the other—'

She blurted out: 'But he didn't do anything. He never took that money.'

Sanjay shook his head. 'It's not about the money. Listen. It's about the bomb.'

She said: 'But all he wants is to work and look after me.'

Sanjay turned his eyes to the floor.

She went on: 'You must tell them. He isn't strong. And what about me?'

Silence. The world seemed to stop. How could they lock away her baba? He was a good man, an innocent man, she knew that. 'I'll tell them myself if you won't. He's just the sweeper-wallah. That's not a crime.'

Sanjay shook his head slowly and sadly. 'Your baba ran messages between Sahib and his friends. He knew everything.' He shrugged. 'Anyway, it's done now. They're sending them away, far away, to an island.'

'An island?' She stared.

'You should be proud, Asha.' He craned forward. 'Things are much worse for Sahib. They want to hang him.'

'What island?'

'The Andamans. Far from here.' He seemed to read her confusion. 'The Sisters didn't teach you that, did they?' He snorted. 'The Britishers are sending their most dangerous prisoners there, the murderers and the freedom fighters also.'

Asha's legs became weak. She imagined her poor baba in chains, forced onto a ship and taken far away, to a dark and distant shore. She sank to the floor. The edge of the rug was laced with dust and strands of stray cotton.

'How can I get there?'

Sanjay shook his head. 'You can't, little sister. You're a clever girl. Maybe one day you can help your baba and help the revolution also. But now you need to keep safe and to learn.'

She made a lattice of her fingers and pressed them against her face. She clamped her mouth tightly shut and concentrated on making her breaths long and even.

His voice sounded softer. 'Soon I will come to live here. Sahib wants it so. I will carry on the fight in his good name. And you, Asha, you can live here as long as you like. You can go to school as your baba wanted. I will provide for you. *Ye thik hai?* That's fine?'

She sat on the wooden floor and looked through the web of her hands at the patterns on the rug. No, it was not fine. Nothing was fine. She didn't want to help the revolution. She just wanted her baba back.

For several years, she carried on with her schooling and studied hard. The Crows no longer beat the backs of her legs. After school, she cleaned inside Sanjay Sahib's house and helped the new cook in return for meals.

In the darkness, different men crept to and from the house through the garden. She watched them from the shack as they scurried, their eyes cast down.

Only Sanjay-ji used the front entrance, as his uncle had done. When she caught glimpses of him, broad-shouldered and grave-faced, it was hard to remember the youth who once lounged, idle, on the grass. One of the few who stopped by the shack on occasion and showed her kindness was Rahul, Sanjay's friend, that same boy who fed her cocoa as a baby. When he married, she made a friend of his wife, Sangeeta, a girl only a few years older than her, and when their son came, Abhishek, she went along after school some days and helped to mind him.

At night, she slept with her baba's spare cotton lunghi under her head and sometimes she dreamt of him. Once they were in their old home in the village and he sat across the room from her, a blurred shape in the smoky half-light. When she tried to call to him, no sound came. When she tried to reach for him, her limbs were too heavy to move. Once he came to her in chains, pale as milk, and begged her to save him and she woke crying in the empty shack. She hid her face in the folds of the lunghi but it had already lost his scent.

Chapter Eight

Isabel

Jonathan's overnight stay stretched into a second, then a third day as the curfew persisted. He returned to The Grand only once, to settle his bill and retrieve his belongings. By the third day, Isabel wondered if his occupation of the spare bedroom was permanent.

Her father barely left the office. When he finally came home, late at night, his eyes hooded and his skin grey, Jonathan poured him Scotch and lit him a cigar. Isabel fell asleep in bed listening to the convivial murmur of their voices from the dining room or the verandah, punctuated by occasional bursts of her father's laughter.

During the day, her mother was artificially cheerful. She shooed them off on early-morning rides, south from Delhi, away from the trouble. After luncheon each day, she dragged them to teas or tennis at The Club and, in the evening, dinner parties. Jonathan made a polite escort, his manners impeccable. He charmed her mother and her friends and they doted on him. And always, Isabel sensed him watching her.

'Isabel Madam!'

Tap, tap on her door. Outside, night was beginning to dissolve into day. She peered at the clock. A little after five.

Tap, tap. 'Madam!'

'What is it?' She pushed her feet into her slippers and reached for her dressing gown.

'Very sorry.' Abdul, the houseboy, opened the door a crack and peered in. 'Indian lady asking at the gate.' His face was creased with disapproval. 'I told her: Madam is not seeing you. It is too early.' He hesitated. 'She is poor only. Crying, also.'

'Did she give a name?'

'Sangeeta, wife of Rahul Chaudhary. She is saying like this.'

'Bring her up to the house. I'll see her in the dining room. And fetch us chai, will you?'

Abdul didn't move.

'Well, go on.'

She padded to her bathroom to wash. The face in the mirror was blurry with sleep.

Sangeeta stood by the dining-room window, her hands fastened together, looking blankly towards the lawns. When she turned to Isabel, her face showed the dirt streaks of crying.

'What is it?' Isabel, speaking in Hindustani, thought first of Abhishek, their son.

'Madam. Rahul is gone.'

'Gone?'

She prostrated herself at Isabel's feet. Her hands, metal bangles jangling at her wrists, grasped Isabel's slippers. Isabel reached down, took the young woman's hands in her own and drew her upright.

'Sit. Have some chai.'

'He's good man. Innocent.' Sangeeta's thin shoulders shook.

'Of course he is.' Isabel steered her to a chair and made her sit. She poured tea, served with the milk separately in the English style, added a heaped spoonful of sugar and set the cup and saucer in front of her. It sent waving tendrils of steam into the air. Sangeeta's breathing was ragged.

'Now tell me. What happened?'

'It was late. The curfew was on but he went to buy cigarettes only. At the chai stall. I waited and waited the whole night and still he didn't come.'

She dried her eyes with the tail of her sari. Isabel sat quietly, waiting.

'An hour ago, Manju, our neighbour, he came to the house. Rahul was taken, he said. By police. They came with lathis and took so many men, Rahul too.' Her voice cracked.

Isabel rose from her chair and crouched beside her. 'We'll get him home, Sangeeta. Don't worry.' She rubbed the heaving shoulders with slow, solid strokes. 'You did right to come.'

Slowly her sobbing quietened. Isabel took the cup of tea and held it to her lips. Her teeth juddered against the fine china rim.

'Your neighbour, did he know where they took them?'

She shook her head. Her eyes were miserable. 'He's a good man, madam. You are knowing.' She grabbed at Isabel's hand where it held the cup and set the tea sloshing. Her fingernails made half-moons where they dug into Isabel's palm. 'Please, madam. Please help us.'

'Darling, there isn't a great deal I can do. I've rather a lot on today.'

Her father helped himself to the covered dishes of eggs

and sausages on the sideboard and sat to eat a hurried breakfast. A cardboard file lay open by his plate. Thin, typed sheets of overnight reports spilt across the linen. His bearer had arrived early and waited now in the porch.

'He's Cook Chaudhary's son. You must remember Rahul. I used to play with him all the time.'

Her father looked up, surprised. 'With the cook's boy?'

Isabel set down her coffee cup. Her father turned his attention back to his papers. He began to frown.

'Isn't there someone you could call? There must be.'

He turned a page, then cut into a sausage and chewed as he read on. Abdul appeared in the doorway with a fresh pot of coffee and leant over to fill his master's cup.

Isabel thought of Sangeeta, sitting with Cook in the kitchen, hands folded in her lap, eyes downcast, waiting for news.

'I can vouch for him.' Her father didn't look up. He looked lost in his work. She raised her voice. 'So could you.'

He lifted his eyes at last. 'It isn't just government property they destroyed. Restaurants. Shops. Businesses. Poor, hard-working fellows are ruined. For what?' He shook his head. 'And these are the chaps who want to run this country? It beggars belief.'

She reached over and put her hand on the file. The papers were brittle and crinkled under her palm. 'What about Rahul?'

He shook his head and sighed. 'That's police business, Isabel.'

'They're counting on us. His wife says—'

'Wives say all sorts of things, darling.' Her father pulled his file free. He speared a final fork of sausage and egg and chewed as he shuffled the papers together. 'You have no idea what your mother would come out with, if she thought it would save my skin.' He scraped back his chair and got to his feet, drank down a mouthful of coffee as he rose. 'Are there children? Give her food from the kitchen. Tell Cook I authorised it.'

He dried his lips on his napkin. His breakfast lay in front of him, half-eaten, a pool of egg yolk congealing across the plate. He picked up his papers, kissed her on the forehead and marched out.

She sat alone at the breakfast table, looking out of the French windows across the verandah at the garden beyond. The mali trundled his wheelbarrow along the gravel path. Birds descended to the lawn from the surrounding trees and hopped from one clump of grass to another.

'Morning.' Jonathan, hearty and cheerful, his hair damp from his wash. He took a plate and lifted the covers on the breakfast dishes, then settled himself at the far side of the table and finally looked across at her. 'You're pale as a ghost.'

He reached across the table and put his hand on hers. He looked more caring than she'd imagined possible. For a moment, she thought she might cry.

He said: 'Is something wrong?'

Jonathan chatted easily to the officer on duty in the dour, cavernous entrance hall of Delhi's main police headquarters. The young constable led Jonathan and Isabel up a sweeping flight of stairs. The cheap flooring and echoing corridors reminded her of a hospital.

'Hargreaves!'

Jonathan raised his hand to greet his friend through

89

the half-open door to his office. It was spacious, with an enormous desk at one end and, at the other, a set of easy chairs gathered round a glass-topped coffee table. Patterned rugs in red and gold were strewn across the wooden flooring. The walls were decorated with large framed pictures of Indian game and a ceremonial sword.

'How've you been, Whyte?'

Isabel hung back as the two men shook hands. They had come to India as part of the same IAS intake.

'Miss Winthorpe, what a pleasure!' Hargreaves was pink and hearty. 'Do take a pew.'

They settled in the government-issue chairs.

'Mr Gandhi is behaving a little better, by all accounts.' Hargreaves gave Jonathan a knowing look. 'Finally.'

'No more hunger strikes?' Jonathan shook his head. 'I must say, I thought we'd lost him last time.'

'Chance would be a fine thing.' Hargreaves turned to Isabel. 'Only joking, of course.'

Isabel looked from one face to the other. Hargreaves was much the same age as Jonathan but already showed signs of a receding hairline and a paunch. Jonathan, physically fitter, was the more handsome of the two.

'They're fools to give in.' Hargreaves blew out his cheeks. 'I'd force-feed the man. Anyway, he's off round villages nowadays, which suits us very well.' He paused. 'Plenty of others to keep us busy.'

A constable brought in a tray of tea and salty biscuits.

'Now, this Chaudhary fellow,' Jonathan said. 'The Winthorpes have known him since he was a boy. His wife's begging for help and Miss Winthorpe here doesn't know where to turn.'

Hargreaves brought over a cardboard file from his desk, untied the string around it and looked over several sheets of thin paper, pockmarked with type.

'It's not good. He was right there in the crowd when it attacked the police. Two constables saw him throw rocks.'

'Rahul?' Isabel craned forward to see the sheet.

Hargreaves gave her an old-fashioned look. 'It's all here in black and white.'

Isabel turned to Jonathan. 'He only went for cigarettes.'

Hargreaves laced his fingers together and slowly cracked his knuckles.

'He appeared before the judge this morning. Guilty on a string of counts. Looking at several years, I'd say.' He closed the file and retied the string. 'He should have thought about his wife before he got mixed up in this.'

Before Isabel could protest, Jonathan cut in.

'Speaking of wives, how's the lovely Dorothy? And how old is James now?'

The men chatted about family life as she sat stiffly between them, her eyes on the paper file in Hargreaves' hand which seemed already to have sealed Rahul's fate.

That afternoon, she and Jonathan sat together on the verandah. It was a beautiful winter's day, bright and warm. The mali was on his knees at a flower bed. His trowel scraped a rhythm from the rocky soil.

'Thank you,' she said. 'Thank you for trying.'

She got to her feet and leant against the rail to look out across the garden. A peacock trailed its furled tail across the lawn. She and Rahul made secret dens in those rhodendenron bushes, climbed those trees. She tried to imagine him in a prison cell.

'I'm sorry I can't do more.'

She turned. Jonathan sat quietly, watching her.

'I can't bear to see you sad.' He got to his feet, stood close at her side, reached for her hand. She let him squeeze her fingers between his own. She felt adrift and his grip was firm.

'I so want to take care of you, Isabel.'

She bristled. 'I'm not a child.'

'Of course you're not. Of course.' He shook his head, broke into a smile. 'That's what I love about you. You're strong and brave.'

She looked down at their joined hands. He said love. Her fingers, in his, were suddenly tense. Before she could think what to say, he sank down onto one knee, there on the verandah, still clasping her hand.

'You will marry me, won't you?' He made it sound as if they'd already spoken of it. 'I love you, Isabel. I think I always have, from the first moment I came striding into the drawing room in Kettlewell and saw you curled there on the window seat, so self-contained, so serious as you pored over your book.'

She tried to laugh. 'I don't believe that for a minute.'

'It's true.' He pressed her hand to his lips. 'Being horrid was the only way I could get your attention. Anyway, that's a long time ago.'

She couldn't look at him. Her eyes were caught by a shifting shadow in the sitting room. Her mother, at the window, bent over an arrangement of flowers and fiddled with the stems.

'You'll love the Andamans,' Jonathan was saying. 'And we won't be there for ever. We can stay in India as long as you like. You'll never be cold again, darling. You will take me, won't you?'

She dared to glance at his face. His eyes were imploring and full of longing.

She heard herself say: 'Of course I will.'

He pulled himself up to stand beside her, his body firm and warm, tipped back her chin and kissed her. His mouth was dry with nerves and his lips half-closed as if he weren't sure of her response. I suppose that's it, then, she thought. I'm going to marry Jonathan Whyte.

'We could get married quickly, here in Delhi.' He seemed breathless. 'You don't mind if it's a bit rushed, do you? I've made some enquiries. I'll have to go back soon, you see, to Port Blair.'

He rattled on, making arrangements for their lives. She stood in a daze, looking out at the sunlight across the lawn, the blue and green shimmer of the peacock's feathers. How odd, the way everything solid could shift and change in a moment. Rahul had been her friend, her brother, a man she trusted with her life. Now he was in prison. And soon she would become Isabel Whyte, Mrs Whyte, a new bride starting a new life in the Andaman Islands.

Chapter Nine

Asha

Asha was summoned to the house to meet with Sanjay-Sahib at nine o'clock. She plaited her hair and covered it with a light dupatta, pushed her feet into sandals.

The houseboy led her down the familiar passageway to Sahib's room at the front of the house. It was locked during the day, one of the few places she was not allowed to clean. Now the houseboy tapped on the door and opened it to her.

The room was deep with shadows. A lamp cast a pool on a polished wooden table near the centre of the room and it swirled with cigarette smoke and dancing dust. The table was strewn with books and papers and a chair was pushed away as if Sanjay-ji had recently risen from his work.

'Don't be afraid.'

She jumped. The shadows shifted and he moved out from behind a high-backed chair in a far corner. His eyes glinted in the half-light.

'You wanted to see me, sahib.'

He smiled. 'I often see you, Asha, running about your business. I hear you are good in English and history and mathematics also. That's unusual for a girl.'

He pulled forward a chair for her and sat in the armchair that his uncle had once used. 'Now, will you drink chai?' He gestured to a stool on the far side of the chair. A tray had been set out there with a chai pot and two cups and a plate of Cook's samosas.

She perched on the edge of the chair as he poured the ready-made chai. His arms were thick and knotted with muscle. He wore a cotton shirt with a lunghi. How strange it was that they lived so close together, on the same piece of land, yet saw each other so rarely.

He handed her a cup of chai. 'I called you little sister once. Do you remember? You were only a child then. Now you're a young woman.'

She looked down into her cup. The air above it rocked with rising steam. A skin made wrinkles on the boiled milk.

'I am very grateful to you, sahib, for a place to live and for food and' – she faltered – 'everything.'

He sipped his chai and she did the same. The chai was thick and sweet in her mouth. He had his uncle's straight nose and sturdy body and the same ability to change a room just by being present in it. He set down his cup, opened a cigarette case by his chair, drew out a cigarette and lit it. The smoke billowed from him in soft, sweet waves.

He seemed lost in thought, smoking and looking up into the darkness above her. She looked round the room. His uncle's glass ashtray sat on the mantelpiece. A book lay beside it with a pair of spectacles on top. An old-fashioned book, leather-bound.

'My uncle's. They sent me his things from prison.' He seemed to read everything in her face. 'The night before they hanged him, he sat up late, reading that book. A volume of Tagore's poems. You know Tagore?'

She shook her head.

'Our greatest writer. A fine Bengali.' He paused, looking at the mantelpiece. 'Those are my uncle's spectacles. I keep them in view when I work.'

'My baba called him a great man.'

He nodded. 'He would be sad to see us now. Our friend Rahul suffers terribly in prison. And his family suffers, also.' He sighed. 'Your schooldays are almost over, Asha. You must be, what, fourteen, fifteen, is it? So tell me, what do you want?'

She blinked. No one had ever asked her such a question.

'I could arrange a decent marriage and fix a dowry for you. No? What about teaching in a school? You have brains, Asha.'

She sat very still. Her mouth dried and her hands shook round the warm bowl of her cup. She opened her mouth to speak, closed it again.

His eyes rested on her face. 'What, Asha?'

She filled her lungs and heard her voice, high with nerves, say: 'I want to go to him. To my baba. On that island.'

His eyes widened. He didn't laugh and she took heart and continued.

'I know it's dangerous. But he's my baba. He's all I have in this world. It's my duty to care for him. Can you help me go there, sahib?'

He put his cigarette to his lips and drew on it. The tip glowed red, then faded again to black. He let out a long, slow stream of smoke. All this time, his eyes never left her face.

'Are you sure?'

She nodded. She felt lifted by a tide of hope that she might again see her baba, however hard the journey.

'I'll make enquiries.' He gave her a half-nod. His mood seemed to shift as he reached a decision. He got to his feet. She hurried to set down her cup on the table and jump up too.

'Thank you, sahib. May the gods bless and protect you.'

As she crossed to the door, he said in a low voice that was little more than a murmur: 'You are a good girl, Asha, and clever. Maybe you can help us there also.'

In a matter of weeks, he made all the arrangements: first the hot, dusty train journey down to Calcutta where one of his associates rescued her from the crowded railway station, then her four-day passage on the SS *Maharajah* out to Port Blair.

As they sailed into port on the final day, she dared to leave the safety of her cheap berth and go up onto the deck to join the passengers gathering along the rail. She had been afraid to see these islands across Kali Pane, Black Water, which people mentioned with hushed voices. Now she was surprised by their beauty.

The sea, which had tossed and scurried against the ship for the last two days, was suddenly calm, reflecting a clear sky with a deep, shimmering blue. A low mist hung about the islands and it was hard, as they first approached, to tell the difference between land and cloud. The ship slid forwards through still water.

Fringes of sandy beach emerged from the mist, followed by a cluster of square stone buildings that defined the waterfront. Behind the port, the red rooftops of smart houses clustered together as they climbed up from the shore. She narrowed her eyes to squint into the bright light. Beyond the houses, some distance from the port and rising out of a thick grove of coconut palms, stood a vast circular building of red stone. A tower stood at its centre and a series of low buildings radiated out from this tower at regular intervals, the double-storeyed spokes of a giant wheel.

'You know what that is?' A young man, beside her at the rail, saw her staring.

She didn't answer him.

'The Cellular Jail. Packed full of murderers and madmen.' He laughed, hoping to scare her. 'You better lock your door, at night, Missy, in case they come creeping.'

She shook her head. 'My baba's there,' she said. 'He'll be out soon.'

'Maybe.' He pulled a face. 'Maybe not.'

Above the jail, the mountain rose steeply. Even when they were close enough to lay anchor, its summit stayed hidden in cloud.

'All coral reef down there.' The young man pointed at the shallows. 'One wrong move and we'd be cut to pieces.'

She hung over the rail as the first passengers were handed down into rowing boats and peered through the clear water at patterns of dark rock, far below, and darting shoals of fish whose sudden movements made shifting shadows on the sand below.

Now that the ship was motionless, heavy, thick heat descended. It was different from the heat she had always known. It had a richer, silkier texture, so moist that it licked her face and pressed itself between her fingers. Smells engulfed her. The sharp salt of spray and dock and the pervasive stink of rotting fish. Richly scented flowers and lush vegetation reaching from the land underpinned by the soft sweetness of woodsmoke. She gripped the warm wooden rail with both hands, closed her eyes and tried to steady herself. My baba is there, she told herself. I will wait for him.

She climbed the harbour steps from the rowing boat and stepped out onto the quayside into a cacophony of shouts and sounds. The waterside was bustling with working men, unloading baskets of flapping fish, bowed down by the weight of wooden cases, scurrying along on errands. Some men had skin so dark it was almost black. Some towered above her. Others were short and squat in stature with light skin and wide, flattened features. The whole scene stank of salt and rotting fish and kerosene. The light, glancing off the water, was dizzying.

Off to one side, a group of men in drab cotton trousers, their muscles flexing across bare chests as they laboured, wielded picks as they dug out a battered section of sea wall, ripe for repair. They worked with steady concentration but there was a deadness in their movements, which made her take a few steps towards them to look. A foreman walked up and down alongside them, shouting commands. It was only when they moved forward with a uniform swinging of legs, which reminded her of a creeping caterpillar, that the chains linking their ankles, each man fastened to the next, clanked and jangled.

'Work-gang.'

She turned. A boy stood at her side. His clothes were faded with overwashing and his hair made clumps on the top of his head.

'It's not so bad. They live in barracks. Better than prison. They don't let the politicals out, though. Too afraid they'll leg it.'

'Politicals?'

'Freedom fighters. Like your baba.' He gave her a knowing look, too old for his age, which seemed barely nine or ten. 'I'm Rajiv.'

She looked him up and down. 'I'm Asha.'

'I know. Amit-ji sent me. Come on.'

He took her bag from her hand and led her off through

the bustle along cobbled streets, which steadily climbed first past warehouses and offices, then shops and restaurants and finally between large houses, raised on stilts. The sun grew hotter and the air more humid as they left behind the breeze from the sea and became surrounded by the fierce closeness of jungle. The wheeling seagulls gave way to darting green-winged birds and red-beaked parrots.

When they had walked for almost an hour, he led her at last down a narrow lane between poorer houses, some barely more roomy than the shacks she had left behind in the Delhi bustee, and through a small restaurant. It was a wooden structure, open to the street. A woven straw roof was supported by solid struts. Rickety tables and chairs spilt out into the lane, then reached back into the shaded darkness of the interior. The men sitting there over chai and pakoras, bidis glowing in their hands, raised their heads as she passed between them. She tensed her shoulders and looked fixedly at her sandals as they crossed the floor.

The boy led her through to the back. The yard was chaotic with cooking. Steam shimmered over pots of boiling daal and subzi. A boy, a year or two older than her guide, ran back and forth between them, fetching, seasoning and stirring. On the far side of it all, sitting under a spreading frangipani tree, sat a lean man. A stiff ledger lay open on his knee and his lips moved silently as he totted up figures and entered them in a series of columns.

The boy stopped in front of him and dropped her bag on the ground with a smack. They waited. He was a sinewy man with a bald patch spreading into his crown. He wore thin-rimmed spectacles which slipped down his nose each time he bent forward to enter a fresh number and which he pushed back repeatedly with his forefinger in an automatic gesture. When he finally raised his head, his eyes were large and solemn.

'Flour is costly. It eats our profits like a beetle. What to do?'

She considered, then looked down at Rajiv. 'What does your mama give you with your daal and subzi?'

He shrugged. 'Rice porridge.'

She said to the man. 'Then serve more rice, fewer rotis.'

'But people like rotis.'

She shrugged. 'Then they must pay more for them.'

He looked at her for some time and the eyes behind his spectacles were thoughtful.

'I am Amit-ji.' He looked down at her bag. 'You have something for me?'

She found the sealed envelope that Sanjay Krishna had handed her when she left and watched as he drew out the paper, unfolded it with methodical care and read it over. 'You read and write?'

She nodded. 'Hindi and English also.'

'Good.' He nodded. 'Bring a chair and sit beside me. Rajiv will bring you food and when you have eaten, you can rest.'

She hesitated, conscious of the men all around her.

'You're safe here, Asha. Krishna-Sahib and I are old friends. I will help you.'

It was a world peopled by men and it took her time to find her place in it.

When Amit-ji's restaurant was busy, she worked in the back, chopping and cooking alongside their cook and washing the dirty pots and plates in a pail. The young boys called her Didi, big sister, and protected her as if she were family.

Late in the evening, after the restaurant had closed and the shutters fastened, men knocked softly and crept through to the yard at the back where they gathered under the frangipani tree to talk with Amit in low voices. She came to know their faces and their stories also. They had all been prisoners themselves who, after serving many years, had been released as tickets of leave. They had the right to settle here and to farm or fish or set up a private business like any other citizen but they were barred from leaving the island to return to the homes of their birth and the relatives waiting there.

Sometimes these men came to her and asked her to write letters to their fathers and brothers back home. They dictated simple messages, begging for news of their relatives, the land, the cattle. Some called on their wives and children to journey out to the islands to join them and share their new life here, if they were willing. Most, it seemed, were not. The men ended their messages by saying how well they were doing in their new lives on the island and how the gods blessed them here. She saw their drawn faces and knew it was a big lie but they asked her to write it and so she did.

At night, she slept in a crawl space above the main body of the restaurant. She lay against the warm wood of the eaves, listening to the snores and shuffles of Amit, the cook and the two boys as they slept near her. She fell asleep thinking of the circular brick building, which loomed over them on the mountainside and of her poor baba, locked inside. He had no idea that she had travelled all this distance to be close to him. She had no idea, as those first weeks passed, whether she would ever see him alive again.

Chapter Ten

Isabel

The sail to Port Blair took four days. On the first morning, Isabel stood at the steamer's stern and, looking back over the receding watery churn and swooping seagulls, said a silent goodbye to her parents and to the mainland as it shrank to a thinning band before vanishing altogether.

She looked down at her hand on the warm wooden rail. The sun sparkled on her rings, the plain gold beside the diamond solitaire, mounted by a Punjabi jeweller in Old Delhi. She had to concentrate to bring Jonathan's face to mind. The few days before their hasty wedding passed in a blur of organisation. Jonathan had rushed back to the Andamans immediately afterwards, leaving her to take her time in packing up her belongings and following. Now, as she contemplated their reunion weeks later, it was hard to feel married at all.

She tore herself away from the stern and walked the length of the steamer to the bow, facing forward into open waters. Here the mood of the sea seemed very different. The wind rose and the waves undulated ahead in unravelling curtains of deep blue, flecked with gold threads of sunlight.

The SS *Maharajah* was a small, shabby steamer with cramped cabins along its upper deck. Isabel met the other passengers at lunch in the cramped first-class dining room where the captain, a middle-aged Scot, presided over a single table.

Several of the men were government employees, travelling to Port Blair on official business for the Forestry or Agricultural Departments, both of which were well-represented on the islands. A businessman was travelling out to visit the sawmills on Chatham Island and a Welshman said he was going on holiday to visit a friend who owned a coconut plantation on the islands.

The only other woman was a timid lady of around sixty years old, with heavily powdered cheeks and sturdy brogues. She pecked the assembled company with sharp, anxious looks as she entered the dining room, then darted into a seat at Isabel's side.

'I feared I might be the only Englishwoman on board this dreadful ship.' She set her handbag on her knee and drew off her gloves. 'How do you do? Agnes Timberley. My sister is married to an officer in the Public Works Department in Port Blair. They settled out there such a long time ago, I've hardly seen her. So when Albert, my dear husband, passed away last year, I thought to myself: Agnes, this is your chance.'

Miss Timberley's chatter forced Isabel to abandon the conversation on her left between the forestry officials and the captain and turn to her new companion.

'I am sorry about your husband.' Isabel gave a sympathetic smile. 'I'm Mrs Whyte.'

'Oh, I know, dear. Fancy choosing a husband in such a far-flung, dangerous place. You do know what they call these waters?'

Isabel shook her head.

'*Kali Pane*. Black Water.' She pursed her lips. 'The Indians say they lose their caste if they cross it. Jolly well serves them right.'

Isabel didn't reply. The waiter reached between them to fill their glasses with claret.

'I don't normally indulge.' Mrs Timberley gave a nervous titter. 'But it does settle the stomach.'

A second waiter offered a platter of boiled beef. When she had served herself, Mrs Timberley added to Isabel in a whisper: 'You do know the place teems with the most unsavoury types. Most of my sister's servants are murderers. I shall certainly take care to lock my door at night. And I suggest you do the same.'

Isabel served herself beef and then vegetables and they waited for the gentlemen to catch up.

'The beef looks rather tough.' Mrs Timberley's whisper was embarrassingly piercing. 'Frankly, this steamer's seen better days, if you ask me.'

'I suppose it's designed more for cargo than for passengers.'

'Cargo?' Mrs Timberley sniffed. 'That's one way of putting it.'

The captain, seeing Isabel's puzzled expression, leant forward. 'I think Mrs Timberley is referring to our livestock in the hold below.'

'Livestock?'

'Elephants. Purchased by the Forestry Department. They put them to work as loggers.'

Isabel smiled. 'They must be quite a weight.'

'Indeed.' The Captain nodded. 'Three adults and a calf in the hold at present.'

Isabel was intrigued. 'Is it possible to see them?'

'See them?' Mrs Timberley pulled a face. 'Smelly creatures, stomping about in their own filth? No, thank you.'

'I'd be delighted to escort you, Mrs Whyte.'

The captain rose to his feet and bowed his head to say grace.

'I doubt your husband would approve.' Mrs Timberley whispered out of the corner of her mouth as she placed her palms together. 'They're not the only nasty animals on board either, from what I hear.'

When the other passengers retired to their cabins to rest, the captain led Isabel down into the hold, far below the sun-bleached decks. The passageways became cramped and dark as they descended below the third-class berths and into winding gangways. Isabel felt her way along the pitching wooden walls, lit only by the weak beam of the captain's lamp. The darkness was drenched in the smell of oil and sea salt.

The captain pointed the way down a rounded steel ladder set in a dimly lit shaft.

'You're quite certain? Then step with care.'

They emerged on a narrow walkway and stopped in front of a thick door. He slid back the bolts and lowered his voice to a whisper.

'Steady, Mrs Whyte.'

As the door opened, the rich smell of dung and the sour, dirtied straw flooded out. The captain insinuated himself through the opening and she slid after him. He lowered his lamp to the decking where it made a splayed puddle of light.

As she blinked in the darkness, shapes slowly grew. An eye flashed as a vast head turned. A trunk, far above her head, lifted and curled. Metal clinked as one of the bigger animals shifted its weight and dragged chain.

The captain murmured, 'They're quite secure.'

The animals became more distinct. Three adults, two larger than the third. Nearest to the door, a youngster. It shuffled its feet and swung round its trunk to smell them.

'May I touch it?' She strained forward to reach for the top of the calf's domed, wrinkled head. She expected softness, it looked such an infant, but the skin was hard and punctuated with coarse, sharp hair. One of the adults shifted and trumpeted and the noise ricocheted round the hold, making the wood shiver.

The captain drew her back through the door and slid the locks and bolts into place.

'I've seen them in parades,' she said. 'But never quite so close.' She tried to find the word. 'They're magnificent.'

His teeth gleamed in the lamplight as he smiled. They made their way back towards the procession of ladders that led upwards. As the captain stood aside to allow her to climb, his bobbing light showed another heavy door at the opposite end of the walkway.

'More elephants?'

At that moment, a cry broke out. A human cry of utter misery, accompanied by the grating of metal. Isabel thought of Mrs Timberley's sour words about other nasty animals on board.

She faltered. 'People?'

'We should leave.' The captain turned away.

'Convicts?' Isabel looked him full in the face. 'Are they cargo too?'

He looked embarrassed. 'They say it's the only safe place for them.'

She nodded, thinking. 'May I see?'

The captain raised his eyebrows, then shrugged and moved towards the heavy door. This time the stench was human, the smell of excrement and stale sweat.

Isabel stood inside the half-open door and peered into the blackness, following the trailing beam of the captain's lamp as it swung through the dark. This interior section of the hold was striped with iron bars, making a single large cage. Bodies within it rose, shuffled and lunged towards the door, restrained by leg irons. The heat and airless fug were oppressive. Brown knuckles whitened as fingers grasped the bars.

Faces shone in the lamplight. Men with rough features and thickset bodies. Some had the height and bearing of Pathans. Others were slight and darker in skin tone. Chests gleamed with sweat. Their loins were covered with tattered cotton. Several men pressed their faces against the flaking metal bars and the rusted iron drew black marks across their cheeks. One called out, begging for mercy.

'We should leave.' The captain spoke quietly in Isabel's ear.

As she started to turn, she saw a face she recognised. He was a striking young man, handsome and broad and, despite the shifting chaos around him, utterly still. His eyes on hers were intelligent and calm. He wore a buttoned grey shirt and lunghi and his skin was light brown, the shade of a Hindustani man of high caste. The door closed and he was gone.

It was only afterwards, as she sat in the lounge over afternoon tea, Mrs Timberley jabbering at her side, that it struck her with force where she had seen him before. He was the man who led the marching crowd during the protest in Delhi and who, when she and Jonathan came under attack, intervened to save them.

*   *   *

They approached the islands soon after dawn on the fourth day. Isabel joined the other first-class passengers on the main deck, eager for a first glimpse of the islands. Mrs Timberley soon appeared at the rail at her side.

'Ah, Mrs Whyte. Isn't it a thrill?'

The SS *Maharajah* entered a narrow stretch of water between two islands, one much larger and more densely populated than the other. Both rose steeply from a white fringe of shoreline set against black rocks, broken only by concrete jetties and moorings. Low government buildings – customs houses, perhaps, or army barracks – dotted the lower reaches.

'That must be Ross Island. Do you see?' Mrs Timberley pointed a podgy finger at the smaller of the islands. 'I do believe that's Government House, the chief commissioner's residence. Isn't it grand?'

Ross looked little more than a mile in length but its lower slopes, close to the water, were crowded with government buildings. Government House was an imposing two-storey residence high above them on the hillside, set in a green splash of gardens. A glass-walled verandah sparkled in the sunlight along its length.

'My sister took tea there with the chief commissioner's wife, Lady Lyons. Did I tell you?'

She had indeed.

'Such views, she said. Quite stunning. I expect I'll be invited too, don't you think? Such a charming lady, my sister said. She put her quite at ease.'

A steam launch, towing a barge, appeared from the harbour mouth.

'And that must be Port Blair. Isn't it splendid?' Mrs Timberley was ruddy with excitement.

Port Blair was a heaving bustle of small boats, godowns and stores. Much of the land looked unnaturally flat compared with the surrounding terrain, as if it had been artificially levelled or reclaimed from the sea. Behind the waterfront rose tiers of red-roofed houses, growing grander the further they sat from the shore. The houses gave way at last to grass-covered downs, mangrove swamp and coconut palms. Buried within, Isabel made out the red-stone circle of the low, sprawling jail complex. Beyond, the island climbed steadily to a summit, which was hung with low mist.

The SS *Maharajah* shuddered as she dropped anchor. A motor launch left the small, wooden jetty on Ross Island and crossed the strait between them.

The captain appeared. 'Mrs Whyte, you have your own transport to shore.'

Mrs Timberley giggled. 'Goodness! Well, au revoir, dear. I'm sure we'll see lots more of each other in future.'

The captain accompanied Isabel to the rail as the launch closed the final stretch of sea and came alongside the *Maharajah* in slaps of swirling, lapping water.

'How do you disembark the elephants?'

'We lower them into the water and they swim to shore.' He smiled. 'But I don't expect my other passengers to do the same.'

'I'm pleased to hear it.'

She climbed over the side and lowered herself onto the metal exterior ladder to climb down to the bobbing launch below. A tall Indian in a crisp white turban helped her into the launch, then saluted.

'Singh, Whyte Madam. Sahib's bearer. Very much welcome to you.'

* * *

110

The house was a two-storey building made of wood, with a deep-red exterior. The ground floor was given over to servants' quarters, kitchen and guard post, threaded together by a verandah, which ran the length of the building and was shaded by a dense row of coconut palms.

Singh led her past the porch to a staircase of broad, shallow steps. Chickens made squawking circles as they approached and a uniformed guard, an elderly man with betel-stained teeth, jumped to his seat to offer her namaste. A rusted shotgun hung on a cord from his shoulder.

Upstairs, the style changed from Indian to European. The interior walls were cream. The heavy wood furnishings had the hallmark of government stores.

The sitting room, the largest part of the house, was light and airy with a covered balcony, which protruded over the porch. A wide passage led back towards a rear dining room. Singh opened the second door off the passage and showed her into a bedroom.

'For madam.' He gestured to the recently made-up bed with embroidered bedspread, then opened the door to show her a small adjoining bathroom. A fresh towel and a bar of soap sat on the edge of the Victorian washstand.

Isabel smiled. 'It's wonderful, Singh. Thank you.' She switched into Hindustani: 'Would you bring me some hot water so I can wash? And some chai?'

He disappeared down a winding external staircase from her bathroom to the ground.

Isabel washed, changed and settled in the sitting room. The heat was moist and eased by a low breeze from the sea, which brought into the room the scent of salt and lush jungle vegetation. She picked out a volume on the islands from the bookshelves, then sat, book open on her lap and chai at her elbow, and gazed.

The mesh of the mosquito screen cut into squares the view over the neat rectangle of garden beneath, bordered by palms. It was divided by plumbago hedges and feathery clusters of bamboo and studded with hibiscus in all shades of red and pink and by jacaranda. Beyond it, the slope descended to a cluster of red rooftops and finally to the harbour and the shining aquamarine of the sea far below.

The light had faded to dusk by the time boots clattered on the staircase and Jonathan's voice sounded, calling in Hindustani to the servants. He burst into the sitting room with a rush of outside energy and set his topee on a side table.

'Isabel! I'm so sorry I couldn't meet you in person.' He put his hands on her shoulders and kissed her on the cheek. He gestured vaguely out at the view. 'Rather different from Delhi, isn't it?' He ran on. 'Are you hungry? I've ordered fish stew for supper. I eat it all the time but you can take charge of Cook now.' He loosened his tie and wiped his neck and face with a handkerchief. 'The electricity's out, I'm afraid.'

Singh appeared with glasses of lime soda and they sat across from each other to drink them. Jonathan's manner was attentive but there was something studied in it, which made her uneasy.

'You must be exhausted, poor thing. How was the SS *Maharajah*? Bit of a rust bucket, isn't she?'

When she tried to answer, he rushed in with a fresh question or remark as if he were afraid of silence.

'I do hope you'll like it here. Everyone's dying to meet you.'

He rubbed at a mark on the toe of his shoe, then sipped his drink before continuing.

'I had to kick up such a fuss today to make it home for

112

dinner. The CC – chief commissioner – he's tasked me with a new project, you see. Rather an exciting one. Delhi wants us to find a way of clearing a whole new section of jungle, not just raiding it for timber but actually turning it into decent agricultural land. They want to convince more people to settle here. But of course, the CC wants the report at once. You know what it's like.'

She nodded and smiled, watching him as he spoke. His face wasn't as she remembered. She thought: on the one hand, that man is my husband and, on the other, he's a complete stranger.

She said: 'It may take me a while to work everything out.'

'I'm sure you'll get masses of advice from the other wives.' He tipped back his head and laughed. 'Probably too much, actually. They're all bursting to invite you to tea. I'm sure you'll be a massive hit.' He reached over and squeezed her hand. 'Look, I am sorry to throw you into the lion's den. You will be all right, won't you?'

Behind him, Singh hovered in the doorway to announce that the water for Sahib's bath was heated.

Later, at dinner, Jonathan kept up a steady stream of chatter, telling her about the household staff and the quirks of the house. He opened a bottle of claret in honour of her arrival and drank off a glass or two at once. She sat quietly and listened as he reeled off anecdotes about life in the Andamans, some of which she remembered from their evenings in Delhi.

Finally, as they sat over dessert, she said: 'They brought convicts on the steamer. Did you know? In the hold.'

He reached for the claret and refreshed his glass. 'I heard there was a fresh batch.'

'I saw them. It was dreadful, Jonathan.'

He looked up sharply. 'You saw them?'

'Chained in the dark, like animals.'

He scraped round the last of his mango pudding, set down his spoon and drank off his claret. The houseboy came forward to clear the table.

When the boy left the room, she leant forward and said: 'I recognised one of them. You remember that day in the slum when the crowd attacked us and a man called them off? It was him.'

Jonathan rolled up his napkin, thrust it through his silver ring and scraped back his chair. 'I doubt it, darling. But if it were, I'm glad. He looked a bad lot.' He stood behind her and set his hands on the back of her chair. 'Look, would you mind very much if I disappear to the study? Sorry to be a bore but I really ought to do an hour or two.' He kissed her on the top of the head. 'Besides, you must be done in.'

She was exhausted but it was too hot to sleep that night. She lay on her back on freshly starched bed sheets, looking up at the pattern of shadows on the ceiling. The oddest thoughts floated through her mind. Her mother's voice, saying of some acquaintance: she's made her bed and now she's got to lie in it.

Outside, the jungle rumbled with low noises. Branches shivered as the night wind crept up from the sea. A wildcat howled. An owl gave a hunting cry. The distant heartbeat of the ocean against the island shore underpinned it all.

She raised her head. As she stared, the outlines of the furniture in her room, hard wood and soft rattan, grew from the darkness. Then the dull outline of the door to her bathroom. This is it, she thought. This is my home now.

Above, the ceiling fan croaked suddenly into life, gathering speed as it rotated. The electricity was back. She lay still, arms out at her sides like a snow angel. The breeze from the blades rippled over her damp nightdress and cooled her. She closed her eyes and her head filled with the soft rattle of the turning fan. As she fell into sleep, she felt as if she were back in her cabin on the SS *Maharajah*, lulled by the squeak of its timbers and travelling, travelling forwards through an endless stretch of black water.

Chapter Eleven

In those first, strange weeks, Isabel woke early to the sound of Jonathan's footsteps on the wooden staircase as he disappeared to work. He returned late each evening. She came to expect Singh's appearance in the doorway in the afternoon, bearing a chit from Sahib on a silver platter to apologise for another absence. Sometimes he blamed his workload for keeping him in the office. Sometimes he said Sir Philip or another officer had invited him to dine at The Club.

It was a small household. Singh, Cook, the cook's boy, the mali and a young houseboy called Bimal. He was a pretty child, perhaps thirteen or fourteen years old, and slightly built. He was of mixed Burmese and Indian descent with strong, broad cheekbones, a delicate nose and brown eyes ringed with impossibly long lashes. When Jonathan worked late in his study, Bimal settled devotedly at his feet.

Bimal spoke seldom. His Hindustani had a peculiar accent, which made him difficult to understand. The fact that he was so young and seemed an outsider amongst the other servants made Isabel feel protective towards him from the start.

That feeling strengthened shortly after her arrival when she emerged from her room early one morning. Jonathan had already left for work. She stepped out onto the balcony in her dressing gown. The jungle foliage shone with overnight dew. A bird, its green wings tipped with red, darted onto a tree branch and she stopped to watch it. Down to her left, something stirred and she stepped forward. The boy lay curled behind the planter in the far corner, his dark head sunk in his arms.

'Bimal?' She crouched down beside him, put a hand on the curve of his spine. His body shook. 'Are you ill?'

He lay still, as if holding his breath. His back tensed where she patted it. A moment later, a sob followed by a shudder as he tried to swallow it back.

She set her hands on his shoulders and pulled him round. His face was blotchy with crying. 'What is it, Bimal? What's happened?'

'Madam?' Singh, behind her, peering round to see what was happening. Bimal lifted his hands to cover his face and twisted away from them both.

'Singh, tell Cook I'll take breakfast out here this morning.'

Singh took another step towards her. 'Bimal, is it? Come inside, boy. Now.' His tone was sharp.

Isabel turned, making a physical barrier between the two. 'That's enough, Singh. He's perfectly alright.'

Once Singh left, his eyes grumbling, she pulled a handkerchief from the pocket of her dressing gown and dried his eyes, his nose, as if he were a much younger child.

'There,' she said. 'Now what is it, Bimal?'

His eyes slid to the balcony floor and fixed there.

'If you're in trouble, you can tell me. I'm mistress here now.'

His breath gave a final judder and settled back into a normal rhythm. He climbed awkwardly to his feet and made to slip past her, his head bowed.

'If it's the other servants, you must say.' She spoke softly so only he could hear. 'I won't have bullying.'

He padded through the sitting room without a word. When he returned with the breakfast tray, his expression had recovered its usual blank calm.

As Jonathan had predicted, the ladies of Port Blair proved eager to clasp Isabel to their bosoms.

'Gracious! Jonathan is a dark horse.'

'We had absolutely no idea.'

'What a whirlwind romance!'

'It was all rather sudden.' Isabel nodded round at the three thickly powdered middle-aged women and sipped her tea. Her host was Lady Harriet Lyons, the wife of the chief commissioner, Sir Philip, the most senior administrator on the Andamans.

Her two fellow guests, Mrs Copeland and Mrs Allen, were stout matrons with double chins and large bosoms and inclined to twitter.

By contrast, Lady Lyons struck Isabel as a shrewd woman, reserved and watchful. Now she intervened to ask: 'And what are your impressions of the islands, Mrs Whyte?'

'I'd heard they were beautiful, of course, but I don't think I've ever seen more stunning scenery.'

As Mrs Copeland gushed about the climate, Isabel looked past her at the view from the glassed-in verandah, which ran the length of Government House. The sun hung low in the sky. Below, the harbour glistened, dotted with fishing boats and light steamers. Beyond, the red roofs of Port Blair glowed. Higher on the hillside, almost touching the edge of the jungle, lay the round tower and reaching arms of the Cellular Jail, casting low shadows over the surrounding ground.

When Mrs Copeland came to a halt, Mrs Allen leant forward and began to dispense advice on local housekeeping.

'Meat is generally very poor. Mutton is the only exception and even that needs considerable stewing.'

Mrs Copeland: 'Considerable.'

'But there are so many interesting varieties of fish,' Mrs Allen continued. 'I have devised a host of methods of preparing fish here.'

Mrs Copeland twisted her lips. 'Your husband hasn't hosted many dinners. We made allowances, of course. His being a bachelor.'

Mrs Allen: 'But no longer!'

'Your cook may need a heavy hand. Start as you mean to go on. Has anyone explained to you about daily order books? No?' She shook her head. 'Each morning, a convict orderly gathers all the ladies' order books – he's perfectly safe, by the way – and brings them in person by ferry to the keeper of supplies here on Ross. He delivers the goods to one's door by four o'clock in the afternoon.'

'Milk, bread and so forth.'

'Stay on the right side of him.' Mrs Copeland arched her brow. 'I know a lady who scolded him once. She had sour milk for a month.'

'Stay on the right side of all the servants,' Mrs Allen put in. 'You've heard about poor Mrs Doyly, surely?'

Isabel shook her head.

'Well! Perhaps Lady Lyons would do us the honour.'

Lady Lyons lifted her hand and her houseboy came across to refresh the teacups and hand round a plate of buttered scones. When he finished, she sent him back to the kitchen to replenish the pot and turned to Mrs Copeland.

'Really, you remember the details far better than I.'

Mrs Copeland purred with pleasure and launched into her tale.

'It was some time ago now.' She looked round to assure herself of the room's absolute attention. 'Mrs Doyly's husband was away on business. She was at home with her new baby and a visiting friend. She had a tiff with one of the servants, a Mohammedan, and called him the son of a pig.'

Mrs Allen tutted in anticipation.

'Well, to a Mohammedan, that's a grave insult. He was a convicted murderer, of course. Later, Mrs Doyly was sitting at her dressing table before dinner. Her friend was dandling the baby in the adjoining bedroom. When what should she spy in the mirror?' She paused for dramatic effect. 'The door slowly opened and on the threshold the Mohammedan servant appeared, creeping into her dressing room, an axe raised in his hand.'

Mrs Allen gasped. 'Goodness!'

'She didn't stand a chance. Hacked to death. It's a mercy the child and friend survived. The murderer was hanged, of course.'

Mrs Allen shook her head. 'I have the sweetest houseboy – you know Mani? He murdered his own mother in cold blood when he was practically a child.'

They sat in silence for a few moments, drinking their tea. Isabel looked out at the dark blot of the Cellular Jail on the opposite hillside. He must be there, the young man who saved them in Delhi, who was transported here like an animal in the ship's hold. They were so close, these men. Yet no one spoke of them.

She turned to Lady Lyons. 'I believe many of the men sent here nowadays are political prisoners?'

'Political?' Mrs Copeland snorted. 'They're thugs. I can more readily understand a man who kills in a fit of rage than one who murders complete strangers because of the uniforms they wear.'

Mrs Allen reached forward and patted Isabel's knee. 'You needn't worry, my dear. The real terrorists are confined to jail and rarely see the end of their sentences. You're quite safe.' She helped herself to another slice of cake and broke off a piece with her fork.

Lady Lyons said: 'It's a curious business, isn't it, joining one of His Majesty's penal colonies?' She regarded Isabel closely. 'It takes a little adjustment.'

'It does indeed.'

'I'm not sure I've ever quite lost the urge to ask people what they did. You know, servants and shopkeepers and so on. They've practically all been convicted of something grisly.'

Mrs Copeland gave a high laugh. 'Oh really, Lady Lyons.'

Mrs Allen turned to Isabel. 'It simply isn't done, asking a person directly. It causes great offence.'

Mrs Copeland nodded. 'One finds out by other means, naturally.'

'Naturally.'

Isabel hesitated. 'There are one or two things I don't quite understand.'

Lady Lyons inclined her head.

'Am I right in thinking that most murderers are likely to be released in due course and allowed to live a free life here?'

Lady Lyons nodded. 'If they behave themselves. We call it

ticket of leave. They can run a shop or farm or whatnot, but they cannot leave the island.'

Isabel continued: 'But not political prisoners?'

Mrs Copeland stiffened.

Lady Lyons said: 'Political prisoners are treated differently, that's true.' She paused, choosing her words with care. 'Some can be rehabilitated, but not many.'

Isabel persisted. 'And is it ever possible to visit the prisoners?'

Mrs Allen looked astonished. 'Whatever for?'

'It is possible to see inside the jail on occasion,' said Lady Lyons. 'But not to meet with a particular prisoner, if that is what you have in mind.'

The houseboy came back into the room, carrying the teapot with care. He lifted the lid to allow Lady Lyons to inspect the water level and stir round the leaves, then she gestured to him to pour fresh cups.

Mrs Copeland said: 'Do you have mosquito boots? I know just the place to have them fitted.'

Mrs Allen chimed in: 'And if you're alone in the evening and boots are simply too hot, put your feet in a nice soft pillow case. Does the trick.'

'Plenty of citronella. A tad smelly, but it works.'

After that, Mrs Allen turned to Mrs Copeland and they began to discuss arrangements for a forthcoming dinner-dance at The Settlement Mess, which also served as The Club.

Isabel sat quietly. Her head moved from one lady to the other as they spoke but her thoughts ran back to the jail and to the men imprisoned there, such a short distance away. She felt herself observed and lifted her head. Lady Lyons' eyes were on her face. As she met her gaze, Lady Lyons changed her expression in an instant from watchfulness to polite neutrality. She leant forward and indicated a plate.

'Another piece of seed cake, Mrs Whyte?'

That night, Isabel was woken by the slow squeak of her bedroom door. She lifted her head, narrowing her eyes to make out a ghostly figure in a white nightshirt. Jonathan crept across the room and eased back the sheet to slide into bed beside her.

His manner was eager but awkward. Dry lips opened on hers and he grasped her shoulders too firmly with moist hands. Isabel submitted quietly as he fumbled his way around her body with brittle anxiety. After a little while, he gave a cry and buried his face between her breasts. She stroked his hair with her fingers, as a mother might caress a child and his breathing gradually steadied and slowed. A few minutes later, he slid out of her bed without a word and disappeared back to his own.

The next morning, he left earlier than usual for the office and returned long after dark when she was already in bed. She reached for her dressing gown, hoping to sit with him for a while but before she could intercept him, he padded softly down the passageway and his bedroom door clicked shut.

He never entered her bedroom again and she, uncertain, didn't dare to risk embarrassing him further by trying to find the words to confront him.

Chapter Twelve

Asha

'I have news, little sister.'

Amit removed his spectacles as soon as she sat beside him and played with them in his hands, bending the arms back and forth as he spoke.

'I have friends inside the jail. Secret friends. You understand?'

She nodded. She understood that the men who came late in the evening to whisper must have some connection with those still locked up within the thick walls.

'They tell me that your baba is to be released.'

Her breath stopped in her throat. 'When?'

'Soon. Very soon. I am waiting for another message to tell us the day.' He smiled. 'You are a good girl, Asha.'

She threaded her arms round her knees and hugged her legs. She had been here for several months now. Without her baba, it had been a time of wasted days.

Amit-ji became serious. 'Sometimes it can be difficult, Asha, when a man comes out. You must try to understand.' He twisted his spectacles in his fingers. 'The body suffers in that place but so too does the soul, shut up alone in a cell, day after day, year after year. No one speaks of it and your baba won't also. He will lock it away inside himself.

Freedom can be hard to bear. Do you understand?'

She nodded but she didn't understand. All she thought was: my baba is coming home. Thanks be to the gods.

'Your baba is a simple man. He has suffered a great deal in prison. You must be patient with him.'

The jail was a vast, forbidding complex, surrounded by high walls. Asha sat in the shade of the frangipani trees and watched the heavy wooden gates. The day was hot and humid and her salwar kameez was damp with sweat, her throat parched. She had arrived soon after dawn and now the sun was high and hard. Other women waited too, heads bowed, eyes fixed on the gate or on the ground and the trails of ants which hurried to and fro in the dirt. They stood or sat separately, each one carefully apart from the others, and although they were equally poor, equally wretched, no one spoke.

The trees burst with flowers and their scent hung solidly in the air. High above, a jungle bird kept up a high-pitched cry. No one raised their eyes to look for it.

Asha ran her tongue round dry lips. Her thighs were numb and she shifted her weight, crossed and re-crossed her legs. Time passed. She had prepared food at home and she wondered if it would keep, if he didn't come. She had spent good money on daal and fresh subzi.

In the afternoon, boots struck stone on the other side of the wall. The women rose to their feet. A metal jangling. The women took a few tentative steps forward. The scraping of bolts, of keys. The vast gates slowly parted to create a meanly narrow gap of a foot or two. The men emerged without energy and the women stepped forward to claim them, one by one.

Her baba was the fourth to appear. He stumbled as if he were blind and unsure of his footing. He looked an old man now, damaged by the rigours of his years in prison and the hard manual work he had undertaken there. He took a few faltering steps away from the gate, then stopped and looked around, uncertain.

'Baba. I'm here.' She went quickly to him, slipped her hand through his arm and drew him away. The arm was all bone. 'Let's go home.'

Home was little more than a crawl space, a triangular lean-to of wood and woven straw down the lane from Amit-ji's restaurant. She had swept and cleaned it well and rolled out rattan matting to make a floor where they could sit and sleep. He sat on the matting and closed his eyes.

She went outside, crouched over the cooking fire and blew life back into it. She boiled up chai and took it to him, then went back to heat the food in the same pot.

'Amit-ji was a prisoner himself once,' she said.

He made a ball of the daal and subzi and lifted it to his mouth between his fingers.

'He owns a restaurant. I help them when it's busy and they pay me. They're very respectful.'

He chewed his food slowly. All his movements were painstaking as if his heart barely beat enough strength round his body. When he was halfway through his meal, he stopped, set down the plate, wiped off his mouth with his sleeve.

'Can't you eat more, Baba?'

He put his hand on her shoulder. 'I have no appetite.'

'You will, Baba. I'll cook for you. You'll soon be strong again.'

He didn't answer. He had a way of looking past her as if she weren't there.

'We could rent a shop, Baba, and sell fruits. They have such plump mangoes here, and coconuts too.'

He didn't answer.

'Or buckets and brooms, maybe.'

'If you like, Asha.' He sighed. 'Whatever you like.'

She took away the food on his plate and scraped it back into the pot for later. Then she crouched beside him, eased off his sandals and brought water to wash his feet. They were the feet of an old man now. It would take a lot of washing to make them clean again.

When she had finished and patted them dry with her dupatta, he reached out a hand and stroked her hair. 'You're a good daughter, Asha. But you shouldn't be here. This isn't what I wanted for you.'

She pressed up against him and put his arm round her shoulders. 'I belong with my baba. We can be together, now you're free.'

He shook his head. 'I am not free, child. I will always be their prisoner.'

She soothed him and fanned his face as he settled down on the mat to sleep. Once he was quiet, she rinsed the dishes in a pail and set them to dry.

She looked at him as he slept. His skin was weathered and stretched tightly over his bones, making his cheeks sunken and his chin sharp. She would feed him well and care for him. They would build a new life here together.

The muscles in his face twitched. He let out a cry and opened his eyes.

'Baba? Are you alright?'

The eyes looked unfocused but full of fear.

'Hush, Baba.' She patted his thigh. 'Hush, you're safe now.'

His eyes fell closed again.

This Baba, who emerged from prison, was not the father she remembered. This was a sick man, listless, broken and easily angered.

In those first days, he lay in their shelter and dozed. She worked in the restaurant and bought good food but he had little appetite. She watched in despair as he failed to gain weight or to take interest in the world.

At night, she slept curled beside him. He woke often with cries but refused to discuss the terrors inside his head. Sometimes, as she held him and stroked his head, he wept into her hair.

A week after Baba's release, Amit-ji came to visit him. It was morning and she sat outside their shelter in the dirt, boiling up daal and crushing garlic and turmeric to season the subzi.

'Bhai! Brother!' Amit-ji rapped on the wooden strut of the shelter with his knuckles. Only her father's feet stuck out and Asha crawled inside to wake him. His chin was prickly with stubble and his hair unwashed.

'Baba! Amit-ji is here to see you.'

He grunted, turned onto his side.

She took hold of his shoulder and shook him. 'Baba! Please.'

Finally he stirred and came crawling out, blinking in the sunlight. His kameez was crumpled and stained.

'Welcome, brother. I salute you. We have friends in

common, I think. In Delhi, I once knew Krishna-Sahib, a man who became a martyr for our cause. Your former master, nah? I am Amit.'

Her father sat cross-legged in the dirt, his large gnarled feet tucked under his legs. His jaw was set and hostile.

Amit sat down beside her father and patted his knee as if they were old friends, then drew a parcel from his pocket. He unwrapped the paper and set it on the ground between them. Sweetmeats. Kaju barfi, one of the most expensive in the restaurant. Their silver tops gleamed in the sun. Her father turned his head away.

Asha said: 'How kind, Amit-ji. Baba, try some.'

'They're too sweet. My stomach is ruined by years of eating filth.'

Amit nodded quietly. 'I was in that place for six years. It's true. The food is not fit for cattle.'

Asha got to her feet. 'Will you drink chai, Amit-ji? Baba?'

Her father didn't answer. She mixed water and milk and blew on the fire to boil it up with tea.

'Tell me, brother. Is there news from that place?'

Her father shrugged. 'How can there be news? Every man is kept apart from the others.'

Amit pushed his spectacles up the bridge of his nose with his forefinger. 'Perhaps that is the worst punishment of all, nah?' He paused, studying the patch of bare ground in front of him. 'Well, I have news. About Sanjay Krishna. You knew him a little, I think, in Delhi, when he was still a young man? Sahib's nephew.'

He leant in and lowered his voice, speaking man to man. Asha, stirring the chai, strained to listen.

'He's here, locked up in that same jail. Had you heard?'

Her baba didn't raise his eyes. Asha's spoon scraped against the bottom of the pot as she stirred, stirred, stirred the swirling chai. Sanjay Krishna here, a prisoner? Since when? Amit should have told her also. Just because she was a girl, no one talked politics with her. But this, she should have known.

Amit continued: 'Not long after your good daughter left Delhi, he led a protest. Our people filled the streets, calling for their rights, and were brutally suppressed by the police and the army even. There were martyrs that day and many men were arrested, including Krishna-ji.'

There was a long pause. Asha poured the boiling chai into clay cups and kept her face hidden. Her hand trembled and the ground turned dark where she spilt dribbles of chai. She saw Sanjay Krishna's kind smile as she handed the men their cups.

Her father set his cup, untouched, on the ground. A fly landed on the rim and he made no move to wave it away. 'You come here to talk to me about politics? Don't you see what pain it has brought me and my family? I'm a simple man. All I wanted was to feed my daughter, to protect her and find her a good husband. Now we both are ruined. For what?'

Amit paused and seemed to consider for a few moments before he replied. 'The Britishers did this to you. Blame them, not us.' He kept his tone level and soft. 'You have friends here. We all have suffered. We will help you and your daughter, as a friend should.'

Her father hunched his shoulders.

Amit continued: 'You have many blessings, ji. You have freedom. You have a roof and food to eat. You have a daughter, a good girl.'

'What makes you an expert on my daughter?'

Amit looked down at the clay cup in his hands. 'I don't want to quarrel with you.'

'Maybe I want to quarrel with you.'

Amit didn't answer. The air sat heavily between the three of them. Asha was afraid to break the silence. Finally she picked up one of the sweets, broke off a corner and offered it to her father. 'Try a little, Baba. Please.'

He raised his arm and knocked the sweet from her hand. 'I want nothing from this man.' His face was contorted with anger as he confronted Amit. 'I didn't invite you here.'

'Baba, please, we only have this home because of—'

'You took advantage of my daughter, didn't you? You knew I was helpless to protect her.'

Amit blinked behind his spectacles. 'No, brother. Not like that. I took care of her only. I swear to you.'

'Took care of her?' Her baba tried to get to his feet. His cheeks were red with anger.

'It's true, Baba. He protected me.' She reached for his hand and he swatted her away. 'Why do you say such a thing?'

Amit got to his feet, his hands spread before him. 'Your baba is right. This is his home. I came without invitation.'

'But we're grateful to you.' She looked, stricken, from the calm face to the other, full of fury. 'Aren't we, Baba? Tell him.'

Amit turned to leave. As he retreated, her baba reached for the parcel of sweets and threw them after him. They burst into pieces as they hit the ground, the silver tops tarnished by dust, the sugar broken into crumbs for the ants and birds to eat.

* * *

131

After that, her baba barely left the shelter. On mornings when she could persuade him, Asha drew him down the narrow lanes to the waterfront where they sat in silence, side by side, on the low walls, watching the fishermen unloading their catch and gazing out across the turquoise sea towards the invisible Indian mainland.

Sometimes he scolded her. 'What place is this for a decent girl? An island filled with thieves and murderers. You should never have come here. Did I tell you to leave Delhi? Did I?'

She hung her head and sat quietly beside him, her hand resting on his thin arm, and waited until the storm passed.

In the afternoons, she went to the restaurant to scour the pots and pans and help Cook prepare food. Now her baba came with her. He sat alone, shoulders hunched, at a rickety table in the shadowy interior and smoked one bidi after another. Most customers sat facing the light and bustle of the lane. Only her baba sat with his back to the outside world, peering through the gloom towards the back of the restaurant and the yard where she worked. At first, Rajiv took him chai and plates of snacks but he refused everything. When she finished work, he pulled himself to his feet and walked back with her in silence, his hand on her shoulder.

Amit observed the way her father followed and watched her.

'It is hard for a bird to be locked inside a cage,' he said. 'Captivity breaks his spirit. But finally, the bird becomes accustomed. Then, even when the cage door is opened wide, it doesn't dare to leave. It sits, comforted by the bars that confine it and afraid to fly.'

She shook her head. 'My baba isn't a bird.'

Amit put his head on one side. 'Maybe not. But once a

man has his freedom taken from him, it may take a long time to learn to be free again.'

In the evenings, after she served her father his food, she sat with her body pressed against his and tried to make him talk.

'Tell me about Mama.'

'I don't remember.'

'You do, Baba.' She waited but nothing came. 'Tell the story about how you named me.'

He shrugged. 'What story? Is there a story?'

'You know. You and Mama waited so many years for a child and finally I came and you called me Asha. Hope.'

He shook his head and looked down at his fingers, bent now and misshapen.

'There is no hope. Hope died.'

In the night, he continued to cry out and she had to shake him to bring him back to her from whatever fearful place he visited in his dreams.

One afternoon, she sat in the shade of the frangipani tree cleaning and chopping a mountain of bhindi for Cook, dumping the discarded ends into a pail for the pigs and goats. Her baba watched her from his seat inside the restaurant, visible only by the glow of his cheap cigarette. Amit sat nearby, his ledger open on his knee, raising his spectacles to the top of his nose as he calculated his sums.

'I have a letter for you, little sister.'

She looked up. Never in her life had she received a letter. Amit had his head bowed over his book. She was unsure if he had really spoken and if it was indeed to her.

'Don't turn to me.' Amit's voice was soft. 'Your baba is watching.'

She focused her eyes back on her hands and the soft vegetable rhythm of pluck and chop.

'I'll leave it when I go.'

The fingers of bhindi swam in front of her eyes. She had to wipe off her forehead with her sleeve and blink hard before she could carry on chopping. When Amit got to his feet half an hour later and took his accounts inside, she pretended to have an ache in her neck and stretched it out by massaging her shoulder, glancing over as she did so at the chair where Amit had sat. A newspaper lay under it.

She worked on with unsteady hands through the piles of vegetables in their pots, bhindi first, then beans, then cauliflower. When she had finished, she got to her feet, stretched, picked up the pail and crossed to dump the discarded ends into the trough there. As she came back, she pretended to stop and peer at something on the ground and, turning her back on the restaurant and her baba's watchful eyes, bent to pick at the dirt. With her foot, she kicked the newspaper. The paper concealed inside was cheap and thin and she swept it into her pail in a single movement, then carried it away.

All the way home, her baba's hand heavy on her shoulder, every scrunch and crinkle of the paper in her pocket terrorised her but he seemed to hear nothing.

All night, she thought about the letter. She could imagine one person who might write a letter to her and she was afraid to read it in case she was disappointed.

The next morning, she went to the fields as usual in the grey half-light before dawn to do her business in private. In the silence there, broken only by the morning song of the birds, she opened up the paper and read.

Little Sister,

How is your good self? How is your dear baba? I hear news that he is free at last and I thank the gods for this great, good happiness. I am a prisoner here also, these last months, but in body only. My heart and soul are free. I do not know what fate lies ahead of me but I send many blessings to you. I pray that you may do good in this world. May you continue the fight for your people's freedom.

SK.

On the back, he had written a few more lines. For a moment, she thought: he wrote a poem for me. Then she saw the name at the bottom – R. Tagore – and remembered the book of poems that his uncle had read the night before he died.

I have come to the brink of eternity from which nothing can vanish – no hope, no happiness, no vision of a face seen through tears.

Her face flushed as she imagined him sitting in a cell and writing this secret letter for her. His hands, warm on the pen, on the paper, his kind face bent over his work. She sat in the dewy field for as long as she dared, staring down at the paper in her hands, filled with hopeless longing for this man who was so much more than she could ever dream of becoming and yet called her his little sister.

One afternoon, as she carried piles of washed dishes from the yard to Cook in the restaurant, one of Amit's friends, a fellow ticket of leave, came slinking over to speak to her. He was a light-skinned man from the north who laboured with his father as a tenant farmer before getting into a brawl, being convicted of murder and sent to the Andamans.

Now he was middle-aged, his back crooked after years of prison work. He made a rough living by hauling panniers for the fishermen when their catches came ashore and heaving boxes of goods in and out of the godowns whenever a ship docked.

He had an awkward manner. Amit had brought him to her months earlier with a request to write a letter to his brother about their inheritance after their father's death. He dictated his letter without looking her in the eye. Now he stuttered and stared down at his long hairy toes, which poked out of his chappals. He pulled a paper from his lunghi.

'Amit gave me a letter,' he said. 'Maybe it is a reply at last from my brother. Could you read it?'

She wiped off her hands on her dupatta and he handed her the paper. It was crumpled and dotted with grease stains as if he had been carrying it with him for some days.

The letter was scrawled in bad English. His brother, no doubt also unable to read or write, must have paid a street-corner letter-writer. She spread it out on her lap and tried to decipher the words. The language was old-fashioned and full of mistakes. The man hunched forward, his brow knitted.

'Is there some dispute between you? About cattle?' She tried to remember the content of the letter she had written on his behalf all those weeks earlier.

'Our father died.' The man knotted his meaty fingers. 'Now my brother and his wife have the house and goats and water buffaloes and everything. I want my share.'

She used the tip of her finger to trace over the words, one by one, her lips moving silently. The light suddenly vanished. She looked up. Her baba stood in the doorway, his arms loose at his side.

'What's that?'

His expression was hidden by shadows but his voice was menacing.

'It's alright, Baba. It's a letter from this man's brother only. I'm reading it for him.'

Her baba shoved the man out of the way and snatched the paper from her hands. He stared at it, blind to the written words. 'What does it say? Tell me.'

She hesitated. 'I'm just trying to see, Baba. It's private. About their family business.'

Her father turned on the man. 'Who are you, anyway? Why are you bothering my daughter?'

She reached for him, set her hand on his shoulder. 'Please, Baba.'

The man shoved her father in the back. 'Mind your manners. I've done nothing.'

Her father crumpled the paper into a ball in his hand and threw it onto the floor. Asha bent to pick it up. As she did, fist cracked on bone and her baba knocked into her, staggering, his hand to his jaw. Father and daughter clutched at each other as they battled to stay upright.

The man laughed. His feet were planted squarely and his face hard.

'Go home, old man. You're making a fool of yourself.'

Her father put her aside and lunged at the man, flying through the air with a howl of rage, teeth bared, fists pounding. The sheer force of his body knocked the younger man backwards and they locked together, arms pumping, hands flailing to find purchase.

'Stop it!' Asha tried to dance round them, to seize her baba's arm. 'Stop!'

The turning, grappling men flung her off and she fell, skidding across the wet floor.

Sweat poured down her father's flushed face as they struggled. His opponent was heavier-set and stronger. Her thin father hung like a vine round a stout branch, tossed back and forth by the man's blows to his face, his chest. He clung on, his own fists hammering with frantic energy. All the anguish, the humiliation, the pain that had festered inside him seemed to burst to the surface and surged now into his juddering arms.

The man grasped her father's hair and smashed his head backwards against the wall. Asha screamed. Blood, massing on her father's skull, made a thickly spreading stain on the plaster. Her father's hand groped in empty air, blind fingers reaching. She ran at the man and tried to pull him off. As he turned to knock her away, her father shifted his weight and his groping hand closed on a cooking knife, shining there on the counter beside her.

She screamed: 'No, Baba!'

His fingertips strained to turn it, to grasp the handle and twist the blade inwards. The man lifted her father's head and banged it again against the wall. A moment later, the man let out a cry, the shriek of a wounded animal. The handle of the knife stuck out from between his shoulder blades, deeply embedded. His grip loosened. Asha's father kicked him away, panting, as the man, clawing behind at his own back, crashed to the ground. His eyes rolled, then became sightless and still. Asha's father slumped to the ground beside him, his head bowed to his chest. Asha's rushing blood filled her ears. Silence pressed down on them all, more painful than the screams.

'Take him home.' Amit stood in the doorway, his face pale. She didn't know how long he had been there or how much he had witnessed.

'He started it. He hit my baba. It was self-defence.'

Amit didn't reply.

Her father groaned and put his hands to the floor, trying to get to his feet. Asha ran to help him. 'We must hide him. Please.'

'It's too late for that.' Amit shook his head. 'Wherever you rush now, they will find him.' He looked at her with slow sadness. 'Perhaps, after all, this is what your baba wants.'

Chapter Thirteen

Isabel

After six months, Isabel felt initiated into the elite circle of expatriate ladies who played tennis at The Club, then sat over lunch there, who hosted afternoon teas or who, outside the typhoon season, led weekend bathing picnics to the more familiar island's coves.

When she could, she spent time alone. In Delhi, she always read her father's daily newspaper. Here, news was harder to come by and she felt increasingly out of touch with events both in London and in Delhi. Instead, she turned to the books in Jonathan's small, humidity-stained library. It was dominated by scientific volumes about agriculture and tropical soils. She read them all. The books she found most interesting were those about the native people of the Andamans, the Nicobarese and Jarawa, primitive people whose lives and habits intrigued her.

She disappeared for long, rambling walks down to the waterfront or through the bazaar and the densely populated Indian quarter that surrounded it. The constant assault of the sing-song cries of hawkers, the bustling women in brightly coloured saris with baskets of mangoes and coconuts and fresh fish on their arms, the smells of garlic and chilli, of frying onions and daal, of unwashed bodies crowded unpleasantly close, it all conspired to remind her powerfully of parts of Delhi and her old life there.

Gradually she made the acquaintance of shopkeepers and their wives who were startled by her fluency in Hindustani. She took them small gifts of food and sat with them over chai, hearing nostalgic tales of the towns and villages they left far behind on the Indian mainland and the troubled histories that set them adrift in the Bay of Bengal.

Wherever she found herself, whether reading on the balcony at home or roaming the poorer districts close to the shoreline, the Cellular Jail always loomed, a forbidding presence on the hillside. Its dark arms reached out to her, waiting for its time to come. Finally, it came.

Mrs Copeland was the first to make reference to the hanging, during a ladies' tea at The Club.

'It's simply awful to ask,' she said, looking round, 'but what are people intending to wear?'

Mrs Allen tittered. 'What a question!'

'But it's a serious matter.' Mrs Copeland shook her head, all apologies. 'I mean, is one required to be in mourning?'

'You've never met the chap! At least, I sincerely hope not.'

'Well, quite.'

Isabel looked from one powdered face to the other, failing to understand.

'Mrs Whyte! You are planning to attend, surely?'

'Goodness, I rather think she doesn't know!'

Lady Lyons leant across to Isabel to explain. 'I'm afraid a hanging is scheduled, Mrs Whyte. A sad case.'

'Sad?' Mrs Allen sounded tart. 'He's a subversive, isn't he?'

Lady Lyons shrugged. 'Poorly educated, apparently. My husband was inclined to be lenient in the first instance and granted him ticket of leave status. Then he stabbed a man to death. All rather unpleasant. He has a daughter who'll be left high and dry.'

Isabel sat quietly, listening. She had heard whispers in the bazaar of an execution. This, she assumed, was it. She pushed away her plate of cake.

'Your husband took such a special interest in the case.' Mrs Copeland craned forward.

'A special interest?' She looked to Lady Lyons.

'Your husband passed sentence on the accused last month, Mrs Whyte, when my husband was in Calcutta. Never a pleasant duty. The death penalty was really the only option.' She paused, reading Isabel's face. 'Perhaps that's why he didn't mention it.'

'Perhaps.' Isabel wasn't surprised that Jonathan hadn't talked to her about the execution. They seldom talked about anything.

Lady Lyons lifted her hand for more hot water to freshen the teapot. 'It is all rather gruesome, I know. But do come along. It's a chance to see inside the jail, at least. There may not be another for a while.'

'Oh, you can't miss it.' Mrs Copeland. 'It's the first for simply an age. But, Lady Lyons, what is the correct attire?'

On the morning of the hanging, the air was taut with tension. As Isabel sat over breakfast, the voices of passers-by, drifting up from the jungle paths below, seemed subdued. Only the birds stayed shrill and raucous.

Jonathan was in the office. She would make her own way to the jail later in the morning, along with Lady Lyons and the other ladies.

The Cellular Jail loomed high and forbidding. As they gathered outside the main entrance gates, flanked by a pair of rounded towers, the ladies gossiped and murmured in low voices. Only Isabel stood in silence. She looked up at the blank face of stone stretching above them in three storeys.

An Anglo-Indian guard, a tall, jolly fellow, came out to greet them and ushered them through the vast doors. One security gate after another was unlocked, then locked behind them as they progressed towards the centre.

The ladies peppered the guard with questions and he answered with a sing-song lilt.

'Many of the prisoners are choosing to come,' he said. 'Better to serve short spell here and then settle as a ticket of leave than be spending all of their lives in Calcutta or Delhi prison, nah?'

He pointed out the structure of the building as they continued down a dismal corridor towards a square of light. 'There are seven wings, with the clock tower at their centre. We'll see that presently. Think of it as a wheel with many spokes.'

The ladies fanned themselves.

He went on: 'The cellular plan is from our American friends. Every prisoner, confined in his cell, is having a window but those windows are so carefully angled that no man can see or communicate with another.'

They emerged, blinking, into a triangular open area, a wedge of land between two of the building's stretching arms of cells. It was bright with sunlight, which was broken only by the reaching shadow of the clock tower.

At the far end, a wooden platform and gallows had been erected. Rows of chairs were lined up in front. Isabel stopped. The stream of ladies flowed past her and chose their seats. The heat fell heavily. She looked up at the dark sockets of windows all around her, running the length of the prison blocks. She felt the eyes of unseen men, locked in the darkness within.

A bear of a man with old-fashioned whiskers appeared from a far door. The chief commissioner, Sir Philip Lyons. He crossed the courtyard to greet the ladies as if he were striding through a country estate. After a few minutes, he nodded to Isabel, then came back to greet her.

'All rather grim, isn't it?' He read her expression at once. 'Needs must.'

Behind him, a cluster of fellow Englishmen emerged and crossed to join them, Jonathan amongst them. He took her arm and escorted her to a place in the front row, then settled beside her.

'Chin up.' He patted her gloved hand. 'I shouldn't look if I were you.'

The prison walls pressed in around her. The area was sheltered from the breeze and the heat squeezed out every drop of life. They waited. Isabel's moist hands grasped each other in her gloves.

A single bell, high in the clock tower, began to toll. A solemn incantation. As they watched, a wooden door opened at the base of the tower and a clutch of men shuffled out. Port Blair's Anglican priest and a Hindu holy man were amongst the party and their mouths moved in prayer.

The condemned man was half-hidden by the burly Anglo-Indian guards who surrounded him. He was a slight, elderly figure, his head bent forward and his back buckled. His legs were shackled by chains and his hands, in front of him, bound with rope. He wore a Western-style prison uniform of trousers and shirt in dun, faded by too many washes. His eyes fixed on his bare, bound feet as the guards propelled him up the rough wooden steps to the gallows.

Isabel lowered her face to stare at her gloves. Jonathan had clenched his own hands on his knees and his knuckles bled white. To her right, Sir Philip Lyons got to his feet and delivered the legal words of condemnation. He had a resonant voice and his words rolled around the open triangle of ground and rose to the windows above. Somewhere beyond in the jungle, a bird started to call, a high, rising caw that pierced the air.

Moments later, a colossal bang. Isabel jumped. Her head jerked up. The trapdoor stood open. The prisoner hung suspended in the vacancy. His legs twisted and kicked. As he grew still, his body seemed to turn, spinning on its rope. A dark patch of liquid appeared at his groin and the stain spread down the inside leg of his trousers. The yard vibrated with tension and time itself seemed suspended.

Then, in an incoming wave of movement, the spectators around her were suddenly on their feet, turning their backs already on the platform, moving to greet friends, colleagues and acquaintances. Prison officers, hurrying forward, ushered the ladies away from their chairs and towards a door in the far building. Tea, someone said. Do join us.

Isabel stood in silence in the anteroom as the party around her jostled for tea and biscuits and the general mood lightened.

Mrs Copeland held a sugar-coated shortbread biscuit.

'You simply must try one.' She sprayed golden crumbs. 'Delicious.'

One of the assistant commissioners made a feeble attempt to tell an amusing story about a botched hanging and the ladies within earshot laughed too quickly to reassure him that they weren't taking offence.

Jonathan appeared, a young, ginger-haired fellow at his side. 'Darling, you haven't met Barnes, have you? Terrible chap. Beats me hollow at golf.'

The young man laughed. 'Oh come on, Whyte.'

'He's the assistant commissioner here. So better be decent or he may not let us out.'

Mrs Copeland pressed in at her side, eager to overhear.

'Aren't you somewhat of a newcomer, Mr Barnes?'

'Fairly new, madam.' He smiled. 'I arrived two months ago.'

'I thought so.' She gave a satisfied nod.

Jonathan put in: 'Anyway, he wondered if the ladies would care to view a cell?'

'May we?' Mrs Allen appeared from nowhere. 'How thrilling.'

Mr Barnes led the small party of women down a succession of short corridors, then stopped in front of a closed cell door. Isabel trailed a step or two behind. The ladies pressed forward round the door and jostled to look through the spyhole.

Eventually the rush subsided and Isabel stepped forward. It took her a moment to adjust to the darkness on the far side of the door. The cell beyond was cramped and bare. The only light was a trail of weak sunshine, which entered from a small, high window. The walls were whitewashed and gleamed in the low light.

She started. A hunched figure sat on a ragged cot. An elderly man, thin and prison-pale, his hair already silver. A blanket lay beside him. A bucket sat in the far corner, under the window. The air escaping from the spyhole carried excrement and stale breath. She stepped back abruptly. She couldn't tell if he knew she was there, whether he sensed her looking.

The other ladies were already moving on. Their voices echoed down the corridor.

'Who's the most dreaded prisoner here?'

Someone giggled. 'What a question!'

Mr Barnes lifted his hand. 'We have eighty-seven murderers at present, madam. Many of them took more than one life. Others committed crimes so repugnant I wouldn't dream of describing them.'

He paused, feeling his command of their silence.

'But most of these men can and will be rehabilitated. A few years on a work-gang and they have every hope of being granted a ticket of leave.'

The ladies nodded.

'But to my mind, the most dreaded, as you put it, are the terrorists. Many are murderers and bomb-makers and thieves and they are difficult to reform. You see why? Because death means nothing to them. They see themselves as martyrs, willing to die for their cause.'

The tour came to an end and the ladies, sated now, walked back through the succession of security gates to the main entrance. Outside, in the bright sunlight, tonga and taxi-wallahs lay across front seats, bare feet sticking out, dozing in the heat as they waited.

The ladies, chattering and laughing as if they had emerged from a party, clustered round the vehicles and began to climb into them, in twos and threes. Only Isabel hung back.

'Lunch?' Mrs Copeland, crammed into the back of a tonga, raised a hand. 'We're gathering at The Club.'

Isabel shook her head. She stood by Mr Barnes as, one by

one, the tongas and taxis shook themselves into motion and bumped off down the jungle track.

Silence crept in. Off to one side, a movement caught her eye. A horse, attached to an idling cart, pulled at long, lush grass. Beside it, a young Indian girl, all in white, stood under the trees. She looked across at them with hard eyes.

Isabel frowned. She'd seen her before but struggled to remember where. 'Who's that?'

Mr Barnes lowered his voice. 'The daughter.' He cleared his throat. 'She's waiting for his effects.'

Isabel looked at the cart. 'And for the body.'

He nodded, embarrassed. As she crossed to the girl, his voice followed her: 'I wouldn't advise, really.'

The girl glared at Isabel as she approached. Her fury is all that's keeping her together, Isabel thought, looking at the flushed cheeks.

'I'm sorry.' Isabel addressed her in Hindustani. 'It's a terrible sorrow to lose a father.'

The girl's eyes flashed. 'You people killed him. He was a poor man only, a good man.'

Isabel nodded. A memory stirred. Rahul and Sangeeta's courtyard. That's where she had seen the girl, younger then, but just as hostile.

'You know my friend in Delhi, Rahul Chaudhary, and his wife, Sangeeta. I saw you there.'

The girl scowled.

Isabel put out her hand and touched her shoulder. 'I can help you, Asha,' she said. 'If you'll let me.'

Chapter Fourteen

Asha

'Thank the gods for good fortune.'

Her baba was no more. How dare he speak of good fortune?

'Don't look like that.' Cook tapped the rim of his mixing bowl with the wooden spoon in his hand and pointed it at her. 'You're safe here, aren't you? And well fed? Be grateful.'

Cook was the kindest of the servants. Singh, Sahib's bearer, seemed to think himself too grand to speak to her and issued orders in a clipped voice, looking at some vacant patch of air above her head as he spoke, as if he were a sahib himself.

As for the mali, she tried to keep her distance from him. His body was strong but his mind was peculiar. When she spoke to him, he didn't reply and when she passed him in the porch or garden, where he knelt pruning and weeding, his eyes shadowed her. It wasn't respectful.

The only other servant was the houseboy, a half-Burmese even younger than she was. He was afraid of his own footsteps.

She sat at the far end of the kitchen table and picked at scraps of discarded pastry littered there.

'What would my poor baba say? Servant to the very Britisher who ordered his death.' Her voice caught. She needed to speak often of her baba, to keep him alive, here in this kitchen with its sugary air and spicy smells. 'I never expected this.'

Cook sniffed. 'What did you expect, then?'

He carried on mixing his pudding. Flour rose in soft flurries and settled along the rim of the bowl and the scrubbed tabletop. Milk was there and butter but no spices.

'Why always so tasteless?'

He shrugged. 'It's what they like.'

Cook wasn't a freedom fighter. No one in the household was, Amit said. They must be murderers. She looked now at Cook as he stooped over his bowl, beating up the mixture until it turned from yellow to white. The muscles in his spoon-wielding arm rose in ridges. A light perspiration moistened his forehead and nose and his lips moved as he muttered to himself. Who had he killed? His wife, maybe. It was hard to imagine. But then her baba became a murderer and he was not a bad man and that too was hard to explain.

'They broke him in that prison. My baba.' Pick, pick at the crumbs on the table. 'He wasn't right in the head when he came out. He didn't know what he was doing.'

Cook nodded. She had told him this many times before. He was being patient with her, she sensed that. Her baba came to her in a dream, just that night, her old baba, gentle and kind, as he was in days past, in Delhi. When she woke, she wept and all that happened broke over her with fresh grief. Now, hours later, he still hung around her, in the fading whispers of the dream.

Bimal, the shadow of a houseboy, slid into the kitchen.

'Is Madam back?' Cook, now spooning the mixture into a pastry case, spoke without lifting his eyes from the floury table.

Bimal nodded. He raised his eyes for a moment and Asha saw how red they were. He cried in corners. More than once, Asha heard Cook and Singh speaking about it. No houseboy stays long in this house, Cook said. Singh, seeing her listening, told Cook to hush.

Now Cook said: 'Where's she been today?'

'I don't know.' Bimal looked embarrassed.

'She was in the native bazaar yesterday.' Cook spoke into his pie dish. 'All alone.'

Asha thought of Madam's trousers, their hems often crusty with salt and sand when she came back from one of her walks.

'No normal memsahib goes there.' Cook lifted the pastry top and settled it over the pie. His movements were deft. 'She hardly bothers whether it's fish or mutton at dinner. The other day she said to me: why don't you decide?' He pursed his lips. 'It isn't natural.'

Cook trimmed the pastry edge with a sharp knife and a long line of scrap unwound onto the table. 'Love matches are hatched by two blind people. Much better Sahib's parents arranged a bride.'

One of the staff bells jangled. Cook turned to Asha: 'That's her. Off you go.'

Asha got to her feet, smoothed down her dupatta and headed for the staircase that led to the upper storey.

'Don't look so miserable,' Cook called after her. 'Madam blessed you, giving you this job. Thank the gods.'

Isabel Madam sat in a planter with a book open on her knee. Her eyes had a distant look. She looked up as Asha appeared in the doorway and smiled.

'Asha, would you run an errand? I need a few things.'

Asha hurried to leave the house. She chose the goods quickly and ran along to the restaurant to see Amit. He was sleeping upstairs, the boys said, so she settled in the shade to wait. Metal pots and spoons clanged.

A trace of her baba seemed to linger here and, however horrid her final memory of him, it was still a comfort. That was where she last saw him alive, there, just inside the restaurant. He slumped to the floor and crouched in a daze, his hands covering his eyes. His shoulders shook and there was blood on his fingers and he wouldn't let her wipe them clean. Then the police came.

The next time she saw him was outside the jail when they brought his body to her, wrapped in cheap cloth, and she took it to the temple ground for cremation. A pyre of dried sticks stood ready in the clearing. Amit was there and the boy, Rajiv, and others from the restaurant. They lowered her poor baba on a bier and settled him in a level place amongst the staves and branches. The Sadhu, his face daubed with ash, began to chant. Her baba had no son, no male relative at all, to light the funeral pyre. It was left to her only.

'Asha?'

Amit stood in front of her, blocking the light. She dried off her eyes and nose with her dupatta and steadied her breathing. He sat down beside her in the dirt and patted her shoulder.

'You got my message?' He looked drowsy. He rolled a bidi and lit it and the soft smoke curled round them both. 'He wants to see you.'

Her body felt suddenly awkward to her, her limbs outsized. She sat stock-still and waited, not trusting herself to speak.

152

'You know who I mean?' He turned solemn eyes on her and she hid her face.

'Krishna-ji?'

He nodded.

'But how?'

'Your half day is Sunday, nah? In the afternoon, go to the jail and ask for my friend. He's a guard there.' He fished in his pocket for a slip of paper and pressed it into her hand. 'See, I've written his name. Tell him you've brought samosas from Amit's restaurant. He'll allow you a few minutes at his door.'

Asha hesitated. The thought of facing Sanjay Krishna made her feel ashamed. 'Does he know I work for Britishers now? For the man who sent my own baba to die?'

Amit reached forward and put his hand on her arm. His fingers were warm and comforting and his breath carried the smell of cigarettes.

'I told you, little sister: your work in that house will be useful. He also thinks it. He's very pleased.'

She twisted away to hide her confusion and reached for her parcel.

'Sunday,' she said. 'I will go.'

The wooden door was thick and studded with metal and she rapped several times on it before footsteps came. A hatch slid open with a bang. Dark eyes moved, looking out at her.

Her mouth was too dry to speak. She held up the brown paper parcel, stained with patches of grease. 'Samosas,' she said at last, 'from Amit-Sahib's restaurant. For his friend, Abhishek.'

The hatch closed. She stood in the dust with the warm bag

in her hand. Eventually, a bolt scraped, then another and a key turned. The door inched open. A stout guard peered out. He looked out beyond her, as if checking that she was alone, then reached out and snatched the samosas.

'Are you Abhishek?'

He scowled, opened the door further to let her slip inside, then locked it behind her and led her down a long corridor. It smelt of lime and disinfectant and the sourness of sweaty, confined men.

They turned a sharp corner and an endless procession of identical doors appeared, left and right. There was no time to stop and look, she had to run to keep pace with him as he strode, the bag of samosas swinging from his fist. Her blood sounded loud in her ears. My baba was here. In this corridor, maybe. In that cell. Or that one. All those terrible, cruel years.

He led her up a stone staircase and along an upper corridor, then stopped outside a door and nodded. Without a word, he turned on his heel and stood guard at the top of the staircase, his back to her. She stood at the door, looking after him for a moment, lost.

The wood was worn. There was a covered hole in the door and she stood on her toes to shift the metal cover to one side and peer through.

Her breath caught in her throat. She knew him at once. He sat on a battered cot, his back straight, his chin raised, his eyes closed. The cell was no bigger than a shack. The upper portion of one wall gleamed where a thin shaft of sunshine fell obliquely from the high window onto the whitewash. He, who once had so much, now had so little. A bucket in the far corner. A grey blanket folded on a single pillow on the cot beside him. She saw the book, open on his lap, and knew it at once. It was the volume of Tagore's poetry which had once belonged to his uncle and brought him comfort in his final hours.

She tapped lightly on the door with the tips of her fingers and he turned his head, opened his eyes and smiled. Her cheeks flamed. She blinked, peering through the peephole, unsure whether to speak.

He got to his feet and came to the door. He dominated the space, a noble creature caged in a tiny, bare cell. She grasped her hands, one in the other. He was broad and handsome, just as she remembered, but the skin around his eyes was dark with fatigue and his cheeks were hollowed.

'Sahib. Are you ill?' Her whisper sounded obscenely loud in her ears and she looked quickly down the corridor. The guard didn't turn.

Sanjay Krishna stood a foot or so from the door and faced her. He couldn't see her, she knew that, yet she felt herself watched by him. He put the palms of his hands together in namaste.

'Little sister, I condole you for your poor baba. He died a martyr. Be proud, even as you grieve.'

Her baba, stooped and shaking on the floor, blood on his fingers. Could she be proud? But Krishna-ji said so. It must be true.

'Have courage, little sister. We have both lost loved ones. We are of the same stuff, you and I. One blood.' His voice resonated with the same deep richness she remembered from Delhi.

One blood. Her legs trembled. She was bound to him. You are all I have left in this world, she thought. You are the only person on this earth who cares for me, even a little. Her eyes filled and she swallowed hard.

'Tell me, sahib. Tell me what to do.'

He smiled, a gentle smile which melted the stone walls and the heavy door between them.

'You are a good girl, Asha, and a brave one.' His voice fell to a whisper. 'You have your part to play. An important part. I know you will make your baba proud. And make me proud also.'

She couldn't speak. She wanted to blurt out: already I have betrayed you and my baba both, I am serving that man, who condemned him to death. She stood, silent and ashamed.

He nodded as if he understood everything, as if he saw not just through the thick door but right into her soul. Her body ached from straining to reach to the peephole. It was hot and airless in the corridor. There was so much she needed to say, to confess to him, but she couldn't find the words.

He said then: 'Your madam. You are knowing who she is?'

She blinked. 'Isabel Madam. Her husband sentenced my . . .' Her voice faltered.

'Her husband made your baba a martyr. That is true. But she herself, you know her?'

He lifted his hand. She couldn't see but it seemed to her that he placed it flat against the wood of the door between them. She lifted her own and placed it too, flat against the worn wood on her own side, imagining that they could touch.

He began to whisper to her.

'Do you remember that day, long ago, when you were a little girl only and your baba brought you to my uncle's house? Rahul was there, my good friend, and he told you

156

about the Britishers' house with the mango and jamun trees where you and he were children? They cast out your baba and sent him to the slum, accused him falsely of being a thief.'

Of course she remembered. Her poor baba bore it all and never spoke of it.

'That was your madam's house. It was her people who destroyed your baba's reputation. They set him on the long path that led him to a cell here and to death.'

Her hand shook on the wood. 'Her people?'

He nodded. His eyes fixed on the peephole as if he could see her.

'They are snakes, these people. Full of kind words but also of poison.'

The wood swam. She felt a sudden wave of sickness and leant her cheek against it.

He said: 'Harden your heart against her.'

She took a deep breath. 'I will leave her. Amit-ji will protect me. I'll clean pans and cook for him.'

On the other side of the door, he let out a low sigh. 'No, little sister. They are snakes but we are tigers. Be strong. Be fierce. And have faith. The day of the tiger is almost come.'

He disappeared from view and, a moment later, a sheet of folded paper, as thin as tissue, slid under the door. She bent, scooped it up and hid it in her sleeve.

He said: 'Take this to your madam. Deliver it in secret. Can you do this?'

At the end of the corridor, the guard turned and started towards her.

'Go now, little sister. Do as I say. Our day, the day of the tiger, will come.'

He lifted his hand and placed his palm flat against the

157

other side of the peephole so it turned pink with flesh and she felt his blessing.

The guard reached her side and pushed her from the door. As she stepped away, his voice came after her.

'We will defeat them. Your baba did not die in vain.'

From that moment, she made a study of Isabel Madam, knowing now that she was doing Krishna-ji's work. Her mistress barely saw her husband, who left early for the office and returned late. At night, he called Bimal to his side and closed the door of his bedroom on them both. In the kitchen, no one spoke of it.

In the mornings, Isabel Madam took long walks, even on hot, humid days. When ladies visited the house for tea, Asha helped Bimal to carry in the trays, pass round sandwiches and cakes and serve milk, sugar and chai, British-style. Isabel Madam nodded along to the ladies' stories but Asha saw the tension in her shoulders. It only eased when the last lady left and Isabel Madam pulled off her shoes, tucked her stockinged feet under her and opened a book, one of the thick volumes on Sahib's shelf.

'Asha, here you are!'

Madam swept into the bedroom from one of her walks, her face flushed and the hair around her forehead damp. Asha stood at the dresser, a drawer open, tidying Madam's clothes. A floppy parcel flew through the air and slapped onto the bed.

'Have a look.'

Asha closed the drawer. The package was wrapped in paper and tied with string.

'Well, go on.'

She spent time unpicking the knots – it was good string – and smoothing the paper. The fabric inside was deep red, trimmed with gold braid. It couldn't come from the derzi. He came to the house for fittings.

Isabel Madam lifted it out of her hands and held up a kameez against Asha's body, measuring the width against her shoulders.

'You like it?'

Asha hesitated. It was a salwar kameez with matching dupatta in fine, good-quality cotton. But why had she bought it? No memsahib dressed in Indian clothes.

'We can take it back.' Isabel Madam's face reflected the doubt in her own. 'Is it the colour?'

'Colour is very nice, madam.'

'Why not try it on? Don't be shy.'

Asha stared. Try it on?

Isabel Madam banged down onto the bed, making the springs bounce. Her head tipped backwards and her teeth gleamed.

'You thought I'd bought it for myself? Oh dear. No, Asha, it's for you.'

Asha looked down at the faded, patched clothes she was wearing. How long had she had them? She didn't even remember. Her hands and feet protruded from the cuffs like overgrown branches. She slipped the tunic over her neck and looked at herself in the dress mirror. A different girl stood there, smarter, richer, illuminated by the bright colours. She blinked. She rubbed the hem between her finger and forefinger. Costly.

Isabel Madam said: 'It's a gift, Asha. If you'll accept it.'

Asha looked again at the girl in the mirror.

Isabel Madam lifted the dupatta from the paper and looped it around Asha's neck.

'You need more than one but I wanted to be sure it fit. I had them make it in my size. We're almost the same, aren't we?' She lifted Asha's arms and weighed the fit at the seam, as a derzi might do. 'A tiny bit loose.'

She stood with her hands loosely on Asha's shoulders, admiring her in the mirror.

That evening, before she settled down to sleep, Asha drew the new suit of clothes into her lap and stroked the cotton. The gold braid shone dimly in the half-light. She tried to think of the last time in her life that someone had gifted her anything.

She folded the new clothes, wrapped them back in paper and stowed them under her bedroll. One day, she might need them. Until then, she would wear her own clothes with pride, however small and faded they might be.

Chapter Fifteen

Isabel

The main salon at The Club rang with gossip. The usual array of cane-topped tables were moved to the sides to allow room for people to circulate. Sir Philip and Lady Lyons only hosted a few parties each year and Port Blair society hurried to attend.

Mrs Copeland and Mrs Allen threaded their way across the freshly polished wooden floor towards Isabel, tilting their heads to the gentlemen they passed. Overhead, newly installed electric ceiling fans stirred between the wooden pillars, creating a pleasant movement of air. The brass along their arms flashed as they reflected light from the chandeliers.

'Goodness, what excitement!'

Mrs Copeland's expression was sly. 'My dear, we were starting to fear you might never come!'

They were late. Jonathan had again been delayed in the office.

'Such a sight, The Club at night, don't you think?'

'No wonder your husband practically lives here!'

The two ladies turned to consider the company, commenting on hairstyles, figures and clothes. Their powdered faces shone.

Isabel looked too but with less interest. Jonathan stood

with a small group of men over by the French windows, which had been thrown open to the lawn. The warm night air was heavy with the scent of bougainvillea. One hand sat loosely in his pocket, the other held his drink. His eyes, lowered, studied his glass as, beside him, Sir Philip spoke. The chief commissioner seemed to be in the middle of one of his lengthy stories. A few moments later, the men burst into laughter. Isabel looked more closely. One of the men, standing with his back to them, was unfamiliar. His hair was closely cropped, with an austerity that was military, as if he'd come just that morning from the barber's. His back, in his evening dress, was broad.

'Have you met Mr Johnston?' Mrs Copeland missed nothing.

Mrs Allen put in: 'She'll be seeing a great deal of him, soon enough.'

'You poor, poor thing. I do hate house guests. Such a bore.'

Mrs Allen: 'How long will he be with you? I'd heard it was a month!'

Isabel managed a smile. As usual, Jonathan had kept her in the dark about the details. 'I believe he's at Government House at the moment, staying with Sir Philip.'

'Oh yes, but that's never for long. He'll move across to you next.' Mrs Allen tutted. 'All those menus. Linen to organise. It's too bad.'

The ladies knew more about the arrangements than she did.

Mrs Copeland: 'And he's come to study your husband's methods, hasn't he? For clearing jungle and civilising the natives and whatnot.'

The two ladies exchanged looks. 'He's a queer fish. One hears such stories.'

Mrs Allen's face became suddenly eager. 'Here's Lady Lyons!'

Lady Lyons turned to Isabel almost at once. 'May I steal you away for a moment?' She nodded apologies to the others. 'I want to show Mrs Whyte the flowering poinsettia. It's doing splendidly.'

She led Isabel through the French windows and out onto the gravel path. The salt tang of the breeze cut through the floral scent of the gardens. Ahead, several couples had spilt onto the sloping lawn and stood in clusters on the shadowy grass. Across the harbour, the lights at Aberdeen glistened along the narrow stretch of water which separated it from Ross Island and The Club.

Lady Lyons lowered her voice. 'I can't abide gossip. It causes such pain.'

Isabel waited for her to continue.

Lady Lyons went on: 'I wanted to speak to you about Mr Johnston. Has your husband told you much?'

'Very little.' She considered. 'I hear he's the Assistant Commissioner of the Nicobar Islands and come to Port Blair to study jungle clearance.'

'Quite.' Lady Lyons spoke briskly as if she were eager to deliver her message before they were interrupted. 'He's half one of us, you know, government servant, and half missionary under the Bishop of Rangoon. He spends all year out there with only the savages for company. Hard to imagine, really, the only white man with all those junglis.' She hesitated. 'I suppose it's made him a little peculiar.'

'Peculiar?'

She didn't reply at once. They reached the end of the path and turned back towards The Club. Light falling through the open doors made broad stripes along the path. The members of a convict band, smart in red and white uniforms, were assembling at the top of the lawn.

Lady Lyons shrugged. 'He's been there some years. I think he sees it as some form of penance. He was married, you see. Tragic. She was bitten by a scorpion. Or was it a snake? Anyway, he was away at the time, upcountry. By the time he heard and rushed back, it was all over. He was devoted to her, by all accounts. Not sure he's ever recovered.'

'How sad.'

'Quite. One must make allowances. It wasn't long afterwards that he applied for the Nicobar post. A sort of self-imposed exile. Philip says he's done jolly well to stick it.'

They approached the French windows. As they re-entered the salon, a servant appeared, offering glasses of punch and flutes of champagne.

'The ladies dislike anyone who's different from the herd.' She gave Isabel a complicit smile. 'I think you understand that, don't you?'

She steered Isabel across the salon towards Jonathan and Sir Philip. The gentlemen turned politely as the women approached.

'Mr Johnston, may I present Mrs Whyte?' Lady Lyons was once again a commanding hostess. 'Mr Whyte kept their whole courtship strictly under wraps, isn't he a dark one?'

If Isabel had imagined a missionary, she might have thought of an elderly man with a beard, rather like the drawings in her books of Bible stories. Edward Johnston could hardly be more different. He was young, barely thirty, and rugged with good health. His cheeks were clean-shaven. His eyes were blue-green and intelligent and when he turned them on her, he gave the impression that he thought a great deal more than he chose to say. He greeted her with a restrained half-smile.

'A pleasure to meet you, Mrs Whyte. I was just congratulating your husband. He's a lucky man.'

Isabel opened her mouth to reply but at that moment, the convict band struck up outside with a popular tune and, conversation suspended, the crowd pressed outside to listen, glasses in hand. Jonathan fussed at Isabel's side with the folds of her shawl. When she looked up again, Edward Johnston had melted away into the crowd.

Jonathan dined late at The Club on Monday evening and surprised her by returning to the house with Mr Johnston unexpectedly in tow. Isabel, already in bed, lay, embarrassed, listening to their low voices and wondering whether she should get dressed again and greet her guest or wait until the morning.

The voices quietened and the house drifted into sleep.

The next morning, Jonathan left early. Isabel was sitting in the dining room over breakfast when Mr Johnston appeared. He sat, eyes cast down, grinding the inside of his cup with a spoon as he stirred his coffee.

'How did you sleep, Mr Johnston? Was the room comfortable?'

'Perfectly, thank you.'

She hesitated. 'I do hope you didn't think me impolite. I mean, not greeting—'

'Of course not.' He spoke without expression. 'We were rude to arrive so late.'

'Not at all.'

He scraped back the chair and served himself from the dishes of sausages and eggs on the sideboard. When he returned to the table, Isabel tried again.

'I'm still adjusting to the humidity here. I grew up in Northern India, you see, which is so much drier. I suppose you've become used to it.'

A grunt, then silence. He took a slice of toast from the rack and fell to buttering. Finally he set down his knife and said, rather abruptly:

'Would you mind very much if we didn't talk? Frankly, Mrs Whyte, I'm not one for polite conversation. Especially not in the morning.'

Isabel considered. 'Actually, neither am I.'

He went on: 'The truth is, Sir Philip and Lady Lyons are delightful hosts but I've been rushed from one social engagement to another ever since I arrived. I'm simply no good at it. I suppose that's why I'm better suited to a remote island than to a settlement. Do you see?'

His expression was strained.

'I'm so glad you told me, Mr Johnston.' Isabel smiled, thinking of the endless chatter of the Port Blair ladies. 'I often feel much the same.'

'Really?' He looked relieved. 'I'm not one for formalities, either, if I can avoid them. Would you mind calling me Edward?'

'Then you must call me Isabel.'

For a while, the silence was broken only by the scrape of his knife on toast and the rhythmical crunch of his eating.

'It may seem strange to you,' he said at last, 'but to me, this is a busy, bustling place. It does me good to come back here from time to time. But it's hard to adapt.'

'I'm not surprised.'

'Aren't you?' His keen eyes seemed to read her in a moment. They lapsed again into silence. Bimal appeared with hot coffee and refreshed their cups.

She sat very still as he ate. Outside a green-winged bird screeched and dived, setting a branch moving. It looked a beautiful day, bright and lazy with tropical heat. She might walk down to the waterfront to watch the fishermen. She would leave him alone to finish his breakfast in peace. She set down her napkin.

'I usually have lunch at about one. You're welcome to join me.' She kept her voice light. 'Or you can eat in your room, if you prefer. I don't mind in the slightest.'

He opened his mouth to reply, then closed it again. Finally he said: 'They don't need me in the office until tomorrow. Do you know Anderson's Cove? I thought I might head there today.' He hesitated. 'Come if you like.'

Isabel nodded. 'Cook could pack us some tiffin.'

'Good.' He looked over her clothes, a simple pair of slacks and a cotton shirt, and smiled. 'Can you manage on the back of a motorcycle?'

Isabel had been on numerous beach picnics organised by The Club committee but they'd been held in well-known spots, not far from Port Blair. Anderson's Cove was different.

Edward's motorcycle was a sturdy machine. It was the first on the islands, he said, which he left with a friend and retrieved during his visits.

He strapped their bags to the sides and took Isabel's hand to steady her as she clambered on the back. He directed her to put her hands on his waist to hold firm. His skin felt warm and firm under his shirt.

Isabel closed her eyes against the onward rush of air as he sped along the roads, then tracks, towards the southernmost tip of the island, an area she had never explored. Her cotton top swelled with wind. As the quality of the track deteriorated and forced him to slow, she opened her eyes a crack. The lush green of the jungle made a blur along the left-hand side. To the right, the cliff fell away to show dramatic lines of black rocks gleaming below in the sunshine, washed by the tide. She tipped back her head and laughed and the sound disappeared into the rushing air.

The final stretch was on foot. Edward parked the motorcycle in the shade and led her, single file, down a narrow, steep path to the sea. The sand was fine white powder, peppered with tiny crabs, which scuttled across the surface and disappeared into dry holes as they approached. His expression was distant, as if he were absorbed with private thoughts, and let her own thoughts wander as freely as if she were alone.

As they swam, shoals of silver and red-striped fishes darted beneath them, startled to left and right by the shadow of their bodies. Beyond the rocks, a line of bleached coral shone in the darkness. For a while, Isabel turned on her back, closed her eyes and drifted, held aloft by the salt water and lulled by the soft swell of the waves.

When she came back to shore, she wrapped herself in a cotton robe and stretched out on a towel in the shade of a coconut palm, a straw hat shading her eyes.

When Edward finally reappeared, he shook himself at the water's edge like a dog and stood on the shoreline, looking out across the flashing blues of water and sky. His bathing suit was worn and fell from its shoulder straps in a sagging half-circle down his back. His body was lean and muscular, broad across the shoulders and tapering to a slim waist. When he finally turned and came to join her, Isabel looked quickly away. She felt suddenly aware of her bare calves and the salt ridges where the water had dried on her skin.

He stretched out his towel beside her without a word and fell asleep. The sunlight, filtered through the palm leaves, mottled his back. Isabel closed her eyes and listened to the slow pulse of the waves breaking on the shore. It was hot but the breeze from the sea made the sun bearable.

Later they swam again, washing off the sand that had coated their bodies and startling themselves back to life in the cool water. They found a flat rock which stuck out into the sea to one side of the cove and sat there to eat a tiffin of hard-boiled eggs and rice balls and flaked-fish sandwiches.

'Do you like it here?'

Isabel considered. 'Yes.' She looked out towards the horizon. 'Very peaceful.'

'I mean, Port Blair. Your life here.'

She gave an awkward laugh. 'Yes, of course.'

He watched her closely as if he read a different answer there.

'What about you? On Car Nicobar.'

He shrugged. 'I belong there now. I'm an outsider, of course, but even so . . .'

She thought of the books she'd read about the primitive people in the islands who hunted with bows and arrows and attacked government teams who ventured into virgin forest.

'What are the people like?'

'Like you and me, really.' He smiled. 'Well, a bit different perhaps.'

She hesitated. 'Do they wear clothes?'

'They wear sort of cotton shorts. Kissart, it's called.'

'Kissart?'

'The men love hats. I give the tribal chiefs old bowlers. The women wear wooden earrings through here.' He fingered his earlobe. 'And rings on their toes.'

Isabel watched the tide suck at the edge of the rock below them.

'How do you protect yourself out there?'

'Protect myself?' He was quiet for a moment. 'They abhor violence. They are strict about some offences. Witchcraft, for example. But I have never known a Nicobarese strike another out of anger or cruelty. Not even a child.'

Isabel fell silent. A moment later, Edward rose to his feet for a final swim before the ride home. She watched him from the shore as he strode out into the water. When he talked about the tribal people, his sadness lifted and he seemed animated. The incoming waves struck his thighs and he dived forward into them. His arms flashed, spraying diamonds, as he swam.

Chapter Sixteen

'Isabel could keep you company. Don't look so alarmed, darling.' Jonathan turned back to Edward. 'She speaks Hindustani like a native.'

'I couldn't possibly impose.' Edward stood, awkward, in the passageway. 'There must be someone from the office, surely?'

'Nonsense. She's always complaining she doesn't have enough to do.'

Isabel bit her lip. Edward was due to visit a jungle clearance site that day. Jonathan had just announced that he had to return after a few hours and abandon his guest.

Edward looked uncomfortable. 'I'm sure Mrs Whyte has her own plans.'

'Nothing she couldn't cancel, isn't that right?' His expression was playful but he sounded determined. 'What is it today, darling? Tea with the good ladies of the parish?'

She swallowed. 'I don't have any engagements, actually.'

'There you are, then.' Jonathan rubbed his hands together. 'That's settled.'

She turned to fetch a hat and scarf. Edward fixed his eyes on the panelled floor.

'What about lunch?'

'All arranged.' Jonathan tutted. 'Don't fuss, Isabel.'

The three of them squashed together in the back of the tonga, Isabel sandwiched between the two men. The breeze was pleasant and, as the houses of the settlement started to thin and give way to villages, set in reclaimed farmland, her spirits began to lift. In the early days, Jonathan talked at length about his work and the challenge of clearing tracts of jungle. It might be intriguing to see it for herself.

Jonathan leant past her to point out features to their guest.

'That area, from the low wall to the start of the slope, was a devil to clear. I had three work gangs on it for four months. Some of the tree roots went down twenty feet.' He redirected his arm. 'That village, over there? All tickets of leave. We held a marriage market for them three years ago.' He laughed. 'Don't look so shocked, darling. That's how it works.'

Edward too looked surprised. 'A marriage market?'

He nodded. 'We sent an officer round the women's prisons in Bengal. Any young woman who faced a life term was invited out. Then we lined them up and the men could make an offer.' He paused. 'The women don't have to accept. But if they do marry and settle here, they're let off the rest of their sentence.'

The tonga driver swerved to avoid a boy who was herding goats down the side of the road with a switch.

'It's a real problem for us out here. Shortage of women. Don't suppose it's the same for your junglis, Johnston.'

Edward didn't answer. He sat back in the seat, his jaw hard.

The scenery gradually changed. The reaches of farmland

grew smaller and the jungle thickened. The villages too became more sparsely scattered. This was the furthest from Port Blair Isabel had come and she peered out at the wild interior, which covered the rising slopes of Mount Harriet and stretched far beyond.

'Hear that?' Jonathan raised his hand. The toc-toc-toc of metal on wood, faint but clear in the still air. 'Almost there.'

The sound grew as they approached. They emerged from behind a final bluff and the scene opened up before them. Isabel strained forward to see.

A large trait of land lay at the foot of the mountain. In another climate, it might have been a natural meadow but here the jungle had claimed it. About a third of the open land was already roughly cleared. Tree stumps, recently levelled, shone white like broken bones. Creepers and vines, chopped and hacked, smouldered in a series of smoky fires, scenting the air with burning sap. Scars ran here and there through the ground where lines of men had dug ditches to carve through the solid network of roots.

They climbed down from the tonga and started to walk across the scrub. The site swarmed with men. Convicts, commandeered into work gangs, were stripped to the waist. Their skin glistened with sweat in the sunshine. The air rang with the clang of spades on earth and axes on living wood. Jonathan drew Edward a little ahead, pointing and explaining.

Isabel looked round. Off to one side, there was a makeshift camp with long canvas tents hung over rows of staves. Men's washing, shirts and lunghis, dried along the anchor ropes. A man crouched by a cooking fire, stirring a large pot. He lifted his eyes to watch and his face swam, distorted by the rising steam.

The men paused and she caught them up.

'Quite a show of force.' Edward indicated a ragtag group of men standing around the clearing, ancient guns in their hands.

Jonathan nodded. 'Prisoners don't escape. They're better off in barracks than prison. And besides, there's nowhere to go.'

'So why the guards?'

Jonathan gave a wry smile. 'Let's just say we're not very popular with the local junglis. We've offered terms but they won't compromise.'

Edward said: 'Do they ever attack?'

'Sometimes. Nothing we can't handle.' He turned to Isabel. 'Don't worry, darling. They wait until after dark.'

Jonathan started to walk on, raising his hand to summon one of the work-gang leaders to talk to them. Edward hesitated. His eyes, sweeping over the land, taking in the swinging axes, the guards and the dark shadow of jungle behind, were troubled.

At midday, the workers sat cross-legged in the shade and ate rice porridge served on leaves. Afterwards, they stretched out on the scrub and slept.

The head of the clearance project, a lanky Anglo-Indian fellow, laid on a special lunch for his guests. He spread a white cloth over the ground and set out china plates and cutlery. Bearers ran back and forth, offering spicy chicken in coconut sauce and vegetables. Soon, the only noises were the cries of bright-winged birds through the jungle and the distant, steady drumbeat of waves breaking along the shoreline.

Jonathan waved a hand over the jungle as they ate.

'One day, all this will be farmland.' He reached over and heaped more chicken on Edward's plate. 'It will happen. Progress is unstoppable.'

Edward chewed steadily. 'And the natives?'

Jonathan shrugged. 'Another fifty years and they'll be clamouring to settle in towns and cities.' He pointed his fork. 'Look at the way the rest of India's changing.'

The order to resume work came and the men stirred, got to their feet, sloped back to their trees and ditches.

Edward said. 'Don't you wonder what will happen here, once India becomes independent?'

Isabel looked up. She no longer talked politics with Jonathan. Their views were too far apart.

Jonathan said: 'You think it really will?'

'Of course. It's already underway.'

'Ah, yes.' Jonathan smiled. 'But you're forgetting the difference between a taste of self-government and independence. I might indulge a child by allowing unimportant choices.' He pointed to the mango. 'Mango or pineapple, for example. But I wouldn't hand over the keys of the house.'

Edward didn't answer. His eyes fell to his coffee and the milk swirling there. Shortly afterwards, Jonathan rose and brushed down his clothes to leave.

'Stop in a village on the way back. See the lives they've made. That's the real argument for clearance.'

After he left, Edward sat quietly for some time, looking round the camp. Isabel drank her coffee, chatted to their Anglo-Indian host and left Edward in peace.

Finally he turned to her and said: 'Do you mind if I leave you for a while? I'm going to venture into the jungle.'

'Into the jungle?' The Anglo-Indian looked taken aback. 'You'll need guards.'

'No, thank you.' Edward's voice was firm. 'I'll be perfectly safe.'

Isabel set down her cup and got to her feet. She pinned on her hat and tied the scarf round the brim, letting it hang to protect her neck from the sun.

'I'll come too, if you don't mind.'

The Anglo-Indian's eyes widened. 'Madam, I am not thinking Sahib—'

'Indeed.' Edward, interrupting him, rose too. 'Let's both go.'

They strode off before anyone could stop them. At the edge of the clearing, Isabel glanced back. The bearers were shaking out the white table-cloth and folding it carefully into quarters. The Anglo-Indian stood, hands on hips, looking after them with a worried frown.

Once they entered the jungle canopy, the air became thick with moist heat. Edward pressed ahead. He seemed to follow a trail that was invisible to her. She pushed aside curtains of creepers. She had never been in such virgin jungle and her heart hammered with a sense of entering the unknown. Clouds of insects hung about their heads. She had to hurry to keep pace with him and was soon slick with sweat. She slapped at insects on her neck and face.

Just as she was tiring, the jungle opened into a small, natural clearing. The atmosphere was at once less oppressive. Blue sky, streaked with white cloud, appeared above their heads. Edward trod the perimeter, eyes on the ground.

'How did you know this was here?'

'I didn't.' He seemed to satisfy himself, then turned to face her. 'But a path always leads somewhere.'

He sat on a fallen tree and she crossed to join him. She rested her boots on a rock, covered with spongy green moss, and drank in the jungle scent of hot sap and rotting vegetation. The clearing had a magical, secretive quality. The sudden downward shafts of air cooled her face and neck. Distantly, a tropical bird cried, a shrill, warning note.

Edward, motionless at her side, was alert, listening to the quietness as another man might listen to a symphony. Something shifted in him. She sensed it. The tension that had plagued him all morning slipped away and he softened.

'Is Car Nicobar like this?' She found herself speaking in a whisper.

'Even more so.' He hesitated. 'Isn't it easy, sitting here, to imagine nowhere else exists? No cities. No towns. Just this, stretching without end.'

She tipped her head and looked up along the rising trunks of the palms to the dark green of the distant leaves that framed the sky. It was dizzying. Somewhere deep in the jungle, foliage crashed and shifted as an animal moved. Close at hand, insects made a solid wall of low sound. The rich scent of the trees, the creepers, the bushes, filled her senses. He was right. It was complete.

'And it's timeless,' she whispered.

He turned to look at her and slowly nodded. They sat on without talking, feeling the jungle absorb them. Her blood pulsed loud in her ears.

Finally she said: 'Will you ever leave?'

He didn't answer and, for a moment, she wasn't sure if he had heard her.

'I don't know.' His tone was solemn. 'I'm not sure I could go back to England. Not now.'

She took a deep breath. 'Because of your wife?'

He frowned. 'Is that what they say?' He shook his head. 'Poor Johnston. His heart broke and he hid himself away with the natives and went doolally.'

She reached down, picked up a large fallen leaf and smoothed it out between her fingers. 'I'm sorry. I shouldn't have—'

'It's alright.' He sighed. 'If we're going to speak at all, we may as well be honest.'

He became quiet for a while and she thought the subject was closed. She ripped the leaf along its veins, section by section.

Suddenly he said: 'My heart did break. But that was years ago now. That's not why I stay in Car Nicobar.'

She tore the leaf into smaller and smaller pieces, then let them flutter through her fingers to float to the jungle floor. Her hands trembled as she waited to see if he'd carry on.

He stood up. 'Anyway, we should head back.'

She said quickly: 'So why do you stay?'

Edward paced round the clearing. He regarded the toes of his boots as he placed his feet with care, his brow creased in a frown.

'Your husband wants to wipe all this off the face of the earth. To civilise the people who depend on it.' He spread his arm, indicating the jungle, which pressed round them in a solid circle of green. 'And it's not just him, it's all of them.'

Isabel looked at the sunlight through the canopy, which coloured the air a dappled green.

'They have every right to live the way they do, don't you see?' He shook his head. 'The Nicobarese, they're wonderful people. Yes, they live differently from us. But why not?' He looked exasperated. 'If you met them, you'd understand.'

'I'd like to.'

He gave her a sharp look, then carried on. 'They've been the same for centuries. What gives us the right to destroy their way of life? Show me that in the Bible.'

She didn't answer. Edward was so different from Jonathan. His warmth. His respect for local people. She realised, feeling the contrast, how much she despised her husband.

'I agree.' She got to her feet. 'You need to be there to protect them. And you're absolutely right.'

She strode past him out of the clearing, retracing their steps through the foliage. Fronds and leaves brushed wetly against her face. His footsteps, his breathing were close behind her as they returned together to civilisation.

Chapter Seventeen

Their lives found a steady rhythm. During the day, Isabel resumed her old ways, with long walks around Port Blair, afternoon visits and reading. Jonathan and Edward busied themselves with work.

And yet, everything was different. In the evenings, during Jonathan's many absences, she and Edward dined alone together. She developed an interest in running the household, which she had never previously known, arguing with Cook about the menus and asking the ladies how best to cook mutton to bring out the taste or how to curry fish.

Over dinner, she talked to Edward about the Indian families in the bazaar and the stories they shared with her. He told her about his meetings. Much of the time, they sat in comfortable silence.

One evening, about three weeks into Edward's stay, they were sitting together on the balcony after dinner, smoking. It was a pleasant evening, the heat made bearable by a light breeze from the sea. Isabel looked out at the hillside and the dark outline of the prison in the trees.

'I hate that place. It looms over everything.' She drew on her cigarette and let out a stream of smoke.

He gave her a sideways glance. 'Have you been inside?'

She nodded. 'I had to attend a hanging there. I hated it.'

Edward sat quietly. There were voices, footsteps below. Locals, jostling and joking.

'When I sailed out here, I went down to the hold and saw the prisoners there. They were chained up in the dark, like animals. I told Jonathan but he didn't want to hear.'

'I doubt there's much he can do.'

She drew on her cigarette. Singh hovered at the screen doors behind them and she lifted her glass to ask him to mix fresh drinks. When he'd delivered them, the silence settled again.

She leant forward and stubbed out her cigarette, said in a low voice: 'Edward, can I show you something?'

'Of course.'

She opened her bag, unzipped a side pocket and drew out a folded sheet of paper.

He bent his head low over the lamp to read. His shorn hair rose in clumps across his skull and into the nape of his neck. The skin below it was red with sunburn. She thought of the elephant calf and the feel of its bristly hide. Finally he looked up, the letter limp in his hands. His face was grave.

'Sanjay Krishna. The terrorist?'

She nodded.

'He says you met in Delhi, then again on board a ship?'

She found she couldn't raise her eyes to meet his. 'In Delhi, Jonathan and I ran into a hostile crowd. A man intervened and saved us. I didn't know who he was.' She took a deep breath, remembering. 'Then when I saw the prisoners in the hold, I recognised him.'

Edward turned again to the letter. 'How did he get this to you?'

'It was just there on the letters' tray one morning. The servants didn't know who'd brought it.'

'Have you shown it to Jonathan?' Edward passed it back to her. 'You ought to, you know.'

She felt herself flush. 'He'd be furious. You know he would.'

'Krishna's a dangerous man.' Edward rubbed his chin. 'Burn it. Forget it came.'

Isabel looked over the lines of small, neat handwriting. 'He says he knows what happened to Rahul, our cook's boy. My friend.'

Edward leant in close. 'Isabel, he's trying to trap you. If you reply, you'd compromise yourself at once.'

'Compromise myself?' She shook her head.

'It's not just your reputation. It's Jonathan's too. He can't have his wife writing in secret to one of India's most dangerous prisoners.'

She got up and went to stand against the rail. An unseen wireless crackled Indian music in the night.

'Rahul was like a brother to me.' She pulled herself against the rail, then swayed away again, restless. 'If I knew where he was, I could at least write to him.'

'I'll visit the prison before I leave.' Edward rubbed again at his chin. 'I'm expecting a consignment of Bibles from Calcutta soon. I always take some to the prisoners. I could ask about Rahul, if you like.'

She clenched her fingers on the rail and stared at the dark roofs against the sky. To one side, the jungle rose. To the other, the buildings of the town sloped to the invisible shore. It was the first time he'd spoken of leaving. She felt sick. She hadn't realised, until he came, how alone she felt here.

He rose and came to stand beside her.

'Another cigarette?'

He took two from his case, lit them and passed one across. His free hand rested on the rail, capable and strong, inches from her own. The heat rising from his body warmed her side. They stood in silence and smoked, looking out at the night.

Several days later, Isabel sat alone in the sitting room, reading. The ceiling fan overhead rippled the heavy air. Singh tapped on the door and brought her an envelope on the silver letters' tray. She knew the hand at once.

'Who delivered this?'

Singh looked awkward. 'I don't know, madam.'

'Someone must know.' She turned over the envelope in her hands. 'When did it come?'

Singh shook his head. 'It was in the hallway just now, madam. I did ask Asha and Cook but neither of them knew anything about it.'

'Letters can't appear from nowhere.' She reached for the opener and slit the top of the envelope. Singh hovered. 'Tell Cook I'd like luncheon at one, would you?'

The paper crackled in her fingers as she opened it up. It was the same cheap ink and translucent paper as Sanjay Krishna's first letter. Her eyes went first to the signature, the initials SK, then she returned to the top and began to read his small, neat hand.

Isabel Madam,
How is your good self? I trust you are well in body and soul and happy now in your new life.

   Did you receive my letter? I feel you did. I have waited these many long days for answer but none has been forthcoming. Perhaps you are already forgetting our previous encounters in Delhi and on the ship? I will never forget them. I feel I am gifted to know a person's heart from their face and I read goodness in yours only.

In my former letter, I am quoting to you some lines from our great Bengali poet, Tagore. Here I am quoting another: *Men are cruel but man is kind.*

Why am I again writing? I fear you are thinking badly of me for offering to tell you the whereabouts of your friend, Rahul. I wanted your reply, it is true, but now I fear I may not live long enough to tell you, person to person, even if you agreed such a thing. Therefore I am telling this: he is still in prison in Delhi at the hands of your government. I am not knowing how long he will be kept from his wife and son. What is it which you Britishers are saying? At the pleasure of His Majesty? I wonder what manner of King takes pleasure in subjugating and punishing men who want freedom only.

We face days of darkness here. My people are dying at your people's hands. As you take chai with the British ladies or sit at dinner with your husband, is there talk of our *bhukh hartal?* A hunger strike is a desperate protest. A man must be driven by despair itself to refuse food and drink when his body craves it. They are forcing tubes down our throats. Do they say that at your dinners? The suffering is very terrible.

One of my men, a good fellow from Calcutta itself, has just passed. The doctors forced milk down his throat and it entered into his lungs. Imagine the pain of his dying.

Forgive me for such hard words, Isabel Madam. I

*would not be wasting my ink and strength in writing
to you if I did not have faith in your good nature.*

   *What can you do? I am not knowing. Only I am
knowing that you will do whatsoever you are able to
give us justice. That I do believe.*

   *I am taking my leave with another line from the
great Tagore:*

   *Faith is the bird that feels the light and sings when
the dawn is still dark.*

   From the brink of eternity,
   Your faithful servant,
   SK

Isabel sat for a long time with the letter in her hands. The
pulsing breeze from the fan rattled the paper.

When Singh appeared to escort her to lunch, she sat alone
at the head of the long polished table. The sunlight fell in slices
through slats of the blinds and set the water jug glistening.

Her mind was full of thoughts of another place. Of Rahul,
confined in some dank cell in Delhi with no idea when he
might be released. And of Sanjay Krishna and his men who
were driven to starve themselves to death by hunger strike.

The plates of soup, mutton and sliced bread sat untouched
in front of her.

Two wooden tea chests arrived for Edward. Isabel sat beside
him in the drawing room after dinner as he rolled back
his shirtsleeves and fell to prising out the nails and ripping
off the slatted lids. He pulled out handfuls of scrunched
newspaper, then reached in further and handed her a black
leather-bound Bible.

The scent of leather and freshly printed ink spoke of England but already it had acquired a hint of mildew. The flyleaf and edges were embossed with gold, which glistened and left specks on her fingers.

'They don't last long out here.' Edward flicked through another volume. 'White ants. Get into everything.'

The print was cramped. 'Can they read English?'

He closed the book in his hands. 'Some can, the ones who attend the Mission School. But even those who can't like to have them. It's the only book they're likely to own, you see.'

'And you'll take some to the jail?'

'The Good Lord knows they need comfort too.'

He opened up a canvas bag and began to fill it with Bibles. Isabel watched his deft hands at work. She said: 'Will you tell me the truth?'

He looked up. 'I hope I always do that.'

She opened the Bible again, flapped the front cover back and forth in her hands.

'Is it true there's a hunger strike in the jail? That we're force-feeding them?'

Edward pursed his lips. She waited, her fingers tense on the cover.

'Isn't that a question you should ask Jonathan?'

'Is it true?'

He sat back on his haunches, his hands full of Bibles. 'Yes, it's true.' His voice was soft. 'Where did you hear about it?'

'And a man died because they forced milk into his lungs?'

He lifted one of his hands and ran its back across his forehead. He looked weary. 'The doctors force-feed them to save their lives but the men struggle.'

Isabel got to her feet and crossed to the windows. Down

below in the garden, the mali was pruning the trees. He was barefoot and stripped to the waist and his back ran with sweat.

'You've had another letter from him, haven't you?'

She didn't turn round. She stood quietly, breathing deeply. The sun glinted on the clippers as the mali swung them back and forth in his hands.

'My father despises revolutionaries. So does Jonathan. They call them murderers.'

'Some of them are.' Edward's voice was gentle.

'What if they're right?' She turned to face him. His eyes, on her face, were sad. 'Sometimes I think we have no right to be here. That Mr Gandhi and all these so-called subversives are only doing what we should do in their position.'

Her father would blanch if he heard such a thing. So would Jonathan. They had such belief in the Empire. Her fingernails dug into the soft leather binding of the Bible in her hands. Edward regarded her thoughtfully.

'Aren't you shocked?'

'The Lord gave us minds for a reason.'

She strode back to the chair and sank into it. 'He has written again. He says we're torturing and killing people who only want freedom.'

His eyes stayed on her face. 'And what do you think?'

She shook her head. 'I don't know. I feel guilty. I feel I ought to do something to help them.'

'To help them?'

'Something to stop all the hatred.'

He smoothed the cover of the books in his hand as if he were caressing them. 'Perhaps if they read these, their hearts will heal.'

She sat forward. 'What if he dies and I did nothing? He saved my life once.'

He didn't answer.

'Could I come with you when you go into the prison? Please, Edward. I want to see him, see what state he's in. I'll just hand him a Bible. You'll do that in any case.'

Edward sighed and turned back to packing Bibles into his bag. 'The prison officers might not allow it.'

'But you could ask.'

He lifted another handful of books from the crate and made space for them. 'On one condition. That Jonathan consents.'

She reached down to him, took his hand and squeezed it. 'Ask him for me. Please? Just say I want to help.'

A shadow shifted at the half-open door. She turned her head quickly to look.

'Is someone there?'

The door eased open. Asha stood in the doorway, the sewing basket in her hands. She looked from Isabel to Edward.

'Did you want something?'

'Nothing, madam. Very sorry.'

Later, Isabel sat alone in her bedroom, looking out at the darkness. In the corridor, Edward's footsteps finally sounded, retiring to his own room. Once the house fell silent, she reached for her dressing gown.

The piles of Bibles were heaped on the sitting-room floor. She opened one to the back cover. Thick, dark paper fixed the bound pages to the leather. She ran her nail along the seam. It would be easy to prise it up with a knife or a sharp pair of scissors.

Her heart thumped. She stood in silence, listening to the creaks and sighs of the wicker furniture. She turned again to the back cover. If she inserted a letter there, there was every chance Sanjay Krishna would find it.

She lit the lamp, drew out her writing case and began to write, before she had the chance to change her mind.

Dear Mr Krishna,
Thank you for your letters. As the wife of a senior officer here, you will understand that I am in no position to pass judgement on the nature of your conviction and imprisonment. But I am grateful for the chance to express my thanks to you for your kind intervention during the disturbances in Delhi, a kindness which I have not forgotten.

I am deeply distressed to hear of the demise of your friend as a result of his refusal to eat. I can only urge you to accept food and drink yourself in order to preserve your own health.

She paused, read over what she had written, tapped the end of her pen against her lips. Insects, attracted by the light, banged against the screened door. Voices drifted up from the servants' quarters below. She turned again to her paper.

I want you to know that, however great the divide between us and whatever the political differences, you are not alone in your suffering. I urge you to address your attention to the Holy Bible and I hope most sincerely that you will find comfort in its pages.

When she finished her letter, she lifted the back cover of the Bible and inserted it inside, pressing her thumb firmly along the join. It was quite invisible unless the book were examined with care.

She put away her writing case and closed the drawer, then picked up the Bible and leant forward to turn out the lamp.

She jumped. A sound. Close, in the shadows. Down to the right, towards the balcony doors.

'Who's there?' Her voice was loud in the silence. Her heart thumped.

She reached out to the lamp and turned it up with shaking fingers. Something moved. The darkness behind the planter seemed to shrink into itself. She went across and pulled out the chair. A small figure sat hunched in the corner, his arms wrapped round his knees.

'Bimal?'

He gazed up at her. His eyes were red.

'Were you spying on me?'

He shook his head. His knuckles shone white where he clasped his hands together.

'What are you doing here so late?'

'Sahib. Waiting.'

She shook her head. 'Go to bed.'

He didn't move. She reached down a hand to him. He stared for a moment, then stumbled to his feet and slunk from the room without a word. His bare feet made soft slaps as he descended the staircase.

She turned out the lamp and stood in the darkness in silence for a while, the Bible in her hand, listening to the murmur of jungle noises drifting in from outside, and thinking about the nature of the man she had married.

Chapter Eighteen

The sky was heavy with cloud. The brick walls of the prison were dark with shadow. Isabel followed Edward through a series of locked gates into a waiting room where a guard checked their names against entries in his ledger.

Edward and the guard carried in the boxes of Bibles and set them on the floor. The Bible for Sanjay Krishna bulged in her handbag and she held it on her lap. If she were searched, she would simply say that it was her own.

A sudden banging made her turn to the window. Pellets of rain struck the courtyard, raising clouds of dust, which turned quickly to mud as the water gathered, spread across the hard ground, then sank finally into the earth. At once, the smell of the air changed, becoming lush and fertile with wet foliage.

Edward's face was tense. 'You're sure you want to do this?'

'Of course.' She rested her hand for a moment on the linen sleeve of his jacket, then turned silently back to the drama of the crashing rain.

An Anglo-Indian gentleman, dressed formally in a cotton suit with a red silk handkerchief in his breast pocket, appeared on the threshold to greet them. He shook Edward by the hand and bowed his head to Isabel as he introduced himself as one of the senior warders.

'I'm afraid we will not be permitting you direct access to the prisoners,' he said. 'I am sure you are understanding. Current situation is most tense.'

Edward nodded.

'Please be following me. I am showing you how to offer up the Good Book without entering the cell. Conversing with these men is not permitted.'

Two guards shouldered the boxes of Bibles and followed as they hurried through the rain across one courtyard to another, pausing while successive gates were unlocked and rebolted after them. Isabel kept her handbag close.

They crossed a further courtyard in the shadow of the central bell tower. Isabel looked round. It was the dismal yard where the hanging took place, now sodden with falling rain.

The warder pressed them through a wooden door to the mouth of a corridor. He stopped at the first cell.

'These are opening, see?' He demonstrated the wooden panel on the door, which could be unlatched from the outside to give access to a small hatch. 'In this way, we are giving eatables and suchlike to the prisoner.'

'May I see?'

The Anglo-Indian guard motioned her forward with a gracious wave of his hand.

She put her eye to the spyhole in the wood. It took her a moment to adjust to the dim interior. A figure lay motionless on his cot, his face turned to the wall.

Edward said calmly: 'Shall we begin?'

He drew out a pile of Bibles from the nearest box and

192

placed the first in the hatch. He closed the panel, then bowed his head. His lips moved in private prayer.

Gradually they fell into a steady rhythm. Isabel stepped forward to each door first, peered through the peephole to glimpse the prisoner beyond, and opened the hatch. Edward, stooping, passed her a Bible to insert, then stood for a moment of prayer before they moved on. Most of the prisoners lay on their cots. Occasionally one, hearing the scrape of the hatch, called out, either with a plea or with abuse. Isabel took her cue from Edward whose movements were steady and methodical. He gave each wretched man, noisy or silent, sleeping or waking, the same prayer.

They completed the corridors that made up the wing and the Anglo-Indian guard led them across a covered inner courtyard to the next. He wrinkled his nose as they mounted the steps to the top storey.

'Revolutionaries.' He nodded down the bare corridor. Rainwater splashed off the rail along the walkway and cascaded in meandering streams down the brick walls. 'Too late for their souls.'

Edward smiled. 'Let's try, anyway.'

He shrugged and stood to one side to allow them to approach the first door. Isabel put her eye to the peephole. The man lying on the cot looked barely alive. His hair was matted and his face dirty with a ragged growth of beard.

'These are the men on hunger strike?'

The guard snorted. 'When they get really hungry, they'll eat.'

Edward didn't meet her eye as he handed her the Bible. They moved on down the corridor. Similar scenes, one after another, of debilitated men who lay in dirtied clothing on their cots, sleeping or too listless to raise their heads. The cells were rank with the smell of unwashed bodies.

They had almost completed the length of the corridor when Isabel put her eye to a door and saw Sanjay Krishna. She started. He lay on his back on a cot under a threadbare blanket. His arms were at his sides. His hair was plastered around his temples and his cheeks had an unhealthy feverish sheen. His eyes were closed. His posture and his utter stillness gave him the look of a stone tomb effigy.

Edward handed her a Bible.

'This man looks ill.'

The guard blew out his cheeks. 'He is most dangerous of all. And cunning also.'

As he turned his head to tell Edward more about his most notorious prisoner, Isabel rounded her shoulders, drew the concealed Bible from her bag with a shaking hand and slipped it into the hatch. She pushed the spare Bible into her bag, then made a show of pulling out her handkerchief and dabbing her forehead.

'Is it the heat, madam?'

'It is hot.' The rain had stopped as quickly as it started and the sunshine was turning the puddles in the courtyards into rising waves of humidity. 'But let's carry on.'

They moved to the next cell. The doctored Bible, with its concealed letter, sat in its hatch. She didn't know if Sanjay Krishna had the will or indeed the strength to retrieve it and, even if he did, if he would search it well enough to find the letter folded inside its cover.

Chapter Nineteen

Asha

Isabel Madam and the Britisher sat alone together on the balcony, talking and drinking alcohol. It was the same every night. Cook and Singh and even shopkeepers in the bazaar gossiped. Where was Sahib, they asked, while his wife entertained another man alone? It was not correct.

Asha sat cross-legged on her sleeping mat in the servants' quarters, listening hard. Behind the partition, Cook snored in a low growl. Outside, a pig snuffled along the wall, nosing at the swill, which Bimal scattered each evening. Asha pinched her cheeks to keep herself awake.

Finally footsteps sounded. Sahib was back. A few moments later, the voices from the balcony trailed off, then fell silent. A shadow passed the window. Bimal crossed silently to the stairs that led to the upper storey and to Sahib. She waited until all was quiet, then got to her feet, reached for her bundle and crept to the door. It took her a moment to adjust to the bright moonlight outside. Silver sparkled on the branches of trees. The moss underfoot was cool and doughy.

A twig cracked. She stood rigid, listening for movement. Nothing. All she could hear was the steady wash of waves on the distant shore and her own heartbeat.

She crept down the side of the building into the shadows. The old chowkidar sat hunched on his stool, head nodding on his chest. His rusty gun was jammed upright in his arms and he leant on it as he dozed. She took a final glance back at the house. A single line of light showed below the curtain in Sahib's bedroom. She waited until she was clear of the house, then began to run.

The restaurant made a solid blot in the darkness, surrounded by a fug of spilt toddy fumes and stale cigarettes. She hung back, watching until a shadow moved, there by the tree. A man stepped forward and the light caught his profile. Amit. He put his finger to his lips, then turned and she followed him without a word down a narrow track into the jungle interior.

Amit drew her further and further away from the harbour, skirting silent villages, setting stray dogs barking, startling rats and hunting foxes. She was hurrying through an endless dream of pacing feet and close, fetid plants and trees, the air lightened only by the salted breeze, which whipped now and then from the sea. Above them, always, loomed the slopes of Mount Harriet, thick with forests of coconut palms and bamboo.

Her eyes started to close, even as she walked. Her head drooped. All her thoughts were of rest, of tumbling down on the ground in this hollow or that bank and giving herself up to sleep.

Just as numbness started to steal over her, the path veered to the right and they began a steep descent. The air changed, carrying freshness and the sting of salt. Sea opened up below, a sudden expanse of shimmering water, flecked with foam where the waves unrolled on a narrow shore. Amit looked back, made sure of her, then twisted sideways, climbing down a sheer hillside with his body almost turned to the cliff and his hands spread to feel for tree roots, plant stems and rocks.

She was panting by the time she reached the shore and flecked with spray. The wind, whipping across the water, was chill. Amit stood in the shallows by a fishing boat. Two men, standing knee-deep in the waves, steadied the keel as Amit turned back, reached out a hand to guide her through the water towards them.

She set both hands on the warm wood of the boat and peered inside. A barrel and a crate were stowed, one at each end. A man lay along the bottom, wrapped round in a long, threadbare blanket. He stirred a little, then settled.

'Is he hurt?'

Amit nodded. 'His leg. Shot. Our doctor friend tended him but you must keep it clean. He needs to lie low for a while, to eat and drink and recover his strength.' Amit gave her a keen look. 'Are you sure, little sister?'

She threw her bundle into the prow. The men, watching her wordlessly, held the boat steady while she pulled herself up and, with Amit's help, climbed in. She opened the flap of the blanket for a sight of Sanjay Krishna's pale, hot face, then settled herself on the planks and lifted his head and shoulders into her lap.

'Where will they take us?'

'Far into the islands.' Amit lifted his hand in signal to the fishermen who started to push the boat deeper into the sea, setting it rocking as the waves took it. Amit's voice, dispersing rapidly in the wind, whispered after them: 'May the gods bless and protect you.'

The fishermen clambered into the boat, splattering her with seawater. They were swarthy, thickset men who stole glances at her, then looked quickly away. They began to row, grunting and straining as the boat creaked into motion. Her ears filled with the whipping wind and the rhythmical lap of water against wood.

She reached into her bundle and put a flask of water to Krishna-ji's lips. He drank a little, let the rest dribble from his mouth. His eyes stayed closed. She wet the end of her dupatta and washed with care his eyes, his forehead, his cheeks, his neck. His face was all pockets and hollows.

She put her lips to Krishna-ji's ear and whispered. 'See how well I care for you, ji.'

She fell to rocking him, her body bending backwards and forwards with the same motion as the steadily rowing men, and watched South Andaman Island shrink until it became no more than a black smudge disappearing at last into the water.

Chapter Twenty

Isabel

She dreaded Edward's departure. When his final day came, she refused engagements in the hope that they might spend his last hours together before he sailed in the evening.

She was sitting on the balcony with him over afternoon tea when Singh appeared in the doorway. His face was tight with disapproval.

'She is gone, madam.'

'Who's gone?'

'The girl.'

'Asha?' Isabel considered. It was true. She hadn't seen her all morning.

'Cook says food is missing also.' Singh's frown deepened. 'Mutton, fruits, sugar and flour. Stolen.'

When Singh left the room, Isabel stared at the piece of cake on her plate, suddenly without appetite.

Edward said: 'You gave her a chance. That's all you could do.'

'Perhaps.' Isabel finished her tea. The cup clinked against the saucer as she set it down again.

Edward said: 'You're really upset, aren't you?'

'I thought we were, well, friends.' Isabel lifted her napkin and set it beside her plate. 'Anyway, we mustn't let it spoil your last day.'

He nodded. 'She may reappear.'

Later, as the light mellowed, Isabel followed Edward from room to room as he retrieved his belongings and packed. His silence had never seemed so impenetrable.

'Are you looking forward to going back?'

He bent to run an eye along the books he'd bought in Port Blair, choosing which to take and which to leave.

'It'll be a relief to be back at work, I suppose. Sleep in your own bed.'

'I don't have a bed, exactly.' He spoke without turning to her.

She knew she would stare at the clock in the days ahead and wonder what he was doing just then, where exactly he was, and find it impossible to imagine. Car Nicobar seemed a world away from Port Blair.

He headed back to his bedroom with the books and she trailed after him. His hair was freshly cut. A line of white skin showed between his cropped hairline and his sunburnt neck. She had an urge to touch it, to feel the spikiness of the newly razored hair.

'I shall miss you.' She tried to keep her tone light. An hour or two and he would be gone. There were so many conversations she still wanted to have, questions she wanted to ask.

He bent wordlessly over his trunk, lifting packets of cigarettes from a stockpile on the bed and pressing them into corners, then adding a layer of clothes. She lifted a bundle of shirts from his hands, smoothed and folded them more neatly before placing them flat in the trunk, one after another. She wondered where he would be when he lifted them out again.

He reached past her for his washbag and began to fill it. His hands were so familiar to her. The long fingers, the tufts of dark hair below the knuckles. The silence stretched.

'Have I said the wrong thing?'

He gave her a snatched smile, then turned his eyes back to his shaving kit. 'Is there a wrong thing?'

'I hope not.' She started, her hand at her mouth. Jonathan stood in the doorway. His face was hard with anger. 'Jonathan! You made me jump.'

She bent over the packing. She had no reason to feel guilty.

'Singh says Asha's run off. Had you heard?' Her voice was falsely bright.

Edward said. 'You all right?'

Jonathan hadn't moved. She lifted her head to see. His cheeks were flushed, his hands in tight balls at his sides. She held her breath.

He said: 'You knew, didn't you?'

His eyes were on Edward. She didn't understand. She didn't recognise this man who quivered with rage. Edward set the shaving kit slowly on the bed.

'I should report the pair of you. Her, I can understand. She doesn't know any better. But you, Johnston.'

His fists rose and for a moment he looked about to strike. He paced across the room and stood with his back to the room, gazing out through the bedroom window.

Edward said softly: 'What?'

'You set me up. The pair of you.' His tone was quieter now and all the more frightening for its calm. 'How could you be such a fool?'

'It's nothing like that, Jonathan. Nothing.'

She had the sense that she was witnessing a scene between the two of them in which she had no voice, no part.

Jonathan pulled a paper from his jacket pocket and handed it to Edward. Her letter to Sanjay Krishna. She recognised it at once although it was crumpled now and stained. Edward unfolded it, bent his head and began to read.

Isabel sat down with a bump on the bed.

'Did you help him escape?'

'Escape?' The room dappled with specks of light.

'But how did she send it?' Edward spoke as if to himself. His eyes rose and searched Jonathan's face. Finally, he nodded and said softly: 'In a Bible.'

Jonathan's lips were thin lines. 'She used you. That's the sort of woman she is.'

'Edward, no! It wasn't like that.' She felt invisible to them both.

Edward said: 'I swear to you on my life, on my faith, Whyte. I had no idea.'

The two men stared at each other. Jonathan looked suddenly limp with exhaustion.

Edward said: 'Who gave you this?'

Jonathan shrugged. 'Barnes, the assistant commissioner. We're pals.'

'What will he do?'

Jonathan blew out his cheeks. 'I don't know.'

'Will he keep quiet, if you ask him?'

Jonathan rubbed his hand across his forehead. 'Dear God, what a mess.'

'And Krishna, he's really gone?'

'Last night. They're searching. He must have had help. One of the guards, maybe.'

Edward moved to Jonathan's side and took his arm, steered him out of the room.

'Keep her name out of it. No one need know.' Their footsteps sounded along the passageway, entered the sitting room. A moment later, the clink of a glass stopper, a drink being poured.

'They'll find him. If he heads into the jungle, he won't last long.' Edward's voice was calm. 'As for this, destroy it. It's foolishness, that's all. Ask Barnes to keep his mouth shut.'

'It'll ruin me.'

'It needn't.' A pause. Isabel, sitting on the bed, strained to hear.

A soft rustle of paper. Then the rasp of a match being struck. The acrid smell of sulphur, then flame.

'There.' Edward. 'Gone.'

'Our marriage is a sham. I've seen you two together. I'm not blind.'

'Stop it, Whyte.'

'Have her, if you like. I don't care. Perhaps you already have.'

'Don't be absurd.' The clink of glass again as another drink was poured.

Jonathan gave a sharp laugh. 'Truth is, I can't stand the sight of her.'

Edward sighed. 'You married her, Whyte.'

'I had to marry. Don't you see? A man without a wife, people talk.'

Isabel tried to get to her feet. Her legs buckled under her. Her face was hot. She would pack her bags. Go back to Delhi. What else could she do? She thought of her parents, of the scandal for them both if she reappeared on their doorstep.

Jonathan's voice sounded thick. 'I won't give her a divorce. I don't care how bloody miserable she is. I'd be finished.'

She reached the doorway. Jonathan sat in the planter, a glass of Scotch in his hand. He drank it off, reached for more. His face was slick with sweat.

'Why do you think I ended up in this godforsaken place? No one's sent to Port Blair unless they want rid of them. That's one thing I've got in common with the bloody revolutionaries.'

'That's what you're really worried about, isn't it?'

Jonathan turned his head as she entered the room and went to stand squarely in front of him.

'That if there's a scandal involving your unhappy wife, they'll gossip about you again,' she said.

Jonathan's eyes took on a hunted look. It emboldened her to carry on.

'You abuse that wretched houseboy, don't you? That's why he cries in corners. He's afraid of you. And what you do to him.'

She was right. She saw it in his face at once as the shaft went home. He raised the glass to his mouth and drank. The glass juddered against his teeth.

'Don't, Isabel.' Edward tried to lay a hand on her arm. She shook it off.

'That's why you married me, isn't it? You thought it would stop tongues wagging. Make a respectable man out of you so you could get promoted away from here. You didn't care a jot about me.'

'It suited you well enough. Solutions all round.'

He seemed to shrink in front of her eyes. She saw again

the bullying schoolboy who tried to hurt her all those years ago. She shook her head.

'Isabel.' Edward was at her side. He didn't look shocked, just terribly sad and the gentleness in his eyes made her want simply to cry. They stood still, reading each other's faces.

'Take me back with you.'

He looked confused. 'Take you back?'

'You need help there, don't you? Just for a while.'

Edward frowned. 'I don't think—'

Jonathan said: 'Take her. Do me a favour.'

Edward turned to Jonathan. 'She's not a parcel, Whyte.'

Jonathan slumped in his chair. 'I'll say she's helping with the Mission School. Everyone knows you're short. Send her back when you've had enough.'

'Apologise for that.' Edward tensed. 'You've no right.'

Jonathan shrugged. 'I'm her husband. I've every right.'

'Don't listen to him.' Isabel touched Edward's shoulder. 'Let me come. I'll teach. Nothing wrong with that.' She paused, willing him to agree. 'Jonathan and I will tear each other apart if I stay.'

Edward didn't speak. He stared down at his hands. He can't want me there, she thought. Then: I don't care. Whatever happens, I need to be with him.

'It's settled, then.' She became brisk, trying to bundle him into agreeing. 'They'll have room for me, won't they? On the ship?'

She left to pack without giving him time to answer.

Chapter Twenty-One

The steamer was a weathered Portuguese cargo vessel. The captain, a European with multicoloured tattoos, showed Isabel to a stuffy cabin on the upper deck. She lay awake for some time after their departure, listening to the shouts of the crew, the creak of wood and the low slap of the waves. Eventually she wrapped a shawl round her shoulders and ventured up onto the deck.

The night sky was cloudy. Black water stretched endlessly on all sides, pockmarked by lightly falling rain. The air was heavy with petrol fumes and sea salt.

Her head was filled with images from the final hours in the house. Jonathan's flushed face as she accused him of mistreating Bimal. Edward's troubled look as she pressed him into taking her away. The breeze was cold and she pulled her shawl more closely around her body.

Jonathan never cared for her, then. It was all pretence. She wondered how many people knew. Lady Lyons suspected, she was sure. The servants must gossip. Perhaps she had known herself, from the first time she found Bimal in tears, and been too afraid of the truth to confront it. She thought of Jonathan's one, awkward visit to her bed. They had lived together as man and wife and yet already she felt far closer to Edward than she ever had to her husband.

Her cheeks became numb but she stayed at the rail, facing down the wind and rain. Sanjay Krishna was out there somewhere, unseen, running for his life. Had he played her for a fool? Even now, she didn't regret writing to him.

As dawn slowly broke, the deck grew busy with European and Indian sailors. The wind drew silver ridges and troughs across the surface of the waves.

'Did you sleep?' Edward appeared at her side. His clothes were dishevelled and his face unshaven. 'Do you want breakfast?'

He came back with two glasses of milky tea.

'There aren't comforts, you know. On Car Nicobar.' He sounded worried.

'I'll manage.'

The prow veered to the right, sniffing out jungle, feeling its way in the dull morning light.

Edward lifted his arm and pointed. 'Almost there.'

She strained to see land. Car Nicobar made barely a smudge on the water's surface. They were almost upon it before she made out a low green bank with only the faintest white fringe separating it from the sea. The ship slowed as they approached dark lines of jagged, black rocks, which protected the island as effectively as teeth.

'Where do we dock?'

Edward gave her a wry look. 'We don't.'

A row of dull-brown shapes stood on a white-sand beach. Beyond stretched jungle. A deep shudder rose from the bowels of the ship as the captain had dropped anchor. Behind them, deckhands brought their belongings out on the deck and stacked them in piles: Isabel's hastily packed bag was dwarfed by Edward's trunk, boxes of dried goods and the crate of Bibles.

Edward pointed and she turned to look. Young black men, wearing nothing but loin cloths, were racing into the surf, propelling half a dozen dugout canoes. The flimsy boats tossed as the men pressed them into the waves. When the water reached chest height, they hauled themselves aboard and paddled furiously towards the ship.

The boats were little more than hollowed-out logs, balanced by outriggers of light wood lashed to bamboo struts. The men had stout muscular bodies. Their black skin glistened with spray. As they came closer to the vessel, she made out their bead necklaces and bracelets.

The sailors lowered their luggage on ropes over the side of the boat. Each piece swung as it waited for a canoe to battle against the swell and position itself beneath, then for hands below to guide it in. Within ten or fifteen minutes, four were loaded with their belongings and the natives fell again to their frantic paddling as they drew away from the vessel, changed direction and headed back to shore.

'We go next.' Edward crossed the deck and started to climb down the slippery gangway that stuck out into nothingness. A rope, running along both sides of the gangway, formed the only barrier between them and the flecking foam below.

Edward hesitated, judging the rise and fall of the canoe beneath. At one moment, it rose so high that he could have stepped into it with ease. A moment later, the sea snatched it away again, leaving a yawning vacancy. He reached back for her hand and drew her alongside him. Her face stung with salt spray and her legs juddered under her. The water bubbled far below.

'Ready?' Edward shouted to make himself heard above the sound of the waves. 'Now!'

They fell through nothingness, stranded for a second in some unknown place between ship and water. Black hands caught her, steadied her as she fell forward into the canoe. A man with stained teeth and dark eyes deposited her on a narrow bamboo seat, even as the canoe whipped round and rose steeply on the mountain slope of the next wave. The bottom of the canoe sloshed with seawater. Cold seeped through her boots. Empty air rose around her as they crested the wave, then crashed with a bang down the opposite side, knocking her breath from her body.

The endlessly tossing boat seemed no more substantial than a splinter on the ocean. When the swell reduced a fraction, a line of black rock streaked past the bow and a white-sand shore rushed towards them. The canoe rode a final breaking wave onto land and the men leapt out at once on both sides, seizing the wooden edges of their boat and dragging it to safety, out of the reach of the next roller.

Her knees gave way, pitching her forward into soft, warm sand. She lifted her head to see a group of black, half-naked men, women and children who stood at a distance, their eyes fixed on hers.

Edward was swamped at once by a cloud of small black children with bone-white teeth who jumped round him, swung from his arms and climbed his thighs. He smiled and wrestled with them, then gestured to Isabel to follow and headed into the jungle, picking his way along a narrow path through the dense undergrowth.

It was a peculiar procession, first Edward and his cluster of bounding children, then Isabel, picking her way through trailing creepers, her wet boots whitening with creeping salt stains, waving flies from her face. The native women crept close behind her, whispering and pointing. Finally the men, shouldering the luggage, brought up the rear.

The cool breeze from the sea disappeared once they entered the jungle and the interlaced canopy prevented the slightest stirring of air. The vegetation sweated, raising the temperature with its own body heat and filling the air with the fetid smell of dank, rotting greenery. Isabel's cotton slacks and shirt stuck to her skin.

Just as she was starting to tire, the jungle broke open and they emerged into a clearing. A pack of dogs rushed barking to throw themselves on Edward and the children. Behind them, chickens ran in squawking circles, disturbed by the general commotion and a family of bristly pigs snuffled and grunted.

The clearing was filled with ten to twelve primitive stilted houses, the shape of giant beehives, woven from coconut matting. A boy, perhaps eleven or twelve years old, ran forward with a young coconut and solemnly presented it to Edward. He had the air of a child who has waited a long time for his moment of glory.

'This is James.' Edward ruffled the boy's hair. 'My shadow.'

James pressed close to Edward's side. His eyes followed every movement as Edward took a machete and sliced off the top of the coconut.

'He's Sami's boy.' Edward drank off a little coconut milk, then gave it to James who carried it carefully to Isabel. 'His father drowned, fishing. I try to make it up to him.'

They perched on a fallen tree trunk. The coconut milk

was cold. As she drank, dribbles of watery milk spilt from her lips and trickled down her chin. The natives gathered round her to watch.

Edward motioned forward one of the women. Her figure was tall and slender with swaying, bare breasts.

'And this is Sami. She helps at the school.'

Edward spoke to her in a curious language, punctuated by hard consonants which seemed to catch in his throat.

'Is that Nicobarese?'

He laughed. 'I was just saying that you'll teach.'

Isabel smiled. Sami did not.

'Does she speak Hindustani?'

'No. The children speak some English.' He looked her over. 'I expect you need to rest now?'

Isabel looked round at the curious faces. 'I'd rather get started.'

Edward nodded. 'Sami will take you to see the school.'

She expected the school to be a building. In fact it was an empty space a few minutes further into the jungle, cleared for learning. Sami rounded up ten children of different ages and sizes, all with the oiled hair and black skin of the Nicobarese. They sat cross-legged on the ground and fixed her with brown eyes as Sami picked up a whittled stick, handed it to Isabel and gestured to the dirt which served as blackboard and easel.

Isabel took a deep breath, smiled round at the watchful children and started to chant the times tables, clapping her hands to the rhythm. One or two pupils haltingly joined in. Sami, arms folded, stood silently at the back.

By late morning, the smaller children slept in the laps of older brothers and sisters, and simply wandered away from the class. When they got hungry, the older children too got to their feet, one by one, and disappeared. When only two remained, Isabel handed the stick back to Sami and they trailed back through the jungle to the circle of houses.

Women crouched at the foot of the beehives, stirring blackened pots over open fires. Children sat around them, eating a mess of rice porridge and vegetables with their fingers from leaves. The smell of simmering rice saturated the humid air.

One of the women beckoned to Isabel and ladled steaming rice onto a leaf, then handed it to her. The leaf was porous and the food leached through to heat the palm of her hand. She lowered her lips to the leaf and ate directly from it, as the children looked on and giggled.

Edward reappeared late in the afternoon, his clothes soaked with sweat. Isabel sat in the shade as he fetched water from a wooden trough and washed himself, then put on a clean shirt. The Nicobarese women again began to cook and the air soon swam with woodsmoke.

He sat beside her. 'How was school?'

'Informal.'

Edward gave her a quick sideways look. 'We can go to the shore tomorrow morning, if you like. To bathe.'

She nodded. Her hair was itchy and her skin frosted with salt. They sat quietly for a moment, watching the bustle of the camp.

'Where are all the men?'

'Fishing, probably. Or cutting coconuts.'

The heat eased as the sun fell and the light turned yellow with early evening. The jungle settled around them. A haze of green-winged birds rose, cawing, and wheeled through the sky, disappearing at last behind a distant clutch of palm trees.

Edward turned his attention to one of his boots, unlacing it and easing the leather along the side of his foot.

'Edward, I am sorry. About the letter.'

He didn't look up. His hands stayed on his boot, threading the lace through the eyes with deft, even tugs.

'But I don't regret sending it.'

His fingers paused in their work. 'Don't you?'

'He needed to know. We're not all heartless.'

He pulled again at the ends of the lace and knotted it with care. 'You used me, Isabel. Worse than that, you used the Bible.'

She lowered her head. 'I just thought—'

'Perhaps, next time, Barnes won't let me hand out Bibles at all. Had you thought of that?'

She shook her head. Her feet, in their Delhi-made boots, made dents in the dirt.

'If I compromised you in any way, I am sorry. That's the last thing . . .'

He sighed and made to get up. She caught at his sleeve.

'You don't mind, do you? That I'm here.'

His eyes were sad. 'It's a bit late for that. There isn't another steamer for a month.'

That night, she slept in a one-room hive with Sami, her elderly mother and four other women, three snuffling infants and two dogs. The crawl-hole stank of dried leaves and the coconut oil with which the women rubbed their limbs and dressed their hair. The only gap was the hole in the base, accessed by a spindly bamboo ladder. She lay awake for some time, sweating, nipped by a cloud of flies, wondering how she'd come to be here.

She woke, disorientated, to the sound of stealthy movement. A soft rustling of feet creeping across coconut matting. A subtle creak. Slivers of light rose through the pitch darkness from the open trapdoor. A tall, slender body, Sami's, was making its way between the sleeping bodies towards her. Isabel closed her eyes.

The footsteps stopped by Isabel's side. Warm, spicy breath fell on her face. Isabel lay rigid, pretending to be asleep. After a time, Sami retreated. The slightest creak suggested that she was again settling to sleep. Isabel lay awake for sometime, listening for further movement but none came.

Her feet sank into the moist sand at the very edge of the dispersing waves. The water bubbled, sucked softly around her toes and pulled sand from under them. Ahead the sun shattered into fragments across the surface of endless crystal waters.

Edward stood beside her in his bathing suit. 'Don't stray too far left. The coral's sharp as a razor.'

She dipped, scooped up a handful of foaming water and threw it at him.

'Stop worrying.'

He raised an eyebrow. 'I haven't mentioned the sharks yet.'

She ran out into the water, the tide slapping at her ankles. The beach shelved gently and the lengthy shallows were as warm as a bath. Finally it grew deep enough for her to fling herself forward onto her stomach and swim. The water reached for her, washing off the filth and sweat of the last two days, cradling her as she struck out towards the horizon.

From the sea, the shore looked a paradise. The sand was bone-white, the jungle a thick screen of painter's green.

There was no sign of human, even animal, existence. The only noise was the swish of water in her ears and the dull thud of waves breaking.

The vastness of the landscape shrank her to nothingness as she floated, surrendered to the power of the waves. She felt an odd sense of detachment, as if she could look back at her life on land and realise how insignificant her own troubles, her own happiness really was. As if there were no protests and riots and struggles. Only this life, here and now, of endless sea and sky. She lay back and let the water fill her ears.

Edward finished bathing and stood on the water's edge, hands on hips, watching. When she finally emerged, he walked with her up the beach. She squeezed water from her hair and the drops made sand bullets where they fell.

They sat together on the sand. The skin on Edward's shoulders and legs was daubed with salty streaks. He reached in his bag for his cigarette case and lit them both smokes.

The hot sun dried off her costume, her skin. Port Blair, Jonathan, Sanjay Krishna all belonged to another world. She was alive. Edward was beside her.

They sat in silence for some time and smoked. She thought of the work gangs in their camp on South Andaman, doggedly digging up tree roots and clearing away jungle for ever. She tried to imagine them here, trampling through the narrow paths with their armed guards and building camps near the houses of the Nicobarese.

'How will you do it?' she said. 'Stop the government teams from coming to clear the jungle.'

He didn't speak for a while. 'I'm not sure yet. I'm praying about it.'

She gave him a quick sideways glance. He looked younger than he had in Port Blair. His features were calm. The sadness, which she had come to recognise as part of him, was no longer there.

He turned suddenly and looked back up the beach.

'I might have known.' He grinned.

She twisted to see. James stood under the cover of the palm trees, watching them. He shifted his feet and took a few hesitant steps towards them. Edward raised a hand and James came running towards them at full pelt, showering sand. He fell on Edward and they wrestled in the sand in a contortion of black and white limbs. Finally, he scooped the boy up, an arm round his waist, and spun him round, then tipped him onto his back in the sand. James rolled over, jumped up and flung himself on Edward for more. Isabel smiled.

Finally, he gave James a light cuff. The boy ran off to scavenge for a stick, then drifted to a rock pool.

Edward's eyes followed him. 'He'll leave soon.'

'Leave?'

'His father's tribe will claim him. In their eyes, he's almost a man.'

Isabel, watching James clamber, sure-footed, over the rocks, said: 'What about Sami?'

Edward shrugged. 'We'll care for her, at the Mission.'

Isabel thought of Sami's stealthy attempt in the night to examine her.

'Do you think Sami minds the fact I've come?'

He cleared his throat and stared fixedly at the sea.

'She's not used to sharing the Mission work. I mean, with anyone apart from me.'

She opened her mouth to ask more, then stopped. It was clear from his expression that he didn't want to discuss it.

The days passed with increasing speed. At first, Isabel thought often of Jonathan and their life in Port Blair. She worried about when she would have to go back there and how she might bear it.

Gradually, she came to understand what Edward had described weeks earlier, when they sat together in the clearing in the middle of the virgin jungle. It began to seem as if no other time existed but the present, as if Port Blair and Delhi, and England too, were nothing more than shadows of her imagination. All that was real was the sea, the sand, the jungle and the Nicobarese.

Each day began with Edward. They swam together in transparent waters, then smoked and talked, stretched side by side on clean, white sand as the sun dried and warmed their bodies. Each day ended with Edward, always at her side as they sat at the edge of the Mission clearing to eat, the women's cooking fires slowly smouldering and night gathering around them all.

Chapter Twenty-Two

Asha

The footsteps came in the middle of the night. She woke at once. A low crick-crack of twigs and stir of leaves.

Asha had hollowed a space for them both in the depth of the bushes, camouflaged by bamboo staves and trailing creepers. She lay there now, listening. Someone moved with stealth. She reached to her side for the sharpened bamboo stick.

She had laid dried twigs near the entrance to act as an alarm. A sudden snap, loud in the silence. The sound of a man's weight.

She crawled to Krishna-ji and shook his shoulder. 'Wake up.'

He moaned and lifted his head. His forehead was hot, his hair caked against his skin. She rubbed his back with soft circular strokes, watching him closely as he struggled to the surface out of sleep. His eyes opened. He tried to focus on her face in the darkness but his look was blank.

'Quiet.' She put her lips close to his ear. 'Someone's coming.'

His mind came back in a rush from whatever dream had taken it, she read the change in his eyes. He remembered first who she was, then where they were, hiding out in the jungle.

She held her breath, strained to listen. Silence. He was there, the unknown man. Just feet away from them, hidden by the foliage that surrounded them. She sensed him peering into the blackness. He was so close, she could smell him.

Sanjay Krishna's breathing was ragged. She kept one hand on his back as a comfort, the other gripped the bamboo spear. When he inhaled, the air rattled through his lungs, catching there. His spine was hot and wet with fever. I can't move him, she thought. Not now.

A sharp snap and the soft rustle of branches. Whoever it was, he knew they were here. She lifted her hand from Sanjay Krishna and felt her way forward, pressing herself softly on hands and knees through the dense undergrowth, the bamboo spear in her hand. The leaves were wet with night dew and slapped against her face, arms and legs as she moved. She peered out through the branches, which formed black bars in the darkness.

'Bhai? Brother?'

A stranger's voice. Cautious. She held her breath. If the man were an enemy, if he were leading the Britishers to them, they were finished.

It came again. 'Krishna-Sahib? Are you there?'

'Who are you?'

He hesitated, then said: 'A friend.'

A rustle. A branch pulled aside and against the lesser darkness of the night jungle, the broad, black silhouette of a man loomed, bent low. Behind her, Krishna-ji let out a low sigh. Could he see this man? Did he know him? She moved a fraction, peering through the mesh of leaves, and lifted her spear.

The man saw her, nodded to himself as if satisfied, then

settled. He was a gangly fellow, stooped and thin and he folded up his legs like a penknife.

Her heart banged in her chest. 'Who told you we were here?'

'Our friends.' He set a parcel, wrapped round in a large leaf, on the ground in front of her. 'It is rice and subzi only. I am poor man.'

Asha nodded. The food she brought from Port Blair had long since gone. She fed Krishna-ji one meal a day, made up of whatever she could pick from the trees and bushes or catch with her own hands.

The man said: 'How is he?'

She made a face. 'He has fever.'

'Can he walk?'

She blew out her cheeks. The leg which the bullet had entered was swollen and hot. 'A little, only.'

The man frowned, leant forward to speak softly to her. His breath was sour. He'd spoken the truth, then, he was a poor man with an empty stomach.

'The Britishers are making some deal with the tribals here,' he said. 'If the Britishers pay them, they will betray you.'

Asha looked round at the lattice of leaves and branches, a poor defence from powerful enemies.

The man said: 'The Britishers have dogs to sniff you out.'

Asha twisted back. They must leave at once. Krishna-ji lay still as if he had slipped again into sleep. 'Uncle, where can we hide?'

The man put his head on one side, considering. 'Not in the village. It's too dangerous. The Britishers will kill us, our women and children, also.'

'So? What to do?'

For some time, neither of them spoke. Behind them, Krishna-ji let out a sudden cry in his sleep. The man jumped, nervous as a cat.

'There is one place,' he said. 'A long sea-cave in the cliff with a narrow mouth. At high tide, it fills quickly. Many men have drowned there and the tribals fear it. They say the spirits of dead men live there. Maybe, if you can make it there, you could hide for some hours, while the tide is low. Not even dogs will find you there.'

Asha picked up the leaf parcel. The rice inside warmed her hand. Her tongue became wet but there was no time to eat.

'May the gods bless you and your family.'

Something stirred out in the jungle and he looked round, full of fear.

'I must go.' He explained to her how to reach the sea-cave, then unfolded his long legs and crawled back out into the night. She packed the food into a bundle and went to rouse Krishna-ji. She had to help him even to crawl. He dragged his swollen leg behind him, biting his lip with pain. Sweat pooled at his temples and ran down the sides of his face.

'We have food,' she said. 'First we must reach a safe place. Then we will eat.'

She tied up the filthy blanket and the food and strapped them across her body, then laced her arm under Krishna-ji's shoulder, taking the weight off his injured leg. His breath was laboured and his body hot and wet against her side.

The path through the jungle was overgrown. Creepers reached in loops for their feet and made them stumble. Once she knocked against him, banging his leg and he cried out in pain. She stood, bearing his weight, and clamped her lips to stop from weeping as he breathed hard, in, out, summoning his remaining strength to carry on.

There had been so many stumbling night walks through jungle since the fishermen first set them on the shore of this small island and they felt their way, joined at the shoulder, blind in the darkness, hearing danger in every sound. She tried to loosen her mind from her body and let it fly free above her, looking down at the girl and man, who struggled together from one step to the next. She felt now what she had known since that first night when Amit helped her climb into the boat to cradle Krishna-ji's head in her lap: I love this man. He is all I have left in this empty world. Whatever the gods require me to give to save him, I will give it gladly. It is a blessing.

The path slowly became steep and led them down the hillside. The air, forcing itself in through the canopy, grew salty and cool and the soft song of the waves on the shore grew louder.

They reached a bluff. Krishna-ji was panting now, his arms running with sweat. She set him on the ground and took a few steps further to the edge of the land. Far below, light glimmered on the sea, which swirled and shimmered round a cliff face.

It took them a long time to find a way down the cliff. Loose stones clattered ahead, making her stop and wait for silence to settle before they continued. The rocks became slippery with spray and the air changed from the sultry heaviness of the jungle to the chill from the ocean. The sea roared against the rocks. If either one of them slipped, they would plunge together.

222

This was the place the man described, she was sure of it. The jagged cliff face, the inlets that made the foam suck and surge. The cave must be somewhere here.

Krishna-ji seemed hot with fever, despite the breeze. The path became so steep that they had to turn to hug the rock face and lower themselves, step by step. She straddled him and guided his weak leg, placing it on one rock, then another. Pebbles peppered the water below.

Finally she saw a crack, just feet above the waterline, and helped him across the rocks towards it. The opening was narrow, a black split in the rock. Asha reached her arm inside, trying to judge the width. If it were the wrong place, she risked being swallowed up by the cliff. She stood for a moment, considering. Beside her, Krishna-ji slumped against a boulder.

His eyes were closed. She stooped, shook his shoulder. Already the sky on the horizon was lightening.

'Come. We're almost there. Then you can rest, nah?'

His lips parted. 'Ah, little sister.'

She reached her hands under his arms and heaved him upright, then dragged him to the crack. She closed her eyes, pressed herself into it and pulled him sideways after her. The stone scraped against her back, her arms, winding her. The gap was so narrow that she had to battle to keep squeezing through, to stop it from holding her fast. She tried to turn her head back to see Krishna-ji and found she didn't have enough room to twist it. Her body juddered in a flash of panic. Rock bulged against her face. A scream rose inside her. She stood still, her blood pulsing in her head, trying to swallow it down. The weight of Krishna-ji's body, plugging the space behind her, made it impossible for her to retreat.

She could only press forwards, further into the cliff.

'Follow me.' Her voice was deadened by stone. She forced herself to wriggle onwards. Every breath swelled her chest tight against the rock. The sides of the tunnel narrowed and she hung there, stuck fast. Then, in a sudden movement, she shifted, her feet stumbling, and staggered sideways, losing her balance as the ground sloped sharply downwards, grazing her cheek as she fell into darkness, banging at last against a sandy floor.

She lay, winded. Brightly coloured streaks of light streamed through her eyes. She clambered up and groped around to find the gap through which she had just fallen. Her hand touched Krishna-ji's elbow and she seized his arm, tugged at him until he came crashing down on top of her. They lay, heaped, fighting for breath.

We will die here, she thought. It came to her with calm certainty. The sea will rise and fill this place and drown us and we will be powerless to escape. We will die here together, as if we had never been. She lay still, crushed by Krishna-ji who sprawled, moaning, across her back and legs, and prayed for them both.

The man had called this a cave. It was a hole. The air tasted stale and fetid. It was a dank, black fissure, which was barely wide enough for them to sit shoulder to shoulder. She managed to sit Krishna-ji up beside her, his head on her shoulder. She took his hand and held it between her own.

Slowly his body stopped trembling. The boom of the waves receded to a dull thud. As her eyes adjusted, the darkness became tempered by weak light from outside, which filtered in tendrils through the narrow entrance.

'We are safe here.' She stroked the back of his large hand. 'Now we can eat.'

She untied the blanket and wrapped it round him. As she opened up the leaf parcel, the rich smell of cooked rice and vegetables made her stomach grumble. She fed it to him, pinch by pinch between her fingers, cajoling him to chew, to swallow.

Afterwards, they sat in silence. Below, deep in the cliff, the sea rushed back and forth in a muffled heartbeat. She didn't know how long it would take for the waters to rise and claim them. She thought of the walls of rock that had pressed against her body, crushing it, and terror seized her again.

He slumped forward and she squeezed his hand. If he slept now, she feared he would never wake again.

'Talk to me,' she said.

'About what?' She sensed his smile in the darkness.

She felt the comfort of the warmth of his shoulder. 'Tell me about your family.'

'Ah. My family.' He shifted his weight and they sat, one against the other, in their world of rock. His voice rasped in his throat as he began to talk. His story seemed to take him far away into the past as he remembered.

'My baba was a good man. He moved to Delhi, to the bustee, when we were children and made business there, buying and selling cloth. He worked hard, day and night, and saved everything he earned and sent it home to us in the village. We were seven children. Every one of us, boy and girl, he sent to school, as my uncle and your baba sent you to school. Education is the best weapon, he used to tell, and I was wondering: why are we needing weapons? Who are we needing to fight? I was young then.'

She squeezed his hand to remind him that she was listening. He paid her no heed. His story was for himself. He was summoning his life to say goodbye to it.

'My baba had a kind heart. He gave money always to his brothers also and helped them make business. He helped my uncle, sahib, who later gave his life for our freedom, as you are knowing.'

He paused. His voice softened. Ahead of them, the first dullness of sunrise expanded the narrow line of light in the rock.

'Finally news came that my baba was very sick. My mama sent me to Delhi to bring him home. I was maybe ten years old.' He paused. 'I was afraid. I found him lying on a charpoy in a dark room. So many books were there and papers also. He had the face of an old man, not the baba I remembered. His skin was grey and his legs were thin as sticks.'

Slowly, as he talked, the darkness in the cave eased.

'He could barely walk. I helped him to the railway station and bought first-class tickets. The station was teeming with every kind of person and my baba looked so frail in the midst of it all. The first-class carriage was empty and I settled him there with water and a blanket. I was only a boy but I loved my baba. Soon, he slept.

'The train was ready to leave the station when a young man came, a Britisher. A loud, arrogant fellow. He was barely twenty years old and he spoke Hindustani badly. He peered in the carriage and saw us there, a sick man and a boy. Then he started to shout at the stationmaster. All manner of insults. "Get these damned natives out." His words were ugly, like his ruddy, shiny face. "This is first class. Europeans only." He screamed and banged on the door of the carriage with his cane and a crowd gathered on the platform, jaws hanging, to stare.'

'So what happened?'

He shrugged. 'The stationmaster poked his head through the window and I showed our tickets and said: "See, we are paying to go first class. My baba is sick." No use. He turned us out and sent us to the third-class carriage, which was already spilling over with passengers. My baba spent the final journey of his life crushed against the side of a carriage by farmers and day-labourers, his face streaming with sweat, his eyes closed.'

He fell silent.

Asha said: 'At home, in the village, did he get well again?'

He shook his head. 'I vowed then that, whatever might come, I would devote my life to fighting these people who treat us like animals in our own land.'

Asha said: 'When will they leave, these Britishers?'

'We have no one to lead us in the fight against them. Do you see? Gandhi-ji has abandoned us. Nehru-ji and the rest are slippery creatures. They think only of themselves.'

He stayed quiet for some time, reflecting. 'I thought freedom would come in my lifetime, little sister. Now I do not think so.' He paused. 'Perhaps it will come in yours.'

He started to cough and the breath cracked and splintered in his chest. She pulled the blanket more tightly round his shoulders.

'Sleep a little,' she said.

He closed his eyes and she fell to stroking his cheek. A strange calm crept over her. Perhaps this is what it means to be happy, she thought. If I could stop time and have only one moment, maybe this is the moment to keep. She stared into the crack of light, bright now in the rock. It bounced with rising spray and mesmerised her.

Something cold touched her foot. She woke with a start, pulled up her knee. Beside her, Krishna-ji stirred. Cold water soaked her toes. She blinked. The air was stiff with salt. Water trickled down into the cave, splashing over the rim of the rock with each rising wave.

'Krishna-ji. Quick. We must go.'

She turned to shake him awake but his eyes were already open. His skin was grey but his look was calm.

'The tide is rising,' she said.

He stretched out his hand and touched her face. The tips of his fingers were hot. When he spoke, his voice was hoarse.

'You must be brave, little sister. Very brave. Can you do that for me?'

'Of course.' Something in his face frightened her. 'But we need to go. Come on.'

She got to her feet, tried to pull him up by the arm. He smiled.

'I am dying, Asha. Don't you see?'

She shook her head. 'You need rest. And a doctor. We'll look for one. Maybe our friends—'

He lifted his hand to silence her. 'It's too late for that.' He patted the ground and she sat reluctantly. He wasn't thinking clearly. It was the fever. A fresh wave set a surge of water sloshing round her feet.

'I told you about my baba, remember?' His face shone pale and sickly in the half-light. 'I wanted so much to save him because I loved him. I couldn't bear to live without him. His passing left the world too small a place.'

228

She frowned. 'That was a long time ago.'

'You are young, Asha. They are not hunting you. Only me. You must leave me now.'

'Leave you?' She wanted to hit him, to scream. She would rather die with him than leave him here to drown. She pointed to the slit in the cliff, flowing now with seawater. 'You can do it. Please. I'll help you.'

'I have decided.' He sounded stern. 'Listen. I'm too weak. If we both try to flee, they'll catch us both. What's the sense in that? You must go alone and go quickly. Go back to your mistress.' He watched her closely. 'Does she suspect you?'

She shrugged. 'She thinks I'm a child only.'

'Good.' He nodded. 'I have a plan. Will you listen and do as I ask?'

She turned her head away. The cave walls shimmered.

'Don't cry, little sister.' He squeezed her hand and released it, then turned her shoulders so she faced him, his dark-brown eyes inches from hers. 'Listen and listen well.'

He spoke his instructions clearly, even as the waves broke over the rocks and poured in runnels down the slope to their feet. The effort seemed to spend the last of his strength. When he finished speaking, he sank back, exhausted and closed his eyes.

'Wait, then.' Her fear made her sound impatient. 'I'll get help. You hear? I'll soon be back.'

She waded through the gathering cold water and pressed herself out through the narrow walls into daylight. She stood for a moment in the brightness, blinking, her face wet. The rocks below, where they had climbed during the night, had already been swallowed by the rising tide.

She pulled her dupatta round her head to shield her face

and climbed, stumbling and crying, between the boulders. When she reached the summit, she set off at a ragged run into the jungle, heading back the way they had first come, racing to find help.

Somewhere in the jungle, a pack of dogs snarled and barked. Birds rose cawing and squawking and wheeled over the canopy. She stopped, panting, to listen. Men cried out, one to another, as they beat their way through the jungle, searching for Sanjay Krishna. They were already close.

She changed direction and started to run again, skirting the jungle now and racing along the edge of the cliff. Far below, the sea crashed and swirled against the rocks. Every time she looked, the waves were higher. She imagined the rising water pouring into the cave where he was trapped, flooding it. Someone must help him. Someone.

The raucous barking became suddenly louder as it broke free of the jungle. She stopped, a pain sharp in her side, and looked back. Men, reduced by distance to the size of children, swarmed out from the canopy and ran along the cliff edge. It was a confusion of movement, backwards and forwards along that same spot where she had been, directly above the mouth of the cave. The dogs, tails wagging, ran back and forth at the men's heels, noses to the ground, searching for a way down.

She fell to her stomach and crawled to the very edge to look. The water had risen quickly. She tilted her head and strained to see along to the bluff where the entrance to the cave had been. It was no longer visible. All she saw was light, sparkling across a mass of surging, foaming waves.

She buried her head in the grass and wept. She should have stayed with him. She tore at her dupatta with wet fingers. She should have drowned at his side. She opened her mouth to scream and tasted grass and dry earth. She never even said goodbye.

She lay prostrate for a long time, without hope, without the will to move. Her mama was taken. Then her baba. Now Sanjay Krishna too. She had nothing and no one left to love.

A thought broke over her, bringing a fresh wave of grief: he knew. He knew this desperate nothingness would engulf her when he was gone. What had he said? I wanted to save my father because I loved him, because his passing left the world too small a place.

She stretched out her arms, pressed her face into the earth and wept.

Chapter Twenty-Three

Isabel

Weeks passed. Isabel lost herself to the steady rhythm of each day. Her body became brown and strong. She taught the children, swam, helped the women to cook, looked always for Edward. She exiled thoughts of Port Blair, of Jonathan, of the day she must finally return, of time itself.

One morning, she was collecting her belongings after class when Edward stepped without warning into the clearing.

'A steamer's due in two days' time.' His tone was brisk and impersonal. 'It's going to Calcutta but puts in at Port Blair on the way.'

Her eyes turned to the ground and the scuffs in the dry mud made by the children's feet and hands.

'It's dropping off supplies,' he went on. 'I've told them you'll join it.'

'So soon?' Her stomach was suddenly cold, her chest tight. She couldn't leave.

'I think it's time.'

She shook her head. The jungle swam in front of her eyes. 'Have I done something? We should talk . . .'

His body was tense, twisted away. He paused, as if he were summoning strength. 'It's been six weeks now. There mightn't be another ship for a month or more.'

She took a step towards him. 'He doesn't want me back.'

He didn't look her in the eye. Her breath became short.

He said: 'They've started to talk.'

'Who has?'

He shrugged. 'Everyone.'

'We've nothing to be ashamed of, Edward. Nothing. What have we done?'

His voice stayed resolute. 'It's time, Isabel. Time for you to go.'

He turned and walked out of the clearing, taking the path that led further into the jungle, away from the Mission where the women, even now, were preparing lunch.

That evening, they ate at the Mission without him, for the first time since she arrived. She sat alone, outside the circle round the cooking fire, until the glow died almost to nothing and the Nicobarese began to disperse, climbing the rickety wooden ladders to sleep.

He's avoiding me, she thought. He wants me gone.

She sat, wretched, waiting for him to return. One by one, the last figures rose. The fire turned to ash and the clearing became dark. The only noises were the crashes and snuffles of wild boar in the jungle around her, the clatter of insects in the undergrowth.

When she finally climbed up into the women's hut, she hunched into a ball. She thought of her bedroom in Port Blair. She wrapped her arms round her body for comfort.

She once longed to know what Edward's life on Car Nicobar was like so she could picture him clearly when he was far away. Now she knew. Every person, every smell, every sound of this place was embedded in her and losing it, losing him, was more than she could bear. She trembled, thinking of the sadness of the following day, her last, and straining to hear Edward return.

The next day, she told the schoolchildren that she was leaving.

They looked confused.

'Where will you be?'

She clasped her hands together and smiled with false brightness. She drew in the mud a rough map of the islands, showing Car Nicobar here, and the Andamans, with South Andaman and Port Blair, over there.

They stared at the drawing, then again at her.

'But why?'

She took a deep breath. 'Everything has a beginning and an end, doesn't it? We read about it in the Bible.'

The children shook their heads, puzzled, struggling to grasp her description of time.

She packed that afternoon, setting out her belongings in the scrub. Her clothes were in tatters after weeks of being washed by hand and dried in the sun. The children, gathered round, watched with solemn eyes. She looked at the lush jungle canopy. This is what she wanted to take, to preserve in Port Blair. She went across to a palm tree, trailed by the children, and picked up one fallen leaf, took it back and pressed it between her clothes.

That evening, her final one, Edward again failed to appear. Isabel sat quietly alone. She couldn't eat. Perhaps he won't come at all, she thought. Perhaps he's arranged for someone else to take me to the shore tomorrow, to see me leave. The thought made her physically sick. The warm air murmured with the sound of women's voices and, always on the breeze, the soft hush of breaking waves on the shore.

She must have dozed. She was jolted awake by a noise, the banging of a rhythm on wood, sounding insistently through the jungle. She sat up, alert. The noise rose, coming closer, solid and forbidding.

The women too lifted their heads to listen, then scattered the embers of the dying fires and gathered in a circle below one of the women's huts, forming an open mouth. A figure appeared at the top of the ladder. Sami's tall, lean figure began a slow descent. When she reached the ground, she stood, surrounded by the women, and reached her arms towards James. His eyes shone in the half-light as he watched.

A figure emerged from the shadows and came to stand by Isabel. Edward. His face was sombre. His eyes were on Sami and he spoke without looking at Isabel.

'This is not our business.'

The jungle swayed and parted and a group of tribal elders, dressed in paint and finery and carrying sticks adorned with bundles of leaves, broke into the clearing, their chief in the fore. He led the men in a ritualistic figure of eight, which encompassed the local women, drawing them into its circles.

Isabel said softly: 'What are they doing?'

'They've come for James.' His face was strained. 'They want to test him, to see if he has special powers.'

Sami began to ululate, her head tossed back. As the chief approached James, the boy's eyes widened with fear.

The chief led James to the centre of the circle and he sank to the ground. The villagers produced a skin of coconut toddy and poured it into shells, drinking and passing it round from one to another. After some time, when the onlookers seemed giddy with toddy, the wise men advanced, one by one, and took it in turns to brandish ceremonial sticks, garnished with leaf bundles. Each, with a cry, pulled a bundle open. A lizard fell from the first, lay stunned for a second by James's foot, then scurried away. The crowd cheered. A shower of shells cascaded from the second, bouncing and rolling over James's arm. Another cheer.

'What are they doing?'

Edward leant close. 'They're drawing bad spirits from his body.' He shook his head. 'He needs to be strong.'

Women began to adorn James. They tucked coconut leaves in his hair and painted his pale face with streaks of ash. He lay unresisting on the ground, his eyes closed.

When the women finished, the tribal men lifted James into their arms. They stretched an awning over him, a cover of plaited coconut leaves mounted on a stick frame and studded at its corners with fresh flowers and young leaves, bright with sap. The chief banged his staff on the ground and the villagers formed into a ragged procession, led by the chief and the elders, then the bearers who supported James and finally the onlookers. Several men lit torches from the dying fires as they moved with purpose towards the far depths of the jungle.

'I'm going too.'

Edward looked uncertain. 'I'm not sure that's wise.'

The jungle became increasingly dark. The smell of rotting fungus closed in. The moonlight was obscured, held off by the dense fingers of leaf and vine and the air thickened with the sickly smell of decay. They walked for some time, following the reflection of the torches. The only sounds were the chatters and screams of the night forest and the swish of bodies brushing against the foliage.

Finally the group emerged into a small clearing. It smelt

rancid. The tree trunks around it shimmered with blue fungus, which shed an eerie, other-worldly glow. Scraps of dirty rags, red, white and black, hung about the bushes and trees. The villagers stood in a close huddle. Women grasped at each other's hands for comfort. Their faces were sharp with fear.

The chief gestured for James to be lowered to the ground. The wise men began to chant. It was a low hum that seemed to resonate through the jungle and vibrate through them all.

James stumbled, as if in a trance, to the edge of the clearing, pushed forward by the wave of chanting. He hesitated, his legs trembling, then, with several dozen pairs of eyes focused on his back, he was swallowed by the blackness.

Isabel gripped Edward's arm. 'Where's he gone?'

Edward's lips were white. 'He'll meet the spirits of his ancestors. That's all I know.'

'Will he come back?'

Edward's eyes closed and his lips began to move as he prayed.

They waited in that strange clearing, clustered together in silence. They seemed balanced on a threshold between the world of the living and that of the dead. As they stood like statues in the dimness, waiting, time lost all meaning.

At last, a subtle shift in the darkness. A movement. Finally, it may have been minutes later, it may have been hours, James returned.

Isabel put her hand to her throat. The young man's eyes were wide. Sweat ran in runnels across his forehead and cheeks. His limbs trembled so violently that he seemed on the brink of collapse.

The wise men rushed forward and hoisted him in their

arms. The chief and elders marched out of the clearing, gigantic in the shadows of the fading torches. The villagers rushed to keep close.

When they reached the Mission clearing, the tension broke. James lay on the ground. His limbs juddered weakly against the earth. Sami sat beside him, stroking his face with the flat of her hand.

Isabel craned forward, trying to reassure herself that James was safe. A moment later, Sami let out a cry. She threw back her head and, eyes blazing, pointed an accusing finger at Isabel. Those around them in the clearing fell silent.

Strong hands grasped Isabel's shoulders and pulled her away. She twisted to see. Edward half-guided, half-dragged her back towards the darkness of the jungle, even as faces turned to follow her. The eyes were hostile. Sami's voice rose to a shout. She drilled holes in the air with a long finger.

'Hurry.' Edward turned her away and bundled her ahead of him into the trees.

Sami's angry shouts pursued them. They stumbled on in the darkness, leaves brushing wet against arms and faces, Edward's arm tight on hers. The creepers around them sweated with fresh sap and night heat.

They emerged at last onto the long beach where they had first come ashore weeks earlier. He pulled her across the cold sand to the cluster of low mud and wicker huts dotted there, prised open a loose section of the first and held it clear while she crawled inside, then followed her.

It was a cramped space, only just long enough for an adult to stretch out. She lowered herself to the dirt floor, and sat, blinking, her arms threaded round her knees as her eyes adjusted to the dark. Needles of light reached in through the wicker panels, pricking the blackness. The only sounds were the crash of the waves outside and Edward's close breathing. The air was stale, acrid with the remnant of smoke, which lay over a sickly cloying sweetness.

'She accused you of witchcraft.' He spoke softly.

'Witchcraft?'

'Of trying to curse her boy. If the elders believe her, they'll kill you. It's one of the few things—' He broke off.

Something scuttled across her arm and she jumped, brushed it off. She put her hands to her face, suddenly made nauseous by the sour-sweet smell.

'What is this place?'

Edward hesitated. 'A death hut.'

'Death hut?'

'They leave their dying here. They want to stop the spirits of the dead finding their way back to the villages, to haunt them.' He paused. 'It's one of the few places they're afraid to look, you see.'

'The ship will come in the morning, won't it?' She strained to see his face in the darkness. 'I can bear it until then.'

The air hummed with the sound of the sea. She thought of Sami's fury.

'She was jealous of me. From the start.'

He sighed. 'Perhaps.'

Their breathing, stirred up by the panicked flight, started to slow and settle and the silence between them deepened. Isabel blinked. Thin strands of moonlight reached down through the woven walls and made patterns of silver lace across her legs. Edward's silhouette gradually emerged from the gloom. He sat, curled forward, his shoulders hunched.

'I thought I'd never see you again.' She spoke softly.

His face was obscured by shadow. 'I couldn't bear it.'

He bowed his head. The close, warm smell of his body, so near her own, cut through the stench of the dead. She reached out a hand, tentatively touched his cheek.

'Why are you sending me away? Why, Edward?'

No reply. She sat with the silence, desolate. In a moment, he might leave and never return. A rustle of dry wicker as he shifted his weight. She held her breath and listened. A shudder, a sudden loud sob, hastily swallowed back. The catch of his breath.

She crawled forward and reached blindly for him, wrapping her arms round his huddled body and drawing him to her. He smothered a cry. His body was hard with tension and he held himself apart from her, even as she pressed her face into his chest. His skin, under his shirt, was smooth and moist. She ran her fingers across the broad muscle of his back and tightened her arms around him.

A tremor ran through his chest and for a moment, she feared he was about to push her away. She clung to him, buried her lips against his neck and kissed the fresh salt of his skin.

He groaned, lifted himself apart from her and searched for her face in the darkness. She pressed her eyes closed. Spangles of white light flew through the black.

Her voice was a whisper. 'Edward.'

Something broke in him. His movements became sure as he took her shoulders and eased her backwards onto the floor of the hut. His hands found their way beneath her clothing to her skin. She arched her back as his fingers ranged the length of her body. A low moan. His breath fell on her cheek.

She opened her eyes. His face loomed over hers, his face strained, his eyes closed. She ran her hands down the small of his back to the curved muscle of his buttocks and pulled them closer, digging her nails into his skin as he held himself above her. They began at once to rock, clutching each other. She lost all sense of herself as they moved, merging in the darkness not just with him but with the waves rising and crashing against the shore.

Afterwards, they clung together in the darkness. His arms were so tight around her that she could scarcely breathe. She buried her face against his neck, damp now with sweat, afraid to move, to break the spell. Edward, she thought. My love. Then, in panic: how can I go back to him now, to Jonathan? How will I bear it, after this?

Finally he pulled himself free and lay beside her. She tipped back her head to see his face in the half-light. His eyes were shut, his forehead tense. She traced his eyes, his cheeks, his lips with her finger.

'Edward.'

He didn't respond.

'I thought you didn't want me.'

His mouth made a hard line. 'How could you think that?'

'You're sending me back to him.'

He sighed and the judder passed through them both. 'You're his wife, Isabel.'

She reached her hand to the back of his head and stroked the short, soft hairs along his neck. 'How can this be wrong, Edward? How can it?'

He turned his face away. 'Of course it's wrong.'

Her mouth trembled as she began to cry. In a matter of hours, she thought, all this will be over. I will be gone.

'Don't.' His fingers reached for her cheek, wiped it. 'Please.' He turned, drew her to him, stroked her hair.

Already the darkness was slowly lightening with the first shade of dawn.

She struggled to speak. 'I don't want to leave.'

'I know.' Silence for some minutes. His voice, when he spoke, was strangled. 'I don't want you to. But you must.'

A breeze blew in from the sea, whipped across the surface of the beach and threw sand against the wicker. The walls pressed in on them both. She closed her eyes against the growing light and buried her face in his neck, hiding from the smell of death all around them.

She thought of the poor souls, men, women and children, who had lain here through the years, each in their turn, alone in the darkness, listening to the same low rattle of sand against the hut and the drumming of the waves beyond and knowing them to be the last sounds they would hear on this earth, their last fragments of life.

Chapter Twenty-Four

Isabel stepped down the gangway onto Port Blair's teeming waterfront. Her clothes were tattered and crumpled, her hair filthy. She hailed a tonga to the house.

Singh lazed on the ground, smoking with Cook. His mouth gaped. He jumped up, squashed out the remains of his bidi and rushed forward to greet her.

'Madam.' He led her up the staircase to the upper storey. The wooden stairs felt grand after the rickety ladders of the Mission. 'Hot water, madam, for bathing?'

'And some chai, please, Singh.'

Isabel sat with her china cup and saucer and silver teapot and looked out over the ordered flower beds, coconut palms and the jungle creepers stretching away up the hillside. It seemed very tame to her now. In the distance, a gramophone played a jazz tune. When she was last here, Edward had been with her. It seemed a very long time ago.

She thought of poor James who had been thrust into the darkness to meet the ghosts of his ancestors and emerged transformed. She closed her eyes and rested her head against the edge of the chair, overcome by a feeling of exhaustion and of emptiness.

Below, on the road, a car horn blared. She awoke in

confusion, uncertain for a moment where she was. Her mouth was parched and her neck stiff. When she opened her eyes, they fell on Jonathan. He sat across from her, one leg crossed over the other, a gin tonic in his hand. She looked down at the table between them. The tea tray had been cleared. Beyond, the sun was low and the light tangled in the coconut trees was yellow.

'I suppose I should say welcome home.' He studied her with the coolness of a cat. 'You look different.'

'Do I?'

He continued to scrutinise her. 'Sunburnt, of course, but more than that.'

She shrugged, looked away. She was different. After all she had seen, all she had lost, she was no longer afraid. 'We need to talk, Jonathan.'

'I won't divorce you. Do as you please, but keep it quiet.'

She wondered how long he had sat there in his chair, watching her. 'You want me to stay?'

'Yes. Play the part.' He got to his feet, set down his empty glass and crossed to lean against the balcony rail.

She looked at him with an odd sense of detachment. He was her husband and yet a stranger. If she left him and returned to Delhi, she would be a long way from Car Nicobar and Edward and the disgrace would ruin her parents.

'Leave the boy alone, Jonathan.' She thought of Bimal's red eyes. 'He's too young.'

He shrugged. 'He's old enough.'

The darkness deepened. In the trees, birds shrieked as they wheeled through the dusk and settled along the branches. Clouds of insects hung above the rail.

Singh stepped onto the balcony, set a mosquito coil on

the table and lit it. The smoke rose and dispersed, bringing bitterness to the evening air.

He picked up Jonathan's empty glass and paused.

'Another gin tonic.' Jonathan looked across at her. 'And for you, my dear?'

'Nothing, thank you.' She tried to force herself to smile. 'I'll go to bed, if you don't mind. I'm very tired.'

She withdrew, leaving Jonathan to drink on the balcony alone.

She woke early the next morning. For a moment, she didn't know where she was. The pillow was crisp and clean, the mattress soft. Above her, the ceiling fan sent ripples of cool air across the room. Then she remembered. She closed her eyes, bitter with disappointment. She couldn't find the will to move.

Jonathan's door opened and his footsteps sounded up and down the passageway. She traced his movements around the rooms until he clattered at last down the staircase, calling to Singh. A woman's tread followed, softer and more stealthy.

At seven o'clock, the bedroom door creaked open.

'Asha?'

Asha carried in a tea tray and set it on the bedside table, then turned to leave.

'You're back?'

'I am just returned, madam.' The girl hid her face, muttered something inaudible.

Isabel sat up. 'Where were you?'

Asha raised her hands to her face. 'My father's cousin, madam. In the village, in the jungle. He was very sick. They sent for me.'

'Why didn't you tell me?' Isabel frowned. It made no sense.

Asha turned her back and tugged at the mosquito screen to open up the window behind it. Warm air, scented with sea salt, drifted in, spread across the room by the turning fan.

'I'm very sorry, madam.'

'How is he? Your cousin.'

She pulled a face. 'He is passed, madam.'

Isabel watched her as she moved about the room, her eyes averted. 'I'm sorry.' She paused. 'But you should have talked to me about it, Asha.'

'Yes, madam.' She disappeared, closing the door with a soft click.

Isabel lay back against the pillows. Sami and the women in the Mission would already have risen, washed themselves in salt water and rubbed coconut oil through their hair. Their fires would be smoking. Soon school would start in the clearing.

In the passageway, Bimal crept to and fro. Singh would be setting her place for breakfast, her knife and fork the only cutlery on the long polished table. Familiar sounds drifted in from below through the open window. Cook's voice, scolding the kitchen boy. The clatter of metal pots. The hiss and sizzle of oil.

'Gracious, my dear! You look so thin.'

'And your skin! Burnt to a cinder.'

Mrs Copeland and Mrs Allen pecked at her, all smiles.

'So you taught savages!'

'Weren't you frightfully afraid?'

They tutted and clucked, herding her into the corner of the verandah until her back touched the rail.

'But my dear, what was Jonathan thinking?'

'Letting you go off like that. Quite absurd.'

The lawn of Government House stretched out behind them, its neatly mowed grass yellow in the afternoon sun. The white canvas of a marquee and its side tents rose on the far side, a sequence of meringues. Inside, Lady Lyons was holding one of her quarterly Ladies' Days, hosting the matrons of Port Blair to a grand afternoon tea.

Mrs Copeland and Mrs Allen cocked their heads and looked at her through narrowed eyes.

'Have you been terribly ill?'

'Banana. Mashed in rice. Always works. Cures the dickiest tummy.'

'Anyway, you shall eat now. Come along.'

They swept her between them, down the steps to the gravel path, which skirted the lawns and along towards the marquee. Isabel, used now to being alone, found the chatter overwhelming.

The interior of the marquee was a fug of overheated flowers. Sunlight bled through the canvas. Lady Lyons received them with warmth. Mrs Copeland and Mrs Allen started to prattle, singing the praises of the decorations, of the plates of miniature sandwiches, which the servants threaded through the crowd to offer.

After some minutes, Lady Lyons directed the ladies to the long tables at the far end of the awning where cups and saucers lay in rows for tea, then placed her gloved hand on Isabel's arm and led her out into the garden, down a gravel path between immaculately kept flower beds. She walked briskly, pausing every now and then to pluck dead leaves or to inspect a bloom.

'You really should garden.' She didn't wait for a reply. 'It's jolly difficult out here but it's important to challenge oneself.'

She paused at a straggly rose bush and lifted a drooping bud between two fingers. 'I had this shipped out from home as a seedling. Doesn't exactly thrive here but it's still alive. Suppose you could say the same of most of us.' She walked on, adding over her shoulder, 'One can always have pots. My father taught me that. He dragged us all over India when I was a girl. My poor mother hated being uprooted so often. Pots. Load them on a cart and off you go.'

The path narrowed on the far side of a copse of trees and revealed the harbour far below, glinting in the sun. The roofs of Port Blair made red blotches in the island green. She paused as Isabel caught her up.

'You were sensible to come today.' She spoke in a low voice, her eyes thoughtful. 'People are talking.' She paused. 'Whatever's happened between you, your husband's not an unreasonable man, you know.'

Isabel wondered how much Lady Lyons knew. They were interrupted by one of Sir Philip's men who came hurrying down the path. His hair stuck to his scalp and his forehead glistened with perspiration as he handed Lady Lyons a chit.

'From Burra Sahib, madam. Most important.'

She tutted to herself as she unfolded it. As she read, her expression changed.

She said under her breath: 'Always the worst possible times.' She turned to Isabel and added: 'We should go. There's a ferry waiting.'

'Go?' Isabel frowned. 'What's happened?'

'Our husbands need us.' She gave Isabel a keen look. 'I

really think it would be prudent of you to come.'

They took a tonga from the harbour directly to the jail and were ushered through the security gates in a flurry of procedure, then escorted to the open courtyard where Asha's father was once hanged. Windows blinked down on them from all sides, framing unseen eyes within.

A knot of uniformed men stood huddled together there, laughing. The group began to part as Lady Lyons strode forward. The laughter subsided as they caught sight of the women and their expressions turned to embarrassment.

The chief commissioner lifted his hand. 'My dear, I do apologise—'

'But what news!'

A body lay, wrapped round in a shroud of unbleached cotton, at the men's feet. The folds around the head were open, showing hair that was matted and littered with scraps of dried mud and debris. One of the officers touched it with the toe of his boot and passed a remark in a low voice.

Isabel stepped forward. She saw at once that these were Sanjay Krishna's features. His flesh was livid and bloated. His eyes were closed, his lips blackened.

Isabel flinched, took a step away, overcome by a wave of sickness.

'You got him.' Lady Lyons spoke briskly to her husband as if the rest of the company were deaf. 'Well done, darling.'

'Tip-off.' He tapped his nose. 'Local knowledge.'

'What happened?'

'He was already dead when they found him. Drowned. Tried to hide in a cave, by all accounts, but he picked the wrong one.' He nodded. 'Anyway, I can't take all the credit. Jonathan here commanded the search.' He gestured to Jonathan with an open palm. 'Top job, absolutely.'

Isabel swallowed down bile in her throat. Her eyes fixed on the ground. The dirt was mottled with boot prints.

The chief commissioner went on: 'We had to send in divers to haul out the body.'

'Why did you bring him here?' Isabel's shock sounded in her voice.

Jonathan said: 'He'll have the proper rites, don't worry. But first, these criminals need to see him.' He raised a hand and gestured round at the dark cell windows. 'They need to know what happens to men like him.'

Isabel turned her eyes back to the ground. A voice cried out, then another. They seemed at first to come from inside her head.

'*Jai Hind!*'

A cry, followed rapidly by answering echoes all around. The voices multiplied as the shout flew between the walls, many voices blending to one.

Sir Philip said: 'Stop that!'

The officers turned and ran, scattering, to the various doorways that led into the cell blocks.

'*Jai Hind!*'

Metal clattered against the bars. Prisoners on all sides, unseen in the darkness of their cells, raised their voices and beat out the rhythm of their chant.

'*Jai Hind! Jai Hind!*'

The mantra of Indian independence. The shouts resonated round the courtyard, bouncing off the brick walls, even as the guards raced into the buildings and down the corridors to silence them.

* * *

Isabel struggled to adjust to her old, solitary life in Port Blair.

Jonathan left early each morning and stayed away until late in the evening. They spoke to each other only in company and then very little.

During the long days, she took solitary walks, losing herself in the noise of the native bazaar and the harbour, where she was generally the only European in sight.

In the afternoons and evenings, she sat in her bedroom, looking out through the thousand squares of the mosquito screen at the stirring leaves of the jungle. In the quiet and stillness, Edward joined her and sometimes her childhood friend, Rahul, and Sanjay Krishna too.

A numbness descended upon her and a sense of powerlessness. I am waiting, she thought. I must endure this misery until change comes. She had no idea what that change would be.

Chapter Twenty-Five

Asha

Asha overheard Singh and Cook talking about her.

'Like father, like daughter,' Cook said. 'I always said so.'

She had her fingers on the handle of the kitchen door, coming to fetch a tray.

'She's a thief.' Singh's voice. 'They should beat her.'

A wooden spoon bang, banged against the sides of a mixing bowl.

'Madam is too soft.'

She pushed open the door and walked in. They saw her and scowled.

That afternoon, when Isabel Madam disappeared on one of her long walks, she dodged Singh and ran to the restaurant to see Amit.

He led her through to his private office at the back and closed the door. It was a dingy room, dominated by a shabby wooden desk, which was piled with files and loose papers. He pulled out a rickety chair and they sat facing each other.

Her mouth was dry. She sat very still, her hands clasped in her lap.

'I failed him. I disgraced my baba's good name.'

'He drowned?'

She nodded. It was her fault. She should never have left him.

'It's true, then.' He spoke softly, almost to himself. 'They took his body to the jail, that's what people say.'

Amit replaced his spectacles on his nose. His hands reached for a pile of papers on the desk at his side and began to shuffle them together. He didn't look her in the eye.

Finally, he said: 'Tell me.'

She stared at the papers and saw water there, saw Krishna-ji flailing as a growing torrent dashed him back against the rocks. She imagined him weakening, swallowing spray, then water, and finally becoming limp, floating, suspended in brine. She couldn't speak.

'It's a shock.' He nodded. 'Asha, you did what you could.'

She cried out: 'He sent me away. I went for help.'

Amit's hand reached out and pat, patted her shoulder. 'He was right to send you away. You have your own destiny.'

She wiped off her hot face with her dupatta. Her breath came in gulps. Krishna-ji told her what to do. She must carry out his wishes. She got to her feet, straightened her crumpled clothes.

'Where are you staying?' He paused. 'There's space for you here, if you need it.'

'I'm again with the Britishers. My madam was away but now she also is back.'

'You could go home to Delhi, to your baba's village even. I could help.'

'One day, maybe.' She considered. 'Now, I need to be with the Britishers. It was Krishna-ji's wish.'

'May the gods give you strength.' Amit put his hand on her head in blessing. 'Be careful, Asha.'

His face was full of concern. She thought: I divided my

heart into two pieces, one for my baba and one for Krishna-ji. These people killed them both. What more do I have to fear?

She planned with care, following the instructions that Krishna-ji gave her.

One afternoon, she went into Isabel Madam's room, opened her wardrobe and took a coat and hat. No one saw.

When Isabel Madam went walking, Asha found letters and papers that her mistress had written and learnt to copy her handwriting. Education is our weapon, Krishna-ji said. She practised the forged note many times before she was satisfied. Then she sought out Bimal.

Bimal hid himself in corners when the house was quiet. She knew the places. It took her only a few minutes to go from one to the other before she found him, curled in the servants' quarters, dozing. His legs were folded under him, his head resting on his arms.

'Bimal.' She crept into the room and sat beside him. 'Mango. Have some.'

He lifted his head and looked at her with suspicion.

She tore off a broad piece. The soft, sticky flesh hung along it in clumps. She flipped it inside out and pushed it at him.

'Come. It's good.'

He uncurled his arms, took the mango slice and started to scrape off the fibres with his teeth. Juice ran down his chin.

'Sweet, nah?' She peeled off a second slice and sucked on it herself. They sat together and slurped, licking the juice off their lips and fingers.

When the mango was almost finished, she said: 'Bimal, I know what Sahib does to you. He's a wicked man.'

The boy stopped eating, became tense.

'Don't you know?' She lowered her voice to a whisper. 'He does bad things to me, too.'

Bimal's eyes opened wider.

She sensed his doubt and added: 'Why do you think I ran away?' She gave the mango skin a final chew, then threw it out of the doorway into the dirt. 'We can help each other.'

He stiffened. Finally he said in his thick accent: 'What do you want me to do?'

'Madam wants to send us both on a very special errand.' She put her fingers to her lips. 'It's very secret. No one must know. Ever. You must promise.'

He put his head on one side, considering her.

She leant in closer. 'Afterwards, if you do as I say, Sahib will never be able to hurt you again.'

The pharmacist was himself a ticket of leave and a friend of Amit's. His shop was in a poor district of Port Blair, near the waterfront.

Asha led Bimal to a nearby alleyway and they waited there until the light began to fade. The first shopkeepers carried out their wooden shutters and slotted them into place over shopfronts, rattling chains across doors and windows. Soon the pharmacist too would close up his shop and disappear to the poky back rooms where his wife and daughter stirred steaming pots of food. Pools of light stretched across the road, catching the faces, the figures of the people who passed by.

Finally, Asha gave the forged note and some money to Bimal and sent him in. A moment later, she pulled Isabel Madam's hat down over her face, lifted the collar of her mistress's coat and stood in the shadows by the front of the pharmacy.

Bimal was inside. His slight body hovered at the counter. On the far side, the pharmacist studied the note, then the boy, then turned to look across his shelves. Her heart hammered. Krishna-ji, she thought, I am doing this for you, just as you asked.

Several minutes later, Bimal crept out with a paper parcel, tied round with string. She drew him into the shadows.

'Did he give you a receipt? A paper?'

He looked anxious. 'Inside the parcel.'

'Did he ask questions?'

'As you said. Why did my madam want datura? Did she know how to use it?'

'And you said?'

'I said as you told me: for the weeds in her garden, maybe. Ask her yourself, if you like. She's there, outside.'

'And he looked? He saw me?'

He nodded. 'Then he again read the note and again counted out the money, then finally wrote the paper.'

She nodded. 'Good boy.' She pinched his arm. 'Now, do you swear on your own life not to tell a soul about this? Whatever happens.'

His eyes widened with fear.

'Swear on your life.' Her voice became sharp. He was an easy boy to bully.

'I swear.'

She relaxed her shoulders. 'Go back to the house now. If anyone asks where you were, say you were sleeping. I will come after.'

She took off the hat and coat, brushed them both down and returned to the house to slip them back in Isabel Madam's wardrobe. She unwrapped the parcel and hid the pharmacist's receipt deep into the mess of papers inside her mistress's writing case.

Then she waited for the right moment, as Krishna-ji had told her.

Chapter Twenty-Six

Isabel

One Sunday, five weeks after her return, Jonathan disappeared for the day to join a seasonal fishing expedition organised by the chief commissioner's staff.

Isabel sat in the drawing room, reading. The shadows lengthened and, as she was thinking about going to bed, Jonathan's boots sounded on the staircase. He appeared at the drawing-room door.

Isabel lifted her eyes from her book. 'How was the fishing?'

His cheeks and nose were ruddy with sunburn. He stepped into the room and crossed to the balcony doors.

'Didn't catch much.'

'Well, you caught the sun, at least.'

He didn't reply. He wanted something of her and she was uncertain what. Singh appeared and placed a measure of gin on the table alongside a squat jug of tonic, then withdrew. Jonathan poured a third of the tonic into the gin, stirred it well, then stood for a time in silence, looking out, drinking. The insect chorus grew.

'We lost sight of the islands for a time.'

He seemed to speak more to himself than to her. She sat quietly.

'When I looked down, through the water, I could see such

a distance. A mile or more.' He sighed. 'There are hidden worlds down there.' He trailed off. His lips fastened on the rim of his glass.

She closed her book and shifted in her seat.

'You wouldn't understand.' His mood hardened.

Isabel rose to her feet. 'Do you want supper?'

'I've asked Cook to fry fish.'

She turned to the door. 'Goodnight, then.'

She left him there, a motionless figure in the gloom against a dark canopy of trees.

A rap on her door.

'Madam! Please!' A man's voice.

'What is it?' Isabel lifted her head from the pillow.

'Madam!'

'What's the matter?' She groped for her dressing gown. Her feet scrabbled for slippers.

'Burra Sahib. *Bimar hai.* Sick, sick.'

Singh was always immaculate. Now, there in the passageway, he looked dishevelled, his beard uncombed.

'Sick?'

The door to Jonathan's room was ajar. Inside, he lay on the bed, covered only by a cotton sheet. His red face was slick with sweat and he was thrashing, his head pitching from one side to the other, eyes closed.

'Jonathan?' She put her hand on his forehead. Burning.

He moaned but didn't speak.

She turned back to Singh. 'Fetch the doctor. *Jaldee!*' As Singh made for the door, she called after him: 'Wake Asha. Tell her to bring a cloth and cold water. Clean water. Make sure it's clean.'

She patted Jonathan's forehead, his cheeks, his neck with a cool flannel. He seemed tormented, tossing under the sheet and grimacing.

The doctor, a retired army surgeon, arrived with a coat fastened over his pyjamas.

He examined Jonathan wordlessly, took his pulse, eased open his eyelids to examine the eyes.

'Last night, did he have much to drink?'

'A gin tonic. Maybe two.'

'What did he eat?'

'Fish, I believe.'

He nodded. 'Has he vomited?'

'I don't think so.'

'He was on that fool fishing expedition, wasn't he?' The doctor looked grim. 'Bet he didn't wear a topee.' He rummaged in his bag and brought out aspirin powders. 'We need to lower his temperature.' He turned to Singh, a dark agitated figure in the passageway. 'Fetch ice, boy.'

For hours, they struggled to cool him. Isabel sponged Jonathan's face and neck. His lips murmured but the words were unintelligible.

Dawn broke, revealing the hard outlines of the bedroom furniture, the hollow contours of Jonathan's face. Below, the first hawkers sang as they passed from house to house, calling on sleepy servants to buy brooms and pots.

The morning sun reached through the gap in the curtains and drew a line across the bedroom floor. Jonathan gave a shuddering sigh, then fell silent. His cheeks became slack. The colour of his skin crept from white to grey. The doctor stepped back from the bed.

'Would you like a moment?'

She didn't understand. 'Should we try more aspirin?'

The doctor looked dull with exhaustion. 'I'm afraid it's too late for that.'

She looked down at Jonathan's still body.

'I'm sorry.' The doctor leant over the bed, lifted the top of the sheet and drew it up over Jonathan's face.

Isabel dropped the damp flannel in the water.

The doctor got to his feet and closed his bag. 'I'll notify the chief commissioner. Is there a friend, someone to sit with you?'

She shook her head. No friend. She looked at Jonathan's body. It was a mistake. People didn't die from fishing.

'But what—?'

'Heatstroke.' He tapped his head. 'He didn't suffer long.'

She said, as if in a dream: 'So that's it, is it?'

The doctor helped her to her feet and steered her out along the passageway and into a chair in the sitting room. Asha followed. He gestured to Jonathan's whisky decanter.

'Pour her one of those, will you? Steady the nerves.'

Asha rushed forward. As Isabel sipped, the rising fumes made her choke.

'I'll be back shortly.' He turned to Asha. 'Stay with her.'

Isabel stared sightlessly at the gold braid that edged the settee. The doctor's footsteps took him away. She had the odd sensation of looking down at herself, of watching the crisis unfold as if she were someone else. She was a widow, then. It made no sense. No sense at all.

Mrs Copeland came.

'You poor, poor girl.' She kneaded Isabel's hand between her moist fingers.

She clapped her hands in Asha's face and told her to fetch tea and be quick about it, then crossed to Jonathan's desk and started to sift through the piles of papers there.

'Now,' she said, 'we need to make a list.'

She settled herself on the settee, drank tea, ate Cook's floury biscuits and scribbled notes with a stubby pencil. 'What about his people?'

Isabel shook her head.

'There must be someone.' She narrowed her eyes. 'Parents? Brothers?'

'A cousin came to the wedding. Bernard. He's stationed upcountry.' She tried to remember. It seemed a long time ago. 'We married quickly, you see, in Delhi. There wasn't time for his family to sail.'

Mrs Copeland made a note. 'They must be informed.' She helped herself to another biscuit and bit into it, scattering crumbs across her plate. 'Had he discussed his wishes?'

'His wishes?'

'I don't wish to be indelicate, my dear, but arrangements must be made. You do understand. In this heat—'

A funeral. Hymns and prayers and a coffin lowered into the fertile wet earth. It wasn't possible. It was all unreal.

'I don't know. I mean, it wasn't something—'

'Of course not.' She bent her head. The pencil made a soft scrabble across the paper. 'I'm sure we can—'

'Madam.' Singh, at the doorway, all concern. 'Please.'

He moved to one side. A British police officer stood in the passageway. Two uniformed constables, Anglo-Indians, lolled behind him. They waited in silence.

Mrs Copeland sat forward and whispered: 'They've come to take him away.'

Isabel thought of the silent body, its features hidden beneath the sheet.

The police officer cleared his throat. 'The chief commissioner has instructed me to proceed. I trust you have no objection?'

Mrs Copeland answered. 'Of course she hasn't.' She turned back to Isabel. 'You haven't touched your tea.'

At noon, Mrs Copeland had Cook prepare lunch. Isabel sat in silence as Mrs Copeland ate.

Afterwards, Isabel withdrew to her room. She lay on her back and watched the pattern of light on the bedroom ceiling. Mrs Copeland's footsteps sounded up and down the passageway. Wooden shudders as she pulled open drawers in Jonathan's study. The scrape of the middle one, which always stuck. The low flap of papers.

Isabel closed her eyes. Her body, on the soft mattress, shook.

Banging at the door. The walls were solid with shadow. Her mouth was dry. For a moment, she was lost, then she remembered. Jonathan was dead.

'Madam.' Singh's voice. 'Burra Sahib is come.'

Sir Philip stood in the sitting room, turning his topee in his hands. Mrs Copeland was at his side. Their expressions were grave. Isabel had the impression, as she walked in, that she interrupted them.

'Bad news, I'm afraid.' His face was tense. 'I've requested a post-mortem. Thought you ought to know.'

Mrs Copeland's eyes were greedy on her face.

'A post-mortem?'

'Cause of death,' said Mrs Copeland. 'Apparently it's not clear-cut.'

Sir Philip frowned, rotating the topee steadily in his hands. 'Best to be sure. I have to advise you' – he coughed – 'better if you didn't leave Port Blair for now.'

'Leave?'

Mrs Copeland: 'I'm sure Mrs Whyte has no plans . . .'

Sir Philip withdrew. The two women stood alone, awkward together. Finally Mrs Copeland crossed the room and guided Isabel to a chair.

'I've told Cook to poach a little fish in milk.'

'A post-mortem?' Isabel imagined a knife cutting through Jonathan's skin, through that same body that was once in her bed.

'Best thing for shock. Poached fish. Mother swore by it.'

For the next two days, Mrs Copeland wouldn't leave. Whenever Isabel emerged from her room, Mrs Copeland appeared, large eyes glinting. She took control of the house, ordering the servants and dictating meals to Cook.

In her room, Isabel lay for hours on her bed. The fingers of light on the ceiling shifted and shrank as the sun moved.

On the third day, Sir Philip returned, this time accompanied by the British police officer. Mrs Copeland, peering out of the window, could hardly contain herself.

'Six constables. Goodness. And a van.'

Sir Philip wore a dark suit. He hovered at the drawing room door.

'It is my duty to inform you that a post-mortem examination of the remains of your husband has revealed traces of datura in the viscera. Therefore I have registered his death as murder, under section three hundred and two of the Indian Penal Code.'

It was his legal voice. She had heard it before, when he pronounced the final judgement on Asha's father.

'Datura?'

The police officer said: 'Poison, ma'am.'

Sir Philip continued. 'Isabel Whyte, I am arresting you on suspicion of the murder of your husband, Jonathan Whyte.'

The police officer shuffled his feet, then took a step forward. Isabel was seized by a rising wave of panic.

'I'll testify.' Mrs Copeland seemed elated. 'I've found evidence, in her writing case. She did it, all right.' She turned on Isabel, her eyes full of spite. 'Never liked her.'

Chapter Twenty-Seven

Asha

After the police-wallahs took away Isabel Madam, the house lost its life.

Singh puffed out his chest and ordered them about, pretending nothing had changed. He made Bimal dust and polish empty rooms. Cook made meals for the servants only. All the talk was of the scandal and of how they might find new positions without references. Cook, in particular, was angry.

'How does it look? A death from poisoning and me, a cook.'

When the house fell quiet after dark, Asha sought out Bimal. He flinched when she found him, hidden away in one of his dark holes.

'If you say anything, you'll hang.' She pressed her face against his. 'You bought the poison. You're as much a murderer as I am.'

His eyes shone with fear.

Asha passed the afternoons curled in Madam's chair. The trees at the window stuck green fingers into the sky. I did it, Krishna-ji, she told him, just as you said. She remembered his face as she saw it for the last time, his brown eyes sunk in their sockets, his body hot with fever. I avenged you and my baba also.

A mutter of voices rose like smoke from the servants'

quarters. The words were indistinct but she knew what the topic would be: how to find work. Where would she go? She didn't know. Go back to Delhi or to your baba's village, Amit had said.

It seemed now to matter so little. Her baba was gone and Sanjay Krishna too and, however long she lived and however hard she worked and wherever she travelled, she would never see them again and her life seemed a spoilt thing because of it.

She slipped on her chappals and went to the Hanuman temple to breathe the incense there and see the wilting flowers hung round the neck of the giant monkey statue and do puja in remembrance of those she had lost.

Chapter Twenty-Eight

Isabel

A thin British man with ink-stained fingers and a worn briefcase visited Isabel's cell. John Scott, he said. Government lawyer.

'Did you know my husband?'

He looked round at the foul-smelling bucket in the corner of the cell, the rickety wooden table and chair, the rusting cot.

'I didn't have that pleasure, Mrs Whyte.'

He wiped over the seat of the chair with his handkerchief, took a yellowing notebook and pen from his briefcase and unscrewed the pen's top.

'I am appointed to act as your defence counsel.'

Isabel sat opposite him on the cot and folded her hands in her lap. 'My husband and I did not have the happiest of marriages. But I didn't poison him.'

He didn't answer. He busied himself with writing a heading, putting date and place at the top of the page and underlining both.

Isabel said: 'Are they certain it wasn't heatstroke? He was out on the water all day. The doctor seemed to think—'

He interrupted without looking up. 'The symptoms of datura poisoning are almost identical to heatstroke. That's what led the good doctor astray. But the tests are conclusive. They sent samples to the government laboratory in Calcutta.'

Isabel looked at his head, bent forward over his notes. Strands of combed hair lay loosely across the pink dome of his skull. She clenched one hand with the other. 'Mr Scott, do you think I murdered my husband?'

His voice was without emotion. 'My personal opinion is really of no consequence, Mrs Whyte. My role is merely to represent you.'

Isabel looked round the cell. Flakes of lime from the walls peppered the floor. A single window, set high, gave a glimpse of empty sky.

She said: 'If you suspect me, is it right for you to take the case?'

He gave a frown. 'I depend on government work.' He made another note in blue, watery ink. 'Besides, no one else would take it.' He set down his pen and cracked the knuckles of his right hand. 'Now, shall we begin? Tell me exactly what happened on the evening of your husband's death.'

Isabel took a deep breath and began. He questioned her insistently on her final conversation with Jonathan.

'Did you quarrel?'

She shook her head.

He lifted his pen from the paper. 'Are you quite sure, Mrs Whyte?'

'Of course. Why do you ask?'

He gave her a queer look. 'We may face testimony to the contrary.'

Jonathan was dead. No one else had been present. 'From whom?'

He paused. 'The prosecution will argue that there was a fierce row between the two of you that evening. That your husband accused you' – he paused, searching for the most delicate form of words – 'of inappropriate conduct with a third party. That he threatened you with divorce and you threatened him.'

'Threatened him?' Isabel stared. 'Who said such a thing?'

'Your maid.'

The walls of the cell seemed to press in around her until they squeezed the air from her lungs.

'You said your marriage was unhappy. Why?'

She hesitated, looked down at her hands in her lap, at the wedding ring still on her finger. 'My husband's sexual tastes were,' she hesitated, 'unorthodox.'

'Indeed.' Mr Scott raised an eyebrow. 'I have no wish to be indelicate, Mrs Whyte, but I must ask you, in what sense?'

She blew out her cheeks. 'Our marriage was barely consummated, Mr Whyte. He seemed to prefer' – she hesitated – 'young boys.'

He set down his pen. 'That's a very serious allegation. Do you have evidence?'

She considered. 'We have a houseboy. Bimal. My husband mistreated him.'

'Will he testify to that effect?'

She thought of Bimal, crouched, tearful, in a corner of the balcony. 'I imagine so.'

'On the question of your own conduct,' Mr Scott looked over his papers. 'Your maid named a gentleman. A Mr Edward Johnston.'

'Edward?'

He gave her a sharp look. 'So you are acquainted with the gentleman?'

'He stayed with us, studied my husband's work.'

The pen scratched across the paper.

Isabel got to her feet and paced to the far side of the cell. Why had Asha dragged Edward into this?

Mr Scott watched as she walked back and forth. 'And how would you describe the nature of your relationship with Mr Johnston?'

'He's a friend. A colleague of my husband's. He's a government officer and missionary in Car Nicobar.'

'So I understand.' His eyes were sly. 'And you recently stayed on Car Nicobar with Mr Johnston, I believe?'

'With my husband's consent, yes. That's no secret.' Her face felt hot. 'I helped at the Mission School.'

He tapped his pen against the paper. 'The prosecution may summon Mr Johnston to testify, Mrs Whyte. If there has been any impropriety between you, it would be prudent to tell me now.'

She shook her head. 'Mr Johnston is an honourable man, Mr Scott. There was no argument that evening. I made no threat.'

'I see.' He closed his notebook.

That night, Isabel lay awake in the darkness. Scraps of moonlight made the lime-washed inner wall gleam with an unearthly glow.

She thought back to her first visit to the prison when Asha's father hanged. Jonathan sent him to the gallows. The girl had every reason to hate them both.

Somewhere in the darkness, a cockroach scratched across the floor and she drew the sheet more closely around her body. She's just a child, she thought. I never understood how she suffered, how she grieved.

She thought of Rahul, imprisoned far away in Delhi. She thought of Sanjay Krishna, striding through Delhi in his demand for freedom, chained like an animal in the hold of the SS *Maharajah*, bloated and defeated at last in a rough cotton shroud at the feet of his enemies. She turned on her side, lifted her hands to her face and wept.

Chapter Twenty-Nine

In the weeks that followed, Mr Scott made frequent visits to her cell. His pen scratched and his file thickened but they seemed to make little progress.

He returned often to the same questions. The prosecution had found numerous witnesses to testify that her marriage to Jonathan was not a happy one. Was she certain that she and Jonathan didn't argue on that final evening, as her maid said? Had there ever been talk of divorce? Her decision to accompany Mr Johnston to Car Nicobar, without her husband, had shocked many in Port Blair. How could it be explained?

She felt his eyes on her face as he repeated the questions, time and time again, and she rehearsed the same answers. Mr Johnston is an honourable man. There was no impropriety.

On one occasion, he said: 'You made certain allegations, Mrs Whyte, about your husband's sexual conduct. I interviewed your houseboy.' He checked his notepad. 'Bimal.'

Her heart quickened. 'And?'

'He denies there was any misconduct. Sahib was a kind man, he said. I quote: I loved him like a father.'

She got to her feet, paced to and fro. 'He was scared witless of Jonathan. Everyone knew it.'

Mr Scott closed his notepad and slid it into his briefcase.

'Everyone may have known it, Mrs Whyte,' he said, 'but if that is the case, it is strange, is it not, that no one will speak of it?'

He gave her his cold smile and got to his feet. He banged on the cell door with the heel of his palm to be released back into the outside world.

'I can only help you, Mrs Whyte,' he said, as he waited to leave, 'if you tell me the truth.'

The trial began.

Isabel was led to a stuffy room in a remote wing of the jail. As she entered, a prison officer grappled with the windows, set high in the outer wall. They seemed stuck fast. His only tool was a long hooked pole and the task of catching the worn ring at the top of each window and hauling it open was not an easy one. His efforts loosened specks of paint, which fluttered down and peppered his hair.

Battered ceiling fans turned overhead. There was a long table at the top of the room and she was escorted to a seat to one side of it. Chains, binding her wrists, were fixed to its arm. A dozen rows of chairs had been set out for spectators and, as she settled herself, she felt a general craning forward in her direction and an intake of breath, followed by windy whispers.

Lady Lyons sat on the front row in a subdued grey suit, flanked by Mrs Copeland and Mrs Allen in a flamboyant new hat. Mrs Allen flinched and looked away when she caught her eye. She knew others too, some by name, some merely by sight. Port Blair society had gathered in full force.

The prison officer released a second window with a bang and was anointed by a fresh shower of paint. At the same moment, a procession of British men filed in from the back, wove a path between the spectators and gathered behind the long table at the front. Mr Scott was amongst them, battered briefcase in hand. He and several other gentlemen stood reverently by their chairs and waited while Sir Philip settled into his place in the centre, grandly flanked by his men as if he were presiding over The Last Supper.

A middle-aged man rose and declared himself to be the chief prosecutor on behalf of the Crown. He was balding and his nose was bulbous and criss-crossed with veins. He tucked his right thumb into the side of his waistcoat.

'I submit,' he said, 'that this was a cold-blooded, premeditated crime.'

Isabel looked along the table to Mr Scott. His chin tipped forward onto his chest.

'Jonathan Whyte was a kind and patient man whose only crime was to marry unhappily.' He pulled his hand from his waistcoat and flourished it. 'The prosecution will show that his wife's infidelity drove him to threaten divorce proceedings against her, provoking such fury in her breast that murder ensued. A cunning murder. Murder with a poison whose symptoms were so similar to those of heatstroke that, had suspicions not been aroused, it might have lain undetected.'

Isabel saw at once how things lay. The ladies were round-eyed with shocked pleasure. This was the most delicious scandal to erupt in the Andaman Islands since Mrs Doyly was axed to death by her manservant. In the eyes of this community, she was already guilty. She closed her eyes as the prosecution began its evidence against her.

One of the most damaging witnesses was Mrs Copeland.

'How would you describe the accused, Mrs Copeland?'

She sniffed. 'When Mrs Whyte arrived in Port Blair,

I made every effort to befriend her. I would describe her, however, as a cold and aloof person.'

She spoke with deliberate care, as if rehearsed. Isabel looked across at Mr Scott. He bent forward over his papers, pen in hand, drawing a series of concentric circles and shading them in.

'How would you describe the accused's relationship with her husband?'

'Most peculiar.' She wrinkled her nose. 'After his marriage, Mr Whyte spent most evenings at The Club, everyone knows that. Why would he rather eat there, all alone, than go back to his own home? Well, it speaks volumes, doesn't it?'

'Indeed.' The prosecutor paused, shuffled his papers. 'You suggest in your evidence that the accused's affections lay elsewhere?'

She sniffed. 'While Mr Whyte dined at The Club, she and Mr Johnston had intimate suppers under his roof. Then she ran off with him to join the savages. It was the talk of the town.'

Sir Philip interjected: 'If you could perhaps confine your answers to evidence you saw or heard yourself, Mrs Copeland?'

'Of course, Sir Philip.' She smiled across at him.

The prosecutor continued. 'Mrs Copeland, you spent some time with the accused immediately after her husband's death?'

'I did.' She looked smug. 'As soon as I heard, I went straight round. Out of Christian charity.'

'And while you were in their home, you happened upon some surprising documents?'

She nodded emphatically. 'Someone had to look through her husband's papers for details of his relatives, addresses and whatnot, in order to write to them. Mrs Whyte was in no fit state.'

Isabel recalled the soft flap of paper as Mrs Copeland rummaged through their belongings.

'And what did you find?'

She looked round the court, savouring the moment. 'First of all, an incriminating letter addressed to Mr Whyte.'

'In fact, I have it here.' The prosecutor pulled a thin sheet of paper from his file. 'A letter to Mr Whyte from Assistant Commissioner Barnes, the officer in charge of the Cellular Jail. The assistant commissioner makes reference to enclosed material with regard to, I quote: your wife's regrettable conduct. He writes: Please be assured of my utmost discretion.' He turned back to Mrs Copeland. 'Did you then, or do you now, know to what this letter refers?'

Mrs Copeland pulled a face. 'I didn't at the time but afterwards I happened to invite Mrs Barnes, the assistant commissioner's wife, to tea and she told me everything. Apparently that woman, the accused, was in correspondence with one of the most dangerous subversives in the jail, that fellow who drowned.' She paused, for emphasis. 'She was a sympathiser.' She looked round the courtroom. 'We might have been murdered in our beds because of her.'

A tutting and bobbing of hats.

'Mr Barnes has made a statement to the court to that effect.' He pulled a sheet from his file and presented it to the court clerk to set before Sir Philip. 'Mrs Copeland, did you find anything else?'

'I did.' She glowed. 'A receipt in Mrs Whyte's writing case. From a pharmacist in Port Blair. For datura.'

'The same substance that was used to poison Mr Whyte?'

'Exactly.' She stabbed the air with a podgy finger. 'It was

275

made out to Mrs Whyte quite specifically. Dated a fortnight before his death.'

The prosecutor looked round the courtroom with satisfaction. 'I would like to submit to the court a signed statement from the aforementioned pharmacist. He confirms the sale of datura to the accused. He saw the accused with his own eyes, waiting outside his shop while her servant made the purchase. Clothing, matching the description he gave, has been found in the accused's wardrobe.'

He turned back to the witness. 'Thank you, Mrs Copeland. You've been most helpful.'

That evening, Mr Scott came to visit Isabel in her cell. He looked doleful as he seated himself at the rickety table and drew out his papers.

'You should have told me about your relationship with Sanjay Krishna, Mrs Whyte.'

Isabel paced up and down in front of him, turning on her heel in the small space. 'He wrote to me and I replied, that was all. It was nothing.'

'But enough to alarm Mr Barnes and your husband, it seems.' Mr Scott shook his head. 'Now, about the poison.' He pushed his spectacles back up his nose. 'The pharmacist is quite certain he saw you outside his shop. Have you any explanation?'

She leant forward and rested her forehead against the wall. The brick was cold and lime flaked onto her skin. She imagined how many other prisoners had pressed against it through the years.

'None.' She lifted her head and turned to face him. He regarded her without expression. 'Mr Scott, I did not murder my husband. I don't know what more to say.'

He straightened his papers into a pile.

'They have one more witness, I believe. Mr Edward Johnston.'

She sat down on the cot with a bump. Her breath stuck in her throat.

'He's here?'

'He's just arrived in Port Blair.' He watched her closely. 'He has made a request to see you.' He paused. 'I'm not sure that's wise.'

'No.' She shook her head at once, feeling panic rise. 'Please refuse the request.'

He slid his papers into his briefcase. 'That's probably for the best.'

'Will he testify?'

'The court won't sit over the weekend but I expect him to be called on Monday.' He got to his feet. 'As you know, he's a man of God. If anyone speaks the truth under oath, I would imagine it might be him.' He gave her a curious look. 'If, as you say, there has been no impropriety in your relationship, his testimony may prove helpful.' He turned to leave.

She said in a rush: 'Will I be required to give evidence?'

'I'm preparing a written submission.' He gave her a tight smile. 'I'm not sure it would be advantageous to call you for questioning.'

'But you will present our case?'

He gave a tight smile. 'Frankly, Mrs Whyte, I'm not sure I have a case to present.'

Chapter Thirty

Asha

Cook found a new position. An Anglo-Indian family, recently settled in Port Blair and amused to tell their friends: our cook was in service with the deputy commissioner, you know, the one who was poisoned to death.

The salary was less, Cook said, but what to do?

Asha walked into the kitchen to find him on his knees, rifling through cupboards. He pulled out dishes and bowls and ladles and wrapped them, one by one, in newspaper and packed them into wooden cases. He hummed as he worked.

'You can lose that look.' He turned, a carving knife in hand. 'Good things, nah? Expensive things. No point in waste.' He wrapped up the knife and slotted it down the side of the case. 'Sahib is expired, may the gods bless him. And don't tell me she'll be needing them, not where she's bound.' He chuckled. 'She won't be needing anything.'

Asha left him and trailed back up the staircase to the upper storey. However much polish Bimal rubbed into the tables, the rooms had died since they became empty. The spirit of the house was flown and the space held nothing but sadness in it.

She ran a hand along the top of the planter where her mistress liked to read. A strand of her brown hair was still caught there in the wicker. It shone in the low light, which pressed through the shutters.

In Isabel Madam's bedroom, she opened the wardrobe, fingered the finely stitched clothing, then turned to the dressing table and slid open the top drawer. Jewellery was packed neatly in boxes. Silver bracelets and gold ones too and necklaces with precious stones, which used to sparkle on her mistress's bare neck in the lamplight. She knew every piece. She had cleaned and polished them for months. She hesitated. She was owed wages, wasn't she? She thought of Cook's words: she won't be needing them, not where she's bound.

In his office at the back of the restaurant, Amit held up first one piece and then another. His eyes bulged behind his spectacles. The light, catching the fine gold and silver chains, sent filaments of sunshine across his desk.

'Are you become a common thief, child?' He didn't look at her, he looked at the jewellery as it twisted in the light. 'What would your dear baba say?'

'Can you sell them?'

He shrugged. 'They'd fetch a lot.'

He spent time arranging the jewellery on the papers in front of him. The chains. A bracelet. A necklace set with a single turquoise. Then the fancier, grander pieces with multiple stones. Rings set with rubies, even a diamond.

After admiring them for some time, he lifted his eyes to her face and said softly: 'I won't sell them. It's a very wrong thing.'

Her cheeks became hot. She scooped up the jewellery and pushed it back into her pockets.

'I need money, Amit-ji. I want to go back to Delhi. I want to become a teacher.'

'A teacher?' He considered her for some moments in

silence, peering at her through his spectacles. 'I will arrange everything. I will give you money also, for your passage and food and all. But leave the jewellery, child.' He hesitated. His eyes became solemn and sad. 'For whatsoever deeds you have done here in Port Blair, may the gods forgive you.'

The trial was almost over. Soon, the verdict would come. Once she heard it, she would sail from that place. But before that, she needed to see her mistress. She needed to be certain that she suffered, as her baba had suffered and Krishna-ji too.

In return for rupees, Amit's friend, the guard, granted her a mercy visit, a chance for the loyal maid to comfort her beloved mistress. That might be arranged, he said as he pocketed the cash.

The smell of the jail stabbed deep in her belly, the sour stink of despairing men, packed close together. She stopped to catch her breath, pulled her dupatta closer round her face. Last time she came here it was to visit Krishna-ji, desolate in his cell. It seemed a long time ago.

The guard led her through the gates, then along a dim passage, dotted with cells and stopped at last beside a heavy door.

'If she kicks up a fuss,' he whispered, 'you'll have to leave.'

Asha shrugged. She was here now. The rest was in the hands of the gods.

He peered through the spyhole, then drew back the bolt, turned the key and opened the door. She slid through the narrow gap.

The room stank. The shabby cot, the slop bucket, the rickety chair and table were as dismal as those she had seen in Krishna-ji's cell.

Her mistress lay on the cot, her eyes closed. Her hair, once so neatly groomed, hung about her neck in rats' tails. She wore a prison dress, a rough piece of serge, which bunched around her slim waist. Asha thought of the fine clothes hanging in the wardrobe at home, clothes that she had stitched and brushed and hung.

Her mistress opened her eyes and sat up.

'Asha?' She seemed lost for a moment. 'Is it morning?'

'Yes, madam.' She said it without thinking, then cursed herself. She was a prisoner now, no longer her madam.

Isabel Madam blinked, stared around her. 'I was dreaming. Dreaming about you, Asha, and here you are.'

For a moment, Asha didn't know what to say. She wanted to enjoy power over her enemy. She expected Isabel Madam to rail against her, even to strike her. In fact she looked pitiful. Stripped of her finery, of her rank, she looked tired and broken.

Isabel Madam lifted her legs over the side of the cot and set her feet on the floor. Her movements were slow and careful. She arched her back, stretched her arms.

Asha thought: Why care for your body when it has so little time left in this world? Soon it will rot in the ground. Like the bodies of those I loved.

'Tell me. Why were you the mistress and I the maid?'

Her mistress looked surprised, then sad.

'I don't know, Asha.' She nodded thoughtfully. 'There's no justice in this world, is there?'

Isabel Madam picked up the one chair, set it near the cot and, with a twist of her hand, invited Asha to sit. It was the way she seated her guests, all those days ago in the old life, for afternoon tea.

Asha sat down, then watched Isabel Madam settle again on the cot. The mattress was threadbare and sagged under her weight. Isabel Madam set her hands in her lap. Her fingers were thin. Her wedding ring fell forward to her knuckle and she pushed it back with an automatic movement.

'I'm glad you came.' Her cheeks were hollowed but her voice was calm. 'I wanted to see you.'

Asha narrowed her eyes. It was a trick. Harden your heart against your mistress, Krishna-ji had said.

Isabel Madam said: 'You did it for your father, I suppose?'

Asha glanced at the cell door. No one knew she was here, only Amit's friend.

'For my baba, yes. And for Sanjay Krishna-ji.'

'Sanjay Krishna?' She looked surprised. 'You knew him?'

'I loved him.' She paused. Isabel Madam's eyes were fixed on hers, alert. 'Those letters he sent you? I was bringing them.'

'But how?' She looked puzzled. 'How did you know him?'

'In Delhi. You Britishers martyred his uncle, that same man who saved me from the slum and sent me to school. Sanjay Krishna protected me when my baba was sent away to prison for so many years. For what? For serving his master, only. He was a simple man, a good man.'

Isabel Madam looked dazed. 'So much I never knew.'

'I ran with him, when he escaped.' She pointed to her chest. 'I did that. I hid in the jungle for so many weeks and fed him, tended him, tried to save him.' She paused, remembering the bitterness of his death. 'Until you hunted him down.'

Isabel Madam slowly nodded. 'When you disappeared. That was it, was it?' She spoke in a low voice. 'I see now.'

They sat in silence for some time. Isabel Madam's eyes settled on her hands, composed in her lap. Her forehead tensed in a frown.

'You hated my husband. I see that, Asha. We did a great wrong, to you and your baba.'

The room blurred and swam. Asha blinked, forced her mouth into a tight line. Harden your heart.

Isabel Madam spoke slowly, choosing her words with care. 'You're a clever girl, Asha. I always knew that.' She paused. 'You poisoned him. I understand. But why pin the blame on me?'

Asha mastered the corners of her mouth at last and tried to smile. 'You don't know, do you? My baba and me also, we were of so little consequence, nah? Crushing an ant under your shoe and walking on without a thought.'

Isabel Madam's face was puzzled.

'Your sweeper, all alone, with a baby daughter to care for? He never stole money. But your mama and baba dismissed him just the same. With no reference, he had no hope of another job. That is your justice, madam. The justice of Britishers. Now you understand.'

She walked to the door, banged on the wood for the guard to let her out. She didn't look again at Isabel Madam. She imagined this as her moment of triumph. In fact, her chest was tight with a suffocating sadness, a pressure she could hardly bear.

Chapter Thirty-One

Isabel

The sky was black that night. Isabel sat on the cold floor, her knees drawn up to her body and her back hard against the door of the cell. She fixed her eyes on the high window. A fragment of darkness was framed there. She imagined dissolving into it and becoming nothing.

Tremors ran through her legs, making her feet judder against the ground. She slid her hands to the floor. It was rough with fragments of grit and grainy to the touch. Death rushed towards her. She felt its coldness, smelt its rotten breath in her face. Not feeling. Not being.

She put her hands to her face and felt the sharpness of the bones, the hollows of her cheeks and eyes. How could it be? It was nonsense, all nonsense. She saw it all so clearly but there was nothing she could do to save herself. Asha was too clever. She was caught fast.

She pulled herself to her feet and started to pace, back and forth across her cell. Justice. How could there be no justice? She banged the flat of her hands against the door until they smarted. The warm wood shivered in its frame. She tipped back her head, opened her throat and screamed. The cry, shrill and other-worldly, echoed round the walls and flew back to her. She slumped back to the floor, sank her face in her hands and wept.

Edward was in Port Blair. He wanted to see her. If she closed her eyes, he was almost there with her, in that bleak cell. His arms tightened round her. His fingers touched her hair. His body, pressing down on hers, smelt warm and close as they clung to each other in the death hut, their last night together.

The pain sat with her for a long time. Slowly, even as she still sobbed, her thoughts began to shift and expand. Rahul and Sangeeta were there. Asha and her father. Sanjay Krishna and the condemned men, chained like animals in the hold of the ship. The prisoner on hunger strike, a man whose name she never even knew, locked in a cell like her own until force-feeding caused his death.

She shifted her position on the hard floor. Memories from childhood crowded round. Her father when she was a child, lifting her onto the back of her first pony and leading her round the paddock and joy so intense that it overwhelmed her. Her mother, resplendent in a feathered hat, presiding over the tea tray in the drawing room, while outside the monsoon threw puddles across the verandah. She blinked against her palms. It was finished for her, this life, but the disgrace would haunt her parents for years to come.

The night was still. She thought of the Mission hut on Car Nicobar, where the calls and caws of the jungle sounded constantly and the air shimmered with the slow, thick breathing of women, generation huddled against generation.

She thought of James, that solemn boy, who crossed the boundary between this world and the next. He entered the realm of his ancestors and returned to rejoin the living, cauterised by knowledge.

But most of all, she thought of Edward. His gentle, strong

presence each evening, as they sat side by side in the darkness, watching the dying fires and the Nicobarese gathered round them. She shook her head. He would be ruined. It was her doing. She would go to her death knowing it.

They would force him to take the witness stand and he would speak the truth, of course he would. He was not a man to lie before God. He would confess his feelings for her, for the wife of a fellow officer. They committed adultery. He would admit it, how could he not? His own reputation both as a man of honour and as a man of God would be destroyed. The prosecution would hound him. He would be left with the knowledge that, in admitting his feelings, he would also, in the eyes of the court, confirm her motive for murder and send her to the gallows. She pressed the heels of her hands into her eyes until the darkness spangled.

Her legs ached from sitting. She got again to her feet, strode back and forth through the faint ladders of shadows drawn on the floor by the barred window, light and shade, light and shade. She would hang. The walls shrank around her. That already seemed certain. But there might yet be a way of protecting him.

She drew the rickety chair to the table and reached for pen and paper. In the half-light, barely able to read the words on the page, she began to write.

Afterwards, her body exhausted, she sank again to the floor and watched for some hours the soft changes in the sky as the night receded.

The jungle stirred and woke and a chorus of birdsong broke the silence. This routine breaking of the day seemed a phenomenon of such great beauty that she felt ashamed to think of all the dawns that she had never risen to witness and all the days she had squandered, little realising how few remained.

Mr Scott lifted his eyes from the papers in his hands. His face was hard with curiosity.

It was Sunday. She had to beg the guard to summon him and Mr Scott had looked cross when he finally arrived.

'You do understand what this means?'

'I am of perfectly sound mind.' She gazed at him levelly. 'You will agree with that, I hope?'

He narrowed his eyes, set the document to one side and considered her at length. 'This furious argument with your husband. It was all about your friendship with Sanjay Krishna, you say.'

She nodded. 'That's why I went to the Nicobar Islands in such haste.' She hesitated, swallowed. 'My husband found out about my letter to Mr Krishna, as Mrs Copeland and Mr Barnes both testified. He was furious. It remained an issue between us, even after my return. That's why I administered the poison. I couldn't bear the arguments any longer.' She paused, then added with some force, 'Any suggestion that my relationship with Mr Johnston was improper is nonsense. Nothing but malicious gossip.'

'I see.' Mr Scott's eyes never left her face. 'Mrs Whyte, do you wish to die?'

Her eyes followed the fragments of flaked lime on the floor. 'No sane person wishes that.'

'But you state quite clearly here that you murdered your husband in cold blood. You leave no room for leniency.' He pressed forward on his hands and pushed himself to his feet. 'When it comes to sentencing, Sir Philip will have little choice.'

Her hands clasped each other in her lap, turning her wedding ring in an endless cycle. 'I understand.'

He crossed to the cell door.

She said: 'The prosecution will be satisfied, I assume?'

'I imagine so.'

On the far side of the door, the bolt scraped back. Mr Scott hesitated. 'I'm curious, Mrs Whyte. What made you change your plea at this late stage?'

'I want to leave this world with a clear conscience.' She steadied her breath. 'That's all.'

When Sir Philip entered the courtroom on Monday morning, his expression was grim. Isabel fixed her eyes on her hands. Edward might be there. She couldn't bear to see him.

The prosecution lawyer read her confession to the court. His voice was strong and his delivery theatrical. The men and women of Port Blair strained forward to listen.

Afterwards, the guard prodded Isabel to her feet.

Sir Philip's eyes were cold.

'Mrs Whyte, is this your own confession, given freely and fairly?'

'It is.'

'You have changed your plea to guilty?'

'That is correct.'

He sighed. The room fell silent as he reached for his black cap. His stern voice echoed through the room.

'Isabel Whyte, I find you guilty of the murder by poisoning of your husband, Jonathan Whyte. I sentence you to be taken from this place and hanged by the neck until dead, so help you God.'

Chapter Thirty-Two

Asha

It was dusk. The fisherman curved forward, then pulled back, tightening the muscles along his arms and legs, forcing the rowing boat through the waves with urgent strokes. He was elderly and his teeth were stained red from chewing betel.

At first, the salty breeze across the water was pleasant but as the setting sun sent red streaks across the dark expanse of sea, it became chill. Asha wrapped her shawl round her head and shoulders.

'Bas, madam. Far enough, nah?' He sat, resting his forearms on the gathered oars, and waited as she twisted round and looked back at the black water. Beyond, further down the coast, the lights of Port Blair shone. Waves slapped against the wooden sides of the boat, rocking them. Below, an endless volume of water threatened oblivion.

'*Thik hai.*' She nodded. 'It's fine.'

He lit a bidi and smoked, his eyes gazing vacantly across the water.

She opened her bag and put together her offerings. She prepared each with care, taking a broad green leaf, adding a pat of ghee, rolling a strand of cotton into a wick and embedding it deep in the ghee, then, finally, placing in the leaf, beside the ghee candle, a bright-yellow flower which, until an hour ago, grew wild in the bushes close to the shore.

When she was ready, she looked down at the swirling water. She blew out her cheeks and lit the first wick, cupping her hand to protect it from the wind.

The fisherman steadied the boat as she leant out and lowered the first leaf over the side. Cold air rose from the depths. The sea, falling away beneath her, smelt of salt and of decay. The leaf swirled in the current and the flame flickered, battered by the breeze, then again raised its head.

'May the gods bless Sanjay Krishna.'

She bowed her head. Pictures came to her. Of the handsome youth who saved her in the chaos of the parliament attack. Of the charismatic man who sheltered and cared for her in his uncle's home. She blinked, remembering. The flame shimmered more faintly in the darkness as it travelled from her on its journey into nothingness. Of the fighter who had faced death alone, sending her from him, back into the world. She wiped her eyes with her scarf, then strained to search for the point of light. It had already disappeared.

She breathed evenly and waited until her hands were steady enough to light the second wick. She lowered that leaf into the water, to follow the first.

'May the gods bless my dear baba.'

The water took this leaf at once. It turned softly, finding its path on the swell.

She seemed to feel again her baba at her side, lying against her for comfort as he did when she was a child, his heavy arm round her, keeping her safe, his breath warm in her hair, her neck.

She sat, hunched, for a long time, gazing into the night, afraid of losing sight of the leaf as the low wind drew it from her. The tiny flame shuddered and vanished at last into the vast ocean, into the great darkness.

Chapter Thirty-Three

Isabel

'You have a visitor.'

'A visitor?' She lifted her head from the cot.

'Your father.'

She closed her eyes. She hadn't expected the news to reach her parents so soon. She shook her head. 'I don't want to see him.'

The guard's footsteps crossed the cell towards her. 'He says he's come a long way.'

He fastened a cuff to Isabel's wrist and drew her out along the corridor without another word. It was the first time she had left the cell since sentence was pronounced. The shouts and moans of other prisoners drifted down the corridor. The smell of bodily filth, roughly covered with disinfectant, pressed in on her, making her dizzy.

She was taken to a small room, bare apart from two chairs and the table between them, all bolted to the floor. The guard attached the chain to a ring in the table and took up a position behind her. Isabel lifted her wrist and felt the weight of the metal drag it down again. She didn't want her father to see her tethered.

She twisted to appeal to the guard but already the door was opening.

Edward, broad and solid in the doorway. She blinked. Her mouth dried. His expression was solemn as he strode in. He was a man built for the natural world and he seemed too large for the small room. His eyes ran across her face, reading everything there, then ranged over her crumpled prison clothes. She tried to struggle to her feet to greet him, tugged back by the chains.

'They said it was my father.'

'I'm sorry. Your lawyer, Mr Scott. He said you wouldn't see me.'

She slumped back into the chair. Her eyes fell to her hands, gathered now in her lap. Her nails were unkempt and rimmed with dirt and she hid them from him.

He took a seat opposite her and motioned to the guard to leave them.

The guard shuffled, hesitated.

Edward said sharply: 'Haven't I paid you enough?'

The guard withdrew. The bolt scraped shut as he fastened the door behind him, leaving them alone. Isabel bit her lip. For a moment, the silence pressed down.

'You shouldn't have come.' Her fingers twisted in her lap. She couldn't raise her eyes to him.

'I've appointed a new lawyer. A private fellow. He's already looked over the papers.' Edward sat forward. His manner was businesslike. 'He plans to appeal. First, we retract your confession. Did they force you to write it? Did they threaten you?'

She shook her head, wretched.

Edward's hands twitched. He reached into his jacket pocket and pulled out a pack of cigarettes, shook one free and lit it. He reached across the table and held it to her mouth. Her lips trembled and she pulled away.

'You know what really happened?' She struggled to keep her voice steady. 'Asha poisoned him. Asha, my maid. She told me. She wanted revenge.'

He straightened up. 'Revenge?'

'Jonathan hanged her father. And my parents wronged her. A long time ago. I was just a child.'

'Can we prove it?' He seemed galvanised. 'Even introducing an element of credible doubt—'

'We can't prove a thing.' Isabel sighed. 'She's too clever.'

He sat for a moment, thoughtful, and drew on his cigarette. He exhaled and the smoke filled the space between them.

When he spoke again, his voice was softer.

'The lawyer wants to go after Bimal. If he agreed to testify that Jonathan' – he hesitated – 'that he behaved indecently, it would show you told the truth.' He paused. 'It might even loosen someone else's tongue.'

She considered this but didn't reply.

'If we could arrange for Bimal to see you, could you persuade him? It would mean contradicting his earlier statement.'

He was such a frightened boy, a child who cowered in corners to cry. 'I don't know.'

'Try to find a way.'

He drew on his cigarette, blew out smoke. The smell took her back to the beach on Car Nicobar, smoking together after a bathe, the sun warm on her skin. She blinked hard.

'So why did you confess?' Edward's eyes were on her face. 'If you knew it was Asha.'

'I can't tell you that.'

294

He frowned. 'We'll argue it was a moment of insanity, that's all.'

She bowed her head and breathed hard. There was so much she wanted to say.

'Go back to the island.' Her words came in a rush. 'Whatever happens, you mustn't testify, Edward. They'll ruin you.'

The guard called through from the corridor. 'Time is finished, sahib.'

Edward shouted: 'In a minute.' He turned back to her. 'I may have to testify. Anyway, that doesn't matter.'

'It does.' Her mouth twisted.

Behind him, the door opened. 'Sahib. Please be coming.'

He scraped back his chair. 'I must go. Don't cry, Isabel.' He paused, looking down at her. 'God be with you.'

She bowed her head and felt him leave her. The door slammed shut. She held on to the sound of his footsteps as they slowly faded down the corridor and waited for the guard to return, to take her back to her cell.

She didn't know how they persuaded Bimal to enter the prison but he did come.

When the guard closed the door behind him, he stood with his back pressed against it. He looked round the peeling walls with eyes full of terror.

'Bimal. Are you well?'

She took his arm and led him to the chair. She sat on the edge of the cot and bent forward to him.

'I'm so sorry, Bimal.' She spoke in a low, steady voice. 'I've thought about you a great deal.' She gestured round the walls, which pressed in on them both. 'I've had plenty of time, I suppose.'

He wouldn't raise his eyes to look at her.

'I wanted to apologise.' She thought of his silent shadow around the house. 'My husband hurt you terribly. I failed to protect you. I'm sorry.'

His mouth trembled. He opened his mouth and for a moment, he seemed about to speak but no words came.

'You're a good boy, Bimal. I know that. I want to make peace with you before' – she paused, feeling her way to the right words – 'before I go.'

He looked stricken. He didn't respond.

She went on: 'I want to leave you something. I don't have a great deal but I'll leave instructions. Do you understand? You mustn't be afraid to take it.'

His face twitched but still his eyes stayed fixed on the edge of the cot.

'It might be enough to buy an apprenticeship, perhaps, or a small shop. When you're older, you can take a wife and have a proper home.'

She got to her feet and rested her hand lightly on his shoulder. It was hard with tension. 'Take it with my blessing. Please.'

He sat with his shoulders hunched.

She walked across the cell towards the window.

'It's a peculiar thing, to face death.' She spoke quietly. 'It forces a person to assess their life, you see. To weigh their sins.' It was bright outside. When she tilted her head back, the sky between the bars was clear. 'The day of reckoning comes for us all, in the end, Bimal. I know that now.'

A shudder. She looked round. Bimal had sunk his head in his hands. His shoulders shook.

'Don't cry.' She crossed at once and reached an arm round him. 'I didn't mean to upset you.'

He resisted at first, then finally yielded as she pulled him towards her. She knelt there for some time, his head against her side, stroking his hair as he sobbed.

When he recovered, he wiped off his swollen eyes and, when the guard returned, he left her without a word.

Afterwards, she lay on the cot as the daylight slowly faded to night. Her eyes ran back and forth, tracing the dark stains across the ceiling until the cell became too dark and they disappeared from sight.

Days passed. There was no word from Edward.

Isabel spent the long hours sitting in a corner of the cell, with her knees raised and her arms, thin now, wrapped round them, and looked up at the small window on the sky. The daily passage of the sun seemed extraordinary to witness. The subtle shifting light of morning and evening, the shrill whiteness of noon. She sat alone and stared, watching with reddened eyes, thinking.

A steady toc-toc-toc drifted in from outside, from the courtyard below. A scaffold was being erected, she knew it without being told. It took her thoughts back to Asha's father's death. She lived it all again, imagining herself in his place. The blackness of the hangman's hood. The coarse rope of the noose, rough against her skin. The sudden bang of the trapdoor. The frantic flailing legs as her body fell away into nothingness, into eternity.

The good ladies of Port Blair would be discussing what to wear for the hanging. Mrs Copeland and Mrs Allen would make reservations at The Club for luncheon so they could raise a glass together as her body cooled.

She was too nauseous to eat. In her mind, she rehearsed

every detail of her meeting with Edward. His manner was so stern. Was he angry with her? Perhaps he thought her capable of murder. She tried to feel his presence in her cell, as she had felt it so strongly when it filled the room. Always, she heard again his final words as he rose to leave. God be with you. They had an air of finality, of an ultimate goodbye.

Sometimes a bird wheeled, high and broad-winged, riding the rising currents of air as another afternoon moved towards its close.

Gradually, day by day, she became weaker. She took to her cot and spent hours lying there, her cheek pitted by the rough blanket. Shards of bright light reflected off the wall. Her body scratched with heat. A fly buzzed close to her ear but she didn't have the strength to sit up, to wave it away. Her head ached.

She didn't have the will or the appetite to eat the food they brought. The sounds of sawing, of hammering, in the courtyard below gave way to silence. The scaffold must be finished. The time had almost come.

Her thoughts drifted, unanchored. She was on Car Nicobar again, the waves booming on the sand. Edward was there, sun-warm and safe. Day and night merged to become a grey shapelessness of fitful dozing, half-dreaming and half-remembering.

'Isabel.' A woman's voice, urgent. 'Wake up.'

Her mind stirred, struggled to free itself, swam up at last to the surface.

Someone was talking, there in the cell. 'She's coming round.'

They had come for her, then. This was the moment. She had thought herself prepared, at peace with the world. Now, as she faced the prospect of dying, panic seized her. Not now. One more day. One more hour. I beg you.

A hand clasped hers. A soft hand. She tried to open her eyes. Lady Lyons loomed over her, her powdered face all concern.

'Isabel, can you hear me?' Her breath was sweet. 'It's alright, Isabel. You're safe. Do you understand?'

She shook her head. A dream, then. Others were there too, crowding the cell, absorbing its light. She twisted her head. Men with solemn faces gazed down at her.

'Mrs Whyte. I have just signed the papers for your release.' Sir Philip's patrician voice. She managed to move her head, to look. There he was, ruddy-cheeked, flanked by guards.

Her eyes moved slowly back to Lady Lyons' face. It swam.

'It's true, my dear.' Lady Lyons' face showed Isabel how pitiful she must look. 'Bimal told Sir Philip everything. That dreadful maid made him buy the poison. She dressed up in your clothes to fool the pharmacist.'

'Poor Bimal.' She thought of the boy's wretchedness when she played on his conscience.

'Try to sit up.' Mrs Lyons lifted her shoulders from the cot and helped her to sit. Her clothes smelt of rosewater. 'I've brought you a little tea.'

A silver tea tray sat on the grimy floor, with a china teapot and matching milk jug and a lidded sugar bowl.

'Just a dash of milk, isn't it?' Mrs Lyons stooped to lift the jug and pour. 'I always remember how people take their tea.'

She steadied Isabel's hands as they raised the cup to her lips. The rim juddered against her teeth.

'You must stay with us for a little while, at the Residence,' she said.

Behind her, Sir Philip shuffled his feet.

Isabel looked more closely at the men clustered round him in the cell. She recognised some. An Anglo-Indian warder. Two of Sir Philip's officers. A guard. There was no sign of Edward.

Lady Lyons took the cup and saucer from her hands and set it down.

'We need to build you up. Heaven knows, it's all been quite a business, hasn't it?'

Chapter Thirty-Four

Isabel rejoined the world slowly, gaining appetite and strength each day. Government House was spacious and well-appointed and her hosts were generous. Lady Lyons was often occupied with social functions. Isabel found herself left to her own devices for long periods and she was grateful.

In the mornings and evenings, when the sun was less fierce, she sat often in a planter in a small pagoda in the west corner of the garden. It gave striking views out over the sloping lawns and splendid gardens of the Residence towards the sharply glistening stretch of water far below, which separated Ross Island from Port Blair.

In the mornings, as she sipped her tea, her spirits were seized by a fluttering lightness. It will be today. Edward will come today. In the evenings, the lengthening shadows and mellowing light reflected her brooding disappointment that another day was ending without sight of him.

She thought often, even as her eyes travelled over the page of some book on gardens from Lady Lyons' library, of her last meeting with him inside the prison. She knew how wretched she looked then, how dirty and unkempt and utterly without hope. He had saved her. He appointed the lawyer who won her appeal and directed him. The fact Edward had taken such trouble on her behalf gave her cause to hope. But his manner had been so businesslike, so impersonal. And now she was free, why didn't he come?

When she allowed herself to lift her eyes, they ranged over the distant bustle of the waterfront. It was too great a distance to make out even a vehicle but she imagined sometimes that she saw him striding there, head high, arms loose at his sides.

Eventually her eyes always crept higher, rising above the terraced roofs of Port Blair to the black blot of the Cellular Jail, which crouched on the hillside with its reaching arms. I was imprisoned there, she thought. In that dark, desperate world from which there seemed no hope of escape.

At times, when she lay in bed, hovering in the half-world between sleep and waking, she felt herself still there, and, overwhelmed by panic, sat upright, eyes staring, blood loud in her ears.

'Mrs Whyte, how marvellous to see you!'

Mrs Copeland bustled into the sitting room at Government House, her arms outstretched. Her lipstick made a thick, bright smear across her mouth.

'Gracious, you lucky thing, even black suits you.'

Isabel rose to greet the new arrivals and Mrs Copeland took the opportunity to look her up and down.

'A little thin, perhaps, but Cook will soon see to that, won't he, Lady Lyons?'

Mrs Allen, a few steps behind, gave a shrill laugh.

'Mrs Whyte! We've been so worried. You simply must write your memoirs.' Mrs Allen inclined her head in appeal to their hostess, Lady Lyons. 'They might publish it in that new women's magazine.'

Isabel settled back in her chair beside Lady Lyons and let the women talk on. She had no desire to see them but Lady Lyons had insisted. She looked now at Mrs Copeland's waving hand, sparkling with diamonds. The summer heat was intense and her round cheeks were flushed. Last time they saw each other, Mrs Copeland had been on the witness stand, trying to send her to the gallows. She remembered the spite in her eyes.

'You're right, Mrs Copeland, of course.' She assisted Lady Lyons by handing out cups of tea. 'Lady Lyons' cook is beyond compare.'

Mrs Copeland reached for a jam tartlet. 'Everyone has quite forgotten those dreadful rumours. The ones about you and Mr Johnston.'

'Such an unpleasant business.' Mrs Allen nodded. 'Your reputation seemed quite ruined.' She leant forward. 'I heard that the gossip reached the Bishop of Rangoon himself. Imagine. His own missionary.'

'As you say, it's all forgotten.' Lady Lyons' tone was brisk.

Isabel gave a tight smile. 'But Mrs Copeland, do tell me your news. Please.'

Mrs Copeland's eyes gleamed. 'You've heard about the fancy new bakery on the waterfront? I wouldn't usually entertain shop-bought bread. One can't employ a cook and let him sit around idle all day. But several local ladies are praising the bread and cakes simply to the skies, so eventually I decided . . .'

Lady Lyons, sitting with a straight back, her hands composed in her lap, glanced at Isabel as the women started to unburden themselves of the talk of the town. Stay calm, her look seemed to say. It will pass.

After some time, the conversation turned to politics. The latest batch of English newspapers, newly arrived in Port Blair, carried prominent reports on Mr Churchill's inflammatory remarks about Germany and Chancellor Hitler and the threat of war.

Mrs Allen lowered her voice. 'One might think the Great War was beginning all over again.'

Mrs Copeland helped herself to a second tartlet. 'It's such scaremongering. I'm surprised they don't silence him.'

'Well, I don't suppose they can.' Mrs Allen's face creased with worry. 'At least we're safe here. Whatever happens in Europe, it shan't reach India.'

Mrs Copeland sprayed crumbs across her plate. 'Normally I have the highest regard for Mr Churchill. But on this issue, he leaves me cold.' She turned to Isabel. 'You're very quiet, Mrs Whyte. Are you unwell?'

'I do have a slight headache.' Isabel gave an apologetic smile. 'How kind of you to notice. It must be the heat.'

'I do recommend lemon water,' Mrs Allen chimed in. 'Drink it tepid, never cold or it chills the teeth.'

Mrs Copeland gave Isabel a shrewd look. 'Will you be repairing to cooler climes, Mrs Whyte? I don't suppose you have reason to stay, now your dear husband has so sadly departed.'

Lady Lyons spoke up at once. 'How funny you should ask, Mrs Copeland. Mrs Whyte plans to return to Delhi at the first opportunity. Her father serves there, of course. Gerard Winthorpe.'

'And your lovely mother was Georgina Hancock before marriage, was she not?' Mrs Allen simpered. 'I had the pleasure of meeting her aunt, Davinia Hancock, in Calcutta many moons ago.'

Mrs Copeland narrowed her eyes. 'Port Blair will certainly miss you.'

'Indeed we will.' Mrs Allen nodded along. 'What a shame.'

They got to their feet.

'It's been such a pleasure,' said Isabel, rising too. 'My husband thought so highly of you both.'

'And we of him.' Mrs Copeland put on her gloves, finger by finger. 'And to think that wicked native girl is still on the loose.' She picked up her handbag. 'One's not safe in one's own bed.'

'Indians.' Mrs Allen gave a soft tut. 'My parents served here for thirty years. Never trusted them.'

Sir Philip's office arranged a passage for Isabel on the SS *Maharaja*. Her departure was just two days away.

One of Lady Lyons' servants brought trunks of Isabel's effects from her former home. She sat amongst them in her bedroom at the Residence and pulled out dresses and slacks, blouses and jackets, making colourful heaps across the floor. One of Lady Lyons' maids hovered at her elbow.

'This one's very gay, madam.' The girl lifted a cerise evening dress, trimmed with silver braid. She held it against herself.

'Take it.' Isabel's mother had chosen it for the wedding trousseau. Isabel had only worn it once, at a dinner party with Jonathan's friends.

'Oh, madam. I couldn't.' The girl hesitated.

'It's no use to me.' Isabel looked over the rest of the clothes, picking out a few pairs of dark slacks, a black linen jacket and a woollen one, two simple grey and black dresses. She put them to one side to be laundered and packed.

As for the vividly coloured clothes, it would be a relief to part with them. From now on, she was a widow with no one to please but herself.

'By the time I'm out of mourning, most of those clothes will look ancient.' She nodded to the maid. 'Please, help yourself. And what you don't want, give away.'

The girl began to trawl through the silks, satins and cottons with fresh enthusiasm.

'What about this dress, madam? For this evening?' The girl held up a full-length black gown. It was a classic style, cut from a pure, shimmering water-silk.

'I don't know.' Isabel reached out a hand to take it. She had worn this dress at The Club, the night she first met Edward, set off by a bright shawl. 'It's a bit much, isn't it?'

'Not at all, madam.' The girl came forward and held the dress against Isabel. 'With a plain black shawl, pinned across the body. Here, perhaps.' She twisted Isabel round to look at the effect in the mirror and gathered the material at her waist. 'I could stitch it here.' She considered. 'I think it's elegant.'

Isabel gave a sad smile. It was a lovely dress but the face in the mirror was weary.

'Well, I have to wear something,' she said finally. 'But do find a large, modest shawl.'

That evening, Sir Philip and Lady Lyons took Isabel to a formal function at The Club. It was her first appearance in wider Port Blair society since Jonathan's death and her last before leaving. She must be seen publicly with them, Lady Lyons insisted, to quash doubts about her respectability.

Lady Lyons looked Isabel over as they gathered in the hall. 'Black can be so unforgiving. But you're still young,

Mrs Whyte.' She led her down the steps to the waiting tonga. 'Too young to be a widow.'

Sir Philip and Lady Lyons made their entrance into The Club's ballroom, with Isabel awkward at their side. The light was already fading, giving way to candles, which set the polished brass fixtures gleaming. Overhead, ceiling fans glistened as they span. Diamonds and burnished gold shone on women's pale throats.

The evening was heavy with the remnants of the day's heat and the French windows stood open, leading the way to the gardens beyond. The strains of an Anglo-Indian band, seated outside on the shadowy lawns, drifted in.

'What a splendid evening!' Lady Lyons greeted the head of The Club's social committee with warmth. 'I do congratulate you.'

Isabel let her eyes slip across the faces, picking out former colleagues of Jonathan's and the wives at their sides. One or two gave stiff nods. They don't know what to believe, she thought. They're not quite sure if I'm a murderess, after all.

A waiter presented a tray of drinks. Sir Philip handed flutes of champagne to Isabel and his wife, took a Scotch for himself. He nodded to a corner where men in evening dress stood in the shadows, further obscured by a fug of cigar smoke.

'I might perhaps . . . ?'

'Of course, darling.' Lady Lyons patted his forearm. 'We'll see you a little later.'

They watched him cross to join the gentlemen. Isabel's breath caught in her throat. Edward was there. Staring right at her. Her fingers ran with champagne as the glass tipped in her hand. He stood on the far side of the group, concealed behind other men. She'd caught a mere glimpse of his face, of his eyes on hers, framed in a narrow gap. She blinked and stared and the moment passed. He had turned away.

'Come.' Lady Lyons steered her towards the French windows and the relative cool of the garden. A light salt breeze rose from the sea below. The musicians, seated to one side in their striped uniforms, shuffled in their seats, lifted instruments and struck up the next tune.

'You're on public display.' Lady Lyons spoke quietly in a voice only Isabel could catch. 'Never forget it.' She lifted a hand and greeted an oncoming tide of ladies. 'Mrs Harris. How lovely you're looking. And Mrs Benning too. What a charming dress. You remember Mrs Whyte?'

Isabel barely heard them. Blood roared in her ears. Her cheeks glowed. Edward was here. It took all her strength to stop herself from turning back into the ballroom and crossing it to join him.

When Lady Lyons moved on through the crowd, Isabel hung back. The chatter, the heat were suffocating. She walked out of the crowd to the far reaches of the gardens where young couples sat on blankets, champagne glasses in hand, laughing and murmuring.

She chose a deserted spot in the darkness under the trees and settled herself on the grass. The shrill band music was muffled by the foliage. Around the flower beds, cicadas screeched. As the pounding in her head settled, the rhythm of the sea, beating against the rocky shore below, rose to comfort her.

She lit a cigarette and inhaled deeply. He had been here all the time, then, here in Port Blair. He must have known she was staying at the Residence. Everyone did. She drew again on her cigarette. She felt sick and a little faint. He saw her, she was certain. He saw her and turned away.

She considered. Dinner would soon be served. She would simply hide in the shadows, then make her excuses to Lady Lyons and leave. Another two days and she would be gone. She need never see these people again.

She pulled her shawl closer round her shoulders and lit a cigarette. After some time, the dinner gong rang out. The young couples rose and drifted away towards the marquee. The night air settled. Isabel lit another cigarette and her nerves calmed. She looked out over the black water. The scent of the jungle pressed in from beyond the garden. It was a cloying smell of fertile vegetation and moist growth. Somewhere out in the trees, wild monkeys barked and branches crashed as they swung through the trees.

'Mrs Whyte?'

She jumped, turned. Edward's voice. She knew it at once. She hadn't heard him approach. He stood just a few feet away, his shoulders broad and square in silhouette.

'Are you well?'

'Perfectly, thank you.' She got awkwardly to her feet. She felt a fool, caught skulking in the trees like this. The back of her dress was damp from the ground. She wasn't sure what time it was. Dinner had ended and voices wafted down from the top terrace where people were gathering to watch the fireworks. The first cracks and zings rang out. Above, the night sky flashed red and white with sparks.

'I'm disturbing you.' He hesitated.

'Not at all. Have you got a smoke? I've just run out.'

They sat together on the grass. He lit two cigarettes and handed one across. There was a time when we shared the same cigarette, she thought. A time when you sat so close at my side, the heat of your body warmed my leg.

'I hear you sail soon.'

She nodded. 'Friday. Back to Delhi, to my parents. For a while, at least.' She blew out a trail of smoke. Overhead, a rocket exploded in a stream of colours. 'What about you?'

'Monday.' He paused, smoking. 'I've just signed up for another tour.'

Her stomach contracted. Another tour. He had bound himself to Car Nicobar for the next four years. She said: 'That's wonderful.'

'A real chance to build the Mission.'

This was it, then. She looked ahead into the loneliness of the coming years, knowing she would never see him. 'Will you come to Delhi ever?'

'I shouldn't think so. I'll be lucky if I get as far as Calcutta. You know how things are.'

She steadied her voice. 'Well, I am glad to see you. I wanted to say thank you.' She hesitated, trying to find the words. 'If you hadn't come. If you hadn't appointed that lawyer, well, who knows?' I'd be dead, she thought, and we both know it.

He didn't answer.

'I've arranged a settlement for Bimal. Not a vast sum but enough for him to get by, if he lives carefully. It seemed the least I could do.'

He nodded without looking at her. 'That's kind.'

'Seems I'm rather well off now.' She laughed but the sound was thin. 'Thanks to my service widow's pension. I don't suppose I need worry too much.'

'I'm glad.' He reached forward, stubbed out his cigarette under the rocking toe of his shoe as if he were preparing to go. She was seized by a sudden wave of panic.

'I didn't mean—' She broke off. What did she mean? 'If I ever harmed you, your reputation, because of what happened, I'm so sorry. I would never deliberately—' She tailed off as he got to his feet.

He thrust his hands in his pockets and stood there, looking down on her. 'It was never your fault. None of it.' His voice was thick. 'I can hardly bear to think about it, what might have happened. It was all my fault, my fault entirely.'

He seemed about to leave, then hesitated and turned back to her. 'I always cared for you, Isabel. I hope you know that.'

He strode quickly away before she could answer, leaving her alone in the shadows, helpless as she watched him disappear.

The porters hurried up the gangplank of the SS *Maharajah*, with Isabel's trunks and suitcases swaying in towers on their heads. Bimal waited on deck to point the way to her cabin. He wore a new jacket and swaggered a little as he directed them. Isabel, watching from the dockside, saw that already the boy was less afraid of life.

'If we find ourselves in Delhi, we shall certainly pay a call.' Lady Lyons was at her side. 'One never knows.'

'My parents would be delighted.'

A whistle sounded. Ship stewards took their places at the top of the gangplank to greet passengers. Men and women pressed forward and started to board.

'My husband bumped into Mr Johnston at the office yesterday.' Lady Lyons gave her a thoughtful look. 'He asked quite deliberately to be remembered to you. He wanted to know what time you were sailing.'

Isabel bent down and picked up her bags.

Lady Lyons scanned the crowd. 'I rather wondered if he were planning to see you off.'

'Oh, I shouldn't think so.' Isabel's tone was light. 'We said our goodbyes at The Club the other night.'

'Did you?' She nodded, her eyes on Isabel's face. 'My husband says that the Mission and those junglis are his whole life. He'll never leave them.' She pressed Isabel's gloved hand. Her fingers were warm and firm through the cotton. 'Anyway, I wish you a smooth sail. The winds are so variable.'

'I don't know how to thank you. And Sir Philip.' She paused. 'You've been so kind.'

'Nonsense.' Lady Lyons became brisk. 'I shan't wait. I've a luncheon at twelve-thirty and I do hate to be late.'

When Isabel paused at the top of the gangplank and turned back, Lady Lyons had already disappeared in the swirling crowd.

On board, Isabel said goodbye to Bimal and headed out onto the top deck. She stood against the rail. The wood under her hands was warm and smooth with wear.

The bustle on the dockside below became more frenzied as workers untied the ropes. Chains wound with a clatter into the hull. The engines, fired up, set the rail trembling. Wood creaked and heaved as the ship shuddered finally into cautious movement.

'You know, it's jolly beautiful, the jungle and mountains and everything, but I can't wait to reach Calcutta.'

A young girl, eighteen or nineteen, in a fresh cotton frock. Her hair, pinned loosely under her hat, fell in blonde streaks around her shoulders. She pulled off her gloves and put out a hand, eyes shining, to shake Isabel's.

'Jennifer Whittaker. Daddy's an assistant commissioner in the Forestry Department. George Whittaker. Do you know him? Well, anyway, I'm engaged, you see, that's why I'm off to Calcutta. It's awfully exciting.'

Isabel smiled. 'He's a lucky young man.'

'Freddy? Well, I don't know about that. But I am looking forward to being married.' She seemed finally to take in Isabel's black clothing. 'I say, I am sorry.'

'Thank you.'

The girl looked at Isabel more closely. 'You look awfully familiar. Did you come to one of Daddy's dinners?'

'I'm afraid not.'

'Or his party at The Club?'

'No.' She hesitated. 'I had my picture in the newspapers, though. Maybe that's it.'

'Did you?' She looked intrigued. 'Are you very important?'

'They tried to hang me. For murdering my husband.'

Her eyes widened, then she blushed and, twisting away, looked fixedly at the rail. Finally she stammered: 'How awful.'

'Actually, it was.'

The girl fidgeted with her gloves, then turned abruptly and disappeared.

Seawater sloshed against the rusting metal side of the ship. Isabel's nostrils filled with the stink of fish, sharpened by salt. The choppy gap between the ship and the dock widened to the width of a stream, then a narrow river. The ship sounded its horn with a single deep note as it pulled away.

Faces on land tilted towards them, brown, weathered circles set along the water's edge. She ran her eyes across the vanishing crowd. Brown-skinned dock-workers in lunghis,

313

their bare chests shining in the sun. Scurrying porters in faded cotton uniforms. Hawkers with trays round their necks, selling snacks. Chai-wallahs weaving in and out with clay cups of milky tea. Here and there, the taller figures of Europeans in topees and long-sleeved jackets.

She stopped, blinked, looked again. A face seemed turned towards her. A European man. She narrowed her eyes, half-blinded by the glare from the water. Was it Edward, that fixed point in the swirling crowd? She strained forward to see, gripping the rail until her knuckles whitened. Already, the figure was too blurred, too far away. She lifted her hand and waved in a broad arc as he and the figures around him softened and melted into one.

The ship gathered speed. She stared doggedly back at the receding shoreline, telling herself it was indeed him, that he stood there still, looking after her. The harbour and the rising hillside with its tiered red roofs shrank to nothingness, overwhelmed by the mass of dark jungle above.

The chill grew as they gained open sea. The vibrations from the engines coursed through her body and numbed her. She stayed at the rail, a solitary figure, as the final traces of the islands disappeared completely, swallowed at last by the vast silence of the Bay of Bengal, as if they had never been.

Part Two

Chapter Thirty-Five

Delhi, 1942

Isabel sat on the verandah with a glass of nimbu pani at her elbow. The shadows were lengthening. It was February, one of her favourite times of year. The late afternoon was cool and mellow.

The newspaper lay across the table in front of her. Nothing today on the fighting in the East. She would ask her father when he came home. She lifted her head, reached for her drink and looked out across the lawn as she sipped.

A light breeze stirred the mango trees and threw shifting patterns across the grass. She saw herself there, a child running over that same patch of lawn, crawling through those bushes, chasing the family of peacocks that strutted there now. Rahul was with her, a boy again, playing hide-and-seek.

The old magnolia tree they used to climb all those years ago was stirring into new life. It might blossom in the spring. Before the war, they gave it up for dead.

Isabel looked at her watch. They had guests coming for dinner but she might just have time to ride before her bath. She called to the syce to saddle Gypsy and went inside to change into riding clothes.

The bungalow echoed with muffled noises. Her mother, calling to Cook. The slosh of water as her mother's bath was prepared. Abdul appeared from the kitchen and padded barefoot down the corridor with a pitcher of heated water. He stooped and his hair was streaked red with henna to disguise its grey. She remembered him from her childhood, a thin, startled boy, sent to the Chaudhary's cramped home in search of her. Now he was a grandfather.

She rode west, taking a path out through the fields towards the open countryside. The land was recently turned, ready for planting. Village women bent low as they weeded and cleared ditches. The plumage of their vivid saris – indigo, turquoise, gold – shone against the dull brown of the earth. Men, stripped to their lunghis, whipped the flanks of bullocks to press them forward through the dirt, dragging plough-blades behind them. Their backs shone with sweat.

Gypsy snatched at the bit, eager to gallop, and she had to strain to hold her back. The path ahead narrowed. An elderly man, strolling towards her, stepped off into the ditch to let her pass and bowed his head. The air was brittle with dying heat and thick with the rich scent of earth. The path powdered to dust where Gypsy set her hooves.

Ahead, the path looped and turned to the right towards a small village and a crossroads there, which would allow her to turn back towards the bungalow. She had ridden further than she planned, she'd be late, but she didn't regret it, it was simply too lovely an evening. A plume of birds rose, cawing, from a cluster of trees off to one side. They wheeled and disappeared over the fields.

The light was full as it turned from white to gold and she felt a surge of well-being. Edward would stay safe. She wouldn't allow herself to think anything else. The war would end and he would come back. Perhaps, if Sarah and

Tom invited him to Delhi, she might even see him again.

Gypsy tossed her head, tugging, and she shortened the rein. The first dark huts of the village came into view. There was a gnarled tree at the crossroads, she knew it from childhood. The old men of the village liked to sit in its shade on wooden benches to drink chai and smoke bidis. She'd known her father stop there sometimes, when they rode together, to greet this man or that and listen to their troubles. Ear to the ground, he told her. Catch a problem before it happens.

She thought of him now as she approached and of the life he'd made for them here. Burra Sahib. How proud she had been as a little girl to ride through the countryside at his side and see men put their hands together in namaste or scramble to touch his boots in respect. He cut a fine figure then, a broad-shouldered man who could swing her up onto her pony without a thought. Now, his knuckles were swollen with arthritis and his bones crooked.

The benches under the old tree were dotted with hunched men. She nodded to them as she turned Gypsy to pick up their homeward path, holding her with care as they passed a shuddering bullock cart, loaded with potatoes and stunted cauliflowers. A village dog ran out and snapped at Gypsy's hooves and she patted the mare's neck with her left hand to steady her.

The copse of trees lay just beyond a dip in the path. She was only a few hundred yards away when the men stepped out. Young men with cloths tied across their noses and mouths. Several held staves, fresh wood, cut perhaps from the same trees. In amongst them, the low light flashed on a knife or sword. Her stomach gave a sudden contraction.

They glared at her and the deliberate way they emerged as a group from the shadows of the trees made her hands shake. She was almost upon them. There was nothing for it, it was too late to turn, she must simply ride on.

'Easy, Gypsy. Calm, girl.' The feeble sound of her voice made her more afraid.

One of the men took a step towards her and raised his club. '*Jai Hindustan Ki!*' His brown eyes gleamed. His cry was taken up by those around him. Others lifted their staves high in the air and waved them in tight fists.

For a second, she hesitated. There were too many of them. Perhaps she should stop, talk to them in Hindustani, reason with them. If they were locals, they must know her, know her father certainly, since they were small boys. The men straddled the path. Their chants grew wilder, their gestures more menacing.

She slackened the rein and gave Gypsy her head, squeezed her sides, urging her forward. She broke at once into a fast trot, approaching a gallop by the time they crashed forward into the knot of men. Staves cut through the air, whistling round them. Gypsy reared, rolled a wild eye, twisted, lashed out with her front hooves in panic.

Isabel focused on Gypsy's neck as she struggled to hold her steady and to keep her seat. Something struck Isabel across the side of the head, above the eye. Gypsy's front legs plunged back to earth and she tossed her mane, snapping, as a man grabbed at her bridle. Thwack. A stick smacked her across the haunches.

Gypsy screamed, pitched forward, flattened her ears and bolted through the men, scattering them with flailing hooves until, a moment later, they were through and beyond, galloping along the open path, Isabel pressed low along Gypsy's neck, breathing the heady scent of the mare's sweating coat, Gypsy's mouth flecked with foam, the men and their shouts already receding, fading to an ugly memory as the calm of early evening again knitted and settled around them.

'Good Lord! Isabel, what on earth—'

'What happened?'

She hoped to creep past them from the stables but they were sitting on the verandah with cocktails: her old schoolfriend, Sarah Winton, John Hargreaves, newly promoted to Superintendent of Police, and his stout wife, Dorothy, and Isabel's parents. The horror in their faces made her lift her hand to her head. Her fingers found the thick stickiness and crust of congealing blood.

'It's not as bad as it looks.' She looked at her bloodied fingertips. 'I'll just clean up.' She made to turn and continue inside.

'But darling—' Her mother was on her feet.

Sarah's face was all concern. 'Did you take a tumble?'

'Not exactly.' She hesitated. 'Gypsy's got a nasty gash. They had nails in those sticks. They must have.'

'Nails?'

Dorothy said: 'My dear girl.'

Hargreaves took a step forward. 'You look awfully pale.'

'Sit down, Isabel.' Her father's voice was quiet and commanding. He was the only one who seemed to understand at once. He placed a gin tonic in her hand and guided her to a planter.

'Now.' His hand was warm on her shoulder. 'Tell us exactly what happened.'

* * *

After dinner, Isabel and Sarah sat out together a little longer, shawls wrapped round their shoulders, savouring the cold night air. John and Dorothy Hargreaves had left. Her parents had retired to their rooms. The garden was heady with the scent of the last chrysanthemums of the winter, gold and white and maroon, now ready to be overtaken by the first buds of bougainvillea.

Sarah opened her case and lit them both fresh cigarettes. They sat back with a creak of settling wicker and blew lazy columns of smoke at the darkness. Isabel was drowsy with rich food and wine but too unsettled to go to bed. The cut above her eye, stained brown now with iodine, pulsed with a low throb. The faces of the young men rose again in her mind, their eyes menacing, their fists raised.

'What kind of person strikes a horse?' The gash across Gypsy's flank was deep. The syce had rubbed ointment into it but she feared infection.

Sarah raised her eyebrows. 'Or a woman.'

Isabel considered. 'It's the idea of their hating me, that's what hurts. You know? I wish I understood what they're thinking.'

Sarah shrugged. 'There've always been troublemakers. The political rows give them an excuse.'

Isabel twisted round to face her. Sarah's eyes glistened in the strands of lamplight spilling out from the drawing room behind them. 'I do worry. Don't you? I mean, Pearl Harbour. Then Hong Kong. Thailand. Do you think it's possible . . .' she paused, reluctant to say the words. 'They're getting closer.'

Sarah shook her head. 'They were talking about it at The Club the other night. They seemed to think the Japanese had been jolly lucky to get as far as they have. There's still a lot between them and us. Singapore, for one thing.'

Isabel looked out at the dark lawn. 'But if the Japanese did invade' – she held up a hand as Sarah opened her mouth to protest – 'I'm just saying, if. Do you think the Indians would really stand by while they slaughtered us?'

'Mr Gandhi seems ready to.'

Isabel shook her head. 'I can't believe that. I mean, not people here. Not Abdul and the mali. They've known us all their lives.'

'You just don't know. Until it happens.' Sarah blew out her cheeks, exhaling smoke. 'Which it won't.'

Isabel lowered her voice. 'What about independence?' It was a topic she daren't raise in her father's hearing. 'I mean, it is on the cards eventually, isn't it? I don't see why they can't just support us through the war and then see.'

'Apparently that's not enough. They want it now.' Sarah wrapped her shawl more closely around her shoulders. 'John Hargreaves says there's hardly anyone capable in the police. Not in the upper ranks. If we upped sticks and left them to it, they'd make an utter botch of things.'

Isabel snorted. 'Hargreaves.'

Sarah gave her a sideways look. 'He's not so bad.'

'He's a buffoon. I pity Dorothy.'

'At least she's got him here. He's not lord-knows-where in some jungle.'

Isabel looked at the familiar contours of the trees and bushes. 'I can't imagine living anywhere else. Can you? I wouldn't go back to dreary England for anything.'

'I just want this damned war over and Tom safely home.' Sarah sighed. 'I don't care where we live, as long as we're together again.'

Out in the gloom, a match scraped and flared as the chowkidar, guarding the gate, lit a bidi.

'Any news of Tom?'

'None.' Sarah aimed a stream of smoke at a cloud of flies above their heads. 'You know how it goes. Nothing for ages and then two or three letters come at once.' She turned to Isabel, her eyes glinting in the darkness. 'Anyway, it's not Tom you're worrying about, is it? It's that other chap. The one who asked Tom about you.'

'Don't be silly.'

Sarah pulled a face. 'What's his name? Jones?'

'Johnston. Edward Johnston. And of course I'm worried about Tom.'

'You don't fool me.' Sarah raised an eyebrow. 'I don't know why you don't just write to him. Send it through Tom, if you like. They see each other all the time.'

'We lost touch years ago. When Jonathan died.' She paused, remembering. 'I doubt he'd even recognise me.'

'You haven't changed that much.'

Isabel hesitated. She was thirty-one. She was being a fool, thinking about him as much as she was. It had just been a shock to hear of him again, after all this time.

'He's probably married.'

'Doesn't sound like it. Anyway, suit yourself.'

Isabel drew deeply on her cigarette, feeling the smoke in her lungs. She wondered what he looked like now. She let out a long column of smoke.

'You know Felicity?' Sarah said. 'She got a letter from George a few weeks ago with the last page missing. Rather queer, she thought. Then, just the other day, a second letter came and, lo and behold, there was the missing page from

324

the first one, tucked in the middle. The censor must have been half-asleep.'

Isabel smiled in the darkness. They sat in silence for a while.

Sarah reached forward to stub out the remains of her cigarette. The fragments glowed red, then died to darkness in the ashtray. She got to her feet, wrapped her shawl more closely round her shoulders. 'The trouble with you, my dear, is that you've given up.'

Isabel blinked. 'On India?'

'On men. You think you had one shot and you blew it and that's it.'

Isabel opened her mouth to protest but Sarah lifted a finger to silence her.

'Don't bother arguing. I know you too well.'

When Sarah had gone, Isabel lay in bed in the darkness. Outside, cicadas screeched, unseen, in the grass.

Her head ached. She lifted her fingers to her forehead and traced the dried blood along the cut there. She tried to imagine where Tom and Edward might be, lying in some jungle camp, plagued by insects, surrounded by sleeping, snoring men.

Her eyes closed and her thoughts drifted. Bright sunshine came and the white-sand beach on Car Nicobar and Edward standing at the water's edge, his back to her, his shoulders broad, smoking a cigarette, as the waves ran in, low and gentle, bathing his feet and swirling sand around his toes.

Chapter Thirty-Six

Asha

Fried potatoes again, spiced with chilli.

Asha tore off strips of roti and pinched them up between her fingers, chewing slowly to savour each mouthful. They sat in a circle in the smoky half-light of the hut, cross-legged, knees touching. A make-do household of women and children. The aunties watched over the children as they ate, slapping their bare legs if they misbehaved, prodding them to finish. They ate little themselves.

'What about you?' Asha pointed to the pot on the dying fire. Already, the potatoes were almost finished.

'Not hungry, Didi.' Her cousin's wife kept her eyes low. Her cheeks had a hollow look now. She seemed older than her years.

Asha considered. Her wages weren't due for another two days but a diet of potatoes meant the money had run out. Nothing had arrived from the men for some weeks. She looked at the pot. 'No sabzi today?'

'Gobi, only, in the market.' The auntie looked embarrassed. 'Too much of cost.'

The oldest boy, Sushil, ten now, said: 'I can work. If I left school—'

Asha reached forward and cuffed him across the back of

the head. 'No one's leaving school.' It was an old argument and she was tired of it. 'They feed you there, don't they? Be grateful.'

The aunties scraped out the pot and gave the boys what was left, then they blew up the fire, mixed water, milk and tea and set the chai to boil. They served Asha each evening as if she were a man because she worked in a clean-hands job and brought good money home. They held their tongues around her.

After dinner, the women crouched low on their haunches in the dust outside. The sounds drifted back into the hut: the slosh of water and clang of metal as they washed the pots and the low murmur of their voices. Asha headed out for a walk.

Her head ached. Her classes seemed restless nowadays. The children were too hungry to concentrate. When they bowed their heads over their books, their hair showed the light streaks of bad diets. In the playground, many were too listless to play.

The day gave way to dusk. Kerosene lamps, hanging from trees and posts along the edge of the bazaar, made yellow circles of muddy light. The hawkers sat quietly on the ground with patient, sloping shoulders. She walked along, her mind barely registering what she saw. The gobis were poor specimens, the size of potatoes only. A meagre pile of beans was there. And bhindis.

'Sister! What about apples? Very good tasting.'

An elderly man with bare, gnarled feet offered her a red apple.

She shook her head. 'No money, Uncle.' His apples were carefully arranged in a pyramid. They looked dusty and undisturbed as if he had failed to make a sale that day.

He wagged his head, still held out the apple. 'Take one anyway. Why not?' He patted the space beside him. 'You're the teacher, nah? My son's boy goes to your school. May it please the gods he learns his letters and numbers and gets a good job. Not like his poor old grandpa.'

She didn't know his grandson but she took the apple, thanked him and sat for a moment. The evening air was cool. They watched together the feet, some in boots, some in chappals, others bare, tramp past along the path.

'No business?'

He shrugged. The folds of skin around his eyes fell in loose pouches. When he spoke, his remaining teeth showed red with betel. 'No one has money.'

'Bad times.'

'No work.' He sucked his teeth. 'My son gets a day's work a week nowadays.' He leant closer to her. 'Bengalis, that's the problem. They'll work for nothing.'

Asha nodded. The aunties complained about Bengali men, hanging around the slum, begging for work. She heard their accents late at night, drunk sometimes and rowdy. 'People are going hungry there. That's what they say.'

'We're all hungry.' The old man rolled his eyes. 'What's so special about their bellies?'

She tutted, bit into her apple. It was sweet and crisp and she fell silent as she ate. Her pleasure in the apple was tainted by guilt. She might have put it in her pocket and taken it home to the children but that would have been rude and besides, it tasted so good.

'Ripe, nah?' The old man, watching her, smiled, then shook his head. 'If they don't sell soon, they'll spoil. I'd feed them to my own family but where's the profit in that?'

She ate in silence and let him talk.

'My good wife departed this life ten years ago, may the gods bless her.' He sighed, lifted a switch and brushed flies off the apples. 'If she could see this place now, foreigners swarming all over the place, I don't know what she'd say. It isn't decent, the way they look at our girls. I tell you, I thank the gods that we had sons, my wife and I. Five healthy boys.'

He gave her an appraising sideways look. 'No tika? No husband yet, nah? Your parents couldn't find anyone?'

Before she could answer, he went on: 'Well, don't give up hope. Some men get lonely enough to marry older ladies, even your age. Go for a widower.' He winked. 'I'll keep an eye out.'

Shouts drifted across from the central section of the bazaar. Asha strained to look. A crowd was gathering, damming up the path.

'Trouble.' The old man cocked his head. 'What did I tell you? Bengalis.' He turned his head and spat a stream of blood-red betel juice into the dust as she left him and moved on to see.

The crowd grew quickly. Young men jostled and pressed forward, their hands on each other's shoulders, calling and jeering. Asha drew her dupatta forward and picked her way round the edge of the throng.

A tall, thin man held a boy by the arm and whipped him with a branch. Nearby, two smaller boys were slumped on the ground. One showed only the top of his head. The other peered out miserably through eyes that were sticky with blood and swollen with bruising. She knew the child. He was Abhishek, Rahul and Sangeeta's boy.

'Bloody thieves!' The man's voice was breathy as he

laboured to keep hold of the wriggling boy and thrash him. 'I'll teach you.'

'Give him a good hiding.' An old woman in the crowd urged him on.

'Call a jawan,' shouted a man. 'He'll sort them out.'

Asha stepped forward. 'Stop it!' She used her classroom voice.

The man paused for a moment, looking up at her in surprise. 'What's it to you?'

'He's only a child.'

The boy hung limp from the man's hand. His shirt had fallen to tatters and his back was striped red with blows.

The man sneered, raised his stick as if to lash out at Asha too. 'If they're old enough to steal, they're old enough to take a beating, nah?'

'Steal? Are you sure?'

'I saw them. All three of them, helping themselves to tomatoes, filling their pockets.'

'I'll pay for them. Let their parents do the beating.'

He narrowed his eyes. His anger was spent and he looked exhausted from the effort but his mood was still sour. 'Who are you, anyway?'

'I know her. She teaches at the government school.'

'Don't listen to her. You teach them a lesson.'

People, gathered tightly around, started to speak out. Most of them knew Asha and her family but they knew the hawker too and it was hard to stand back and see a public beating end so soon. Especially if you had a good view.

'She's Ramesh's cousin. Don't you remember her father?'

'That sweeper-wallah who got sent to prison?'

'That's right. She was a girl then.'

'I lost good oranges last week. What're you waiting for?'

Asha took another step forward and held out her hand for the stick. The man was so close that his sour breath blew in her face. He stared at her open palm. Something in her manner made him uncertain. A moment later, the fight flowed out of his limbs and he let go of the boy's arm. The boy staggered forward and Asha pushed him behind her.

'I will pay you,' she said. She didn't want the man to lose face in public. 'You can trust me.'

She turned her attention to the boys on the ground and stirred them up with her toe. The smaller of the two finally raised his head and she bit her lip to stop herself from crying out. Sushil. Her own nephew. The line of his small nose was crooked with swelling.

'Come.' She reached down and lifted the two boys by the hair. Once they were away from the crowd, she cuffed Sushil.

'Go home,' she said. 'I'll deal with you later.'

Rahul's stall was in the far corner of the bazaar, squashed between a fruit hawker and a chai stall. It was a narrow bunker with walls of bales of cotton and silk, inlaid with trays of buttons, ribbons and lace. The low shafts of light from his overhead lamp picked out motes of cotton hanging in the air.

Asha held his boy by the arm. 'Rahul?'

In the gloom, a figure stirred. Rahul emerged from behind the bales like a ghost, pale and lean. He held bunches of cloth samples in his hands as he stepped forward and peered through narrowed eyes.

'It's me. Asha.'

He had known her before she even remembered, when she was little more than a baby and they all lived as servants in the grounds of the Britishers' house. Then again, years later, when he hung around Sanjay Krishna's home with the young freedom fighters and she, alone by then, slept in the outhouse there. He was approaching middle-age now. His stomach had thickened and his eyes were spoilt by long days crouched in poor light, chalking, pinning and stitching, by hand or with his battered sewing machine. A worn tape measure dangled round his neck.

He put a hand out for the boy. 'Abhishek?'

'They caught him stealing tomatoes.'

His face darkened. 'Is it true?'

The boy hung his head. Rahul lifted his chin and looked him in the face, reading his eyes. 'What happened?'

The boy didn't speak.

Asha said: 'The sabzi-wallah thrashed them. My cousin's boy, Sushil. He was there too.'

Rahul shook his head, put his hand in his pocket and drew out a handful of coins. 'Please, give the sabzi-wallah this.'

Asha put her head on one side and considered. She wanted to refuse him, to wave the money away, but the truth was, she didn't have any herself and she had promised the hawker in front of everyone.

'I'll pay back my share,' she said at last. 'When I get my wages.'

Rahul pressed the handful of coins into her palm and closed her fingers round them. 'No need. I'm grateful.' He turned to the boy. 'Go home, Abhishek. Tell your mother you were in a fight only. Don't make her ashamed.' His voice was more sorrowful than angry. The boy slunk away. Rahul stood for a moment, looking after his son. 'He's a good boy,' he said. 'But he needs to learn.'

He shook himself and turned to Asha. 'Come, little sister, sit with me. I seldom see you nowadays.'

He settled again at his workbench at the back of the stall and she sat on the ground near him. He bent his head over his work and listened as she told him about the school and the way she worried about the children's hunger and her cousins and their older sons, so far away now in Burma, labouring for the Britishers there and sending home money when they could. At first it had been good money and the men's absence had seemed worthwhile but now they heard rarely from them – no money for so long already – that they wondered why they were hungry, all these women left alone with young children, and if they were abandoned. And how was she to stop young Sushil from stealing tomatoes when his belly was empty, even if he knew it was a wrong thing?

He listened in silence, his eyes fixed on his stitching. He was adorning a fine piece of cloth with sequins. His head was tilted towards her and his hair was thin on the crown and flecked with grey, as the cloth in his hands was flecked with white and gold, and it seemed a secret that she was privileged to share.

She paused in her story after a while and felt the pleasure of the quietness between them. She liked to watch him sew. He had long, slim fingers and they played the cloth as if it were alive and happy to be worked. She wondered if this was how it felt to be married and thought of the old man with the apples and his betel-stained teeth and his promise to find her a husband and laughed out loud.

Rahul looked up and smiled. He had a sweet smile. 'What?'

'Nothing,' she said.

He fell back to sewing and they sat in silence a while longer.

'How's your business?'

He puffed out his cheeks. 'With the price of cloth now, it's hard to make a profit. I need rich customers.'

She pursed her lips. 'Who can afford to buy daal and subzi, let alone fancy clothes?'

He inclined his head, his eyes never leaving his work. 'Britishers only. They have money.' He lifted the cloth in his hands to make his point. 'A piece like this, I can ask a lot for it. What Indian could afford it?'

She felt her insides tighten. He should work for his own people only. For their betterment.

He said, as if he read her mind: 'What to do? I have a wife and child to feed. And, praise to the gods, another son on the way.'

'Another one?' She smiled. 'Congratulations! How is Sangeeta-ji?'

He hid his face from her and she sensed his blush. 'Very fine. The baby isn't due until the summer.'

She nodded. 'A few years and I'll see him in school, I hope?'

'If the gods allow.' Rahul lifted his eyes to her. 'Can you find places in school, Asha?'

She shrugged. 'It's crowded but we can find a way. Besides, he isn't born yet. Who knows how things will be in the future? Maybe the Britishers will be gone and we'll be living in their houses, nah?'

Rahul hesitated. His needle, usually plying so quickly through the cloth, slowed. 'But for other children. The poorest, even. Are there places for them?'

Asha gave him a shrewd look. 'What, Rahul? What plans are you hatching?'

He lifted his eyes to hers. 'After school tomorrow, come with me, will you? Let me show you.'

The following day, Rahul sat at the front of his stall, his long-fingered hands idle in his lap, waiting. His face was set and his eyes solemn as he got to his feet without a word and led her out across the slum.

They strode through the sprawling network of shacks, a collection of crawl spaces like her own home, some made of wooden struts and topped with sacking, others with scraps of metal and scavenged iron as roofs.

The winter sun was warm and she raised her dupatta to her face to filter the stench. The cobbles underfoot were slippery and cut through with open drains. A toddler, the ironmonger's youngest, lifted curious eyes as they passed.

She struggled to keep pace with Rahul. 'Where are we going?'

He didn't pause to answer, just hurried on. Cloths, hung as curtains across doorways, were tied back to let in air and sun and the shacks gave up sudden pictures of the worlds inside. A mother, squatting on her haunches, dandled a half-naked baby. A wrinkled old woman crouched over a steaming cooking pot. A fat-bellied man snoozed on a charpoy in the shade.

As they neared the edge of the slum, Rahul led her out towards waste ground, far from her walk to and from school. Beyond, there was little but open land and rubbish dumps. She paused to catch her breath.

On the corner, a man with a straggly beard and blood-spattered apron hacked apart a chicken on a wooden board. The visceral tang of bloodied guts quivered in the air. She pulled her dupatta closer round her face.

Rahul hurried on. Beyond the slum, the ground rose towards a raised ridge of road. It was a fetid, unhealthy area, dotted with low-lying marsh and rife with mosquitoes. Asha climbed the ridge and stood beside Rahul, looking out.

The expanse was covered with new shacks, even more shabby and cramped than the ones they had just passed. Low plumes of smoke rose from cooking fires. To one side, rising beside them, lay a vast rubbish dump, a grey cesspit of rotting filth. Black scavenging birds, stray dogs and ragged children poked through it.

'Banaras people.' Rahul paddled the air with his fingertips. 'They weave silk. The best.'

He pressed down into the maze of shacks and picked his way along a narrow mud track, then finally turned, ducked through a low doorway and disappeared to the right.

A small courtyard opened up in the centre of a cluster of meagre buildings. It was stuffy and dimly lit, overshadowed by the structures that had grown up round it. The air puttered with soft mechanical clacking. The space was dominated by four wooden looms. Women and girls sat cross-legged at each, their heads covered, their backs hunched over their work. They pulled their scarves closer round their faces as Rahul walked amongst them.

Asha looked more closely. Many were children. She stopped at the loom of a girl who looked barely six years old. The child strained forward over her work. Coloured metal bangles – red, gold and silver – jangled at her wrists as her hands flew back and forth. A shiny stud glistened in her nose. Her hair was tied back, veiled by the cotton scarf that covered her head.

Her loom was simply made: a bed of taut strings running between thin strips of wood. Her tiny fingers picked their way along a row of coloured silks, weaving each by turn in and out of the strings. Her movements were fast and sure and she plucked the silks with grace.

Each time she reached the end of a row, she pulled a bamboo bar towards her in a single, swift movement to compress the threads, then began, a second later, at the start of the next row. Asha tried to imagine how her hands and back must ache.

In the corner, behind the looms, three old ladies squatted together in the dirt. They were rotating circular spindles on bamboo sticks. The spindles chirped and danced. Each one tugged a fast-spinning, clattering drum of silk thread, mounted to one side on a bamboo frame, which the women wound into skeins.

Rahul gestured to her to follow him into a small brick building at the far side of the courtyard. It was the only structure with proper walls and a door, propped open with a stone. It was dark inside. She stood for a moment on the threshold while her eyes adjusted, blinking back rods of light.

Rahul held up a piece of cloth. It swam through his fingers, a delicate aquamarine patterned with grey and gold flowers. The silk shimmered in the half-light like flowing water. He handed it to her. Warm and impossibly soft. As her eyes began to adjust to the gloom, she blinked and looked around. The silks were raised above the ground on boards and protected with matting. There were thirty or forty stacks, which made up a rich rainbow of colour.

'Those girls did all this?'

Rahul shook his head. 'Other families too, all from Banaras. Mothers, aunties, cousins.'

'Why haven't they sold it?'

'Sometimes local merchants come to buy. These people get a poor price but what to do? They're outsiders and afraid to argue.'

The silk caressed her hands.

'I'm borrowing everything I can,' he said, 'and buying it myself. I give a better price than the merchants and I can stitch it into dresses, blouses, scarves. Few people have money to afford such fine stuff, nah? But if I could sell to the Britishers . . .'

She refolded the aquamarine silk and let it float back onto the pile. Her fingers ached for its softness. Rahul, reading her, pawed through the pile and selected a golden strip. He raised it to the light to judge the weave, then ripped it along the thread in a sudden violent motion and handed it to her.

'For remembering,' he said, 'how beauty comes from suffering.'

In the courtyard, the six-year-old girl hadn't shifted position. Her fingers flew on and on without pause.

They stopped off, on the way back, at a chai stall, which overlooked a piece of waste ground at the side of the new slum. Metal cauldrons were propped on bricks over wood fires. Bare-chested men, bodies glistening with sweat, dipped and stirred raw cotton inside, twisting it in the boiling dye with staves. Their faces shimmied and shook in the rising steam.

The chai-wallah, a scrawny boy, brought them glasses of

milky tea. Specks of black rose and fell in the cloudy liquid.

'So.' She sipped at her chai, sweet and milky and warm in her empty stomach. 'Those are the children you want me to teach in school?'

He nodded. 'In the mornings, only. In the afternoons, they weave.'

She considered. 'Their parents agree?'

He sipped his chai. The ground at their feet was stained with spilt tea and splashes of betel and buzzed with flies.

'They respect me,' he said. 'I give them money.' He paused. 'And at school, the girls can eat also. They'll have more strength for work.'

Asha looked at his long toes in his sandals, as delicate as his fingers. The toes of a kind man. 'I can't teach every poor child, Rahul-ji. The school would burst.'

He nodded. 'Not every child. Just these.'

It might be possible. So many children were pulled out of class now, even at their age, and sent to work. There were always spaces.

She watched Rahul as he sipped his chai. He was such a scrawny youth once, ready to tease her. He was so passionate about politics, about fighting the British for rights. Somehow, life had tamed him and she wondered at it.

'Was it so hard in prison?'

He looked surprised. He never spoke of it and she never asked. 'Hard for me, and for Sangeeta also. Abhishek was young.'

She nodded. People said he lost his uncle's mithai shop because he was shut away in jail. When he finally came out, he ran errands and sold onions in the bazaar while he learnt at night how to sew.

'Is that why you abandoned the fight for our freedom? You're afraid of prison?'

He drained his glass and set it down. 'Now I have a different fight. To feed my family.'

Asha narrowed her eyes. He was a good man and a clever one. He could help them, she was sure of it.

'If I take these children into school, will you do something for me?'

The chai-wallah collected their empty glasses with clinking fingers. They waited while he wiped down the bench with a dirty rag and left.

Asha leant in closer. 'A new chapter in the fight is beginning. Come with me to hear our leaders. Will you?'

Across the waste ground, the dyers fished with their sticks and hauled out lengths of red cotton, which hung, dripping, from the wood. The blaze of steam engulfed everything. The cloths became entrails, bleeding heavily into the cauldrons below. She blinked and they became cotton once again. It was simply illusion, conjured by the upward rush of swimming air.

Chapter Thirty-Seven

Isabel

The tennis court was one of the few places where Isabel could forget the war. That afternoon in particular, she had to focus to win.

Her opponent was the daughter of one of her father's friends, a strapping girl and barely twenty. Some of her strokes were poor but what she lacked in technique, she made up for in fitness. However carefully Isabel placed her shots, sending the girl dashing from one corner of the court to another, she seemed cheerfully tireless as she chased after them.

When the match finally ended and they turned back towards The Club, Isabel caught sight of Sarah, sitting to one side on the terrace, which overlooked the courts. Sarah lifted her hand to wave and Isabel went across, racquet in hand.

'I was beginning to think you'd never win.' Sarah gave her a wry look.

Isabel pulled on her cardigan. 'So was I.' She sat beside Sarah, facing the courts. 'She made me feel very old.'

'I'm not surprised.' Sarah snorted. 'She only looked twelve.'

Isabel shrugged. 'It's hard to find partners.' She ordered a nimbu pane and settled back in her chair. Two middle-aged women were engaged in a genteel match on the adjacent

341

court. Her eyes idly followed the ball back and forth, soothed by the tap-tap-tap of ball striking racquet. The air was cool but the weak sun pleasant on her skin.

'You meeting someone?' Isabel didn't often see Sarah at The Club so early. She wasn't known for her love of sport.

'I was waiting for you. Your mother said you'd be here.'

Isabel turned. Sarah's eyes were shining.

'News from Tom?'

Sarah grinned, opened her handbag and pulled out a crumpled envelope. 'Just come.'

Isabel leant forward. 'And?'

Sarah drew out the letter and unfolded it. Tom's cramped, spiky handwriting sloped across the page. 'He's fine. Well, you know, fine-ish. He says there's a lot of illness in camp. Malaria, dengue fever and whatnot. Touch wood, he was well when he wrote.' She hesitated, considered. 'Although that was weeks ago. It's taken an age to get here.'

'Even so.' Isabel gave a tight smile. 'That's good news.' She waited to hear more, swallowing back what she most wanted to ask. If Tom made any mention of Edward, if he were safe.

'Anyway, that's not all.' Sarah pulled out an inner sheet, written on the same thin paper. It was clear at once that the neat, even letters were from a different hand. 'He sent this.' She thrust it towards her. 'For you.'

Isabel's stomach gave a sudden, cold contraction. Her eyes fixed on the note.

'Well, go on, take it.'

Isabel didn't move.

'Oh, for heaven's sake.' Sarah leant over, lifted Isabel's hand and pushed the folded paper into it. 'I'll read it if you don't.'

The waiter arrived with her drink, set it on the table and withdrew. Sarah picked up Tom's letter and began to look over it again.

Isabel sat very still, her eyes on the note in her hand. The ink was smeared in places. She set it flat on the table and bent over it, hiding her face from Sarah as she read.

January, 1942

Dear Mrs Whyte,

I hope you will forgive me for writing to you after so many years. Captain Tom Winton is a good fellow and assures me that he and his wife are closely acquainted with your family. When I asked him to convey my good wishes to you, he encouraged me to set them down on paper myself. I trust my letter finds you in good health and as untouched by the war as anyone may be.

As for us, we stay in good spirits. We seem always to be moving. We dissolve camps no sooner than we establish them. I am being punished, I think, for all those years on the islands when I was such a passionate advocate of life in the jungle. Now, after months of jungle camps and marches, with mosquitoes and leeches in equal measure, I laugh to think of my old enthusiasm. Perhaps you see the irony too.

These are good men. They bear their trials bravely and without complaint and I think I speak for Tom too when I say we are proud to lead them. Each time a fresh order comes through, they rouse themselves and start once again to dismantle. They pack and box supplies at an extraordinary speed and with barely a grumble.

One of my young subordinates, Bateman, heard last week that he has become a father. A fine boy, by all accounts. Imagine his longing to be home now, to see his newborn son. It is etched in the lines of his face. We did our best to make a party of it. I laid hands on a small bottle of gin and we shared it out amongst us to wet the baby's head. They've named the little chap James, after his grandfather.

Oddly, we speak little of the war here, apart from wishing it over. Some days, the enemy's aircraft are constantly overhead and the jungle resounds to the thunder of falling bombs. On other days, we get word from men upcountry of Japanese raiding parties. They make forays deeper into our territory each week and, by all accounts, use the most deplorable tactics.

Often, though, we are simply undisturbed by the outside world, as deep inside a jungle as a fellow could imagine himself, wooed by the coughs of monkeys as they crash through the canopy and the shrill whooping of birds. They dive and swoop far above our heads, splashing colours of the most extraordinary brightness against the green. At such times, it is almost possible to forget there is a war to fight. I sometimes imagine it may already have ended and the generals have simply forgotten to send word.

Forgive my ramblings. If you have dear ones fighting, please know I pray for their safe return and for your health and happiness always.

Yours,

Edward Johnston

'Well?' Sarah's eyes were sharp on her face.

'It's from Edward Johnston.'

'I rather assumed that.' She blew out her cheeks. 'What does he say?'

The letter fluttered in her hands. 'The jungle, you know. The war.'

Sarah frowned. 'That's all?'

Isabel hesitated. 'He says he prays for me.' She looked down at the letter. 'For my health and happiness. And for the safe return of my dear ones.'

'Your dear ones?' Sarah laughed. 'He just wants to check you're unattached.'

'I'm sure that's not—'

'Of course it is.' Sarah shook her head. 'Izzy, you are hopeless.' She paused, reading her face. 'You must write back.'

Isabel felt her breath quicken. 'I don't know.'

'Why not?'

She was chilled by a sudden wave of panic. 'I'm not sure I want . . .' She trailed off.

'What? To renew his acquaintance? He's in Burma, Izzy.' Sarah folded her own letter and put it back in the envelope. 'I'll get a letter off to Tom tomorrow. Write the poor chap a note and I'll pop it in. It doesn't have to be much.'

Isabel kept her eyes low. 'It was a long time ago.'

'Just cheer him up, can't you? Honestly, Izzy.' Sarah leant towards her. 'He's at war. Don't you see? He might not come home.'

Isabel spent the evening in her bedroom, writing and rewriting her note to Edward.

Dear Mr Johnston,
Thank you for your kind letter. It was such a pleasant
surprise to hear from you again after so long.

She read it back, screwed the page into a ball and threw
it at the waste-paper basket where it found its place among
those already scattered there. She lit a fresh cigarette, crossed
to the window and opened it.

The cool night air flowed in, diluting the fug of smoke
inside. She stood with her arm resting on the sill and smoked,
trying to calm herself. Damn Sarah. She should never have
let herself be bullied. She would simply forget the whole
thing, tell Sarah tomorrow that she didn't intend to reply.
She drew on her cigarette. Sounds drifted down the side of
the bungalow from the kitchen. Pots clanged and scraped.
A woman's voice, Abdul's daughter-in-law, scolding a child.

She imagined Tom's awkwardness when the next letter
came. Sorry, Johnston, nothing for you. She bit her thumbnail.
Sarah was right. Edward might not make it through the war.

She turned back into the room and paced round it, kicking
the balls of paper. She couldn't bear to write a formal letter to
him. All those polite phrases, the small talk about tennis and
the weather, it was such nonsense. She'd rather not write at all.

She picked up his letter from the table and stood, smoking,
looking over it. She practically had it by heart now.

Often we are simply undisturbed by the outside world,
as deep inside a jungle as a fellow could imagine himself.

She nodded. They had sat together once in a clearing in the
virgin jungle on South Andaman, separate from the world. It

was the day Jonathan took them to visit the project there. She remembered tipping back her head and tracing the endlessly rising lines of the palms to the distant canopy that framed the sky. Edward was motionless beside her. The only breach of the silence was the sharp cry of a bird and the low hum of insects. The magic, the mystery had overwhelmed her.

She stubbed out her cigarette, sat at the table and began to write at speed.

Dear Edward,

I fear for you, out there in the war, facing the enemy. I read the newspapers every day, searching for news of Burma, but we hear so little and always, it seems, weeks after the fact. I try to imagine you in jungle camps with all those soldiers trampling down the mud and building shelters and cooking rations. I'm afraid I struggle to see it. But poor Bateman. How cruel to be so far from home as his son comes crying into this world to find him.

And I envy you too – is that very strange? When you hint at the eternal silence and stillness of the jungle. You showed me that once, a long time ago. I've never forgotten it.

I wish there were somewhere here to hide away and find peace from the world. There is such tension in Delhi. This country, our country, is a delicate silk, a cloth of rare and exquisite beauty, which seems now in danger of being ripped into pieces. I was born here. I always felt I belonged. And yet now, for the first time in my life, I have started to feel a stranger.

I understand, you see. I catch the looks between the

servants. I hear gossip in the streets and understand that many Indians are hungry and desperate and also angry. We are preparing to fight our own war here and no one quite knows where the battles will be fought or what the weapons will be. I fear for the future.

She paused, considered, then lifted her pen again.

And I fear for you, Edward. I pray for you. Please come home safely.
Yours
Isabel

She sealed the letter hastily, without reading it back, and left it for a servant to deliver to Sarah the next morning. She lay awake for a long time, her heart racing.

The following afternoon, as her mother napped, Isabel took a tonga down to The Club where a group of ladies had arranged afternoon tea. She didn't often attend their gatherings but she was restless and wanted a distraction before she went for her ride.

The afternoon was tight with pre-summer heat. The route took her along the grand avenue of Rajpath, through India Gate, majestic in the hazy sunshine, and out beyond, cutting between the open lawns which rolled on either side of the road, set with neat lines of tended trees.

The grass was fresh and lush. Off to one side, a stone monumental fountain played and brown-skinned youths, stripped to the waist, splashed and washed in its bowl. Hawkers paced across the lawns with trays of cigarettes and nuts and sweetmeats in twists of paper. Others were barely visible behind multicoloured bunches of balloons.

Near the trees, some distance from the path, boys ran in zigzags, trying to persuade home-made kites to fly in the still air. Teenage boys sauntered companionably with their arms loosely round each other's shoulders. Here and there, monkeys darted to seize discarded food or sat on their haunches, as content as the humans in the spring sunshine, grooming each other's fur, the young tumbling and scrambling round the adults.

It was a familiar scene and it soothed her. Already she regretted the candour with which she had written to Edward but it was too late, the note had gone. Perhaps he wouldn't reply. She looked at the children racing in circles in the sunshine. She should never have expressed her fears for India. On a day like this, it was impossible to imagine Japanese tanks swarming down Rajpath and the people of India cheering while the British were rounded up.

The tonga-wallah called to her over his shoulder in Hindustani.

'Please, madam. Problem is there.'

'Problem?' Isabel leant further out to look. Ahead, on a broad lawn, close to Parliament House and the buildings that housed the main government ministries, the myriad dots of individual people were converging to form a crowd. At the far side, close to the trees, there was a solid, rectangular shape. A platform. Was there a festival? She frowned. She couldn't think of one.

'What's happening?'

The tonga-wallah slowed the horse to a walk. 'I am not knowing, madam.' He sounded worried. 'Perhaps – am I turning back?'

'I'm sure that's not necessary.' They were so close to the heart of government. No one would plan anything dangerous right under the noses of British officials.

Voices echoed across the ground, distorted by megaphones.

'What are they saying?'

The tonga-wallah cleared his throat and spat to one side. 'Political slogans, madam.' His face creased into a frown. 'I think it might be best—'

Isabel tapped him on the shoulder, suddenly animated. 'Set me down over there, would you? By those trees.' She dug out coins and handed him a generous fare. 'You can have twice that if you wait here for me.'

The horse dropped its mouth in a clink of bridle to the grass along the verge. The tonga-wallah looked down at the money. '*Shukriah*, madam, but—'

She climbed out of the tonga and started across the grass.

All around her, men, young and old, hurried past. The crowd grew with surprising speed. As she approached, a figure in white flowing robes, his face dominated by a bushy whitening beard and moustache, appeared on the platform and the air rang with a cheer, then settled into ragged chanting. Fists struck the air. Men began to run, as if anxious not to miss the start of the event. Her own steps quickened too.

She circled the crowd, trying to avoid being pressed close amongst the men. A handful of women in brightly coloured saris stood together under the trees, a little apart from the crowd, and she went to join them.

On the platform, the stout man in white had started to talk. He spoke slowly and clearly as if he were used to addressing large gatherings.

'My brothers and sisters of India.' She strained to follow his Hindustani. 'Listen! Our time is come.'

Men on either side held a cloth canopy over his head to shield him from the sun. It was attached to poles, which were wrapped around with brightly coloured streamers. The sound was punctuated with high-pitched electronic squeals.

She reached the women. 'Excuse me, madam. Who is this?'

A middle-aged woman turned and looked Isabel up and down. Her face was stony. She twisted away from Isabel and spoke to a younger woman on her other side, her daughter perhaps.

Isabel said again in Hindustani, a little more loudly: 'What is the good name of the man who's speaking?'

The young woman moved a step closer. Her eyes were curious.

'Baba Satya.' She spoke in English. 'Surely you must be knowing?'

Isabel shook her head. 'Baba Satya.' Father of truth. She had heard that name before. She couldn't remember where. 'But who is he? A guru?'

The young woman laughed and said something under her breath to the others. They stared at Isabel. Their mouths smiled but their eyes were cold.

She turned and looked out across the crowd. The men were focused on the platform, their eyes on Baba Satya. Far behind them, in the shade of the trees, police officers on horseback were assembling, drawing a line of mounted khaki. When the megaphones screeched, the horses stamped and shifted. A larger group of police officers on foot were taking up positions behind. Their lathis were drawn and raised in their hands. Beyond, a fire engine shone in the sunshine. She frowned and turned back to the women.

'He's for independence, is he?' They ignored her. 'Is he a radical?'

On the platform, Baba Satya held his arms aloft. That simple gesture stilled the noise of the crowd. Isabel too held her breath. The silence was more powerful than the clamour had been. Softer sounds reasserted themselves. Birds cawed in the trees above them. Bicycle bells and rickshaw horns drifted in from the road. Somewhere, distantly, a dog howled.

On the platform, Baba Satya began again to speak. His voice crackled across the park, sharpened by static. 'Thank you for coming here today.'

Isabel looked from the baba to the back of the crowd. The line of police horses inched forward, stamping their hooves and tossing their necks against tight reins. The police officers on foot pressed close behind them. She lifted her hand to her mouth.

'There is a dawning of hope, dear brothers and sisters. Do you feel it? A day of great change is drawing near.' Baba Satya's voice was strong and steady. He teased the crowd with pauses and, as he spoke, the swell of his voice rose and crashed over them all. The men near Isabel strained forward to catch every word.

'The end of the Great British Empire is almost upon us. The end, I say! I call on you all, each and every man, woman and child, to stand firm. Follow the teachings of the Mahatma. Until and unless the British make full and immediate concessions on the matter of our independence, stand apart from them. Give nothing to their war effort. No Indian hand shall be raised to defend them.'

Isabel looked over the faces. The crowd stamped and

murmured. Someone sent up a cry of: 'Home Rule!' It ran on for a while, then died back as Baba Satya began again to speak.

'Brothers, sisters, how can we believe their words? They mean to keep us in servitude. Believe that only! Let them lose their war and learn bitter lessons from it. Their Empire is dying! Change is sweeping the world, bringing new order, new hope. And with that change only will India again be independent!'

Baba Satya raised both hands high and his robes fell in folds about his body. The crowd, intoxicated, roared and pressed forward. Isabel took a step backwards, moving instinctively away from the restless audience. She turned and looked again to the police lines.

John Hargreaves was there, mounted on horseback, his arm raised. In his helmet and uniform, he had the hard, unyielding look of a statue. The sunlight glinted on the gun in his hand.

Baba Satya ended his speech. He stood, encased in white, his arms reaching for the heavens. A chant rose from within the crowd and spread quickly through it. A rallying cry that was already familiar. '*Jai Hindustan Ki!* Victory to India!'

The sound burst against the sky and scattered in echoes across the belly of the cloud. The birds rose from the surrounding trees and swooped, cawing, in a black flurry across the lawns towards India Gate.

A shot rang out. Even as she turned, the police horses bolted forward. For an instant, time seemed suspended. The men's mouths hung open, their chants silenced. They stared at the approaching horses, hooves flailing, at the mounted police officers with their lathis held high. Then the moment of stillness burst and the men, shouting, scattered and ran, tumbling past each other, arms groping as the horses bore down on them, the lathis chopping and cutting through the air to left and right, cracking against skulls, shoulders and fingers.

The men at the front roared, then too began to flee, knocking Isabel and the watching women as they hurtled past. Isabel pushed through the stream to the trees and stood with her back pressed against a trunk, unable to tear her eyes from the scene.

As the crowd scattered, the police constables on foot charged after them, beating heads and shoulders and backs. The fire engine rumbled forward down one side of the park, forcing those in its path to throw themselves out of its way. The officers waited until they were almost level with the raised platform before unwinding their hoses and letting loose an arc of water.

The force knocked the men on the platform off their feet. Hair, beards and clothes were soaked in an instant. The men on either side of Baba Satya dropped the canopy to grasp him by the arms and steady him, struggling against the storm of water as they led him, step by step, away from the front of the platform and down a narrow flight of wooden steps at the side. The gay streamers lay limp and sodden round the poles.

A girl screamed. The older woman, who earlier refused to speak to Isabel, lay on the ground, her daughter pulling at her arms as men pressed round them. Isabel ran to help and together they lifted the woman clear of the kicking boots and chappals and sat her, dazed, against the tree.

The lawn was a mess of panic. Many had already vanished.

Others ran to and fro in confusion, trying to dodge turning, rearing horses and the lathis. Some, ready to fight, grappled with the police, wrestling them or punching and kicking. A young boy, perhaps five or six years old, stood screaming in the chaos.

Across the grass, Baba Satya was being marched away by police, his wrists cuffed. One of the officers had his hand on Baba Satya's head, forcing it down towards his chest. He stumbled as they propelled him forwards. A dark streak of blood ran down the side of his face. To one side, Hargreaves sat tall on his horse, his face impassive.

'Is she alright?'

The daughter didn't answer. She sat with her arm round her mother's shoulders, her head cradled against her. The woman sat with her eyes closed but her breathing was calm.

'I'll stay with you,' Isabel said. 'Help you home.'

The daughter shook her head. 'We are not wanting your help.'

Isabel leant against the far side of the tree. Sodden debris lay strewn over the grass. The lawn, usually so tranquil, had the look of a battlefield. Men groaned. Others curled silently, drawing their legs to their stomachs. A sole chappal stuck up in the mud. The sun picked out a lonely scrap of blue, a scarf perhaps, forgotten.

To the side of the platform, protesters huddled together, penned in by a tight circle of police officers. A lathi swung, catching one of the prisoners across the side of the head. Another followed. The men, powerless to escape, ducked and cringed as blows fell. Faces twisted and turned.

'Rahul?' She pushed upright. Her feet began to carry her across the ground towards them. Was it Rahul? The face fell back into the melee. The police officers, many bruised and bloody themselves, panted with exertion as they struck out.

'Rahul!'

There he was, she knew him, she was sure, older now, his cheeks fuller, the skin around his eyes lined and weathered, but Rahul, just the same, that same boy she'd known as a child, that same young man she visited at his uncle's mithai shop.

'Not him.' She was pointing, shouting, wild. Eyes turned to stare. 'Let him go. I know him.'

'Isabel!' Hargreaves, lofty on horseback, looked disapproving. 'What on earth? Go home. Don't you know—'

She tilted up to look him full in the face. 'This man.' She pointed. Rahul turned his face away. 'He's not one of them. He's done nothing wrong. Please, I know him.'

Hargreaves shook his head. 'Really, Isabel. What would your father—'

'My father knows him too. He'd say the same. Please.' Her words tumbled out, barely coherent. 'I'll take him with me. I've a tonga waiting.'

The police officers goggled, listening without understanding. Finally Hargreaves blew out his cheeks and pointed with bad humour.

'This man. Let him out. Tie the rest.'

Rahul was ejected from the group. He stumbled out, looked back as the line again tightened. Isabel seized him by the arm and started to pull him away.

'Come on.' She tugged, half-dragging him as the police officers herded the other men into two lines and began to rope them together.

She didn't expect the tonga to be still there but it was, a

solid, comforting shape, which grew on the distant edge of the grass once they emerged from the trees. The tonga-wallah stood by his horse, one arm protectively round its neck. He looked out through narrowed eyes as they approached.

'So much of trouble,' he said. 'So many fellows saying: take me. Ladies also. No, I said. Not possible. Madam is coming.'

'Shukriah. You did well.' She would pay him handsomely, he needn't worry. She climbed into the tonga, her legs suddenly shaking. Rahul hesitated, then finally, reluctantly, climbed up beside her. He looked back across the vanishing ground as the tonga-wallah pulled up the horse's head and slapped its flank with his switch.

They sat stiffly. She looked ahead at the horse's bobbing back, its bony rump, the long line of its mane and tossing ears. How many years must it be since she and Rahul last saw each other, sitting in the dusty courtyard behind the shop, drinking chai and nibbling sweets as Sangeeta swept and their baby son played in the dirt? Jonathan was there, that last time, eager to court her. How long ago it all seemed. How little she'd understood.

She wanted to turn to him, to say: What did they do to you in prison? Do you forgive me for being British, is it possible we could still be friends? But she was afraid. He seemed unwilling to look at her.

The tonga-wallah set him down at last, on the far side of the Civil Lines. He climbed out and, for a moment, he seemed ready to let her drive away without a word.

'Thank you.' He struggled to say it.

'Don't.' She shook her head. 'We know each other better than that, don't we?'

He stood there by the wheel, all awkwardness, his eyes on the ground.

'You can't think—' She broke off. She didn't know what to say. The horse shook its head and the bridle jangled. She reached down towards him.

'Rahul, come and visit me at the bungalow, won't you? Bring Sangeeta and your son. How about next week?' She was babbling, trying to find a way of reaching him. 'Abdul's still with us. Come on Wednesday afternoon. Please.'

She turned abruptly to the tonga-wallah and urged him on before Rahul could refuse.

At home, she bathed and sat alone on the verandah in the warmth of the afternoon sun, all thoughts of The Club now abandoned. Rahul looked older. It shocked her. A middle-aged man with a tired face and slackening skin. He had been such a sharp-eyed, energetic boy, then a handsome young husband. She put her hand to her face, reading the changes there too.

She would find ways of helping his son, of proving herself to them both. He could show his boy where he'd lived as a child. It was modernised now and given over to Abdul's family. The bushes where they'd played hide-and-seek and the mango trees where they used to gorge themselves in the hot season and the old magnolia, with its low-lying branches, where he'd taught her to climb to the top of the world, to see into the past and the future.

She hesitated, remembering his stiffness. She had no idea if he would even come.

Her father sent a chit.

Her mother, waiting to tell Cook to serve dinner, looked vexed.

'Well, really.' She shook her head, peered at Isabel over her reading spectacles. 'I do wish he'd give a little more notice.'

Isabel shrugged. 'I don't suppose he can.'

Her mother set down her book.

'We'll have to dine without him.' She reached for the servants' bell and rang for Abdul. 'He seems to have no idea when he'll be back.'

Isabel went to her mother's side to escort her into the dining room. Her mother wore one of her old-fashioned gowns with a high neck and it rustled as they walked.

'We're not the only households managing without men,' she said. 'England's full of them, apparently.'

Her mother seemed preoccupied. After dinner, she retired early to bed, claiming a headache.

Isabel sat alone in the sitting room, a book open on her lap, waiting for her father to come home. Her eyes ranged over the print without seeing it. She wondered how long it would take her letter to reach Edward. They shifted camp so often, he said. Perhaps it would never find him.

Gradually her mind drifted to the events of the early afternoon. Baba Satya and his supporters would be in jail now. She imagined the mothers and wives and children who must now be waiting, as Sangeeta once had, with little hope of their men's return. Rahul at least was with his family. She was glad. Hargreaves might complain to her father about her but she didn't care.

It was almost eleven when her father's footsteps finally sounded in the hall. He pushed open the door and she put down her book.

'My dear.'

His thinning hair stood in furrows where he'd raked it with his fingers.

'You're very late.' She got to her feet, kissed him on the cheek. 'Are you hungry?'

He sank heavily into his armchair. 'Have you heard the news?'

'Baba Satya?'

He shook his head. His skin looked grey. My poor father. He is old now, too old for this. Edward and the other young men should come home from this wretched war and let him retire, before it's too late.

'You haven't heard, then.' He lifted a hand to gesture to the evening drinks' tray. She poured him a Scotch and added soda, then perched on the arm of his chair as he took it. His hands had a slight tremor and his wedding ring rattled against the cut glass. He let out a long sigh. She sat still, suddenly afraid, and waited.

'Singapore.' He spoke at last. 'The Japanese, you see. It's fallen.'

Chapter Thirty-Eight

Asha

'The tide is turning.'

Asha sat cross-legged on the floor, her fingers alternately pleating and smoothing the edge of her dupatta in her lap. The young man had fire in his eyes. He paced up and down in the dim, airless room as if the world were too small a place to contain him.

He made the older men, the familiar faces who usually attended the meetings, look tame and comfortable. Those others, slack-jawed now, knew her from her childhood when they crept to and fro in the twilight to visit with Sanjay Krishna's uncle, then with Sanjay himself, in those early Delhi years. They petted her like fathers and would help her if she needed them. None, she felt, took her seriously.

'You understand?' The eyes ranged across the room and, when they came her way, she lifted her head and looked straight back at him, showing she was not afraid.

'The Britishers never thought Hong Kong would fall. But it fell,' he said. 'The Britishers thought it was impossible to take Singapore. But the Japanese outwitted them. Now that too has fallen. Our British masters are shaking in their smart leather boots. The Japanese are at their door. They feel Japan's breath on their necks.'

Anil, they called him. He only came to Delhi recently. He was in prison in Bombay for years, people said. A political prisoner, some told. A murderer, whispered others.

At her side, Rahul shifted his weight, then scratched his neck. He seemed bored and she pulled away from him, regretting bringing him here.

'Already our brothers are holding talks with the Japanese.' Anil lowered his voice. 'Believe me, they want our help. They will take India and with our help, the fall will be easier and faster.'

A thin man with wire spectacles said: 'What do we get in return?'

'What do you think?' Anil opened his arms wide. The room sang with his energy. 'Once the war ends, they set us free.'

An older man said: 'What about Baba Satya? And our comrades? Is there news?'

Anil stood to one side and another fighter rose to answer. Forty-seven men had been brought before a magistrate that morning, he said, Baba Satya among them. They faced all manner of charges, including sedition. The trials would be quick, with little chance of justice.

The conversation moved on. Asha's eyes stayed on Anil, standing now to one side. His body was sleek with muscle. He reminded her of Sanjay Krishna in his youth. He had the same courage, the same vitality. There were some men who rose above the rest. I had thought freedom would come in my lifetime, Sanjay said to her as he lay dying. Now perhaps it may come in yours.

The men around her stirred and started to creep away. Their meetings were always short. Every minute added to the risk.

Rahul rubbed at his ankles like an old man. He leant forward: 'I don't know, Asha.'

He made such a contrast with Anil that, for a moment, she despised him for being so ordinary. 'What?'

He whispered: 'We don't trust the Britishers to keep their promises and give us freedom after this war. Why should we trust the Japanese?'

She turned away, embarrassed. Where were his guts? Sanjay Krishna faced death alone in a dark, dismal cave, he gave his life for the struggle, for the freedom of others. She wouldn't betray his memory.

'You do as you like.' Her tone was sharper than she intended. 'There are always people who let others fight and die in their name, nah? Then reap the benefit.'

Rahul looked stung. 'I didn't say—'

She brushed him away. She wanted to go home, to lie quietly with her own thoughts in the darkness, as the women and children slept around her. Anil had stirred too many feelings in her, feelings she thought had already died.

Rahul parted from her in the heart of the slum and she walked on alone, tense and alert to danger. As she turned into a dark alley, close to their shack, she sensed cautious movement behind her. She pulled herself into a doorway and waited, straining to hear every sound. Her heart throbbed. Silence. She waited a while longer. Nothing, after all. Her blood settled and calmed. She stepped out.

'Ha!'

She let out a cry. Anil. His teeth glinting as he smiled, lying in wait in the shadows.

'Don't be afraid, little sister.'

'I'm not.' She scowled. At least it was dark. Her cheeks burnt and she was glad he couldn't see. 'And don't call me that.'

He looked amused. 'I remember someone who used to call you that.'

She narrowed her eyes. 'You do?'

He raised a bidi to his lips and lit it. He blew out a plume of pungent smoke.

'You don't remember me, do you? I was a scrawny boy then, a chai-wallah. Sanjay Krishna was my hero too. I heard what happened to your baba. And what you did in the islands. I salute you.'

She shook her head, confused. Had he really known her in those days, known her baba, known Sanjay? 'I must go.'

He settled himself on a rough stone wall, patted the place beside him. 'Sit with me a while. I want to talk to you.'

She hesitated. 'Is that why you followed me home like a stray dog?'

He lifted his hand. 'Be careful what you say.'

Something in his tone frightened her. She went at once to sit beside him. The stone was cool and the stench of the gutter, of rotting rubbish and waste, rose around them.

'He was a great man,' he said. 'He and his uncle also. We must think often of them in the coming days. We must be worthy of them.'

She looked down through the darkness at the shape of her hands in her lap. It was her own thought, of course. He seemed to know her.

'Our friends tonight, they say all the right words.' He spoke in a low voice, his mouth so close that his smoky breath warmed her cheek. 'But I wonder how much courage they really have. This is a time for heroes. For strong men to carve their names in our country's history.' He paused. 'And strong women also.'

She couldn't speak. He drew on his bidi and the end glowed red in the darkness. Behind them, on the far side of the wall, claws scuttled. A rat, perhaps.

'What about you, little sister? Will India remember you?'

She couldn't speak. Her breath stuck in her throat, choking her as surely as if his hand were on her neck.

'Someone is talking. He must be stopped. Will you come with me, now?'

She thought of Sanjay, of his courage as he faced death, and forced her head to nod.

'Good.' He dropped his bidi to the ground and crushed it into the dirt with the toe of his boot. He tipped back his chin. 'You say you have guts? Show me.'

He had a way of moving quickly and quietly through the slum, drawing her behind him through shadows and down narrow passages. She hurried to keep pace. If her sandal struck a stone or caught a clod of loose earth, he turned and frowned. It was late in the night now and few lamps burnt. Doorsteps, where men liked to sit in the evening to smoke and drink country-made toddy, were deserted.

They reached a distant quarter of the slum, an older, settled area where families were well established and the shacks more elaborate. He slowed his pace. Her ears throbbed with listening to the silence and the low fragments of sound buried in it: the murmur of lovers' voices, the distant mewling of a baby, the scream of a wildcat.

He lifted his hand and motioned her forward and pointed. A wooden door, set in a neat frame. A faint line of light showed in the cracks along its edge. He put his lips to her ear.

'Knock. See if he's alone. If not, bring him out into the darkness to speak to you.'

He drew something from his lunghi. A fragment of light caught it as it moved. A sharp-edged knife. He stepped to one side and flattened himself into the shadows beside the closed door.

For a moment, her feet didn't move. She steadied her breathing. Sanjay, she thought. Give me strength. Help me honour your name. She crept forward, raised her knuckles to the wood and tapped. Silence. All she could hear was her own blood roaring in her ears. She found the strength to tap again, more loudly. A pause. Cautious steps inside. A low voice.

'*Kon hai?* Who is it?'

She put her mouth to the crack. The wood was rough against her lips and tasted of tar. 'A friend.'

A bolt scraped back. The door opened an inch. A searching eye. 'Who?'

'Asha. The schoolteacher.'

He adjusted wire-rimmed spectacles on the bridge of his nose. She recognised him. A tall, thin man who came often to their meetings.

'My wife is sleeping,' he whispered.

She put her finger to her lips, then beckoned. He looked puzzled, gave a final glance back over his shoulder, then stepped into the alleyway, pulling the door closed behind him.

Anil pounced at once. His hand seized the man's head from behind, tilting it back and stopping his mouth. At the same instant, in a single movement, he plunged his knife into the man's chest. The eyes, fixed on Asha and magnified by the spectacles, crooked now across his nose, widened in surprise, then horror. He seemed unable to understand, to

366

calculate how Asha, this young woman, stood, separate, before him while a knife pierced his ribs.

Anil, calm and sure, withdrew the knife and struck him a second time, slightly higher. A low gurgle sounded from the first wound as the knife came out, a ghastly sighing of the heart, followed by a spurt of blood. A dark fountain pumped through his white dhoti and flew out across the ground. Asha moved her feet out of its path. The man's eyes rolled until he stared glassily at the sky. He hung limply now in Anil's arms. His spectacles slipped and fell to the ground, bouncing, then settling on their side for his wife to find for him, one final time.

Anil eased the body to the ground and pulled out the knife. He wiped it with care on the man's clothing until it gleamed clean, then pushed it back into his lunghi.

He raised his eyebrows to Asha and gave a half-smile and, in it, she read: see, we are bound together now, are we not?

He has done this before, she thought. Many times. It means nothing to him.

He pointed behind her, back down the alley, and, finding her feet suddenly able to move again, she started to run from him, from the dead man, from the unknown wife, back through the darkness, past innocently sleeping families, to her own shack and her own family and her own bed where she lay, eyes staring, body shaking, terrified, until the first watery light bled in through the cracks and the aunties, grumbling, started to stir around her, shaking off their sleep and rousing themselves to fetch water and light the cooking fire for chai to start another day.

Chapter Thirty-Nine

Isabel

Isabel wandered across the lawn, cigarette in hand. A bird hopped ahead of her.

A rustle. Something stirred the bushes. Her eyes drifted idly over the rhododendrons, then the line of mango trees. Her thoughts were elsewhere.

In the past week, all the talk was of Japanese advances in Burma. The newspapers said little but she heard the gossip in The Club. Our boys in Burma, the wives whispered. The Japanese are bombing them. There are constant raids.

Some made secret plans to ship their belongings and tried to secure a passage Home. No one spoke of it openly but the anxiety was clear. It seemed almost inevitable that if Burma fell, a Japanese invasion of India would follow.

Isabel drew on her cigarette. The bird hopped onto the soil and pecked. It was already three o'clock. No sign of Rahul. She'd had Cook bake a cake, prepare scones and sandwiches. A feast, she thought. Now she roamed restlessly round the garden, smoking, feeling a fool.

Only a month ago, her father had laughed when she'd expressed concern about Tom and others fighting in Burma.

'Why would the Japanese bother up there?' he'd said. 'It's jungle.'

Now, though, since the fall of Hong Kong, then of Singapore, he laughed less. He came home late at night and spoke little. India was preparing to defend itself, that was clear. The London newspapers focused on the war in the Middle East. The chance of external support in India's battle with Japan seemed low.

Voices drifted across the drive from the gate. She stopped to listen. The chowkidar scraped back the bolt and opened the gate. She dropped her cigarette, ground it into the grass with the toe of her shoe and went with a quick step to meet her guests.

'I'm so pleased. I wasn't sure you'd come.'

Rahul stood uneasily on the drive, holding a boy of about ten years by the shoulders. Abhishek. Last time she saw him, he was a wide-eyed toddler. Now he had grown into a lean youth, all bones and joints. His eyes were sharp with suspicion as he regarded her. A Western-style shirt was buttoned over his lunghi. The pattern was faded with repeated washing and it strained across his chest. His hair was slick with oil. He didn't want to come, she thought. His father dragged him here. I may be the first Britisher he's actually met.

She raised her hands in namaste to greet the boy and said in Hindustani: 'Welcome, Abhishek. When I last saw you, you were a child only. Now you are almost a man.'

The boy stared. His father poked him between the shoulder blades until he raised his hands in namaste.

'Can you ride a horse?'

He hesitated, then nodded.

'Nonsense.' Rahul gave the boy a light cuff about the ear. 'He climbed on the tonga-wallah's horse, maybe.

That's all. Or did you hitch a ride on a water buffalo?'

'Well, the syce will saddle my horse for you, if you like. Gypsy. She needs exercising.' She paused. 'The syce will help.'

The boy tilted his head back to read his father's face. Rahul didn't respond.

'Only if you like.' Isabel herded them into motion along the drive. The bungalow, looming, suddenly looked impossibly grand. The tended pots and the manicured, watered lawn seemed lush, compared to the arid landscape outside the compound.

Her voice chattered on. 'I thought we'd have a picnic on the lawn first and call it tea. Cook's cut some sandwiches and baked a sponge cake. Do you like cake, Abhishek?'

She spread a picnic blanket on the grass and called to Cook. He and Abdul carried out trays of food. The two servants glanced at Rahul as they set the plates on the grass but didn't greet him. Abhishek hung to one side. As Cook straightened up to leave, his eyes ranged over the boy with a stern, disapproving look.

'Was it dreadful in prison?'

She spoke in a low voice, almost afraid to ask. Rahul pulled at the loose skin round his fingernails. For a moment, she thought he hadn't heard, then he sighed.

'It was a long time ago.'

She put a hand on his arm. 'I tried to get you out, you do know that? I went everywhere.' She hesitated, remembering, and drew on her cigarette. He disapproved, she sensed it. Indian women didn't smoke, it wasn't considered decent. After tea, she had taken him on a tour of the garden and pointed out the rhododendron bushes with their dry, hollowed centres where they'd made dens as children.

Now they sat halfway up the old magnolia tree, resting against the trunk, looking over the empty lawn below. Abhishek was with the syce, being led on Gypsy in endless rounds of the paddock.

'I'm sorry Sangeeta couldn't come.'

Rahul shrugged. 'We're expecting another child. May the gods make him another son!'

Isabel stared. 'That's wonderful, Rahul. When?'

'A few more months only.'

'You sound worried.' She considered. 'Isn't Sangeeta strong?'

He blew out his cheeks. 'Not that. The situation is poor, that's all. So much of hunger. So much of joblessness.' He paused, gave her a quick sideways look and added quietly: 'So much of politics.'

'How's the mithai shop?'

He looked away. 'I'm a derzi now.'

'A tailor?' She stared. 'Is it a good living?'

He spread his fingers and rocked his hand. 'Not so much. I'm buying silk. Beautiful silk, very fine quality. I was wondering, perhaps—' He turned to her, embarrassed.

'I'd love to see it. What will you make?'

He shook his head. 'Whatsoever people are buying.'

'We'll organise a tea.' She nodded, overly enthusiastic in her eagerness to help. 'My mother knows everyone. Her friends send parcels back to England, you see. You can't get a thing there now. The government takes all the silk for parachutes and whatnot. You'll have plenty of orders.'

He looked again at his hands. 'You're very kind. I don't know . . .'

371

She shoved him with her shoulder. 'Just say yes, won't you? You'd be doing me a favour.'

They sat in silence for a while. From the tree, they looked across at the tops of the boundary walls and the monkeys climbing there. New babies clung upside down from their mothers' stomachs or perched on backs as the adults went about their business. How many generations of monkeys there must have been, she thought, since they were children. She'd missed them desperately when her parents sent her Home to live with the Misses Ellison. She had missed Rahul too.

'I used to think I was really Indian, you know,' she said. 'That you and I were brother and sister. I used to ask God every evening when I said my prayers. If I were really good, please could I be a Chaudhary? That's why I tried so hard to learn Hindustani.

'One day, I thought, I'd be eating supper with you, just as we used to, and no one would come to fetch me. I'd somehow be Indian and stay with you for ever.'

He looked at her in astonishment for a moment, then turned away. 'You wouldn't want it now.'

'Wouldn't I?' She bit her lip. The afternoon light was thickening and where it caught the fresh buds on the magnolia tree, they gleamed.

'They're ancient, you know. Magnolia trees. Go back millions of years. I was so pleased. This one always looked so gnarled. I imagined it here long before we came along, with dinosaurs sniffing its branches.' She pulled herself up to stand on the branch where they were sitting. 'Do you think we could still do it? Get to the very top.'

He shrugged. 'We're not children.'

'But you do remember?' She looked up into the branches at the sharp criss-cross sticks of light striking the wood, the leaves. 'It's another world, up there, that's what you said. Look that way, back towards the house, and we could see hundreds of years into the past. And there' – she pointed ahead across the garden – 'into the future.' She looked down at him. He hung his head, his eyes on his hands. 'You haven't forgotten?'

When he lifted his head, his eyes were sad. 'Perhaps better not to know the future.'

Her surge of excitement evaporated at once. She sat beside him on the branch and let her legs dangle. 'I'm sorry. It's seeing you again, after all this time. It brings back so many memories.'

Rahul faced away from her towards the low outbuilding where his family had once lived. It was bigger now, enlarged in the last decade to accommodate Abdul's growing family. Even so, the wooden roofs looked tiny from above. A fraction the size of the stables on the other side of the bungalow.

She thought of the smoky darkness inside, pierced by shafts of weak sunlight. And Rahul's mother: the strength in her brown arms as she washed, swept, cooked. Cook Chaudhary was never there. He was working in the cookhouse, kneading loaves or making pies or icing fancies for afternoon tea.

Her thoughts ran on. 'I know I was just a girl but life seemed easier then. No war. No hunger.'

'There's always been hunger. For common people.'

Abhishek appeared, down on the lawn. He picked out a dead stick from the back of the flower bed and started to thrash the bushes.

'You will come back, won't you? I mean it, about the silk.' She stubbed out the butt of her cigarette against the bark and started to lower herself to the bough beneath. Once she reached it, she looked back at him. 'I mean, all the things Baba Satya said, about hating the British. You don't hate me, do you?'

He didn't answer.

She filled the silence, afraid of what he might say: 'Everything's changing so quickly. I feel as if the world's spinning out of control. You know? What with the struggle against the British and the war.' She paused. 'It will end, I know that. But when? And what sort of world will we be left with afterwards? I shall miss India so much. You can't imagine. If we are forced to leave.'

He sat in silence, an odd expression on his face.

'And who'll be climbing the tree then?' She started to climb down. 'Abhishek, perhaps. With his little brother.'

Chapter Forty

The following week, one of Sarah's servants ran to the bungalow with a letter. Abdul brought it out to the verandah where Isabel was lunching alone.

She took it, nodded, waited for him to withdraw, then finally opened it.

The writing on the envelope was in Sarah's hand. Her note was short.

Izzy, This just came in a letter from Tom. Seems they're on the move again. Our last may not reach them. Yrs S

Isabel's hands shook as she opened the second sheet to see Edward's hand. His writing was unmistakeable but she saw at once that it was rushed, in comparison with the neat lettering of his earlier note. The edges of the paper were brittle and peppered with specks of dirt. The letter was dated almost two weeks ago.

February 21, 1942

Dear Mrs Whyte,
There is great uncertainty here. I cannot say more.
I have lost many men in recent days. Good men. I

write the same tired words of condolence to parents and wives and sweethearts and wonder what they think of me, as they read such poor phrases.

Bateman is one of those lost. I wrote of him before. A kind lad. He wanted so much to see his newborn son. Now his young wife is a widow and little James is without a father.

The aide has come. I must hurry. How can a letter find its way through all this chaos to Delhi and to your hands? I must have faith.

I stare now at the page and struggle to know how much to say. I have little time to try. My darling Isabel. May I call you that? Can you forgive me? It may be the last chance I have in this world to speak tenderly to you.

You cannot know how I curse myself for all the wasted years, when I might have written, when I might have come in search of you and did not. Please understand, it was never lack of love, never that. It was fear, pure and simple. Fear of damaging your reputation more than I already had. Fear, as the years passed, that you had forgotten me, that you had married another.

Pray for me. Know how much I love you. May God be with you.

Edward Johnston

She sat very still. The letter was limp in her hands. He had loved her, then, all this time. The loneliness of the last eight years, the heaviness of each day, pressed in on her. They were fools. Utter fools. Both of them.

Her hands started to shake. He was gone. Disappeared into the jungle. Even if she wrote now, it would never reach him. She let out a cry, bit down on her lip to silence herself. He would never know.

The letter slipped from her hand to the wooden floor. Her fingers raked through her hair, grasped it in clumps as she rocked back and forth. Her lips whitened where she clamped them together between her teeth.

By the time Abdul came out onto the verandah to clear away the dishes, her face was again composed.

'Cook will be angry.' Abdul looked dismayed. 'Isabel Madam has eaten nothing.'

'Never mind, Abdul. Tell him I have a headache.'

She got to her feet with care and withdrew to her room where she hid Edward's letter at the back of a drawer. For the rest of the day, she lay on her bed, clinging to the comfort of a pillow, her face pressed into its softness.

Several days later, Isabel's father left for the office without his tiffin. Normally Abdul would be sent but the main government offices were under curfew and he would find it difficult to penetrate the cordon. So Isabel, glad to make herself useful, set off by bicycle with the tiffin carrier and a box of Cook's sponge fancies strapped in her basket.

It was the end of the first week in March and already, although it was only ten o'clock in the morning, the heat swelled and gathered. The sky above was yellow with dust and hard sunshine. She stopped to tie a scarf round her hair to protect it as her wheels sent up clouds of fine, dry grit along the road, parching her mouth and throat. As she cycled on, her shirt and slacks stuck to her skin.

The heat would steadily worsen for weeks yet before they could hope to see the monsoon. The fighting season. That's what her father called it. The time of year when tempers were short and the slightest quarrels, between husband and wife, between brothers, between colleagues, turned quickly to violence. And this year, with the Japanese closing in and political arguments furious, tensions were already high.

The traffic was unusually spare that morning. It was a relief to be out and alone. The lines of the first checkpoint came into view in the distance as she cycled down the grand, straight avenue of Rajpath, through India Gate and past the broad stretches of lawn where Baba Satya's protest was disrupted. Barricades made a low metal wall, looping round the entrance. Three or four army trucks stood to one side, with covered troop vehicles. The soldiers were watchful as she approached. Shards of light splintered on their weapons.

To one side, a group of Indian men sat cross-legged, staring out along the road without expression. Day-labourers, she thought, waiting for work. She drew closer. No, they had a determined air. A protest then. She dismounted and wheeled her bicycle for the final stretch, going first to the Indians. The cool eyes of the soldiers ranged over them all.

'Namaste.' She put her hands together.

There were seven or eight men, lean and muscular, dressed all in white. The leader, seated in the centre, had a weathered face.

'*Kia ho raha hai?*' she said. 'What's happening?'

He hesitated, looking her up and down, taking in the headscarf, the neatly pressed blouse, the smart slacks pinned at the ankles by cycling clips.

'A dharna?'

He nodded.

'Why?'

A young man answered in English. 'Until now Baba Satya and so many fellows are staying in prison, madam. This dharna is for their release. Please be telling.' He nodded his head back towards the blank windows of the government building.

'Are you fasting as well?'

He shook his head. She dipped into her basket and pulled out the box of miniature cakes, resting the bicycle against her hip. Cook had sent a dozen and she offered them now but the leader, suspicious, shook his head.

She lifted one to her mouth and bit into it. Soft, sweet cake, crisp at the edges, iced in pink rounds. She offered again. Still the leader refused. She licked the crumbs off the tips of her fingers and tucked the box back in her basket.

'See you again.'

As she approached the barricade, the young British officer stepped forward to stop her. 'Miss?'

'Hello. All quiet?'

He shrugged, unfriendly.

'Mrs Isabel Whyte.' She lifted a hand from the handlebars but he didn't move to take it. 'DO Winthorpe's daughter. I've brought his tiffin.' She pointed to her basket and he raised his chin to see inside, then nodded, gestured to the Indian jawans to move aside and waved her through.

She secured her bicycle and entered the hushed cool of the building, crossed the atrium to the staircase, the tiffin carrier and cakes in her hands. The wood of the banister was smooth with wear. Sun filtered in through long stained-glass windows, bathing the marble walls and floors in a surreal, underwater light. A nineteenth-century portrait hung on the first landing and the eyes of a forgotten British commander followed her to the next floor.

The door to her father's office was ajar. Male voices murmured within. As she approached, his personal secretary, a Sikh with an imposing turban and thick beard, appeared in the corridor and nodded to her.

Inside, her father sat behind his voluminous desk. It was stacked with cardboard files of typed paper, faded by the sun and loosely tied round with string, which he was gradually moving from one side to another as he read and signed the documents inside.

'You forgot this.' She set the tiffin carrier and the cardboard box on top of a polished wooden cabinet. 'Cook sent cakes. He seemed to think you'd need them.'

A map of Delhi was fixed to the wall, studded with coloured pins. She leant in closer to look.

'Everything alright at home?' He spoke without looking up from his papers. His pen was poised in his hand, ready to signal amendments.

The government office was easy to find on the map. Three long rectangles, arranged in a horseshoe, set close to the circle of Parliament. She traced her route home along Rajpath with her eye and entered the Civil Lines, looking for their bungalow.

'Did you really need to call out the army?'

Her father closed one file with a sigh of paper and reached for the next. Thin pages crinkled in the stir from the ceiling fan.

'There could be fifty protesters by evening,' he said. 'Besides, it sends a signal. That we mean business.'

She crossed behind him and stood at the window, looking down at the front gate. From above, the protesters shrank to dark, seated dots.

'What's Baba Satya like?'

'A hothead. A troublemaker. London wants me to set him free but I can't say I agree. He's better behind bars.'

'They're impatient, that's all. They want independence and they don't trust us. I'm not sure I blame them.'

'Isabel.' He twisted round, frowned. His expression shifted as they looked at each other. His eyes softened from stern to concerned.

'Darling, I'm glad you've come. We need to have a talk. I was going to wait until things were a little clearer but perhaps. . .'

His tone alerted her at once. Bad news. She lifted her hand to the window ledge to steady herself. Tom, perhaps. His luck had run out. She stood very still. Perhaps Edward too. Her panic fixed itself on the polished swirls of her father's desk. For a moment, she didn't breathe.

Her father pointed to a chair near the wall. 'Maybe you should sit down.'

The quietness in his voice made it worse.

'Is it Tom?'

'Not exactly. Well, yes.' He made no sense. 'I mean, I'm getting reports from there. Rangoon, you see. Well, it sounds as if it's lost.'

'Lost?'

'Fallen to the Japanese.' His eyes were on hers. His hand set down his pen.

'So where's Tom?' And Edward, she thought.

He sighed. 'The army's moved north, apparently. I have to say, it's not looking good.'

No wonder Edward's last letter had been harried.

'Will they make it out?'

'It's all very confused, frankly.' He blew out his cheeks. 'It's not just the army, you see. People are pouring out of Burma in their thousands, tens of thousands, and not in good shape. Indians, I mean, you know, road workers and so on.' He tapped one of the files on his desk. 'We're setting up camps for them. Heaven knows, there's precious little food as it is.'

She sat very still. Gunfire, bursting through the jungle, shattering the stillness. Bloodshed. Men, wounded, lying in the mud. Edward. Her hands grasped each other in her lap.

'As for Tom . . .' Her father's eyes were sad. 'Well, I don't know.' He paused, watching her. 'You must think how to tell Sarah.'

He picked up his pen and turned his eyes back to his work. A tap at the door. The office chai-wallah carried in a tray of tea. He set out cups and saucers, teaspoons, a plate of yellow biscuits, bending over the low table, then crept away.

Her father, his tone falsely bright, said: 'Have a biscuit, darling. Or a cake, if you like.'

The tea was thick. The milk, boiled to white streaks, swam across the surface. The rich, sweet smell sickened her. She closed her eyes. She seemed to pitch forwards, falling into nothingness. Edward was gone, then. And Tom. The Japanese were storming across Asia. They were unstoppable. India would be next.

She forced herself to open her eyes, to focus. Her father's head was tilted forward over his papers. His crown showed a mottled brown and pink where his hair had thinned. She had trusted him, since she was a child, to look after them all, to guard his own small corner of the Empire. Now he seemed suddenly frail and rather lost, an ageing man whose time had already passed.

'We must be ready for them.'

Her father murmured, deep in his papers. He didn't look up.

'We must pull together. It's our only chance.' She got to her feet, leant forward and planted her hands squarely on the edge of her father's desk. 'Don't you see?'

He looked up. 'See what?'

'Let me talk to Baba Satya.'

His eyes widened. 'What on earth—?'

'We need to stand firm. British and Indians together. He must understand.' She nodded, trying to convince them both. 'Don't you see? He doesn't trust you. And he won't lose face. But talking to a woman. It might be different.'

Her father shook his head and frowned. 'Darling, I really couldn't—'

'Why not?' She pushed back from the desk and turned towards the door. 'What on earth is there left to lose?'

The empty police van that took her through the centre of Delhi to police headquarters was stale with rancid milk and the smell of constables' feet. The building looked more austere than she remembered. The watchtowers and rounds of barbed wire gave it the look of a fortress.

John Hargreaves came down to the main entrance to meet her, acting under her father's orders. His face was sullen. Last time she had seen him there, she was with Jonathan, pleading for Rahul's release, and he was a recent recruit. Now he was Delhi's Superintendent of Police.

'Was he always here?'

He shook his head. 'Transferred last week.'

He led her down chipped stairs to the basement and along a dank stone corridor. An Indian constable kept a respectful distance behind them. She blinked, adjusting to the gloom. An unpleasant fug of sour air and human waste. The men's boots and her lighter shoes slapped on the floor as they walked and the sound awakened noises ahead, high cries and low murmurs. Pale fronds waved in the half-light. They came into focus as they grew nearer. Hands, stuck out through the bars of cells, reaching. Her stomach tightened.

Hargreaves stopped at the furthest cell. The constable stepped forward to unlock the gate. She stepped in smartly and the lock clicked shut behind her. She stood still for a moment. Blood thudded in her ears. The bars made a metal wall at her back.

A low murmur of chanting. The darkness swam and shapes emerged from it. He was hunched on the ground in the far corner. His legs were crossed in a position of Hindu meditation, his heels close to his body. His elbows balanced lightly on bent knees, his hands rested, one in the open palm of the other, in his lap. His robes, once so white, were streaked with dirt and his beard looked unkempt. His eyes were closed. She thought of the imposing figure she'd seen on the platform on a sunlit lawn and wondered if this diminished creature could really be the same. The low incantation ran on and she stood, motionless, and bathed in its rhythm.

When it finally stopped, the cell fell silent.

'Is Rahul Chaudhary your spy?' His eyes stayed closed.

She was startled. 'Why would you think that?'

'Why did you rescue him? Why pull him from the crowd that day?'

'He's like a brother to me.'

'An Indian brother?' He snorted.

She lowered herself to sit beside him, her back against the

wall and legs crossed in front of her. The ground was warm and unpleasantly moist.

'Why are you coming here?' His voice was cold. 'This is, I am thinking, an official visit?'

'If it were, would they send a woman?'

'Perhaps.' He seemed to soften a little. 'They are full of trickery.'

'You men see yourself as different from each other, don't you? Indian and British. But to me, you're much the same. Pride first, common sense afterwards.'

Silence. His face was calm. She couldn't tell if he were listening. She shifted her weight on the hard floor.

'I love this country. I want to grow old here and, when my time comes, to be buried here, however different it may be in the future.'

She spoke carefully and deliberately. 'India will have independence. Everyone knows it. The questions are when and how.' She took a deep breath. 'Mr Churchill needs to find a compromise. He's sending an envoy. Have you heard? Sir Stafford Cripps. A sensible man, people say. He'll be here in a few weeks.

'So how will you meet him? Here, dirty, in rags, in a damp cell? Or clean and well fed, at a negotiating table, meeting as equals? Which, do you think, shows you in a better light? More importantly, which will bring the better deal for India?'

He opened his eyes slowly and looked her full in the face. His expression was alert.

'All you need do is tell them you won't stir up trouble,' she went on. 'No agitation. No fiery speeches. Stay within the law. They want to release you, don't you see? Make it possible for them.'

He looked at her closely. 'Your husband should keep you in check, madam.'

'My husband was murdered in the service of his country, sir. And yours too.'

Baba Satya spread his hands in his lap. His head was bowed, his eyes on his hands. The veins at his wrists were prominent and swollen. Her father was right, then. She was wasting her time.

Finally he lifted his head. 'I don't need a woman to tell me about this man's visit. I doubt he has anything of interest to say. But if Gandhi-ji and Nehru-ji and others agree to meet him, so do I. I see no reason to urge my people to violence until we know what message he brings from London.'

He paused and, even in that small, dark cell, he seemed to swell for a moment into the charismatic figure she saw earlier when he addressed the open crowd.

'But be aware. If this man comes empty-handed and stirs up hope for nothing, you will pay the price. Indians already fight shoulder to shoulder with the Japanese. And with every British lie, every piece of deceit, more are driven to join them.' He smiled, his teeth catching the glister of light. 'Have you counted, madam, how many we are, we Indians?'

She got to her feet. Steps sounded in the shadows of the corridor as the constable came forward to unlock the gate for her.

As she stepped through it, his voice followed her.

'Rahul Chaudhary should take care. Tell him that. He has a wife and child.'

She walked down the dim passage with Hargreaves by her side. Outside, in the fortified courtyard, he handed her back into the police van without a word.

Chapter Forty-One

Asha

Asha's body was slick with sweat as she walked home. It was late afternoon and the May heat pressed down on her head, her limbs, with the weight of the dead. Her feet were swollen and dusty in her sandals.

School would break for the holidays in another week and already the children suffered. They sat listlessly at their desks, too hot to concentrate and too thirsty also. The windows stood wide open but there was little stirring of air. All that flooded in were smells and sounds of the slum.

Sushil came pounding round the corner, arms flapping, and banged into her.

'Asha Auntie!' He was breathless and red-faced.

'What is it?' There was no normal reason to race about in this heat.

'Uncles are back!'

She stared. 'Uncles?' Was it possible? 'Who said such a thing?'

'They sent word. Now Mama and the other aunties are sweeping, crying, talking. They said to fetch you quick-quick.'

She wiped down her forehead with the end of her dupatta and quickened her pace.

The shack was in disarray. One of the aunties sat outside, blowing on the embers of the cooking fire. Her face was speckled with drifting ash. A pot sat ready by her side with a handful of chopped vegetables swimming in water. She looked up as Asha approached and covered her face with her scarf.

Inside, the other aunties huddled together on the floor, bent forward as they rocked, wailing and ululating.

Asha took one of them by the shoulder and shook her. 'What?'

They wailed all the more.

'Tell me. Are they here?'

Finally one of the older aunties wiped off her eyes and mouth and managed to say: 'A boy came, just now. Ramesh and Kumar and Sunil are shifted to a government camp, outside Delhi. Food is there and medicines also.' She shook her head. Ramesh took four sons with him to Burma, all leaving wives behind and children also. She had named only two. 'He gave no word of the others.'

'The boy, where is he? Can he take me to this camp?'

She blew her nose on her scarf, pointed outside the shack.

'Please,' she said, grasping at Asha's hand. 'Bring them home.'

They hitched a ride on a cart to the outskirts of the city, then walked north-west, following a road through the wheat fields, which gradually shrank to a dirt track. The first harvest had just been gathered in, snatched from the threat of the coming monsoon. Now the fields looked bald and dirty with spilt dust.

From time to time, she glanced at the boy. He was a

half-baked child, thin and shy. His shirt hung in shreds, revealing a back striped with scars. He seemed too afraid of life to be a trickster but she wondered, all the same, if his story were true.

The sun was falling. She stopped to catch her breath, wipe off her face and neck, shielded her eyes to look out across the endless fields, hazy with sun, dotted with the last labourers who tied sheaves and threw wheat onto carts and urged tired water buffaloes into motion.

She turned again to the boy. 'How much further?'

'Soon.' He pointed forward, as he always did. 'Here only.'

She sighed and pushed herself on.

A black stain appeared on the horizon, blotting out the gold of wheat. The boy turned, nodded, pointed. He too seemed relieved.

As they approached, dark shapes started to take form. Unstable, ugly homes, thrown together from wooden staves and sheets of sacking and discarded metal sheets. They stretched far back from the track, covering half a dozen fields. All across this land, stolen from farming, hunched figures were building shelters from the sun. Their movements were dull as if they were on the seabed, weighed down by an ocean of water. Children sat, bellies distended, staring vacantly at their drowning parents. The air was still but the whole scene was eerily quiet. The children lacked the energy even to play.

Two police-wallahs stood at the entrance to the camp with long switches in their hands, ready to give someone a beating. The boy hung his head as they passed and kept close to Asha's side.

A small girl, perhaps six years of age, stood close to the

path, her arms wrapped round her body. Her cotton salwar kameez showed red along the seam. The rest of its colour was bleached white by repeated washing. Fragments of a broken pattern of sequins hung around the lower part of the sleeves. They glinted in the sunlight as the fabric rippled.

The girl turned to face Asha as they walked by. Her head was covered with a dark dupatta that swamped her shoulders. She had the grave, still look of a widow. Her eyes, as they met Asha's, were deadened, the sockets too large for her small face. Her lips were thin and pocked with scabs.

Asha raised her dupatta to cover her head. The boy trotted along beside her. Off to one side, in a broad expanse of dirt, men cooked in iron pots. A wall of heat swam sideways from the cooking fires. They stirred in the rising steam with ladles as long as paddles. The air carried the smell of thin rice porridge. Beside them, other men sat cross-legged on the ground surrounded by pyramids of chilli, cauliflower, bhindi and potatoes, which they peeled and chopped into metal basins. Three police jawans sat on stools alongside, tapping their open palms with lathis.

The boy's attention was all on the food. She stopped, pulled at his arm.

'Where are they, these men?'

He stepped down from the raised path into the field, off to the right, and they started to thread their way between the shelters. Families huddled together, inert. Young women held babies too sick to suckle, small bundles of bones wrapped in rags. Half-starved children pressed against their mothers' sides. Men lowered their faces in shame. Here and there an elderly woman with rheumy eyes lay against a bedding roll or bucket, staring out without interest, her hope already exhausted. These ghost-people wore clothes that revealed bone-thin limbs. Joints protruded in painful swellings at ankles, knees, shoulders and wrists.

The boy stopped at a shelter, a piece of sacking stretched over wood to make a crawl space, and pointed. She shook her head. This old man was no relative of hers. He tilted back his head and seemed to struggle to focus on her.

'Asha?'

'Ramesh?' She crouched. Ramesh was always a strong man, a hard worker who liked to drink and afterwards use his fists. This man's body was wasted. She tried to hide her shock.

'What happened?'

He beckoned her closer. His breath was sour with hunger and his voice was little more than a whisper.

'Japanese,' he said. 'We fled. Walked. Week on week. No food. Berries and roots and whatsoever we could steal. No water. Just streams, puddles.' The effort of speaking seemed to exhaust him.

She looked behind him into the dark shelter. Two men lay there, as thin and listless as he was himself.

'Kumar and Sunil are here?'

He nodded.

'And the others?'

His eyes became rheumy. 'Dead. Left there, wheresoever they fell. May the gods forgive us.'

He started to shake. He has lost his senses, she thought.

'Your families are waiting. Come. We'll hire a cart, get you home.'

'No.' He managed to shake his head. 'Food is here. Water also. Not another step.'

She sat beside him and pulled him sideways to rest against her shoulder. As a girl, she was afraid of Ramesh Uncle. He bellowed at her baba. He beat his wife. She remembered it all. Now she wrapped her arms around his bony shoulders and rocked him, crooned to him in a low, rhythm as if he were again a baby.

Baba Satya's devotees fluttered around him, passing him a cup of water, a snack, placing a pillow behind his back. As more men arrived, they dipped low to touch Baba's feet in respect and felt themselves blessed by his hand on their heads.

Asha, come early, sat with her back against the wall, her legs crossed, and watched. Her stomach was hollow with nerves. Her eyes flickered to the door each time it opened, seeking out Anil. He had failed to attend their last meeting, leaving her to creep home, flat with disappointment. Something had happened to him, she thought. Some fight. Some accident. Or perhaps he was bored by them all, these ordinary men, and left them.

Again the door opened. She looked up. Only that dull old man with the withered arm who kept a chai stall. His solid wife waddled in behind him. They bowed low to Baba Satya and found their places in the circle. Faces shone pale in the low light from the oil lamp on the floor. Faces hollowed out by tiredness and lack of food.

Baba Satya raised his hand in greeting. 'Brothers and sisters.' His voice filled the small room. 'Have faith. Our leaders send word to us to be patient, to be calm.'

Asha found her eyes falling to her hands, pleated in her lap. She thought again of the way Anil had sprung from the shadows and seized the man he called a traitor, his hand sure and firm round the knife as he plunged it into the man's chest. She looked quickly round the room, afraid her thoughts were in her face. But all eyes were on Baba Satya as his voice ran on. No one paid her any heed.

She hadn't seen Anil since then. Twice, she thought he was following her as she picked her way through the slum to and from the school. Once she hid herself in a doorway, trembling as she pressed against the wood, expecting him to burst out and surprise her. Nothing.

At night, she decided he had abandoned her. Was it even possible to feel forsaken when they had barely spoken? Was he angry with her? She blinked. Afterwards, when the man lay dead on the ground, he raised his eyebrows to her, a complicit gesture. What had she done wrong? She had proved herself.

The door opened. Her eyes darted to it at once. Blood quickened in her ears. Him. Anil. Finally. Tall and strong in the half-light, his short black hair smooth against his forehead. He glanced unhurriedly round the room as if judging whether the meeting were worth joining. Heat flared in her cheeks and she pulled her eyes away from him, focused hastily on Baba Satya who paused, turned, nodded a greeting to Anil.

He came in and stood against the wall. He was the only one of them who didn't stoop to touch Baba's feet, to offer him allegiance.

Baba Satya carried on. 'Our leaders know we are loyal. That Britisher, Cripps, he brought nothing, nah? We sent him home to Mr Churchill in disgrace. A meaningless offer. But they heard our voices.

'Now more talks are coming. In the meantime, the Britishers watch us. You, brother, and you. Every last one of us. They want an excuse to move against us. Do you see? We must be patient a little longer.'

'Patient? You make me laugh.' Anil's voice, cutting through the room. He lolled against the brickwork like a prince. 'What do you take us for?'

Faces turned. Silence. Anil stared directly at Baba Satya. His body was tense with muscle. The room held its breath to see what Baba Satya might say.

'Brother, you are passionate.' Baba Satya had the air of a father checking an unruly son. 'When it is time to fight, you will lead us into battle. I know that. But that time is not yet come.'

Anil tossed his head. 'Have you seen, Baba, the skeletons who crept home from Burma? Tens of thousands of our brothers and sisters. So many died along the way. Have you not seen them?'

Baba Satya lifted his hand but Anil, ignoring him, carried on.

'The Britishers left them to die. Masters had their servants rush to pack their trunks and travelled back safely by train, leaving their servants to fight for their lives alone, to struggle back on foot. To walk how many hundreds of miles? Walk! Even as the Japanese advanced. Are you deaf? So many stories are there! And you tell us to be patient?'

The air shook with his anger. Asha clasped her fingers so tightly together that they turned white. No one stirred.

Baba Satya sat without expression, his eyes thoughtful on Anil's face. He knows, Asha thought. He knows Anil's raw power and how to harness it. Finally he smiled. 'Anil, I salute you. I say again, when—'

A bang on the metal roof. Men, startled, jumped to their feet. 'What's that?'

Another bang. And another. Hard. Stones, she thought. Some boys are there, throwing stones at us. A man dashed to the door, pulled it open. People were chattering, nervy and afraid. She looked across to Anil. He stood, unmoved, his back against the wall, the only point of stillness in the general dither and panic. She watched, fascinated. He turned and looked directly at her across the bustling room as if he had known all along that she was gazing at him, as if he expected nothing less. She was about to pull her eyes away, embarrassed to be caught, when he tipped back his head, opened his mouth in silent laughter. His teeth gleamed, sharp and long. Over their heads, the bangs drummed on, fast and insistent.

A man darted back in. 'The rains are come!'

The room was all movement as some rushed out to greet the rains and others ran back inside to spread the news.

'The gods be praised!'

Finally, after so many weeks of parched, dusty waiting, the monsoon had broken.

'Come. Leave these old men.' Anil at her side, his voice close in her ear. He turned and she followed without hesitation. He cut a path out through the jostling, shoving people, out of the shack and into the narrow street. Men danced there, arms splayed, faces upturned to the falling rain. In the houses around, people stirred, roused from sleep, and voices called from house to house, sharing the news: 'The rains are come!'

He led her down a side street. Raindrops pitted the surface of the dusty path. He paused in a corner where two blank walls met. For a moment, she was afraid of him, of the quiet corner. He bent and pulled a large stone up against the wall, searched for another and stacked it on top, then a third. He took her hand and steadied her as she climbed his stone stairs, then boosted her with his shoulder to climb up onto the top of the wall.

He scaled it too, then led her along the wall, then higher across a roof, finding his footing with confidence as they clambered along the tops of walls and across a rising ladder of metal-sheeted roofs, slick now with falling water. He commands these places, she thought. These high, hidden spaces. He uses them as the rest of us use paths. Her breath became short as she rushed to keep pace with him, her face lowered to watch her step. Water broke over the back of her head, ran down her forehead, cheeks, her nose, wet her lips and splashed at last down her neck to soak through her kameez.

He climbed a ledge and stopped, turned to take her hand, to help her. She tried to read his expression but his face was impassive. He settled on a narrow stone ledge, overhanging a three-storey building, the tallest in the slum. He sat there, his legs dangling, as if he might step out at any moment into endless air beneath his feet. She hesitated, peered forwards to crane over the lip. The soft pull of the ground so far below made her dizzy.

'Here.' He patted the stone beside him.

She paused. It would be too easy to fall.

He frowned. 'Don't you trust me?'

She sucked in her breath and held it tight in her lungs. She crawled forward, stooping low towards the roof, and forced herself to sit beside him. The ledge fell away to nothingness in front of her. Coldness fluttered in her chest and she tried to ease her weight backwards as if she could anchor herself there.

He was so close, his leg damp and warm against hers. He smelt of cigarette smoke. Rainwater streamed down his head, his face, his shirt, sticking the cotton to his chest. He smiled and leant close to her, placed his hand in the small of her back. She shivered, held herself rigid, tense, waiting.

A sudden shove. She let out a cry, grabbed at him in terror. She twisted and her mouth fell open in panic. For an instant, she seemed to feel herself already pitching forward, falling from the rooftop, helpless, clutching at the wet air as she plunged. Her stomach turned.

'No!'

How could he? He was laughing now, holding her against his solid chest, tightening his arms around her.

She struck him with a fist. 'How could you?'

He shrugged, still smiling. 'But I didn't, did I?'

He pulled away again, leaving her with a sense of the lack of him. Steady fingers of cool rain ran in where the warmth of his body had been.

They sat for some time in silence, listening to the pattern of distant noises across the slum: the shouts of men, barks of dogs.

'Look!' He craned forward, pointed.

She held herself away from the edge as she peered over. A group of men had run into the alley. Their contours were softened by distance, by the falling rain, but there was menace in their movements. They dragged something. A sack, she thought at first. She narrowed her eyes and strained to see. It fell to the ground amongst them. A man lay twisting on his side. They made a circle round him, kicked at his stomach, his back, his head. He writhed like a worm.

'Who are they?' She was shaking.

He shrugged, indifferent. 'What does it matter?'

'We should do something.'

His eyes, when he turned to her, were amused. 'You could jump.'

She pulled back. She couldn't look. It might be anyone. Someone she knew. What if he died down there and she'd watched and done nothing?

'He's probably dead,' he went on. 'What's the point?'

She stared at him. He lifted his hand and ran a finger down the curve of her cheek.

'They're not like us. They kill for sport only.' He spoke quietly as if he were sharing an important truth. 'We're different, Asha. You and I. We are made of the same stuff. Don't you see?'

Chapter Forty-Two

Isabel

'I hate the monsoon.'

Sarah gazed out over her garden. The lawn was sodden with falling rain and the verandah echoed to the steady cascade of water from the overhang to the wooden floor.

'Every year, the same. The flower beds flood.' She shook her head, reached for her teacup. 'Mud gets simply everywhere.'

Isabel smiled. 'I like the drama.'

'And the beasties. They come crawling out of all the nooks and crannies. This morning, the floors were positively alive.'

'But finally it's cool enough to sleep.'

Sarah raised her eyebrows. 'Honestly, Izzy. You're the only memsahib I know who refuses to complain about the climate. It isn't natural.'

Sarah's manservant brought in a fresh pot of boiling water and poured it into the teapot. Sarah reached for the long-handled teaspoon and stretched forward to stir the leaves. The teaspoon made rhythmical clinks against the side of the pot. Rising steam softened the contours of her face.

'I've hired two new chowkidars, did you notice?' Sarah straightened again and offered a plate of cakes. 'One's a cousin of the old chap who's been here for years and almost as old, frankly. If anything did happen, I think they'd have heart attacks. The other's a young fellow. He's strong but I don't know if I really trust him. I mean, if the Japanese come.'

Isabel took a vanilla fancy. 'Let's hope it doesn't come to that.'

'At least your father's here. I'm just a solitary memsahib.'

They hadn't heard from Tom and Edward since those hurried letters at the end of February, just before the fall of Rangoon. That was more than two months ago. Sarah rarely spoke about her husband. At times, though, the strain showed in the lines around her eyes, the tightness in her jaw, even now as she frowned to herself and replaced the lid of the teapot.

Sarah leant forward and lowered her voice. 'I've bought a handgun.'

'Do you know how to use it?'

'Not really.' Sarah cut a cake in half, scattering crumbs. 'I had to ask John Hargreaves to show me. I don't think he approves.'

'I don't suppose he would.'

'I'm a terrible shot. But it might frighten them off.'

Isabel sat quietly for a moment, taking this in.

'I lock it in the safe during the day and get it out at night. I've been sleeping with it under my pillow.' Sarah frowned. 'Do you think I'm a fool?'

Isabel hesitated. 'Well, it doesn't sound terribly comfortable.'

'It isn't.' Sarah laughed. 'It's like the princess and the pea, only worse.'

The downpour was easing. The cascade of rain down the edge of the verandah slowed to a trickle. Isabel looked out across the bushes and trees. They shone with water in the strengthening sunlight.

'I always wondered why you stayed, Isabel, after that awful business in the Andamans. I'd have left on the first ship.'

'Really?' Isabel considered. Sarah seldom referred to Jonathan's murder and her trial. No one did, at least not in her hearing. Was that what people asked each other: I wonder why she stayed?

'Was it because of him?' Sarah's voice was soft. 'Because of Edward Johnston?'

Isabel hesitated. 'Perhaps a little,' she said. 'But I might have stayed anyway. My life is here. Isn't yours?'

Sarah shrugged. 'Maybe not any more.'

Isabel turned her eyes to her plate. She cut her cake into two and bit into half, savouring the sweetness. She chewed slowly. It was odd to think back to the Andamans. Jonathan's death seemed old history to her now. If she grieved, it was for Edward, not for him.

Sarah said: 'Do you know, I was secretly pleased when I heard we'd lost Burma. I mean not pleased, exactly, but I thought: now Tom will come home. Stupid of me, wasn't it?'

The wicker creaked as Sarah lifted the teapot and refreshed their cups. The rain finally came to a halt. The verandah resounded with a low drip-drip-drip as the final drops rounded and fell. A black cat, a mangy stray, slunk out from its shelter in the depth of the bushes and crept across the lawn. Light spray rose from its lifting paws.

'That rich, warm smell after the rain,' Isabel said. 'Wet grass and leaves and earth.'

Sarah didn't answer.

* * *

A sharp crack startled Isabel awake. The room was dark. Still fuggy with sleep, she reached a hand from the tangled folds of the mosquito net and peered at the clock. Twenty to two. Her heart pounded. She lay back on her pillow. Perhaps it was a dream. She closed her eyes and lay still, listening. Her body started to relax back into sleep.

A second crack. A gunshot. She sat up at once and swung her feet to the floor. The room swam a little, then settled. She pulled on slacks and a shirt.

The bungalow was silent with sleep as she crept down the passageway and found her boots. Her father was hard to rouse nowadays. She thought of Sarah's handgun. Perhaps she should have one too.

The outside air was cool on her face. She stood in the shadow of the porch and looked. A dark shape moved near the bushes. A thwack sounded, followed by a cry, then a low moan. She crossed the path. The gravel crunched under her feet, loud in the stillness.

She passed the mango trees and emerged onto the lawn. A man was silhouetted there, dark against the grass, pointing a gun at the ground. She moved closer. The chowkidar, his old back crooked. He heard her and turned.

'Please be fetching Burra Sahib, madam. Quick-quick.'

Isabel went closer. 'What is it?'

Last time the chowkidar had opened fire at night, some years earlier, he'd killed a large monkey.

'Some fellow is there.' The chowkidar shook with excitement. 'See!'

She had almost reached him. A figure lay curled on his side on the ground, half-concealed by the rhododendrons. 'Is he shot?'

Another low moan. The chowkidar poked the man in the back with the barrel of his gun.

'Dacoits. Three fellows. I saw them, creeping towards the house.'

She looked round. 'And the others?'

'Gone.'

She turned her attention back to the figure on the ground. It looked more boy than man. She ignored the chowkidar's frown and bent down, put her hand on the ribcage. Every bone stood proud under the skin. A half-starved boy, then. His breathing was laboured.

She said in Hindustani: 'Are you hurt?'

A groan reverberated through his chest.

She ran her hands gently over his body, feeling first his chest, his torso, his legs. Her fingers came away clean. She reached for his shoulder and pulled him gently towards her. He rolled onto his back in a sudden heavy movement, one arm trailing. His face gleamed, unnaturally pale, in the low light. Blackened streaks ran around his ear and down the side of his cheek. She leant in to look.

'Abhishek?' Rahul's boy. 'What are you doing here?'

He opened his eyes and stared up at her, afraid.

'You clipped his ear.' She spoke back over her shoulder to the chowkidar. 'Lucky it wasn't a few inches further in. You'd have killed him.'

The chowkidar shuffled uneasily. 'Burrah Sahib. Please be telling.'

'Nonsense.' Isabel reached down to Abhishek, took his arm and pulled him to his feet. He rested against her shoulder. The chowkidar raised his gun and muttered.

'Go back to the gatehouse now.' Isabel nodded. 'I'd

keep this quiet, if I were you. This boy's a friend of mine.'

An hour later, she sat on a chair in her bedroom, looking down at the boy. He was sleeping now, lying curled on her rug, covered with a blanket. His ear was cleaned, the skin stained purple with iodine. The glancing bullet had cut out a small piece but he seemed able to bear the pain and the bleeding had stopped.

She sat for a few moments, studying him. His skin was smooth, his eyelashes long and dark, twitching lightly as he dreamt. He looked still a child but his cheeks were sunken and his chin jutted.

She would make sure he ate well at breakfast, then deliver him safely home to Rahul. She locked the bedroom door before getting back into bed and slipped the key under her pillow.

Abhishek was silent and sullen. Twice, when the tonga slowed, he tried to jump out and run. Now, finally, he leant forward to the tonga-wallah and pointed down a side street along the edge of the slum. The tonga-wallah drew up his bony horse. Abhishek strained away from her as she twisted to climb out of the tonga, her hand grasping his wrist as she drew him behind her.

Isabel asked the tonga-wallah to wait. She hadn't been into the slum for years, not since the war broke out and riots became common.

She stood for a moment, looking round. Abhishek hung at her side. The dirt road was slick with splatters of slime, which shone in the morning light. Filthy water spilt out from a central gutter, swollen with rain. The air swam with the stink of human excrement and the sour-sweet smell of rotting flesh. She lifted her scarf to cover her nose and mouth.

A vegetable hawker sat on the side of the road behind a meagre display of undersized tomatoes and onions. He lifted his eyes as she pulled the boy past. The dark shapes of stacked bales of cloth appeared ahead and she quickened her pace.

'Rahul? Are you there?'

It was a tiny space, barely wide enough to enter. The interior was eaten up by stacks of rolled cloth. She stood at the entrance and peered into the gloom. Towards the back of the cave, a figure stirred and rose.

'*Kon hai?* Who is it?' A moment later, Rahul emerged, blinking. 'Isabel Madam?' He seemed unable to believe his eyes for a moment, then his expression changed and he peered past her at the boy. 'Abhishek?' He seemed to take in the sight of his son's red, swollen ear and frowned. 'What happened?'

'I'm sorry.' She hesitated.

Rahul reached, took his son by the arm and pulled him into his stall, past a cramped working space where a length of cotton lay, interrupted in its flow, pinned by the needle of a battered sewing machine. She followed without a word through to the back and into a dark, narrow passageway, which led to a wooden gate in the wall. The courtyard beyond was cramped and gloomy. On the far side, two women sat with their backs to them, hunched forward on a low charpoy set against a shaded wall.

'Sangeeta?'

Sangeeta turned at the sound of her husband's voice, saw Isabel and scowled. She looked much older than the young woman who had swept the yard behind the mithai shop all those years ago and tended her sick mother-in-law. Her face was hard and prematurely lined. A baby, wrinkled and impossibly small, lay sleeping in her arms.

Isabel put out a hand, embarrassed. 'Sangeeta. I'm sorry. I shouldn't have come. But your son—'

Her eyes sharpened as they moved to the boy. 'Abhishek?'

The boy skirted his mother as he slunk into the yard and heaped himself against the far wall, wrapped his arms round bony knees.

Rahul picked up a broken stool from the corner, brushed it off with his sleeve and set it beside the charpoy. He gestured to her to sit.

'I'll send for chai.' He seemed tense.

Isabel hesitated, wondering whether simply to go. The boy was delivered. Perhaps, after all, there was little more to say. She looked round the courtyard, reading it. A round stone wall, covered with a metal sheet, showed a communal well. On the far side, a row of metal pots stood along a rectangle of bricks, which were blackened with smoke from a cooking fire. They had their own space before. Now they shared with other households.

'I won't stay.' She looked at Rahul, standing tense and expectant beside his wife and newborn. 'Congratulations. Now you are doubly blessed.'

He shrugged. 'A girl.' Not, then, the second son he wanted. 'Rupa. We are naming her after her grandmother.'

'Rupa.' She smiled. 'That's a beautiful name, Rahul. You must be very proud.'

The second woman sat hunched forward since Isabel entered the courtyard. Her scarf was raised, covering her head and held forward to conceal the side of her face. Now, as Isabel made to leave, the woman shifted and twisted to look. A sharp pair of eyes. Hard and unrepentant.

'Asha?' Isabel's legs trembled. Her breath stuck in her

406

throat and she found her hand at her mouth. The air in the yard shifted. Rahul frowned, looking from one woman to the other. The boy, curious, lifted his head and stared.

Rahul stepped forward. 'Thank you for bringing home my son.' He spoke softly to her, blocking her sight of the women. 'I'm sorry if he is' – he hesitated, groping for the right word in English, then turning to Hindi – 'museebat.' Troublesome.

He escorted her back to the tonga. As she was about to climb inside, she hesitated, turned to him.

'Is that why?' Of course, Rahul knew Asha. They had all lived together at the bungalow, all three of them, when Asha's father was their sweeper. Isabel's world shifted and found a different shape. The sight of Asha brought back a flash of memories. Of Jonathan, of her trial, of the long, dark nights in a prison cell where she sat alone and faced death.

'Is it because of her?' she said now to Rahul. 'Is that why you won't let me help you?'

He hung his head, looked at the ground.

She thought again of Asha's hard eyes. Last time she saw them, she was in prison. Then, too, they had been without mercy.

'But why, Rahul?' Her voice sounded weak and insubstantial. 'We were such great friends. Weren't we?'

He didn't raise his eyes to look at her. 'Of course, madam. You are very kind. It is difficult, only.'

Her voice caught in her throat. 'Like brother and sister.' She swallowed, gathered her breath. 'I loved you like a brother, Rahul.' She hesitated, tried again to speak. 'Did it mean nothing?'

He didn't answer. The crown of his head showed streaks

of grey. We grew old, she thought, and we grew separately. How did that happen?

The tonga rattled back through the unmade road of the slum. Her stomach was tight. Her hand gripped the door and her knuckles whitened where they clutched at the handle.

In all this time, she had tried never to think of Asha, of where she might be, of what had become of her. Now, to be confronted by her again, so suddenly and without warning, felt like an assault. She and Sangeeta, sitting calmly side by side. Both women hated her, she knew it. She shook her head, wiped off her eyes with the end of her scarf. Rahul was lost to her. She saw that now. The past was dead.

The stalls and hawkers passed by the window in an unseen blur. She shook her head. I wanted to help him, that was all. She thought again of the new baby girl. Her tiny, puckered face. Her skin so clear it was almost translucent. Rupa. Named after the grandmother who had once welcomed Isabel into her home and fed her alongside her own children. This was another Rupa, born into a new and different world.

Isabel sat rigidly, her head held forward towards the back of the tonga-wallah's head and the torn, bobbing ears of his old horse. The tonga led her home, out of the cramped Indian quarters to the broad, grand streets of the Civil Lines. She had no wish now to look back.

Chapter Forty-Three

Asha

'What are you, a common thief now? You bring shame on this family.'

Sangeeta wanted to thrash the boy. If it hadn't been for the baby in her lap, sleeping through it all, it would have been hard to stop her. Asha sat with her hand on her friend's arm, keeping her in her seat.

'Why did you go there? Have you no brains at all?'

The boy sat sullenly with his arms wrapped round bent legs, his head buried in his knees.

'It's your father's fault. He's too soft on you.'

The boy's hands were locked together tightly and his bent head trembled.

'Why did you go?' Asha kept her own voice soft. 'Who went with you?'

Sangeeta said sharply: 'Maybe he went alone.'

Asha shook her head. 'Sushil was there, wasn't he?'

The boy looked up, startled, and her heart quickened.

'Is he hurt?'

'He got away.' He sounded sorry for it, angry that he was the only one caught. 'He and Ajay both.'

Her breathing steadied again. Not shot, then. Sushil needed a strong hand but he was not a bad boy. She would speak to him later.

'But why did you go there?' Sangeeta again. 'Have you no pride? They already look down on us, these Britishers.'

Rahul, back again in the yard. His shoulders sagged. 'I took him there. He saw how much they have.'

'They didn't believe me,' Abhishek blurted out. 'That I rode the horse. I wanted to show them. And Ajay said, when he saw the mango trees, why not take some?'

'You think she's a friend?' Sangeeta turned now on her husband, stabbing the air with her finger. 'Where was she when the Britishers sent you to jail?'

He shrugged. 'She says she tried to help.'

Sangeeta spat into the dust. 'Tried to help.'

Rahul crossed to his son. He gave him a cuff across the head, which knocked the boy sideways. He lay, stunned for a moment, sprawling in the dust.

Sangeeta got to her feet, the baby still sleeping in her arms, and crossed the yard towards their room. 'Act like a man,' she said from the doorway. 'Give him a proper beating. One he'll remember.'

Once she disappeared, Abhishek scrambled to his feet and bolted for the street. Rahul let him go. He lowered himself onto the charpoy beside Asha, where his wife had just been sitting, and rubbed the heels of his hands into the sockets of his eyes.

'She worries.'

'She worries?' Rahul shrugged. 'Do you think I sleep? I earn barely enough to feed one person.'

'He's a good boy.'

'He used to be. Now he makes so much of trouble. Maybe she's right. Maybe I should beat him.'

They sat together in silence for a few minutes. Overhead, clouds were gathering, darkening the sky.

'She is right about the Britisher.' Asha spoke in a low voice. She didn't want Sangeeta to hear. 'Don't see her again. It's dangerous.'

'Dangerous?'

She leant closer to him and whispered. 'Some of our friends are impatient. They won't wait while the British talk. What do they say? Just empty promises.'

He narrowed his eyes. 'What do you mean?'

She slid her eyes away from his. 'Keep away from her. Don't be a traitor to your own people.'

'A traitor?' He shook his head and let out a slow, sad sigh as if his chest were punctured. 'We were friends once, when we were children. That's all. She might be foolish but she tries to be kind.' He paused. 'Who would condemn me for that?'

Anil, she thought. He'd condemn you with a knife. You don't know him. She got to her feet.

'Make up with your wife, nah? And as for the other thing, there's a meeting tonight. Make sure you come.'

He raised his head. His eyes were bloodshot with tiredness and his expression weary. 'I need to work,' he said.

'You must.' She paused, not certain if he understood how serious she was. 'Show your loyalty.'

The usual meeting room, in the back of the chai stall, was barely big enough for the crowd that gathered that evening. Asha arrived early and sat with a small knot of women on stools ranged against one wall, a little apart from the main body of the room, watching as it steadily filled with men. The windows were striped with iron bars, coated in the remnants of flaking paint. It had rained all afternoon and the puddles and runnels in the alley outside slowly gave back their water to the hot steaming air. Inside, men came with bare arms and chests, groins wrapped round by lunghis, dirty feet pushed into chappals. The room swam with stale sweat, toddy fumes and the smoke of cheap bidis.

Asha didn't look directly at the men as they poured in through the doorway, smoking and spitting and hollering, but she screened them with small, covert glances, scanning the faces for Anil.

Many of the men were known to her. Traders and labourers, hawkers and stallholders, dhaba- and dhobi-wallahs from the neighbourhood and beyond. Her cousin Ramesh came, his sons Kumar and Sunil following. They were home now, their bodies still thin and weak. There was no work to be had, even at the lowest wages, and Ramesh was drinking. Their household, which had been for so long a place of women and children, was again furious with male snores and shouts and quick fists.

Still they came. When the room seemed almost bursting, the men jostling each other for space, the women drawing their stools into a tight, protective circle and shrinking into their corner, a gang of ten or twelve men, young and strong with ruddy faces and coarse voices, pushed their way in. Anil strode behind them. He surveyed the room coolly, as if noting for himself who was present. Asha slid her eyes down to her fingers as his glance strafed the room. Her face became hot.

Finally, Baba Satya's men cleared a path through the crowd and led him, imposing in his orange guru's robes, to a chair. He stood beside it, raised his hands and the room quietened as they waited for him to speak.

'My friends.' His voice resounded through the small

space. 'The Britishers have promised much. What have they delivered? Mr Churchill sent his man all the way from London to talk with us and he brought us nothing.'

A murmur of agreement.

'We have listened enough. We have waited enough. Now we must take action.'

Men nodded, pushed forward.

A man at the back shouted: 'Teach them a lesson.'

Another cheered.

Baba Satya raised his hands and commanded quiet.

'A dharna,' he said. 'We will hold fresh protests, there at their gates. I myself will fast also. Every day as they go to and from their offices, to and from their meetings, they will see us and blush.'

A few murmurs in response. A dharna? Was that all?

Baba Satya seemed to sense the disappointment. 'The Britishers in London hear everything. Our protest will anger them. Slowly, slowly, we will win this battle for freedom.'

His men, flanking him, raised a cheer but the echo from the assembled crowd was feeble. A pause. Outside in the alley, two men argued as they passed the open windows and fragments of their anger drifted in.

'A dharna? You call that taking action?'

The crowd shifted. Anil stepped forward and faced them all. His eyes were calm. His voice was defiant. Asha's stomach tightened.

'Your day has passed, old man.' He shook his head at Baba Satya. 'No more talking. No more dharnas and rallies. What have they brought? Nothing. They laugh at us, the Britishers.' He cupped his hand to his ear and made a show of listening. 'Can't you hear?'

The faces in the crowd were fixed on Anil. He knows, she thought. He knows these people and what they need. He has them.

Baba Satya lifted his hands. 'I understand your impatience.' He had the air of a weary teacher. 'But listen to me when—'

Anil's hand was still at his ear. 'Is someone talking?' He looked round, his face mocking. 'Such a thin old voice, I can't hear it. It is drowned out by the noise of the Britishers, laughing, cursing us all.'

The boorish young men who came with Anil started to heckle Baba Satya.

'Go home, old man.'

'Tell us, Anil. What to do?'

Their faces were shining with heat, perhaps with toddy also. Their fists punched the air. The small room seemed to rock with rising anger. The women shrank closer together.

Baba Satya opened his mouth to reply but his words were drowned by the growing commotion. A second later, he flinched and wiped off his cheek with the corner of his robe. A woman near Asha gasped. Someone had thrown a rotten apple. The insult to such a guru was unthinkable. The room seemed to hold its breath.

A moment later, a second missile streaked through the air. Then a third. Asha's breathing quickened. They came ready for this, she thought. Anil watched now with a curious half-smile on his face.

The crowd frothed and shifted. Some men ducked their heads, whispered to each other. They seemed embarrassed to see the guru shamed. Others caught the rising mood of rebellion.

Anil's men raised slogans.

'Home Rule!'

'Jai Hind!'

A forest of fists rose to beat the air.

Baba Satya's men gathered round him, forming a shield and ushering him sideways towards the door to safety. The debris rained down on their heads like arrows. Still Baba himself twisted back, even as they propelled him out through the doorway, trying to reason with the men. News of this humiliation will spread rapidly, she thought. He is damaged by it, finished even. From this moment, he is yesterday's man.

Once they had gone, Anil stepped to the front. He stood where, moments later, Baba Satya had been. The floor around his feet was littered with cabbage leaves, smears of apple pulp and broken tomatoes.

'Will we fight?'

The room rocked.

'Let's teach our enemies a lesson, nah? Not words, not protests, but fists and sticks, guns and knives. Fight for our rights like real men.'

The men were agitated now, whipped up with alcohol and heat and the thrill of witnessing the father of the slum overthrown by an angry young warrior.

'They don't think we have the balls. Do we?'

The crowd roared. The woman beside Asha put her hands to her ears and lowered her head. The throb of the shouting shuddered through the fabric of the room. The wooden stools trembled under them.

Anil's face was a mask of quiet control and yet his voice reached every corner of the room.

'What are we waiting for? What do we have to lose?'

A scuffle broke out. A punch was thrown, a man staggered

and the crowd bunched as it made space around him.

'Save yourself for our real enemies.' Anil smiled. 'You know who they are. Not Britishers only but Mohammedans also, those brown-skinned traitors who hide amongst us and work with the British for themselves.'

He looked across the men, reading faces. Some looked uncertain.

'Bhai, perhaps you know them? A butcher, a tanner, a labourer? Do not be deceived. These people are enemies in our own neighbourhoods.'

'Curse them!' A shout from Anil's men. They jostled and strained.

Anil continued in the same commanding tone. 'Why do you think these talks achieve nothing? Why? Because the Mohammedans plot against Hindustan. They work in league with the British devils.'

'Kill them!'

'Traitors!'

'Are you men? Will you follow me and fight for freedom? Come, then! Come! Now. Tonight.'

Anil raised his hand. Light flashed. A knife. Asha froze. On all sides, the men pressed forward, shouting support. The anger was infectious.

'Prove yourselves now, to your brothers, to your wives, to your sons!'

He turned to lead the baying crowd out into the night, his hand held high. Through the chaos of the crowd, the shifting bodies and flashing fists, his eyes found hers and his look was deliberate and full of power. See, it said. See what measure of man I am and how I command them and I will command you also.

Then he was again moving and the crowd pressed after him, screaming and pumping the air and the energy seemed to drain from the room as they surged out. Their cries became muffled and returned as echoes, which bounded off the walls of the alley and came back to them through the rusting windows.

A woman cried softly, her face in her scarf. Asha sank to the floor and wrapped her arms round her body and found herself rocking. She was spent, exhausted by a heady, confusing mixture of pride in this man who reached for her, who claimed her as his own, and fear at what he might do.

That night, she lay still on her bedroll inside the shack, straining to hear. The air was thick with heat. Inside, the only sound was the steady pulse of the aunties' breathing and the low snuffles and dream-moans of the children curled against their sides.

Outside, a faint echo rose, diluted by distance. A clamour of male voices. Screams. Once or twice, the crack and pop of fire. She held her breath, listened. Where were they? She wasn't sure. Beyond the body of the slum. But what of the Mohammedans? Some twenty or thirty came to the government school, including the pale, solemn children of the weavers from Benares. What of them?

Late in the night, Ramesh and his sons crept into the shack and settled themselves for bed. They smelt of smoke. Asha lay on her back as they stretched on their bedrolls and began to snore. She was too afraid to ask them where they had been, what they had done.

In the morning, the aunties, back from the well with water and crouched over the cooking fire, were hushed.

417

Asha, washing her face and hands, felt the slap of their silence. It was strained and unnatural and it stretched across many households, many shacks. The air was acrid with hanging ash. The children rubbed their eyes and coughed as they woke.

When she set off through the slum, eyes slid away. Faces turned to the ground. Something terrible had happened. Everyone knew it and no one spoke of it.

She found her feet leading her off her usual path to school. No one would hurt a child, she thought. And the weavers, they're no threat to us. The children who came to school were stunted by too little food, too little sleep. But they had large brown eyes and quick fingers and the smallest girl drew endless pictures of horses in her school book, horses galloping in mid-air with crooked legs and flowing manes and she took pleasure in the drawing, Asha could see it, whatever else she learnt.

She reached the rubbish dump and the stones underfoot became slippery with slime. The ash swirled more thickly, stirred up by her sandals. There was no sign of the scavenging boys who picked their way across the black, sodden rubbish. Only a pair of mangy dogs who sniffed and nosed and paid her no heed. A second smell now, keener than ash. She raised her scarf to cover her nose and mouth and took a moment to place it. Burnt hair. She knew it well. Sometimes the aunties, sitting by the cooking fire, raked through their hair with their fingers and threw the loose strands into the embers where they sizzled and gave off a pungent, visceral scent. The memory came back to her now.

She skirted the dump and followed the path down to the far side. She stopped, stared in horror. The single-storey landscape had been levelled. The shacks ahead lay in tatters. Walls had been smashed and contents scattered. A blackened, upturned pot here. There, in the ash, the handle of a ladle, the broken shaft of a spoon. She hurried on. Charred wood cracked and split under her weight.

There was no sign of the weavers nor their children. She picked her way through the debris, which was once their home. Only the brick storeroom was still intact. Its door hung open. Inside, fine ash rose in a cloud, disturbed by her footsteps as she approached. The smells were overpowering. Of singed cloth and burnt fibres but also of kerosene. A dark mound rose against the far wall. She walked across and prodded it with a stick. What had been a pile of silk, the most gorgeous, precious silk, fell into a hundred blackened, sooty fragments. Someone had taken pains to burn it. She let the stick drop.

Outside she stood for some time in the remains of the courtyard. The charred frame of the charpoy lay on its side, its rope lattice tattered and hanging in shreds. That was where the young girl sat, the child whose thin fingers drew galloping horses.

She wrapped her arms round her stomach and closed her eyes. The sun fell hot on her face. A bird cawed and flapped and the sound of its wings faded to quietness. She started to shake, lowered herself finally onto her haunches and crouched there, trying to breathe and waiting for the trembling to pass.

He had done this, Anil. She gripped her body tightly. Violence meant nothing to him. She had seen it with her own eyes, the day he knifed a man to death in front of her, daring her to be afraid. But to burn out families, with small

419

children? Bile rose in her throat and she bent double as she retched.

When she recovered, she wiped off her mouth with her scarf and opened her eyes. She started. A girl, barely three, stood in the wreckage, staring at her. A strange child. Her salwar kameez was grey with overwashing and sagged at her neck. A jagged piece of salvaged wood hung from her hand. Her eyes were deadened.

'Come, child.' She held out her hand. 'Where do you live?'

The child simply stared.

'Where's your good mother?'

Finally Asha took a step towards her, hand outstretched as if she were coaxing a wild dog. The girl, startled out of her trance, turned and scrambled away through the shafts of broken wood, raising clouds of ash with her small feet.

The Mohammedan children didn't arrive for school. The remaining pupils spread themselves more liberally along the benches and filled the empty spaces. By lunchtime, it seemed as if they had never been.

After school, she went in search of Rahul. He sat at the back of his stall. He seemed to be sewing but when she sat beside him, she saw that his hands, always so busy, lay empty in his lap. His cheeks shone pale in the half-light and his eyes were sunken.

She bought chai from the boy at the stall and they sat together.

Finally she said: 'You've heard?'

'Those poor girls.' His voice was broken. 'They called me uncle.'

She opened her mouth to speak, then closed it again. The

stall was cramped and airless. Motes of dust from the cloth danced in the weak shafts of light falling around them.

'I am ruined.' He was unnaturally calm. 'I borrowed so much to buy silk yarn for them to weave into cloth. It was my dream, to make money for Sangeeta and the children. Was that a wrong thing?'

He seemed dazed. He lifted his chai-glass to his mouth but seemed to forget to drink. A cart rumbled past along the path.

'Who did that? Do you know?' He sounded suddenly fierce. 'They were just children.'

She shuffled on her seat, buried her face in the rising milky steam from her glass.

'Maybe they went back to Benares.'

He gave her a pitying look. 'We talk about freedom and all we do is kill one another. They preach madness, these hotheads and goons. And no one has the courage to stop them.'

'Hush.' Asha put her hand on his arm and looked warily towards the street. 'Do you want to be next?'

He shook her off. 'So still I must be afraid to speak truth? Then they're no better than the Britishers.'

She thought of Anil and the look he gave her as he led the men out into the slum to take revenge on their enemies.

'Think of Sangeeta and the children. They need a husband, a father.' She paused, turned to face him in the cramped space. 'Listen to me, Rahul. No one must know about your business with the weavers. You hear me? These are dangerous times.'

His face was sullen but she felt his attention and went on.

'You don't understand these men. You are one of two

421

things to them: a friend or an enemy. Don't be a fool. Never speak of those children. We must carry on as if we know nothing.'

He blew out his cheeks. 'What sort of world am I giving my daughter? Tell me.'

She shook her head. 'Please, Rahul. For your family's sake, be careful what you say.'

Chapter Forty-Four

Isabel

Isabel was sitting over a late breakfast with her mother when the commotion sounded on the drive. The frantic ringing of a bicycle bell. A woman's voice, shrill, calling her name.

Her mother set down her cup and frowned.

'Don't get up, Mother.' Isabel set aside her napkin and rose to her feet. 'I'll go and see.'

Sarah, red-faced and breathless, skidded to a halt in front of the bungalow. She rapped on the dining-room window with her bare knuckles, still astride her bicycle.

'Goodness.' Her mother peered. 'Whatever's the matter?'

Isabel ran outside. Sarah, bent double over the handlebars, struggled for breath. Isabel took her by the shoulders, helped her off the bicycle and guided Sarah to rest on the window sill.

Sarah opened and closed her mouth, barely able to speak, then pulled a crumpled piece of paper from her pocket and thrust it forward.

'Tom?'

Sarah nodded.

The paper shook in Isabel's hands as she unfolded it. It was a short, printed notification from the Red Cross. It took her a moment to understand. Captain Thomas James

Winton. A prisoner of war of the Imperial Japanese Army. The name of the camp meant nothing to her but the place did: Singapore.

'Oh, Sarah.' She reached for her friend, pulled her close. 'I thought—'

'Alive.' Sarah's voice was muffled. 'Thank God.'

Isabel hugged her, then turned to look again at the paper. 'There's hope, Sarah.' She paused, not yet able to believe the printed words. 'The war won't last for ever.'

Sarah nodded, drew out her handkerchief. 'Singapore. It's so far away.'

'Come inside.' Isabel pulled Sarah to her feet. 'We're finishing breakfast.'

They walked into the cool of the bungalow. Isabel called to Abdul to set another place and pressed Sarah to eat.

'Such a blessing.' Her mother, grand at the head of the table, opened her arms in welcome and embraced the news. 'We went through this whole business in the Great War.'

Sarah took a seat and the very English business of breakfast closed calmly around them all.

Her mother took the lead, advising how to put together a parcel. How soon the war would be over. How quickly Tom would be home.

Isabel was silent. Her toast sat uneaten on her plate.

When they finished breakfast, her mother got to her feet.

'Sarah, you must come at once and write to him. Use my writing desk. The Red Cross people will know how to send it.' She turned to sweep out of the room, calling over her shoulder: 'Letter first. Then we'll think of a parcel.'

Sarah looked across at Isabel. 'You write too, Izzy.' Sarah

hesitated. 'Write to Edward. Maybe they're both there.'

Isabel forced a smile. 'I'm so pleased for you, Sarah. Really.'

Delhi, August 1942

My dear Edward,

Sarah has word that Tom is a POW in Singapore. She is writing to him now and orders me to write to you too. She holds out hope that the Red Cross may somehow find you there as well, in one camp or another.

It is late morning. We sit indoors with the French windows thrown open. The verandah is simply baking. Outside, the mali is pacing the lawn, sending an arc of spray across the grass from his ancient watering can. The soft patter of falling water and the rich scent of hot, moist earth drift in. The garden is quite ruined. The first monsoon came late this year and the sun is so relentless that all the plants are limp and yellow.

It is so difficult, my darling, not to know where you are. I try to believe you may be alive. I try to believe that, one day, this wretched war will end and we will be together. But there are times when all I feel is darkness and silence and it frightens me. What fools we were, to waste so many years. I was afraid too, Edward. Simply afraid. You seemed happy in Car Nicobar, happy without me.

My father wants me to leave Delhi and see out the war in England. Not in London – the blitz sounds too awful – but with my aunt. I won't go. For all its troubles, this is my home. I shan't quit India, whatever Mr Gandhi says.

Mother, of course, won't leave my father's side. She

was never one to abandon even the leakiest ship. So be
assured that when this is over and you come to claim
me, as I hope you may, I shall be waiting for you here.
I pray with all my heart for that time to come soon.
    Isabel

Her father came home late that evening. Her mother had already retired to her room, leaving Isabel to wait up alone in the darkness of the sitting room. Outside, the trees cast long shadows across the moonlit lawn.

She sat in silence, thinking.

She and Sarah had taken their letters to the Red Cross office that afternoon. It was a hot, hectic place, staffed by volunteers.

They waited in a long queue. A middle-aged woman, her hair tied back in a silk scarf, perched on a tall stool and entered details from the envelopes in a ledger.

She accepted Sarah's letter without question, then studied the envelope for Edward. Isabel had written: Captain Edward Johnston, POW, Singapore.

She lifted her eyes. 'Camp name? Prisoner number?'

Isabel felt herself flush. 'I don't know.'

The woman narrowed her eyes. 'Didn't you get a letter?'

Isabel shook her head.

'How do you know he's a POW, then?' She peered at Isabel. 'What is he, husband? Brother?'

Sarah leant forward. 'Family friend.'

The woman frowned. 'We're not the General Post Office.'

Sarah put in quickly: 'Send it to the same camp as my husband, can't you?' She pointed to her letter to Tom. 'We heard he's there.'

The woman sighed, copied the details and threw both letters into a brimming cardboard box to one side.

'It will find him.' Sarah took Isabel's arm and led her away. 'Have faith.'

Now, alone in the dark sitting room, Isabel raised her head. Voices at the gate. The clank of metal bolts being drawn. The engine of her father's car sounded on the drive. The car door slammed and her father's footsteps crossed the gravel to the front door. He paused in the hall, reading the quietness.

She called from the drawing room: 'Have you eaten?'

He appeared in the doorway. My poor, dear father, she thought, seeing him there. He had the silhouette of an old man, his shoulders stooped and his eyes, fading now, peered forward into the gloom.

'Georgina?'

'Isabel, Father.' She got to her feet, padded across to kiss his cheek. It bristled with white stubble. 'Everything alright?'

He sighed. She guided him to his armchair and crossed to the night drinks tray to fix him a Scotch. While he drank it, she put her hands on his shoulders and tried to rub a little tension from them. He was all angles, all bone.

He didn't speak for some time. The house was heavy with the day's heat and it weighed down on them both.

Finally he said: 'They've arrested the lot of them.'

She went quietly to sit on the end of the settee, close to his chair and waited.

'Mr Gandhi. Mr Nehru. The whole pack. Rounded up and jailed.'

She shook her head. 'For sedition?'

He shrugged. 'Probably. Something of that sort.' He

lifted his hand, raked through his thin, whitening hair. 'What did they expect? I mean, how much more did they expect us to take?'

She thought of the Japanese, so close now, in Burma, eager for allies, looking to invade.

'What will happen?'

Her father lifted the glass to his lips. His hand trembled.

'Riots, maybe. Bloodshed. Worse than anything we've seen.'

She sat very still in her chair. Her father had never spoken like this before. He seemed mired in despair.

'Hindu against Mohammedan. Brown man against white. When I imagine the future, I fear for this country.'

She tried to steady her voice. 'There've been arrests before, haven't there?' She paused, afraid of the answer. 'Need things be so much worse?'

'Isabel.' He leant forward to pat her hand. His palm was warm on her fingers. 'You love India as much as I do, don't you?' He smiled with such sad fondness that the breath caught in her throat as he added: 'My poor, dear girl. What have we done?'

Chapter Forty-Five

Asha

A boy came to her classroom with a chit from the principal.

'Your good brother is coming,' it read. 'Please be attending most urgently.'

Her brother? She had no brother. She crumpled the chit in her hand, told the children to copy the poem on the blackboard and walked down the shabby corridor to the principal's office.

She looked through the cracked window as she approached and knew at once that it was Anil. From the back, Asha made out his broad shoulders, smart shirt, neatly combed hair. He sat at ease in the visitor's chair.

'You were never telling about your brother!' The principal seemed charmed.

Asha tried to smile. He took such trouble to trick his way into seeing her. She was flattered but also afraid. He knew everything now: her home, her work. Nowhere left to hide.

'Little sister!' He rose to his feet, all performance, stretched out his arms in greeting. 'Don't be angry with me, now! So sorry to interrupt but our cousin is sick and calling for you. Can you come at once?'

She hesitated. Did he really expect her to leave her class and rush away, just because he wished it? She thought of the spaces on the wooden benches where the Mohammedan children had been.

'A little difficult, brother,' she said. 'Perhaps after class—'

'What are you saying? Your brother takes time from his work to come all this way to fetch you and you stand there, gawping. Of course you must go.' The principal clapped her hands. '*Jaldee!*'

The principal had already taken his side. He had won her over with his good looks, his false smile, his flattery. She looked again at the stout middle-aged woman, her waist rolling to fat beneath her sari blouse, her fingers thick with rings. Always, for so many years, she respected her superior. Now she did not.

His manner changed as soon as they left. He pushed her into the back of a rickshaw, climbed up beside her and ordered the rickshaw-wallah to take them to the far end of the slum and to keep his eyes forward and mind his business.

Once they were moving, the rickshaw swaying to the horse's feeble trot, he turned to her and pulled out his knife. The blade gleamed in the sunlight and he twisted it this way and that. She squinted, tried to turn away.

'Your good friend,' he said. 'The derzi.'

Rahul, of course. Anil had seen them together at the underground meeting. She shrugged. 'Rahul Chaudhary?'

He caught her chin in his free hand and held it hard in the pincer of his thumb and forefinger, letting the light pierce her eyes. 'How well are you knowing him?'

She squirmed. 'We were children together, that's all. So many years ago.'

'I don't like him.'

She closed her eyes and waited and, after some time, he loosened his grip and pushed away her face. He looked different. The bright sun showed the hardness in his face. His eyes, on hers, were suspicious.

'He's making trouble.'

'Trouble?'

'About the Mohammedans. He needs to stop.'

She bit her lip. 'He's a good Hindu,' she said. 'A good man.'

He raised his eyebrows. 'Is he loyal to his own people?'

She nodded. She thought of Sangeeta, nursing the new baby, of Abhishek playing in the dirt with Sushil. 'You have my word.'

'*Mujhe asha hai.*' His eyes bored into hers. 'I hope so.'

Finally he turned to face forwards and cleaned his fingernails with the tip of his knife. She waited, watchful, trying to force her breathing to settle back to the same plodding rhythm as the horse's hooves.

The slum grew around them, its fetid smells of bodies, of smoky cooking fires, of waste, reached for them through the air. The rickshaw-wallah pulled at the nose of his bony horse to slow him to a walk and pointed towards the rubbish dump.

'I have a job for Rahul Chaudhary. Listen.'

Anil reached across to whisper orders in her ear. His breath was hot on her neck. When he pulled away from her and called to the rickshaw-wallah to pull up and stop, he tapped the tip of her nose with his knife.

'Make sure he does as I say,' he said. 'You know what I do to traitors.'

He gestured to her to climb down and pointed across the filthy open ground where crows circled round the dark mounds of the dump. Heavy overnight rain had loosened the stink within it and the air was saturated with the sweet-sour stench of rot. She lifted her scarf to her face and lowered herself to the side of the track. Almost at once, the rickshaw-wallah whipped up his tired horse and moved on, leaving her alone.

Ahead, a knot of men and boys stood to one side, watching something. As she approached, they nudged each other and shuffled apart to let her pass. The mountains of debris had collapsed into a noxious pulpy mulch. Rivulets of black water ran off on the sides and shone in threads at her feet. Contaminated water seeped into her sandals and made dark stripes along the ridges of her toenails.

A grating, scraping sound ahead. She walked on, skirting the first mound. Rahul was there, his back bare in the sun, shovelling beside two strangers. She crossed to him.

'What are you doing?' She pulled at his arm. 'Stop that.'

The other men, curious, stopped to stare.

She lowered her voice. 'Come away, Rahul. Please.'

His face was solemn. He didn't answer, just pointed to the ground before him, where the shovels were slowly, painfully shifting the dirt. She stared. Feet. A pair of bare, discoloured feet. The short, slim toes of a young girl pointed to the sky. She craned forward to see more clearly. This corpse was still half-submerged but three others lay beyond it, which were already unearthed and lying silently in the waste. The figures of a man and two more children. They lay on their backs, arms straight by their sides, legs extended. Hellish mud creatures, pasted from head to foot in black slick. Hair plastered wetly against their heads. A low cloud of flies played over them, sometimes hovering, sometimes settling.

Rahul's voice was quiet. 'They called me uncle.'

She steadied herself. 'It's too late for them. But your own children, think of them.'

His eyes seemed glazed as he looked over the mulch. 'They need a better grave than this.'

The shovels sucked and scraped as the three men resumed their work. The faces of the dead were stiff. Their eyes were closed, their features masked with drying dirt.

'Please.' She pulled again at his arm. 'You don't understand.'

Anil had spies. She looked around. Those men and boys, perhaps, who stood still and silent on the line of the rise and watched them all.

The fear in her voice seemed to reach him and he turned finally.

'Don't cry, little sister.' His voice softened. 'It's too late for tears.'

She wiped her eyes with her dupatta and let out a long breath. 'I'm not crying for them,' she said. 'I'm crying for you.'

He refused to leave but she managed at last to draw him away to one side and they stood there, their feet in the wet, warm dirt, while she tried to explain why Anil had sent her.

'Tonight. They plan to attack your friends, the Britishers.'

He looked startled. 'Isabel Madam?' He paused, reading the answer in her face. 'Why?'

Asha tutted. 'Why? Her father is Burra Sahib, nah? Our enemy. Haven't you heard what they are doing? So many of freedom fighters are thrown into jail.'

He frowned. 'He is not my enemy. So why are you telling me?'

She leant in closer. 'You must help Anil. Tonight. Wait, Rahul. Listen to me. Please.' She paused, reached again for his arm. 'You know the house, the garden. Go with them. Show them how to get inside. Show them hiding places. Help them.'

He shook her off. 'It's a very wrong thing to kill. Did

your baba teach you nothing? I remember him. He would be ashamed that you ask such a thing.'

She closed her eyes. Her baba was there. His face a little faded now in her memory. There was the kind, gentle baba she remembered when she was a girl. She slept at night curled in the hollow of his body, his arm heavy across her. Then that other baba, the bitter, broken old man who quarrelled for no reason and killed a man and was hanged for it. They had done that to him, the Britishers. Maybe Anil was right. Violence knew only violence. The blade of Anil's knife glinted in the sunlight. She opened her eyes again.

'You must set aside what you think, Rahul, and help him tonight. You must.'

'I won't.'

She put her face close to his. 'Listen. He is testing you. If you fail him, he will kill you. You and Sangeeta. Your children also.' She hesitated. 'Perhaps me.'

He blinked. 'My children? What kind of man is this?'

She pointed across the waste heap. The two men had resumed their slow, steady work, scratching through the dirt. One crouched now behind the body of the unearthed girl and made to lift her head and shoulders. She rose with a dull suck. Her matted hair swam with mud.

The second man bent to grasp her feet, her legs. They swung her through the air and laid her beside the dark figures of her father, her sisters. The men wiped off their blackened hands on rags, picked up their shovels and began again to search for the disappeared.

'What kind of man?' she said. 'That kind.'

Chapter Forty-Six

Rahul met them late at night at the entrance to the slum, as Anil demanded.

'So brother, not a traitor after all?' Anil slapped him on the back.

Rahul didn't smile. He looked down at his feet. His chappals were split and mended with string.

'Have you forgotten what they did, bhai?' Anil said. 'Hanged our good friend, Sanjay Krishna-ji, and his uncle also and so many brave men besides. And now, when we call again for freedom, they start again. Do you know how many they've thrown into jail now? Nehru-ji and Gandhi-ji both. So many are there.'

He paused. Some of the men gathered round him murmured agreement. Only Rahul kept his eyes low and did not speak.

'Let's teach them a lesson tonight.' Anil turned to Asha. His eyes were hard and his gaze direct. 'You too, little sister. Come with us and see what we do.'

The men carried cans of kerosene and the liquid made a low slosh against the metal as they hurried. The Burra Sahib's compound was set back from the road and bounded by a high wall. The lines of the bungalow's roof gleamed through the trees in the moonlight.

Anil pulled at Rahul's arm. 'You know the chowkidar? See if he's awake. If he is, give him a bidi. Keep him talking.'

She shrank back with the others as Rahul walked along to the gate and called softly through the bars to the chowkidar. The guard's hut was dark. He waited a while, then called again, a little more loudly. Finally, he shrugged and came back to join them under the trees.

'Sleeping,' he whispered. 'He's an old fellow now and deaf also.'

'Old and lazy.' Anil pointed ahead to the wall. 'So show me. Where should we climb?'

Rahul led them quietly to a secluded spot further along the compound, away from the gates. A plane tree grew against the stone. Anil nodded and gestured to the first man to climb. In a matter of minutes, they were all shinning up the knotty trunk, swinging their bodies over the top of the wall and lowering themselves with a dull thud to the grass beneath. Rahul climbed beside Asha, ready to steady her if she slipped. His face was tight with tension.

They gathered again in the bushes on the other side. Anil lifted his hand to them to be still and they watched and listened. The house stood proudly in the moonlight. It was a grand home with a lengthy verandah, set with wicker chairs. Despite the summer heat, the gardens were lush and neatly kept. The slum stank always of bodily waste and sweat and rotting vegetables. This world was bathed in the rich perfume of blossoming trees and blooms in terracotta pots.

Asha strained through the branches to see. This was my home too, she thought. My baba brought me here and found himself disgraced and that was the start of everything. She hoped to feel some dim memory of early childhood stir as she looked out over the trees and bushes and lawns towards the veiled windows of the house but none did.

All was silent. Anil lifted his hand and motioned them forward. Within minutes, the men, silent and bent double, had poured thin trails of kerosene along the verandah and down the side of the house. Its oily stink polluted the air.

Anil gestured for the men to throw down their cans and flee back to the bushes. He struck a match and threw it onto the verandah. Then another and a third. The kerosene flew at once into life, popping with flames which ran like mad creatures along the edge of the house and rose greedily to the woodwork.

Anil ran back to join them. They watched, mesmerised, as the fire rushed and spread through the dry wood. An explosion, then a crash as the first window shattered and fell. No movement inside the darkened house. Still the chowkidar slept.

Rahul's eyes were wide and filled with horror. He whispered: 'They'll burn alive.'

Already the blazing fire was unstoppable. Anil turned to Asha. His eyes shone red, dancing with flames.

'See!' He laughed and his look was feral. 'See how the British palace burns and the Britishers with it. This is just the beginning, little sister. Oh, the fun to come!'

He opened his arms as if to embrace the burning house and kicked up his feet. The men around him joined in with the same mad joy. One drew out a flask of toddy and they passed it from mouth to mouth.

Asha stood stock-still. My baba, she thought. Is this revenge for him? She looked back at the house, shimmering now with flames. Sparks flew like firecrackers into the night sky. My baba was a good man, she thought. A kind man. She shook her head as, around her, the men frolicked and danced and drank. He would take no pleasure in burning a family to death.

'Where is he?' Anil stopped dead, scowled. The men, wary, watched as Anil took a step towards her. His face was menacing. 'Where's he gone?'

Asha looked round, bewildered. Rahul had vanished. She found herself stammering. 'Please, brother. Maybe—'

Anil gave her a sharp push backwards and she stumbled. He set off, moving quickly round the side of the house towards the back, creeping from one clump of trees and bushes to the next. The men followed. Asha, winded, trailed behind.

For a moment, she saw nothing. The back of the house, not yet licked by flame, was veiled and dark. A sudden movement caught her eye. A swish of curtain. Then a figure, clear against the open window, climbed out of the room onto the sill and dropped to the ground. It was Rahul. He ran to the trees and started to make his way in a broad loop back to the front of the house. Anil and his men crept silently behind him. As Rahul made to swing himself up into the low branches of a tree, close to the compound wall, Anil jumped on his back.

'No!' Asha ran forward, grabbed at Anil's hand.

His fist flashed with the blade of his knife. He swung his arm and knocked her to the ground, turned again to Rahul. One arm pulled back Rahul's neck.

'Thought you'd trick me, did you? Save your Britisher friends?'

He plunged the blade into Rahul's chest. When he pulled

it free, it drew sucking air. Blood bubbled in its wake.

'Not just you,' Anil said. 'Your wife. Your children. Wherever they hide.'

Asha jumped to her feet, hung on Anil's arm. She sank her teeth into his wrist. He let out a cry, dropped Rahul and turned on her.

'You too?' He slapped her across the face. 'You'll pay for this.'

She shrank against the ground, crawled backwards, her eyes on the knife.

He spat, turned again to crouch over Rahul who lay writhing on the grass. Blood, fast-pumping now, soaked through his shirt and pooled on his chest. Anil stuck him again with the knife. His chest rose, sighed, sank. Rahul fell back and became still.

Shouts from the house. The chowkidar, finally wakened, went running down the drive, his arms flailing. Figures staggered out onto the grass. A man, stooped with age, had his arm round a woman, guiding her out onto the lawn.

Asha pressed herself low against the earth and crawled backwards into the darkness of the bushes.

Anil knelt and wiped off his knife on Rahul's wet shirt. He turned to his men. 'String him up. Then get out.'

Fresh noises from the house. Cries, a woman's screams, the crash of breaking glass.

Asha, deep inside a hollowed bush, peered through a latticework of branches.

Anil turned. His eyes pierced the darkness, searching her out. She closed her eyes, held her breath. Her body trembled against dead, dry leaves. A memory flickered. The smell of rich earth and mildew and rotting foliage, the prick of dry

439

bark against her skin as she hid from other children, taut with the fear of being found.

When she opened her eyes again, Anil and his men were gone. Rahul's body hung by the neck from the low branches of a tree, turning slowly. She forced herself to crawl out from the bushes in silence, climbed through the trees to throw herself over the wall and, when she reached the grassy verge on the far side, she started to run.

The city was ablaze. The night sky shone an unearthly red and yellow. Sudden flashes of light from explosions, from collapsing, burning buildings, lit the dense smoke, which swam silently through the darkness.

Asha ran at full tilt, her scarf flapping around her face, her feet chafing in her chappals. Her chest ached from panting.

Sirens sounded across the Civil Lines, drowning out the cries of men and the screams and wails of women. She listened, through the chaos, for the sound of feet pounding behind her. Anil would come after her. He would kill her. She knew it. She ran for her life and for the lives of Rahul's family, also.

Police gathered on street corners. They had the pale, strained faces of men who had been roused from their beds at an ungodly hour and ordered to work. They set up roadblocks on the broad avenues and roundabouts, working with efficient weariness. She pulled her scarf low round her face and crept over verges, through hedges, to avoid them.

Trucks, filled with standing soldiers, careered down otherwise deserted roads. The army was called out of its barracks. A curfew would follow. Her lungs burnt but she forced herself forward through the Civil Lines, then beyond them, gradually leaving behind the grand houses, set back from the avenues, the office buildings as imposing as palaces, the roundabouts with their tended lawns and stone fountains.

Now the roads became narrower and the buildings meaner and there were fewer policemen. The roar of burning buildings retreated to a distant rumble and the air around her settled again to the natural heat of an August night, unsullied by ash and burning grit.

At the entrance to the slum, she paused to rest, wiped off her face with her scarf and looked back. The sky above the Civil Lines was a dome of shifting red and yellow streaks. The moon and stars were blocked out by dirty smoke.

The slum alleys were quiet. A dog jumped up and barked as she ran through. A drunk raised bleary eyes to watch her pass. She fell at last on the wooden door that led into the courtyard and pounded on it with her fists.

'Sangeeta. *Jaldee!*'

The wood was rough against her hands. It jumped and strained as she struck it. She wanted to claw it to pieces but already her hands were bruised. She pulled a chappal from her foot and banged the flat of its sole on the door, shouting more loudly.

'Sangeeta. Wake up.'

A sleepy male voice inside shouted: 'Be quiet, can't you?'

A woman murmured.

Asha began again to bang and shout. Finally, a hinge creaked and a screen door slapped shut. Footsteps. The door to the compound opened a fraction. A wary eye shone in the gap.

'Who is it?'

'Asha. Rahul and Sangeeta's friend. The schoolteacher.'

Words tumbled out. 'Please, bhai, let me in. She's in danger.'

A pause, then the man opened the door. He was stout and unshaven, covered only by a lunghi. He scratched at his tousled hair.

'Well, come in, if you must.' He shrugged, let her pass. 'Just be quiet, can't you?'

Sangeeta lay raised on one elbow on a charpoy. Baby Rupa curled against her, wrapped round with a cloth. The boy, Abhishek, lay sleeping on a mat on the floor. Sangeeta stared, blinked, as Asha rushed in.

'What?' Her face was strained as she tried to read Asha's expression. She turned and looked at the empty space on the charpoy beside her. 'Arrested again?'

'Not arrested.' Asha crouched low and took Sangeeta's hand between her own. 'He is gone, sister. I saw it with my own eyes. We must leave Delhi at once.' She looked down at Rupa, deep in sleep against her mother's warm side. 'If Anil finds us, he will kill us all.'

The rickshaw driver lay asleep across the back of his rickshaw, his dirty feet sticking out over the frame. He was angry when they woke him. His breath smelt of stale toddy and spices.

'Double,' Asha pleaded. 'We'll pay double the fare.'

He hesitated, looked more closely at their small group. Rupa hung in a cotton sling across Sangeeta's chest. Abhishek, sullen, shouldered a bundle of possessions.

'No trouble.' The rickshaw-wallah's eyes narrowed with suspicion. 'I don't want angry husbands coming to beat me.'

Asha tutted. 'Nothing like that, bhai. It's our poor Mutter-ji only, back in the village. She's so ill.'

He stretched, scratched his stomach and finally, slowly, heaved down his legs and pulled himself out of the back. 'Double? Get in, then.'

Delhi railway station was shrouded in sleep. An untidy line of rickshaws ranged down one side of the stone steps, their drivers spread, snoring, across their vehicles.

Inside, the main hall smelt of urine and the sour breath of empty stomachs. Through the lofty ticket hall and along the railway platforms, small groups huddled together. Some lay stretched on the ground, sleeping with heads on bags and clothes. Others sat upright, gazing out with glazed eyes, watching over sleeping children and bundles of belongings, wary of creeping thieves and dacoits. A hawker picked his way silently between the prone bodies, selling chai in clay cups from an urn slung across his shoulder.

It was still some hours before the ticket office opened. Asha led Sangeeta and the boy to a far corner of the platform and they squatted there to wait. The stone floor was stained with dried splatters of betel juice and chewing tobacco. Already the first flush of dawn along the tracks turned the blackness of the sky to a fading grey.

Sangeeta settled Abhishek to sleep, cradled Rupa against her breast, then turned to Asha. 'Tell me,' she said. 'What happened to my husband?'

Soon after Asha finished her story, commotion broke out on the forecourt. Desperate passengers crowded round, shouting with stale breath, pleading for tickets. Behind the bars of the ticket window, a station-wallah batted his hands on the counter, palms down.

'Go home,' he shouted into the clamour. 'No trains.'

He wiped off his sweating face with a cloth. A man at

the front of the queue pushed his hand through the bars and waved money at him, too much money.

'No trains!' The station-wallah sounded exasperated. 'What to do?'

Asha searched the faces crowded there. Anil would track them down. She knew him. He would find them.

She ran out of the station building and round to the back of the offices. Two porters squatted there, smoking bidis. They looked up warily as she approached. One was an old man, his legs thin and bent from a lifetime of labour. The other was young. His face showed a picture of the old man's past. His son, then.

'Bhai, what's happening?' She pressed her palms together in namaste and bowed her head respectfully to the old man. 'Please, ji, are you knowing?'

'I know you.' The old man narrowed his eyes. 'You're the schoolteacher, nah?' He nodded, considering her. 'My grandsons go to your school. Three good boys. Already they are reading so many of words. Writing also.' He thought for a moment. His eyes were pale and rheumy. 'What lives they will have, these boys. How the world changes.'

'But the trains, ji, what about the trains?'

'Some big problem is there.' He shook himself, coming back to the present. 'Go home, schoolteacher. No travel today. It's not possible.'

Asha took a deep breath. 'But I must. My poor uncle is dying. I must reach him.'

He scratched his stomach, dropped the stub of his bidi to join a host of others littering the ground and pulled himself to his feet. He beckoned her a little closer. His teeth were stained red with betel.

'These freedom fighters, they're on the rampage. Haven't you heard? The whole night, they're lighting fires. Burning houses and offices. Attacking the railway tracks also.' He lowered his voice to a whisper. 'Already, early in the morning only, one goods train is derailed.' He shook his head in disbelief. 'Two bogies are smashed. Driver is hurt, that's what they are saying. Dead, even, who is knowing?' He sucked his teeth, fixed her with his eye. 'Such times we are living in.'

Asha stooped to touch his gnarled feet and beg. 'Please, ji. We must go. My sister is here with her tiny baby and her son. Help us.' She reached into the folds of her kameez, pulled out a handful of money. 'Please, ji.'

He tutted, pushed away her hand. 'Well, if it's like that, schoolteacher—' he broke off, looked around as if to be sure no one was listening. 'There is some talk. One train may leave. But it's not safe.' He sighed, paused. 'How would my grandsons be learning without a teacher, nah?' He nodded, drew himself up, reaching a decision. 'Go fetch your sister and her children. Carriages are there, out of sight, in the sidings.' He jutted his chin. 'I'll take you. With so much of confusion today, you can creep inside maybe and hide yourselves.'

Chapter Forty-Seven

Isabel

She opened her eyes, dredged up from the bottom of a dream. Something had woken her. Not a noise. A sense of someone. Of someone else in her silent bedroom.

Edward? She managed to raise her head, struggling against the weight of sleep. Of course not. She peered into the gloom. A figure. A man. There, against the pale rectangle of the window. The curtain lifted and billowed and twisted. The window, then. Open.

The man moved towards her. His feet seemed to glide across the wooden floor. She blinked, stared. Her heart quickened. The dark, shadowed features of an Indian.

'Who is it?' She sat up. Her voice sounded in the stillness. Her mouth was parched. She looked round, alarmed, fully awake. Her nose pricked with an acrid smell. The soft flesh at the back of her throat stung. Smoke.

'Isabel Madam.' A familiar whisper. 'Quick.'

'Rahul?' She saw him now. She pushed back the bedclothes, swung her legs to the floor.

'Quick.' His eyes were anguished. 'Please.'

'What's happened?' She reached out to touch his arm. He pushed her away at once. He twisted and looked over his shoulder towards the open window, his face full of fear.

'What?'

He seized her hand and kissed it. His lips were dry. 'Little sister. May the gods bless you.'

He turned, hurried back towards the window and, in a single fluid movement, was gone. She ran to look after him. The back of the garden was dark with shadow but flickers of movement caught her eye. Dark shapes shifted amongst the trees as if the trunks themselves swayed from side to side. She blinked.

Light, stinging ash peppered the side of her face and she turned, narrowed her eyes. Pouches of smoke puffed black down the side of the bungalow. A muffled sound drifted through the heavy night air. The distant screams of horses in the stables. The crash of their hooves on splintering wood.

She pulled on slacks and buttoned a shirt over her nightdress, pulled at her bedroom door. Dense smoke rushed at her from the passageway, acrid in her mouth and nose. As it eddied, the red glow of fire swam through it, a low rumble from the other end of the house. She stumbled across the passage to her father's bedroom door and wrenched it open.

'Get up!' Her opening mouth filled with smoke. It pressed the words back into her throat.

A figure stirred, murmured.

'What is it?' Her father, still in sleep.

'Quick. Get up! Fire.'

He sat up, dazed. Isabel ran past him, flung back the curtains and levered open the French windows, which led to the garden.

'This way.'

Her father got unsteadily to his feet.

'Get out,' she said. 'I'll wake Mother.'

A porcelain ewer stood on the chest of drawers in its matching bowl. Isabel doused her hair with water and poured the rest over one of her father's cotton shirts, snatched from the back of a chair. She pushed past her father before he could stop her and ran back into the smoky hall, the wet shirt pressed against her face.

As she moved further into the heart of the bungalow, the wood beneath her feet began to bubble and blister with heat. Ash, flying thickly through the air, burnt her forehead, her cheeks. She grasped the handle of her mother's door and pulled away with a cry. Her palm throbbed where the skin had burnt. She bit her lip, wrapped the wet shirt around her hand and managed to force the door open.

A wall of smoke and intense light hit her at once. Heat roared in her face. Flame jumped, red and yellow. The air pounded with the crack of fire and shattering of wood. Her mother's young maid, a village girl, crashed against her, arms flailing. Her headscarf burnt on her head. Isabel pulled the wet shirt from her hand and threw it over the girl's flaming hair and pulled her close, suffocating the sparks.

The maid's eyes shone wide with terror. 'Madam is there.'

Isabel flung herself across the room to the partitioned section where her mother slept. Her mother sat upright, her face full of fear. Isabel helped her out of bed and held her mother close against her side. Her bones seemed frail.

Isabel fumbled with the window latch. Firmly locked. Her mother started to cough. Smoke surged round them. Isabel wiped off her stinging eyes against the top of her arm, then tightened her grip on her mother and groped in the darkness.

A hairbrush. A water jug and glass. A chair. She reached

down and her fingers closed on the low stool beside it. She swung it up, hurled it against the window. Her mother screamed. On the third blow, the glass shattered, showering them both in shards of flying glass. Isabel pressed herself out through the ragged hole, which tore at her shirt, her slacks. Her arms tightened around her mother as she guided her through. The outside air, cool and fresh, hit them at once.

She and her father eased her mother onto the back lawn where she sat, coughing. Dirt mapped the wrinkles and contours of her face. Isabel sank beside her and held her tightly until her breathing calmed and gave way to low sobbing. Her mother's hair smelt of smoke. Her eyelashes were clogged with ash.

Isabel lifted her head. The front of the bungalow was gutted. Flames poured out of windows and through collapsing walls. On all sides, funnels of smoke spread upwards, twisting like tornados in the spiralling draughts.

She said to her father: 'Is everyone out?'

He nodded. As they watched, a section of roof collapsed in a Catherine's wheel of sparks. The jagged lines of the remaining brickwork scrawled black lines against the night sky.

Male voices shouted and a commotion of vehicles came tearing down the drive. She turned to look. The police had arrived and firemen too, with ladders and hoses. She sighed and turned her eyes back to the blaze. The red glow lit the night. She knew every inch of those rooms that were crashing into flames.

'Thank God.' Her father gazed in disbelief at the burning wreckage. 'Thank God you woke up.'

She blinked, remembering. Rahul had woken her. That

was no dream. He blessed her and called her 'little sister'. She shook her head, too dazed to understand, and gently stroked her mother's gritty, smoky hair.

Dawn broke over a steaming, smouldering building. The police and firemen had laboured through the night, pumping streams of water from fire engines and soaking every room. Now their faces were black with ash and soot, their eyes pouches of lost sleep.

Isabel and her father stood on the dewy lawn amongst a jumble of salvaged possessions. A fireman had carried out drawers from her father's study and they were sorting through files of official papers and notebooks, packing them into boxes.

'Sahib?' The inspector, a young chap, came striding from the front of the bungalow. 'Please be coming.'

The young man's expression, a mixture of distress and embarrassment, prompted Isabel to follow too. He led them past the kitchen and the servants' quarters, then across the lawns at the front of the bungalow where clouds of rhododendrons were backed by mango trees.

The old magnolia tree rose behind them, splendid now with pink and white flowers. As they approached, a knot of men came into view, gathered under the tree, faces upturned. Isabel strained to see in the half-light. A ragged, sagging figure hung from a bough, twisting quietly on its binding as the men below reached for it. A bonfire guy, she thought, or a scarecrow. It wore Indian dress.

Her father said: 'Is he known?'

The inspector shook his head. They were almost there. Two men gripped the legs, taking the weight between them.

Another man slid out above, along the branch, and began to cut through the rope.

Her father's voice was grim. 'Any idea when?'

The inspector shrugged. 'Poor fellow is quite cold, sahib.'

Isabel gave a cry. She broke into a run. The men looked round as the rope snapped and the figure pitched forward, its clumsy fall broken by the men beneath. They staggered under their burden, pitched the corpse sideways onto the grass.

The men drew back as Isabel propelled herself towards the body and threw her arms across it.

'Rahul. Not Rahul.'

The front of his shirt was hard with congealed blood. When she tried to grasp him, to pull him towards her, he slipped heavily to one side. His head slumped, his eyes staring and his hair matted.

She wrapped her arms around his chest and tried to rock him. His body was stiff and unyielding. Where she touched it, blood flaked into dark specks on her fingers.

Full-blown magnolia blooms were thick in the grass and the warm air was sickly with their sweetness. She closed her eyes. The scent of their childhood, of those endless, hot days when they climbed so high together, tried to see the future.

'My brother.' She bent over him, touched her hot, wet cheek to his cold one. 'My poor, dear brother.'

The wooden door was unlatched. Inside, the courtyard was empty. Isabel stood, breathing hard, looking round. Even the charpoy, there in the shade, was abandoned. She crossed to peer into the windows on the far side.

'Gone.'

Isabel started, stepped back from the window. A thin, elderly voice from the shadows. A shape there shifted and settled again.

'Packed up and left. Children also.' The old lady wheezed, coughed. 'No sign of that husband of hers. He'll be busy stitching, I suppose. Stitches away all night, some nights.'

Isabel narrowed her eyes and strained to see in the gloom. The old lady sat on the floor against the wall, wrapped round in a shawl. Her eyes glinted in the half-light. Never again, she thought. Those long, delicate fingers will never stitch again.

'Where was she going?'

'How do I know?' She shook her head. 'That baby's too weak to be going anywhere.' A thought seemed to strike her and she peered out at Isabel. 'Is she in trouble?'

'I have news, that's all.' Isabel turned away, unable to look the old woman in the eye. 'About Rahul, her husband.' She hesitated, thinking about the body that now lay, wrapped in white cotton, in a corner of their garden. 'My friend.'

Out in the lane, the rickshaw-wallahs dozed in the shade of their rickshaws. They looked at her with suspicion as she described Sangeeta and the children, asked if they'd seen them.

'Delhi railway station,' said one at last. He looked her up and down. 'I took them there myself, so early.' He held out his hand as Isabel fished in her pocket for baksheesh.

'Such tamasha is there.' The next rickshaw-wallah chipped in. 'So few trains, everyone is telling about it. Just people only, fighting each other like animals to get out of the city.'

She ran back to where her tonga was waiting. As she

climbed into the carriage, she wavered. She could simply go home. Go back to the smoking wreckage of the bungalow and to her poor father, waiting there. Leave Sangeeta and the children to fend for themselves.

She closed her eyes and saw again the shadowy figure of Rahul in her bedroom. His eyes were filled with fear as he turned back to the open window to leave.

She sat forward and called to the tonga-wallah. 'Delhi railway station. *Jaldee!* Quick as you can.'

He lifted his switch and urged his old horse into a ragged trot.

Chapter Forty-Eight

Asha

They were crammed inside the carriage like animals, pressed tightly together in that small, airless space, adults and children, sweating against each other on all sides.

Baby Rupa fell quiet. She was exhausted. She had screamed since the train was first shunted from the sidings into the station and they crawled out from their hiding places beneath the bench seats and shrank back and all manner of shoving, fighting people started to pour on board.

'What to do?' Sangeeta stopped jigging her daughter and settled her to sleep on her shoulder. The baby was hungry but there was nowhere to feed her. She'd suffocate in that crowd. The pressing tide had drawn Abhishek apart from them and into another corner.

Pounding feet sounded along the platform and faces stuck in through the windows, tearing at the door handle, begging to be let in.

'No room. Are you blind?'

Knuckles grasped at the open sills and men inside, close to the door, banged on the fingers to drive them away.

A whistle sounded. People braced themselves against door and walls. Bold young men on the platform jumped onto the outside of the door and clung there as the train started to move. Asha turned her face away. Anil might be there. Even now, as they stoked the engine and set off, he might spot her and all would be lost.

The train shuddered as it gained speed. Gritty smoke, billowing down the sides of the train, blew into the carriage. The men by the window drew back a little, coughing and spluttering, and Asha, seizing her chance, pushed Sangeeta forward into the space. They found themselves rammed against a window, which was covered only by fat metal bars. They lifted Rupa, her eyes closed now, higher in Sangeeta's arms so she could breathe the rushing outside air. Smoke from the engine blew past in sudden patches. Ragged figures along the track lifted their heads and stared. As the train gathered speed, their faces blurred and melted into the parched fields beyond.

'We'll find my home village,' Asha said. 'My baba was telling about it always.'

She paused, remembering her baba's stories, long ago when he was still well. They had relatives there, he said. Aunties and uncles and scores of cousins.

'They will hide us.' She tried to imagine village huts, set in fields. A mud crossroads with a chai stall. A village well where women gathered at dawn and dusk to draw water and exchange gossip. Water buffaloes and goats and peacocks.

'I can teach there.' She considered. 'Or if there's no school, I can start one.'

Sangeeta didn't answer. She faced out towards the passing world but her eyes were dead.

'I'll teach Rupa also.' Asha reached to stroke the wispy black hair on the baby's crown. 'Better to live in the village than the slum. They'll have a good life, your children.'

Sangeeta's eyes closed. She leant her head against the dirty surround of the window, with Rupa limp in sleep on her shoulder. Her face looked altered. Her skin was grey and lifeless. Already, Asha thought, Rahul's death has tainted her. Outside, the day was heavy with haze and the gathering heat of the sun.

Thoughts of her baba came to her as she stared sightlessly out at the streaming fields. The young Baba, who curled against her at night when she was still a girl and fell asleep even as she chattered to him, that Baba's face was distant now. But she remembered his gentle voice and the scent of his skin, a mixture of bidi smoke and sun. Slowly she closed her eyes and let her head loll.

Bang. Her forehead smashed forward against the bars. Shards of light made a falling tunnel of coloured streaks. She clawed at the air. She felt herself scream but the sound disappeared in the high-pitched shrieking all around. At her side, someone crashed against her, pinned her arm. She heaved, twisted, wrenched it free. Muscles in her shoulder tore.

The world tipped under her, then shuddered and became still. Shouts. Moans. A great scrambling and jostling of limbs, of bodies, as the passengers, pinned one on top of another, fought to get upright. Asha put her hand to her head. Her fingers came away hot and sticky with blood. Her shoulder ached. She looked round, dazed. She pressed back against the sloping sides of the train, struggling to get on her feet again.

Rupa, shaken awake, bawled on her mother's shoulder. Her face was red with fury. Sangeeta didn't move. The crash had pitched her into the side of the window. Asha took hold of her shoulders and tried to prise her back.

'Sangeeta.'

She didn't respond. She lay slumped forwards, heavy and silent. Her head was gashed along one side. Rupa seemed pinned between Sangeeta's body and the side of the carriage. Asha prised her loose and took her in her arms.

'Hush, baby girl.'

The child screamed.

'Hush now.'

The fields and tracks had disappeared from the window. Instead, she saw a broad expanse of sky, cut through by an arching tree branch. She lifted one hand from the baby to grasp the window bars and, steadying herself, turned to look back into the carriage.

The metal shell had twisted. Everything hung at an angle. On the far side, passengers, old and young, scrambled in a misshapen heap, writhing and climbing on each other to get purchase, to find some way to stand again. An elderly hand protruded from the mess of bodies. It opened and closed uselessly. A young man, pulling himself up, trod on it as he scrambled through.

She blinked, swallowed, tried to breathe. Somewhere deep in the fabric of the train, a deep metallic grinding sounded, as if the Earth's plates shifted beneath them. Shouts swelled in her ears.

'Open the door.'

'Get out.'

The metal frame of the door had buckled. It lay low to the ground. Men stood on the fallen and shouldered each other aside to take turns at heaving on the handle. The door was stuck fast.

'Help us.' A woman's voice, in the far corner. 'Someone. Please!'

Women struggled to find children in the chaos, husbands to find wives. Broken limbs hung at odd angles. Faces ran with blood. The screams became more desperate.

Asha twisted. One hand clasped Rupa against her neck. The other held fast to the window bar and clung to it as she pulled herself higher. Her eyes followed the line of the tree branch down to the trunk until the edge of fields and the roofs of shacks came into view. The wheels of the carriage along this side were raised clean off the track. The whole bogie had tipped onto one side.

A guard ran past, his eyes wild with panic. His turban was splattered with dirt and the fingers of his white gloves were streaked with soot. Thick black smoke, peppered with burning ash, blew in his wake. Woodsmoke. Asha strained to listen through the chaos, the shouts. The low crackle of approaching fire.

Her stomach contracted. She heaved at the metal bar in a frenzy. It didn't even shudder in its frame. Flakes of paint cut into the flesh of her fingers.

Finally, she pulled her hand away and sucked at the bleeding. She pressed Rupa's wet face against her neck and stroked her fine downy hair, trying to comfort the child as she screamed.

Chapter Forty-Nine

Isabel

The stationmaster was polite but firm.

'One train only was leaving today, madam. Fifteen, twenty minutes ago.' He shook his head. 'Very bad business.'

They were alone in the first-class waiting room. Overhead, the fan beat out a steady rhythm as it turned.

'My friend is an Indian lady. She had a new baby with her. And her son. A boy about this height.'

The stationmaster's face was blank.

'Did you see them?'

He spread his hands in a gesture of helplessness. Muffled voices drifted in to them from the pressing, jostling crowd in the main concourse.

'Please, madam.' He shook his head. 'We are having so few men. What to do?'

Isabel took a deep breath. 'Where was it heading?'

'Down train, madam.' He lifted a gloved hand and seemed about to say more when the telephone in the box on the wall started to ring. His face clouded as he listened.

When he replaced the receiver, she said: 'What is it?'

'Nothing, madam. Nothing.' He looked shaken as he opened the door to usher her out.

Isabel hesitated. 'Something's happened to that train, hasn't it?'

He looked anguished. 'Please, madam. I must—'

'Where is it?'

He shrugged, helpless. 'Almost reaching first station. Madam, police are coming.'

The tonga-wallah urged his horse to the next point along the line and set Isabel down outside the small station. She ran through the noisy concourse to the platform on the far side. Families sat amongst piles of battered bags and cases, tied round with string. Children bawled. Boys ran helter-skelter through the chaos, snatching and chasing.

She was the only European in sight and many of the Indians, huddled there, drew back from her as she pressed through the crowd and made her way down the length of the platform to its end. She climbed down rough steps to the side of the track. A couple of ragged boys, picking at rubbish by the sleepers, lifted their heads and stared.

She walked briskly along the grassy verge, which skirted the track. Her boots chafed her feet. A rat ran out of the undergrowth in front of her and disappeared with a flourish of tail into the ditch.

As the station fell away behind her, the morning air settled, solid and still. For some time, the only sounds were the dewy swish of grass at her feet and her own laboured breathing as she hurried.

There was a curve in the track ahead, bordered by trees. As she emerged from the copse, dark shapes rose. They were low and shimmered with smoke, which hung heavy in the sky. She quickened her pace. Noises reached for her. Screams and cries. She began to run.

The engine had careered right off the track, gouging a thick brown scar down the embankment. It was engulfed in a dense cloud of black smoke, streaked with flashes of red where fire raged and spread. The driver and the stoker stood above, on the top of the embankment. Their faces were masks of shock. The flames threw red and yellow patterns across their skin.

The engine had dragged the next few carriages off the rails. They were such a mess of mangled wood and metal that it was hard to tell where one section ended and the next began.

The first carriage blazed. Its metal skeleton shone white-hot in the flames. Its doors had burst open and flapped now at odd angles, like broken limbs. Isabel looked away. If anyone were trapped inside, it was already too late for them.

She climbed, panting, along the bank. Here and there, passengers, who had thrown themselves from the burning carriage or been dragged from it, lay on the grass. A man writhed, his arm torn open. White bone glistened in the sunlight, surrounded by shredded muscles. Beyond him, a severed foot had caught in a train wheel. Its skin was crepe paper, wrinkled and thin.

A woman leant forward over her child, holding it in her arms and rocking it with a steady, calming motion. The child's eyes were closed and its body still.

A Sikh in railway uniform ran back and forth. Isabel crossed to him. His eyes were wild and his temples bubbled with sweat.

'Sabotage.' He grasped her arm. 'Look.' He lifted his leg. His trousers were stiff with blood.

Isabel tried to lead him away from the burning wreckage. As he dragged himself after her, his face became confused.

'So many of people. Poor people, only.'

461

He seemed to teeter and lose his balance. A moment later, he sank abruptly to the ground and sat there, dazed.

Isabel eased him onto his side in the grass and he lay, eyes open, staring sightlessly at a clump of weeds growing out of the bank.

The air swarmed with soot and sparks. The fire was moving quickly. Already a second carriage blazed, shrouded in thick smoke. It was a third-class compartment with caged windows. White knuckles shone on the bars as hands within grasped and tugged.

For a moment, Isabel stared, her hands at her face, unable to move. The dreadful wailing and crying reached a fresh pitch. She clambered down the bank towards the carriage and reached towards the window. As she seized the bars and tried to prise them free, to loosen them, unseen hands within grasped at her fingers. She pulled back. Her hands were slippery with the blood and sweat of those trapped inside. The flaking paint blistered with the heat of the encroaching fire. Desperate, screaming faces swam in the smoke.

She stood back, looked hastily around, then picked up a stone, angled it between the bars, pressed against it with all her strength. It broke into two in a cloud of dust. Her hand flew along the bars as she slipped sideways, skinning the backs of her fingers. The metal seemed barely scratched.

She shook her head and wiped off her eyes with the top of her sleeve.

'Please God.' She turned away from the imploring faces within. 'What can I do?'

The flames whipped through the carriage. The air was thick with the smell of scorching cloth and hair.

She pulled away, scrambled round the carriage to the far

side, angled upwards towards the sky. Here, people seemed even more densely pressed together. Hands waved through the barred windows, reaching for her. She ran her fingers round the frame of the window, searching for gaps, for anything to prise away. Nothing. The bars were heavy and solidly welded.

'Isabel Madam!' The voice, calling in English, penetrated the din. 'Here!'

Isabel craned forward and peered into the jumble of twisting bodies. Asha's face, tilted, gazed up at her from the pit of hell. Sangeeta's baby, impossibly small, screamed at her neck.

'Where's Sangeeta?'

Asha nodded back at the darkness behind her. She lifted the baby and thrust it forward, scraping its small body out between the flaking paint of the metal bars.

'Take her.' She raised the child as high as she could beyond the window. 'The gods have mercy.'

Isabel climbed down, steadied herself against the bank and strained forward to reach. She managed to get enough purchase on the bundle of cloth to lift the baby clear. It weighed almost nothing. She drew the child to her and clasped it against her chest.

Flames flew forward in a fiery ball from the other end of the carriage. Smoke billowed. Hands jumped from the metal bars as they became hot.

'Help is coming, Asha!' Isabel screamed down into the chaos. Her voice seemed lost in the thickening smoke. 'They're coming.'

Asha didn't reply. Her upturned face swam in and out of sight as the smoke swirled about her. Her eyes were points of calm stillness in a sea of clawing hands and screams. A moment later, a streak of flame shot through the carriage in a sudden booming rush and engulfed it all.

'Asha!'

Smoke ballooned from the windows. The face had gone.

The narrow streets, some cobbled, some rutted with dried mud, opened suddenly onto an expanse of river. Dusk approached and the sunlight was thickening, dappling the surface of the flowing water with streaks of gold.

Isabel climbed down from the tonga with slow, careful movements. Rupa, fed and bathed and swaddled in clean cloths, slept in her arms. She hugged the small bundle against her body.

Around them, people emerged on foot from the slum and made their way in small knots down the broad, steep steps, which led to the water and out along the stone shelves of the ghats.

She stood to one side for a moment and watched. The ghats swirled with activity. Old men in orange robes, their foreheads painted with streaks of ash, sold garlands of cream-coloured flowers, which clustered thickly round their necks and along outstretched arms. Others carried trays of holy paraphernalia: beads and brightly painted statues of multi-armed Hindu gods. Lakshmi was there and Hanuman the monkey and Ganesh with his elephant's head.

The air was hushed. The only sounds were the cries of the birds, which wheeled overhead, swarming along the curve of the darkening river.

The stone steps extended into the river itself. Here and there in the shallows, men and women stood, ankle-, knee- or waist-deep. Some dipped their hands into the brown water, tipping it reverently over their heads, then raising their palms to the sky, eyes closed, lost in prayer. Others ducked beneath the surface in a moment of complete immersion, then rose a moment later in a rush of spray. The women's wet saris clung to their bodies. The river, fast-flowing and patterned by swirling eddies and currents, slid slowly past it all, unheeding.

Isabel's eyes rose from the waterline and ran along the ghats where a series of funeral pyres had been built. Bereaved families, solemn and still, congregated round neat piles of sticks and branches.

Over to the left, a ragged procession turned onto the ghats from a distant set of steps and made its way towards one of the pyres. It was led by a tall, imposing man in white robes, flanked by acolytes. Isabel took a few steps closer and strained to see. A moment later, the robed man turned his head and rising light from the water caught his features.

It was Baba Satya. His hair was drawn back from his scalp and knotted at the nape of his neck and his beard was neatly combed. A garland of flowers hung round his shoulders. His face was daubed with streaks of holy ash.

Isabel picked her way with care down the steps and out towards the pyre. The mourners, men and women, walked with eyes downcast. In their midst, a bier, carried at shoulder height, supported the long outline of Rahul's body, wrapped in its shroud. The white cotton shone in the deepening gloom.

As Isabel approached, the low murmur of prayer reached her. A brass pot sat in the crook of Baba Satya's left arm. He dipped his right hand into it with a fluid, musical motion and sprinkled water over the corpse. His toes stretched long and crooked in his chappals.

Isabel paused at a distance from them and sat on the

cool stone to watch. The ceremony continued. In her arms, Rupa stirred, snuffled, then sank back into sleep.

'You can't keep her, Isabel.' Her mother looked exhausted. 'It's simply not on.'

That morning, she had taken Rupa to meet her parents in their suite at The Grand. So many houses had been damaged in the riots, they were lucky to have rooms there. She and Rupa had taken refuge with Sarah.

'I know you mean well.' Her father sat back in his chair. His eyes were thoughtful. 'But you must think what's best for the child.'

Isabel didn't answer. She focused on trying to encourage Rupa to feed from a bottle. Once she latched onto the teat, she sucked in eager gulps. Milk dribbled from the corners of her mouth.

'She's a determined little thing, isn't she?' Her mother watched with suspicion. 'Couldn't you find a wet nurse?'

Isabel kept her voice low. 'One of Sarah's servants has children. She's been a tremendous help.' She paused to wipe milk from Rupa's chin. 'She's the one who suggested goat's milk.'

'Goat's milk?' Her mother looked aghast.

'That's what they give in the villages. If a mother can't feed her baby.' Rupa continued to suck noisily. 'She seems to like it.'

Her mother shook her head. 'She must have someone. A cousin, perhaps. Or an auntie.'

Her father nodded. 'We can always help. I mean, financially.'

'She does have someone.' Isabel's eyes stayed on the scrunched face. 'She has me.'

466

Her parents exchanged glances. She sensed their communication without lifting her face to look. Her mother, her nerves frayed, appealing to her husband for support. Her father, priding himself on staying calm, reassuring her: leave it to me.

When Rupa finished feeding, Isabel wiped off her mouth. Rupa's eyes fell closed, drunk with milk. Isabel spread a cloth on her shoulder and rested the baby there. She rubbed her back in steady, rhythmical circles, as Sarah's servant had taught her. The child's bones were as delicate as a bird's and as fragile.

Her father cleared his throat and sat forward in his chair.

'I'm proud of you, Isabel.' He spoke carefully. 'You saved her life. That's a wonderful thing. But she needs to grow up with her own kind.'

'Think of the future.' Her mother sounded frantic. 'You can't take her back to England. She simply won't fit.'

Isabel said: 'I'm not going back to England.'

'You may have to.' Her father frowned. 'India may not be safe.'

Her mother continued: 'And even here. Think about it. She couldn't set foot in The Club. She'd be excluded from everything.'

Rupa had fallen asleep now, limp on her shoulder. Isabel lifted her, wrapped the swaddling cloth closely round her body and laid her along her legs, the tiny head resting on her knees.

'I know it won't be easy.' The wrinkled face twitched in sleep. 'But we'll manage.' She paused, thinking. 'We'll have each other.'

'You won't be able to marry again.' Her mother sniffed. 'You do see that, at least? No normal Englishman will take on an Indian child.'

Isabel thought of Edward, rolling on the beach on Car Nicobar with James, their limbs entangled.

'I know,' she said. 'But I never wanted a normal Englishman.'

Now, out on the ghats, the sun was low in the sky, reaching red fingers to stroke the flowing water. As the light waned, a low breeze blew up from the river.

The prayers ended. Rahul's shrouded body lay on its bonfire of sticks and branches, close to the water's edge. Baba Satya stooped and touched a light to the pyre. Flames crackled and spread as the dry wood took. In a matter of minutes, the fire raged, shifting rapidly from yellow to red. Thick smoke rose into the darkness and swelled in the breeze.

Isabel fixed her gaze on the long, white shape of Rahul's body in the flames. The outline shimmered and swam. As the fire began to consume him, the bier jerked and the wood beneath it shifted and fell, tipping the corpse with sudden force.

For a moment, Rahul seemed to raise himself for a final look at the world, at the black waters of the river as they flowed through the country he loved and would never, in this life, see again.

Rupa stirred in sleep and Isabel bent over her. She touched her lips to the child's forehead, her nose, her cheek.

'I knew your father,' she whispered. 'He was a wonderful man.'

Moments later, the bier, the shroud and the body within were engulfed by fire and committed at last to eternity.

Chapter Fifty

Delhi, 1945

Finally, the announcement came. The war with Japan had ended.

Isabel and Sarah rushed down to the Red Cross office in the hope of news. The crowd there was already dense. The small rooms echoed with the clamour of shrill, excited voices.

A stout Englishwoman with hairs on her chin climbed onto a stool and raised her hands. 'We have no information.' She shouted into the din, exasperated.

A young woman near the front waved a letter.

'No letters.' The stout woman shook her head and made a shooing gesture. 'Go home.'

Sarah, near the door, pressed against Isabel. 'I thought, once it ended,' she said in a low voice, 'I just thought he'd be home.'

Isabel nodded, reached for her hand.

Days became weeks.

In late September, Sarah, Isabel and her parents met for afternoon tea on the verandah. Rupa, proud in a party dress splashed with pink roses, twirled in erratic circles on the lawn.

'I shall miss this place.' Her father's tone was sad.

Isabel looked across at him. The tea was to mark his birthday but no one seemed in the mood to celebrate. Her father was almost entirely bald now. His face was puckered and pouched with age. The war, she thought. Both wars.

'I wonder where we'll be next year.' Her mother was wrapped round in a shawl, despite the heat. She too seemed shrunken. 'Might we still be here?'

Isabel's father pulled a face. 'I rather doubt it. Not the way Mr Atlee's talking.'

Her mother tutted, looked vaguely back at the bungalow, newly built since the fire.

'Such a shame,' she said. 'All that work.'

Isabel refreshed the teapot with hot water and stirred the leaves. She offered the plate of sandwiches to Sarah, then to her mother.

Abdul appeared at the French windows.

'Telephone, sahib.'

Isabel's mother sighed. 'Not the office, surely.'

Her father got to his feet. 'I should imagine so.'

On the lawn, a cat crept out of the bushes and started to slink across the grass. Rupa turned and gave chase, trying to crawl after it as it disappeared under the rhododendrons.

'She'll ruin that dress.' Isabel's mother shook her head.

Isabel smiled. She remembered being three years old herself, running with Rahul in bright sunshine, crawling through those same bushes.

The three women sat for some moments in silence, drinking their tea, each with their own thoughts of the past.

'Sarah!' Her father's voice was animated. He strode quickly, calling as he came. 'It's Tom. He's in the military hospital. Go at once.'

For a moment, Sarah didn't move. She blanched. A hand

flew to her mouth. The plate on her knee slid sideways to the wooden floor, spilling a half-eaten sandwich.

The military hospital was a mass of single-storey buildings. Isabel stood inside the entrance to the compound, Sarah stiff with tension at her side, and tried to decide which way they should go.

The scene was frantic. Nurses, Indian and European, rushed to and fro. Visiting civilians jostled in and out of the hotchpotch of wards and swarmed along the paths that skirted them.

Off to one side, a hawker sat on the ground beside buckets of full-blown flowers. Their scent was sickly in the heat. A chai-wallah sat on his haunches, ladling boiling chai into glasses. A row of rough wooden benches stood nearby.

Isabel touched Sarah's arm. 'Sit there a moment, would you? I'll be straight back.'

She pressed forward into the first building, one of the largest. It was oppressively hot inside and smelt strongly of urine, undercut by powerful disinfectant. The only relief came from the ceiling fans overhead, which slowly churned the air.

Narrow beds were packed closely together down each side. She strode through, weaving past nurses and trolleys and other visitors. Many of the men were heavily bandaged and lay motionless. Others, sitting, called out to her as she passed. Their expressions were jaunty but their eyes looked bright with fever. Their jutting cheekbones and chins were unnaturally sharp where hunger or illness had melted away the flesh.

I won't recognise him, she thought. He could be any of them.

A nurse came hurrying down the ward and Isabel put out a hand to stop her. The young woman looked annoyed. She held a tin basin in her hand, filled with darkly soiled cotton.

'Can you help me?' Isabel swallowed. 'I'm looking for

someone. Captain Thomas Winton. He was a POW in Singapore.'

The nurse shrugged. 'When did he come in?'

'Today, I think.' She hesitated. 'Or yesterday.'

The nurse pointed to the far end of the building. 'Turn left, left again at the flagpole, second or third tent on the right.'

She indicated a sheaf of paper, which hung on a piece of string just inside the ward. 'Check name against bed number as you go in.' She gave Isabel a meaningful look as she pushed past her. 'You may need to.'

Tom always struck Isabel as a large man. He towered over Sarah when they married, his shoulders broad and solid. She knew his physical power on the tennis court and the polo field.

Now she stood at the foot of his neighbour's bed, looking across at him, biting her lip and trying to steady her breathing. The figure lying there was so slight that its contours were barely visible under the blanket.

Tom was on his back, his shoulders raised by pillows. One arm lay limp on the top of the covers. The fingers, the wrist, the forearm were little more than bone. His head looked too large for the shrunken shoulders. His hair had fallen away into wisps. His cheeks and eyes were dark pits.

She took a deep breath and forced a smile as she approached him, took his skeletal hand between hers.

'Tom. Thank God.' She paused. His eyes were open but they struggled to focus on hers. 'It's Izzy.'

He blinked, his thin face suddenly anxious.

'Sarah's here. I'll get her.' She reached down and kissed his forehead. The papery skin was hot and damp. 'I just needed to find you first.'

Once she had settled Sarah at his bedside, Isabel left them

together. She walked methodically through the rest of the hospital, crossing from one ward to the next, reading through the lists of printed names hanging inside each doorway. Her mouth was dry and her hands shook as she turned page after page but there was no listing for Captain Edward Johnston.

'Does he talk about it?'

Sarah shook her head. 'Not a word.' She stooped and made a show of dead-heading a yellow rose, then moved on to the next bush.

Isabel looked back towards Tom and Sarah's bungalow. Tom lay in a planter on the edge of the lawn, a blanket tucked round his legs. His body had the frailty of an old man. He was performing tricks for Rupa who stood, rapt, at his side. As Isabel watched, he made a coin disappear, then pulled it from Rupa's ear with a flourish.

'He has awful nightmares.' Sarah straightened up. Her voice was low. 'He screams. When I wake him, he just stares as if he doesn't know me. Then he closes his eyes and goes back to sleep.'

'We don't know what he's seen.'

Sarah paused, moved slowly towards the next rose bush. 'At least he's putting weight on.' She shook her head. 'God knows, he needs to.'

Isabel waited as Sarah reached through for a dying bloom and snipped it off, dropped it into her basket.

'And he's home.' Isabel took a deep breath. 'Have you asked him? I mean, about Edward.'

Sarah turned to face her. Her look was strained.

'He says Edward was taken away. A lot were, apparently.' She paused, her eyes on Isabel's face. 'He doesn't know what happened after that. I'm sorry, Izzy. Really.'

Isabel looked down. Her shoes were wet from the undergrowth. Dark half-moons had formed across the toes where water had soaked into the leather.

'We've got a passage home.' Sarah sounded embarrassed. 'I've been meaning to tell you. The doctor told Tom he was fit to travel and then it all happened rather fast.'

Isabel's heart quickened. 'When do you sail?'

'October the fifth. It is rather sudden, isn't it? After all these years.'

Isabel tried to smile. 'Home for Christmas.'

They turned and started to walk slowly back towards the bungalow. There seemed little left to say.

'What about you?' Sarah said, at last.

'I'm looking for a house.' Isabel raised her eyes. Rupa was giggling, fumbling the coin as she tried to master the trick. Her dark hair flew. 'We don't need much.'

Sarah hesitated. 'And school?'

Isabel kept her eyes on the grass. Anglo-Indian schools refused to accept Rupa. 'I can always teach her myself.'

Sarah turned, touched her friend's arm. 'I know you're waiting for him, Izzy. But what if he doesn't come home?'

Isabel shook her off. There were stories in the newspapers all the time about men returning unexpectedly. Men who escaped, who survived in the jungle, who had been given up for lost. She said quietly: 'He will.'

Chapter Fifty-One

Warm air washed across the Civil Lines, coloured by the faint echo of voices. Isabel, sitting on the verandah, strained to listen. There were other sounds. The distant heartbeat of a drum. A whistle.

She lit a cigarette, drew deeply and felt the warmth of the smoke in her lungs. A wedding procession, perhaps. Or another political rally.

It was late afternoon and the first shadows surged along the edge of the grass. Rupa ran out from the side of the bungalow and zigzagged across the lawn, wielding a stick. Her body was small and strong and her black hair, tied in a stout plait, bounced at her neck. She speared the bushes and set the leaves rustling.

Isabel lifted her pen and started to write the latest of many letters that could never be delivered.

My dearest Edward,
All the talk here is of politics. The elections are set
for December, despite the bitterness between the
Congress Party and the Muslim League. Sometimes
I wonder how they'll ever do business together once
independence comes.

She broke off. Clouds of mosquitoes hovered under the trees. The ayah would come soon and call Rupa inside. Isabel looked down at her letter. She didn't want to write about politics. The future held too much fear. She sat for a moment, her eyes on Rupa, crouched now by the flower bed, and the gnarled branches of the magnolia tree behind her.

The old magnolia struggles on. It makes me think, of course, of poor Rahul. I mention him often to Rupa, although it's hard to know what she really understands. She accepts quite stoically that her parents are gone but still tells everyone that I am her mother.

She played all morning with Abdul's grandchildren. I heard her shouting in Hindustani like a native, calling Abdul 'Dada-ji', just as the others do. A little later, she ran to me and spoke in flawless English. Already, she lives in two different worlds. Perhaps she will never belong entirely in either. But she gives me such hope, hope that this country's future can be more than hatred and bloodshed and division.

She paused, imagining Edward there beside her, then added:

You will love her, Edward, I'm sure of it. And she you.

At the far end of the drive, bolts scraped and the gate swung open with a clatter. Isabel sat upright. A figure appeared, a man walking wearily towards the bungalow, as if he were at the end of a long journey. She craned forward. For a moment, in the hazy light, she saw Edward there, gaunt and stooped but alive, come at last to claim her. She blinked, her eyes tight on the figure as it grew nearer, then she sank back into her chair. It was only Abdul, returning from the bazaar, weighed down by bags. She drew on her cigarette, forced herself to breathe evenly again, then turned again to her letter.

Edward, I am the only one who knows you are still alive. I keep hope, even now, that you will come back. To think anything else would be impossible. If you were no longer in this world, I would know it. It would break me. But I feel you with me each morning when I wake. I feel you with me each evening when I settle to sleep. We are one, you and I.

She closed her eyes and, in that stillness, time seemed to twist and turn and lose all meaning. She was a child again, playing in this same garden with her Indian brother, Rahul. She was floating, arms outstretched, in the soft waters of Car Nicobar, knowing that Edward waited for her, there on the white-sand beach.

'Mummy?' Rupa stood at the bottom of the verandah steps. She lifted her weight onto the first step and hung on the wooden handrail. 'Can I sit in the tree?'

'Isn't it time for your bath?'

Rupa twisted, swinging, waiting for Isabel to set down her pen.

They crossed the lawn together. Isabel looked down at the bobbing head, the set jaw. Her tiny, swaddled body had been so light, so frail once, as she lifted her away from the train. She thought of Asha's eyes, calmly fixed on

Isabel's even as flame engulfed her, and took Rupa's hand.

Once they reached the magnolia tree, Rupa pulled Isabel's fingers into a stirrup and set her foot in it, heaving herself towards the lowest branch. She scrambled, pulled herself up, then sat astride it and kicked at the empty air.

'I climbed to the top once,' Isabel said. 'Your father helped me.'

Rupa tipped back her head and stared into the uneven ladder of branches, stretching endlessly to the sky.

'Rupa!' The ayah's voice, from the verandah.

Rupa stiffened. The ayah, seeing them, started out across the grass.

'Time for bed.' Isabel opened her arms as Rupa, frowning, swung her leg over the branch and slid down. She kissed the top of the girl's head. 'Don't forget to clean your teeth and say your prayers.'

Isabel stood quietly under the old tree and watched Rupa trail back across the grass to the bungalow, a slight but determined figure at the ayah's side.

Pray for this grand, beleaguered country, she thought. In the stillness, the low beat of the drum and the boom of male voices came to her again, a little louder now in the darkening air. Pray for us all.

Acknowledgements

I was helped by a range of memoirs and personal accounts which give first-hand insights into daily life during the final stages of the British Raj. Charles Allen's comprehensive oral history *Plain Tales from the Raj* is an invaluable guide. The British Library's archive collection of unpublished papers from the period gave me further details of daily life in the Andamans, of conditions inside the Cellular Jail and of missionary work in the Nicobars. These include memoirs by L. V. Deane, Ernest Hart, P. W. Radice, Frances Stewart Robertson and Theo Stewart Robertson.

My thanks to Susie, Lesley and the rest of the wonderful team at Allison and Busby.

Thank you as always to my agent, Judith Murdoch, the best in the business.

And to my family for all their love and support.